Also by Carole Walker Carter

<u>Aztarian Series</u>
AZTARA, The Mastel Kingdom
SURTEES, Science Rules
AZTARA, A Galactic Love Story
AZTARA, Secrets Revealed

<u>Evers and McFarlan Detective Series</u>
Final Alumni
Shadowy Faces
Nine Points of a Circle

<u>Fantasy Books</u>
The Child Rowanda, Little Dragon
The Child Rowanda, Return to Arolsen
The Child Rowanda, Underworld
The Child Rowanda, Dragon Princess

<u>Children's Books on www.walkercarter.com</u>
Tinker Robot
Grandma's Magic Scarf
Granny Nell
Alec the Astronaut

FINAL

ALUMNI

Vol. I

Evers & McFarlan Detective Series

Carole Walker Carter

WALKER CARTER PUBLISHING, LLC

Cover Design and Layout by Donald E Carter
Cover Photos © Fotolia by Adobe

Final Alumni / by Carole Walker Carter
Evers & McFarlan Detective Series / Volume 1

ISBN 978-1-947734-24-1

9 8 7 6 5 4 3 2 1 17 18 19 20 21

[1. Women Sleuths, 2. Mystery, 3. Detectives, 4. Mystery Suspense Thriller, 5. Paperback Mysteries, 6. Action Adventure Romance]

WALKER CARTER PUBLISHING, LLC

Please check out my website at <u>www.walkercarter.com</u>

To my girls Jennifer and Lisa, my grandson Nixon, my granddaughter Alex and my husband, Don.

In memory of my mother and dad, Elda and Dean Walker.

I will always love you!!!

ACKNOWLEDGMENTS

I wrote this book in cooperation with my best friend, and husband, Donald E. Carter, author of _Concurrent Engineering, Product Development Environment_ business books. Don's inspiration helped to create characters for the Evers, and McFarlan Series, and researched all the technical information.

The first book in the Evers and McFarlan Series is _Final Alumni_. The second is _Shadowy Faces,_ and the third is _Nine Points of a Circle._

Janis Lane supported me with my writing by cheering me on to tell my stories. Don and I worked diligently to edit this book over the past year.

My girls, Jennifer and Lisa Coyle, provided several useful resource books. Without their support and prodding, this book may still be in draft form. Jennifer, with a keen eye for graphics, helped Don with the cover art.

Without my older sister, Linda Sturgill, and younger sister Janel Walker, giving me love, support, and resources, I would not be able to write. They each spent hours proofreading and editing the _Aztarian Series_ Books, _Evers & McFarlan Detective Series_ Books, and The _Child Rowanda Series_ Books. I will forever be grateful for my family's encouragement and dedication to my creations.

Special Thanks to all those that donated to my GoFundMe page, Linda Sturgill, Elda Walker, Janel Walker, Judy Mathiesen, Linda Maddex, Afsaneh Fowler, and Carol Royce Davidson. These donations kick-started my venture by allowing me to acquire editing tools, printed proof copies, ISBN numbers, audio equipment, and final publication costs.

TABLE OF CONTENTS

CHAPTER ONE 13

CHAPTER TWO 17

CHAPTER THREE 21

CHAPTER FOUR..28

CHAPTER FIVE 40

CHAPTER SIX 48

CHAPTER SEVEN 51

CHAPTER EIGHT..53

CHAPTER NINE 66

CHAPTER TEN 73

CHAPTER ELEVEN...83

CHAPTER TWELVE 93

CHAPTER THIRTEEN 103

CHAPTER FOURTEEN..107

CHAPTER FIFTEEN 116

CHAPTER SIXTEEN..126

CHAPTER SEVENTEEN..135

CHAPTER EIGHTEEN...143

CHAPTER NINETEEN...154

CHAPTER TWENTY 160

CHAPTER TWENTY-ONE 172

CHAPTER TWENTY-TWO 179

CHAPTER TWENTY-THREE 190

CHAPTER TWENTY-FOUR...206

CHAPTER TWENTY-FIVE...218

CHAPTER TWENTY-SIX 229

CHAPTER TWENTY-SEVEN 237

CHAPTER TWENTY-EIGHT..252

CHAPTER TWENTY-NINE 266

CHAPTER THIRTY 275

CHAPTER THIRTY-ONE 291

CHAPTER THIRTY-TWO 301

CHAPTER THIRTY-THREE 313

CHAPTER THIRTY-FOUR 316

CHAPTER THIRTY-FIVE 334

CHAPTER THIRTY-SIX 340

CAROLE WALKER CARTER 353

CHAPTER ONE

I walked out of the locker room from my high school gym rather late. The other players took off right after the football practice. The coach wanted to run over a few new plays to make sure I, as the quarterback, understood them before the playoffs. I was feeling guilty since my best friend, Tish, was waiting for me out in my truck.

It was dark. The winter of 1991 came early this year. I figured Tish would be huddled up in her blanket asleep as I started walking towards the parking lot.

Out of nowhere, a hooded figure ran towards me with a baseball bat. I heard Tish shout, "Scotty, look out!" I barely had time to see the movement before the figure was on the ground, kicking and screaming. Tish was holding him in an armlock from which he was not going to escape.

"Get off me, bitch!" I recognized the voice as one of the school hoods, Jesse.

"What the heck do you intend to do with that baseball bat?" I said as I motioned for Tish to release the moron. I had no doubts Jack sent his minion to take out my knees; that way he could quarterback the state tournament playoff games.

"I wasn't going to do nothin," was Jesse's come back as he got up off the ground, rubbing his arm. "I should press charges against your crazy bitch, that is what I should do. I was just minding my own business when she took me down for no reason. You are one crazy freak." He said to Tish. I was used to Jesse's bad mouth; however, I was not going to stand by while he insulted my best friend.

With that, I bitch-slapped him hard across the face. "You better watch your mouth! You are the crazy one here. Did Jack send you to mess up my knees?"

"You both are crazy!" Holding the side of his face, Jesse whined, "I'm going to tell the coach you attacked me."

"All right, let's go…the coach is in the gym…It will be my pleasure to personally march your ass over there," I replied, grabbing the little shit under his arm.

Jesse wrenched free and took off for his truck. I grabbed the bat…giving it a perfect toss; I bounced it off the ground smacking Jessie behind his knees, knocking him down. He got up, running until he reached his truck and jumped into it. Jessie burned rubber and wheel hopped the rear tires of his dilapidated truck as he exited the student parking lot. Predictably, his driveshaft broke. Feeling both disgust and fear, Jessie jumped out of his truck and ran into the city park next to the high school.

Jesse is definitely one of Jack's minions. He is a weasel in every sense of the word. Jesse stands about 5'6" and weighs approximately 130 pounds. He has mousey brown colored hair that most girls would dye to be rid of it. Barely passing a couple of classes, and the rest, Jesse is looking at F's. The only reason he has not dropped out of school altogether is that he can covertly peddle drugs on campus.

Jack finds him an easy mark to get his criminal acts accomplished when Jack doesn't want to do it personally or get his hands dirty. Jack and his father campaigned for my quarterback position on the team for the past two years. Now that our senior year is upon us, they are getting desperate.

I know Jack is the reason I am no longer with Heather. A few weeks back, Jack paid Lucy, the class slut, to undress and spread her naked body all over mine after Jesse drugged my soft drink at the team's football party at Jack's house. Jack had his camera ready.

I did not know Jack's parents were going to be out of town. One of my more stupid moments was staying at the party instead of leaving the minute I found out it was not chaperoned.

Don't get me wrong; I am not an Eagle Scout or anything like that. Nevertheless, I had a feeling that night was not going to end in my favor. No girls were invited except Lucy Loose, as we like to call her, and her slutty girlfriends. Jack wanted to take Heather away from me for a couple of years as well. Jack indeed planned his sneak attack better than the one Jesse just failed to achieve.

I digressed...I am still a bit upset and...yes...hurt that Jack took Heather away from me.

Of course, Jesse might have succeeded if Tish had not been watching him from my truck. Later that same evening, while we were studying, she told me she saw Jesse drive up, stop next to Jack's truck, and then he got out to talk to Jack. She saw money pass from Jack to Jesse. Next thing, Jesse reached into Jack's truck bed and took out the baseball bat. A couple of minutes later, Jack drove away, and Jesse positioned himself where he could see the gym doors.

Tish told me she followed Jesse at a discreet distance and sneaked up behind him without his noticing her at all. Tish has been training in martial arts for years. She is as quiet as a jungle cat when she is in ninja mode.

Tish also said, the moment I came out of the gym and started walking toward the parking lot, Jesse pulled his hoodie over his head and got a grip on the bat. As he leaped out of hiding and started running towards me, Tish tackled him from behind and took him down to the ground in an armlock. The rest is now history.

There is no way Jesse is going to complain to anyone, except Jack. I can only imagine how angry Jack is going to be when Jesse reports his failure. Jack is not one to accept anyone else's incompetence. Jesse will get an ear full and maybe a bit more. At a minimum, Jack will want his conspiracy money back.

Jack has been a bully since grade school. He was always bigger than the other boys until I got my growth spurt. Suddenly, the boys on the playground had a champion against Jack. I wouldn't stand for Jack pushing my friends around. Jack started to hate me, and I think one of his goals in life was to make me miserable anyway he could.

Jack, being the sheriff's son, was convinced he was privileged and above the law. He took his role as little Mr. Deputy Dufus seriously. I don't know whether his father encouraged his behavior. All I know is Jack made life miserable for a lot of the smaller boys.

Jack would shake down the guys for their lunch money, and if they did not hand it over, he would beat them up. For some reason, he got away with his behaviors for a long time. I learned from early on, small towns have their own rules. One rule is our sheriff, and his family are not to be questioned under any circumstances.

I suspect Jack was getting a lot of pressure at home from his father. No doubt, the sheriff was embarrassed that his son was sitting on the bench this entire year. Jack stands 6'0" and weighs about 200 pounds. He doesn't work out enough to carry his bulk well. Frankly, Jack lacks not only the confidence but the skills to be an athlete. His character lacks the drive needed to excel. Drive is the critical attribute found in most college quarterbacks.

The coach gave Jack a chance to show his skills as a quarterback in our junior year. Unfortunately, Jack did not seem to have the courage to stay in the pocket and take a hit with our delayed style pass plays. He was afraid of being sacked and would just throw the ball away. The outcome was he would throw an interception or fumble the ball. The coach finally sat his ass on the bench.

I overheard the coach telling the sheriff more than once that the team was working hard to win the State Championship, and Jack was not the quarterback for the job. I have a lot of respect for our coach to ignore one of our town rules and not to cave into the sheriff.

CHAPTER TWO

My senior football season was exceptional. The coach had the pass plays and the ground game that the other teams could not figure out. He said part of the reason for the success of the team was my arm, my legs, and my head. I hate to sound immodest; nonetheless, I do have a heck of a throwing arm. I played sports since before I could walk…okay, I exaggerate a little. I did play many of the major sports most of my childhood. My dad would pass a football with me, throw baseballs for me to hit, and kick a soccer ball around the yard.

You name the sport; my dad would take the time to explain and play the game with me patiently. Not only did he teach me sports, but he also taught me how to swim, hunt, shoot, and survive in the woods. He even instructed me through my pilot's license. Best of all, he taught me sportsmanship and how to be a gentleman. My dad is the best dad ever. I know I sound like a Hallmark card.

My dad is a bull of a man. He isn't as tall as me. However, he is built. Even at his age, his middle is trim, and he sports a six-pack. Being an ex-Navy Seal, he encourages me to live an active lifestyle. He works out daily, and I am usually at his side.

I am purpose-built to play football. I stand 6'3" and weigh 220 pounds when I am training. I have dark brown hair and dark blue eyes. Pretty typical for an Irish-American who is not a redhead. I wear my hair a bit long on the top and short on the sides. My mom says my naturally wavy hair is a blessing. I know that Heather liked to run her fingers through my hair all the time when we were together.

Heather was the love of my life. I've had a crush on her for years. We dated exclusively for two years. Heather is petite, a red-haired hotty with hazel eyes that flash when she's mad. Her eyes have been flashing at me a lot lately.

My recall is walking into Algebra class during my sophomore year, and hearing all the chatter about this cute new girl…and in she walked. It was love at first sight…for me, probably not for Heather. I guess I acted like a dumb ass, trying to get her to notice me.

It wasn't until after the homecoming game in our sophomore year that she finally acknowledged me. I was the quarterback even back then. The coach said I was a natural phenomenon. It turns out I was really pretty good. Heather made the cheerleading squad. Making the squad as a sophomore is unusual; she bragged to anyone that would listen.

At any rate, we won the homecoming game against Dobbins 43-0. I went stag to the Homecoming Dance and was brave enough to approach Heather while her girl-pals surrounded her. I guess I did not look as much like a fool after winning the game. She said she would dance with me…the beginning of our big romance.

For the next twenty months, Heather and I dated every Friday and Saturday night like clockwork. We would go to the movies, dances, or out for a burger and a malt. In the summer, we would go to the lake and lay on the beach. She was a knock-out in her swimsuit. It was hard for me to keep my hands off her. She was a good girl and told me 'no means no.' I figured I could wait since we would no doubt get married someday.

Heather was the love of my life until Jack sabotaged our cutest couple calling. We were voted cutest couple our senior year for the yearbook. After we broke up, the editor needed to make a hasty replacement since the yearbook was due to be sent out to the publishing company. Ray and Rose Lee took the honor from us. I can't complain since they are good together.

Everyone was talking about Heather breaking up with me. Heather's girlfriends all thought I was a cad. Other girls were thrilled I was available once again. I will admit I didn't mind the flirting; it was incredible. It did hurt knowing I had no chance to get Heather back no matter how many girls threw themselves at me. She was just too mad to be jealous.

Once she saw the pictures of me in bed with a naked Lucy Loose, it was all over. It did not matter that I told her I was drugged, and the whole thing was staged. She just did not believe me. I moped around for several weeks.

Tish poked me in my side to bring me out of my reverie. She could tell I was thinking about Heather again. "Scotty, will you stop mooning over Heather. She is with Jack now, and you look like a whipped dog watching her all the time."

Well, a whipped dog was not what I wanted to be. Heather is with Jack. I need to resign myself to that situation. I admit it is hard for me to watch that creep walking my girl down the hall with his arm possessively around her shoulder. Tish keeps telling me Jack would dump her in a moment if Jack thought I was no longer interested in Heather. Tish challenged me to act like they don't exist. I have tried. Tish is helping me to work harder at putting this behind me.

Tish has been my best friend since 4th grade. Describing Tish in words without sounding like a predator is difficult. She is gorgeous. It wasn't that she recently became gorgeous...she has always been beautiful. Tish also holds a 3rd Dan Black Belt in Taekwondo and Combat Hapkido. She is not only beautiful, but she is dangerous.

I remember this one time in Jr. High, when Jeremy, one of the school's bullies, had me pinned on the ground and was pounding the crap out of my face. Suddenly, Tish was on his back with her arms wrapped around his neck and her long legs locked around his waist. Tish tightened her grip and wouldn't let go. Jeremy's face was turning white, and his lips purple. Jeremy was silently crying, desperately trying to shake her off and break free. Just before Jeremy passed out,

Tish whispered in his ear, "touch, tease or interfere with my best friend, and you might not wake up the next time." The lights went out on Jeremy, but not before the fear of dying welled in his brain.

Tish is not only tuff; she is eye candy. She stands 5' 10" in bare feet and weighs in at strong and powerful 126 pounds. Her caramel-colored skin is flawless. Tish's simple short hairstyle is highlighted with thick yet wispy feathers, jagged bangs, and a beautiful ultra-shine finish.

Tish hates to fuss with 'girlie' stuff like her clothes and nails, however, makeup, now, that is another thing. Her skin color, hairstyle, green eyes, naturally long eyelashes, and signature black cherry lipstick with smoky burgundy eyeshadow, makes her the most stunning girl in school. You can believe me when I say she does not need anything more. She doesn't even need make-up; she is that pretty.

Tish's daily attire is black jeans with black or burgundy pull-over tops. If it is cold out, she adds her black leather jacket. The only 'girlie' thing about her, besides hair and makeup, is she buys shoes…well, boots, like there is no tomorrow. She must have 20 pairs or more. She really likes the ones with studs. To most people, Tish looks like a biker-chick. What I can tell you, Tish is definitely not a biker chick. Although, she does have a rad 1973 Ironhead Harley Sportster. Ok…so…Tish is a rather cool chick.

The playoff games are coming up, and I need to be at my best. I have no time to think about Heather. I am glad to have Tish to keep my mind on what is essential. Tish's comment about acting like a whipped dog and a few other derogatory terms help more than it hurts, but it does still hurt.

CHAPTER THREE

The other thing, besides Tish that keeps my mind off Heather, are the up-coming state football championship games. In the first few games, our team had the home advantage. St. Anthony came to us. The guys were revved-up, belly bumping, and high-fiving in the locker room. The coach came in and gave us a pep talk.

The coach's pep talk sounded like this: "We have practiced and worked hard to overcome all of the different looks their offenses and defenses will throw at us. We have the knowledge and know-how to defeat them. We have the strength and stamina to outlast their best. To win...we must have the greater will...and we've got to believe! Now get out there and play hard, make yourselves proud! I want everyone where they are supposed to be on every play. I want glue on your hands...no fumbles...no dropped balls. I want my runners to run like the devil is chasing them. You got it?" The coach barked some more rhetoric and told us to get out there and fight, Fight, FIGHT!

We tore up the field winning 14-0 against St. Anthony on Nov 15th, sending us to the semi-finals. We bested Elton High 20-0 on Nov. 22 and ended up at the finals with Arceloa High this coming Saturday, November 30th, at 9:00 a.m. at Illinois State University in Normal, Illinois.

On gameday, the bleachers were filled with friends, family, and fans from both towns. Cars had been cruising down the main street all morning with our school colors, maroon, and gold, on pendants flapping in the wind. The school band was assembled and playing loudly as the last of the people filed in to find standing room only. My parents, Tish, and her parents all came together wearing our school colors. They sat on the 50-yard line 5 rows up on the center bleachers.

The temperature at game time was 55 degrees, and the wind was terrible…25 mph straight down the field. None of us played in a game with that much wind, and neither team played on astroturf. The coach stopped me and said quietly, "We are going to make this a ground game. They will be looking for you to pass the ball. I want you to use your head and your legs.

We came storming out of the locker room led by our mascot with the cheerleaders leading the crowd in cheers of welcome. The noise was deafening, however exhilarating. Arceloa was favored to win this game, and we weren't going down without a fight.

The coaches for both teams were legends. They each coached over 18 years at only one school. Both coaches' track records were amazing…our coach, Jim O'Rourke's record, is 235-53-1 with four trips to State and one win in 1979. Arceloa's coach, Terry Smith's record, is 178-84-2 with four trips to State. For sure, the entire state will be watching this game as this is the first time these two coaches have their teams playing against each other.

As the game started, our team was hyped up and ready. The kick-off was sent down to our 20-yard line. Tommy caught the ball on the run and zigzagged through Arceloa's defense before being tackled at our 34-yard line. The wind was howling in our face making any pass risky. We set up our offense for the Pistol Wing-T, which allowed us to have the fullback behind the quarterback and two halfbacks set wide to the left and right of the quarterback. With the two tight ends, this gave us a minimum of five option plays.

Our first down play was called the Buck Sweep Right. The right tight end setup behind our right tackle. The instant the football was hiked, the tight end and the tackles pushed all the right-side defensive linemen to the left towards our center. At the same time, the left halfback would swing right in front of me for the handoff and then follow behind the blocks of the fullback and the right halfback around the right side of the playing field.

Tommy Gillespie, our left halfback was a fireplug of a guy; he stood 5′ 6″ and weighed 160 pounds. He was all muscle with enormous thighs. His lightning-fast speed sent him around the right corner in an instant with a gain of 9-yards before Arceloa's backfield took him down.

The second play would show us how tuff Arceloa's defense was prepared to play. We set up for the Guard Trap Left play. Our weakside lineman would push the left side of the defense to the left, and the strongside lineman would push the right side of the defense to the right, opening a hole up the middle for a handoff to Wally, our fullback. Our lineman did their job correctly, no perfectly, with one exception our center tripped on his own feet and fell right smack in the hole. Arceloa's backfield came toward us through the hole and took Wally down behind our line of scrimmage for a loss.

It was now 3rd down and 4 yards for a first down. The coach sent in a pass play to my surprise. We would set up for the Waggle play with Chuck, our right tight end. In this play, our offensive line would contain their defensive counterpart, and I would fake a handoff to Tommy, our left halfback. I would then roll out to my left and throw across the field to my right side to Chuck, who was waiting on the right sideline. It all played out again as planned except a wind gust stopped the ball, and it fell short. I was upset at myself...we turned the ball over to our special teams to punt the ball.

Fortunately, our punter, Ray, kicked the ball to their 5-yard line putting Arceloa's backs against the goal line. With the wind at their backs, they came out throwing the ball. Our defense was radical; they protected against the pass better than they had all year.

The rest of the first quarter was back and forth with us running the ball and Arceloa passing the ball. The defense on both teams was incredible.

At the start of the second quarter, Arceloa still held the ball with the wind now in their face. It was third and long, and Chuck, who played both tight end on offense and cornerback on defense, was ready for a pass to their number one receiver. Chuck jumped in front of their receiver, right when their quarterback released the ball. Surprising everyone, Chuck caught the ball for an interception, running 46-yards straight down the sideline for a touchdown.

Our field goal kicker stubbed his toe on the astroturf in practice, which meant we would be going for the two-point conversion. The coach sent in another pass play. It was a Wildcat Right Reverse play. Our offense line would line up offset to the left. Our right tight end would be lined up far-right. On the hike, I would slide left, handing the ball off to Tommy, our left halfback. Tommy would run straight right across the field to the right, turn and pass the ball to me on the left side of the field. I would then pass the ball to Chuck, our tight end, as he was rolling right into the end zone. Yay! Two more points! Their defense was really confused, running into each other as they tried to follow the ball moving left, right, left, and then right again. The score was 8 - 0 in favor of Stanton!

Our punter kicked the ball to their 25-yard line, where their kick returner was immediately tackled back on the 22-yard line. Their next two pass play attempts ended in the quarterback being sacked. They ran around the left side of the field on the third down. Doug got his helmet on the ball, knocking it free directly into his arms for a fumble recovery.

Our first down play was the Guard Trap play to the right, on their 25-yard line. The only difference was it would be a quarterback keeper play. I faked the handoff to the fullback then the left halfback. Using my bulk and legs, I barreled thru the hole on the right side of the line behind my teammates. Before I knew it, I was in the end zone dragging four of the Arceloa players behind me. We failed to get the two-point conversion and settled for a 14 - 0 lead at the end of the half. I could hear our crowd in the bleacher screaming and waving towel and pom-poms. I remember seeing Tish and my mom. My Mom was jumping up and down, yelling, "That's my son, that's my son!" Tish was belly laughing at my Mom

The start of the third quarter had Arceloa receiving our kick. It was a feeble kick. Their kick returner Callahan got thru our line like it was butter. Our kicker, Ray, redeemed himself and tackled him at their 45-yard line. To our surprise, they ran the ball using Callahan as their fullback. He tore our linemen apart, getting a touchdown on just two plays. Fortunately, they were unable to convert. The score was 14-6 with 12 minutes 30 seconds left in the 3rd quarter. It really took us back; in all our previous 13 games, we never allowed a score in the 3rd quarter.

Coach O'Rourke called timeout. He gathered us up on the sideline to let us know he is proud of us and to reach inside ourselves for the will to take this game home. I rarely speak at these team huddles. I told the team, "I feel it! I feel it in my bones and in my heart that we will win this game and the State Championship!" We all broke the huddle with a 'HOORAH!'

Arceloa punted the ball directly to Tommy. He ran his ass off straight-arming, juking, and jumping over every defender for an 85-yard kick-off return touch down! Again, we were unable to convert...but the score set the opposition on their heels. Our score now was 20 - 6, and we still had 11 minutes to go in the third quarter. Our punter got off a high and long kick that placed them inside their 20-yard line.

Chuck and Doug defended or kept each pass attempt to a minimum, and the front line sacked their quarterback two more times. On fourth down, their punter kicked the ball directly into the backside of one of his own blockers, popping the ball straight into Doug's arms.

In his confusion, Doug began running the ball in the wrong direction before he bounced off one of our linemen. Realizing his folly, Doug ran the ball into the end zone for another touchdown. Doug may never live this one down. We called him 'Wrong Way' Doug from then on. Again, we failed to convert for the two points. 'Geez,' I thought, 'they are tuff in the red zone.'

We ended the third quarter with a score of 26-6. The fourth quarter opened with both teams running the ball, taking time off the clock. Whenever Arceloa's quarterback tried to throw the ball, our defenders sacked him for a loss. They would sack him four more times for a total of eight sacks, breaking the all-time record for sacks in a State Championship game.

Each time we took possession of the ball, we gained more ground getting closer to their side of the field. The coach decided to try the Guard Trap play this time to the right. It worked perfectly. I found myself in the end zone once again for my second touchdown.

The game ended with the score of Stanton 32 and Arceloa 6. The team went nuts, and the crowd went wild. I gathered the guys together and told them how proud I was of them and how this was clearly a team win! I took the lead to walk over to Arceloa's quarterback, shaking each of their team members' hands with my team doing the same behind me.

The coach praised us all for a great game; he awarded me with two of the game balls and the most valuable player trophy. I felt that the championship trophy belonged to Tommy, Doug, or the entire defensive or even the offensive line. From the corner of my eye, I could see Jack throwing his helmet and his pads in anger.

When I saw my Mom and Tish, I handed them each one of the game balls and the MVP trophy to my father. I thanked them for all their support.

I was the big man on campus for the rest of the winter and well into the spring of my senior year. I took it all in stride, being taught by my dad that team sports are just that…a team. I was no better than anyone else on the team. I tried to act like that was the case…deep down inside, I was proud. Yes, I was proud of my team, as well.

Tish was always there to knock me down to size when I got too big for my britches. With all my swagger, I still had not found anyone to take to the Senior Ball. I did not want to date anyone except Heather.

In late spring, my mom asked, "Scotty, the Senior Ball is not far away. Have you asked anyone yet?"

I told her that I had not, and she told me I had better get the lead out of my pants. I don't know what it is about the women in my life. They keep worrying about my trousers.

"Scotty, why don't you and Tish go as friends? I was talking to Dorothy today, and she said Tish wasn't planning to go to the dance at all. What a shame for a girl to miss her Senior Ball. It would be nice if you asked her."

"Mom, you are talking about Tish. She is my best friend. She is like one of the guys," I whined. I knew, though, that once my mom made up her mind about something, I had best just concede.

Thinking about the idea made me realize it would be fun to go with Tish. I liked the plan, the more I thought about it. I wouldn't need to put on airs or act like anyone other than myself. It was the perfect solution.

I phoned Tish and ran it past her. Once she got over laughing her head off and listen to what I had to say, she agreed it might be fun. It was a date. Tish and I were going to the Senior Ball as a couple.

CHAPTER FOUR

Tonight is the Senior Ball for the class of 1992. Mom rented the tux and bought the corsage for Tish. There was no backing out at the last minute like I wanted to do. Glad now I didn't.

Tish, as I said before, is drop-dead gorgeous in a mysterious and exotic sort of way. When I saw her coming down the stairs, I almost forgot she was my best friend. Wow! She looked stunning in her long gown. It hugged every curve, and her eyes caught where my eyes were watching. Awkward…. Don't get me wrong. I noticed her curves before in those tight black jeans and snug tops. Most of the time, Tish was…ah…well, Tish. Tonight ah…ah…Tish was a supermodel.

She had tiny diamonds in her hair that caught the light and glimmered. Her eye shadow and blush glittered as well. She seemed to sparkle all over. I came back to earth when she said, "Shit! I feel stupid. If I fall off these heels, you'd better catch me, or I'll punch you!"

"What are best friends for" was the best come back I could handle, as I pinned the corsage onto her dress as carefully as possible. I did not want to stick her with the pin. I knew what I would be in for if I did.

I know, it was early in the afternoon to be picking Tish up. I wanted to surprise Tish with a special flight from our hometown airport to Palwaukee Municipal, where we would take a taxi to a famous seafood restaurant. I checked in with the aviation weather center and filed a flight plan with flight services. It was going to be a CAVU night. The skyline would be fantastic when we flew into Chicago. I told Tish my plans for dinner when we got into the car. Tish could hardly contain herself with excitement. When I told Tish, we would be taking the Crusader, she became almost giddy.

Driving to the airport to fly to the restaurant, I started to think about all my hours of flying. My dad teaches at the flying school part-time. Being an ex-Navy Seal pilot, he began to teach me to fly at a young age. By seventeen, I held a Private Pilot Single, Multi-Engine Land, Instrument Airplane, and Helicopter license. My flight school for graduation gifted me with two hours of flight time in a Cessna T-303 Crusader cabin-class twin-engine airplane.

Tish's father is an instructor as well; he flew helicopters during his time as a Navy Seal. Tish has some training and has soloed. She doesn't have the hours needed to get her Private Pilot's license. Her energy has been taken up by her martial arts training. I know she will want to fly more when she isn't busy with everything else. In the meantime, she is my co-pilot.

Flying somewhere for dinner might be extravagant. I thought we only have one Senior Ball night in our lives. Since Tish and I decided to go together, I might as well make it the best prom night ever. To me, flying is on par with winning football games. Flying is a step above football. There is nothing like being up in the clouds and leaving the world behind. To me, it is the only place where one feels entirely in control and close to God.

I glanced at Tish again. She was incredibly beautiful. One can appreciate art with one's eyes without having to touch it. That is how I feel about Tish. She is art, and I am not touching.

She caught me in the act of glancing over at her. "I know. I look like a clown. My mom helped me with all the extra makeup. I told her it was too much. She insisted I needed more in the evening.... I feel stupid."

"No, Tish, you look great. Every guy at the dance is going to notice you differently." I said this innocently, meaning it as a compliment.

"What do you mean? Notice me differently. If you mean they are going to see me as a sex object, you can turn around right now. I won't go to the gym if that is what you are getting at. I am still me, and no one is going to treat me like a sex object!" She was almost foaming at the mouth as she said this.

"Tish, you can't be blind. You look great! No boy at our school would be stupid enough to treat you like a sex object no matter how sexy you look. They all know you could knock their block off. Believe me, they might look. However, none of them will even think about touching. Besides, I told you. I've got your back." I said this to try to keep her calm. She isn't the easiest person to get un-riled once her dander is up. "Come on, let's go and have fun, OK?"

Tish seemed to calm down faster than usual. I suspect it had something to do with the gown she was wearing. How could Tish act like a hard-ass when...geez...she looked like cotton candy? I think even she knew her look did not match her attitude. You are what you wear or something like that…once again, she would prove me wrong.

The early-evening sunset was perfect for flying. As we entered the Chicago air-traffic control space on the way to Palwaukee Municipal, we could see the Navy Pier extending into Lake Michigan off our right-wing. The harbor was full of millionaire yachts. The high rises outlined the Chicago skyline and seemed to be twinkling a greeting. We could also see Wrigley Fields, home of the Cubs. That was always the most exciting for me to view.

My mom made a few phone calls, and I was assured a cab would be waiting for us at the airfield to take us to Bob Chin's Crab House. The restaurant boasted some great crab meals. The fresh crabs came from different places around the world, and I wasn't about to let Tish have anything but a fairy tale evening.

I had plenty of money from working an after-school job; still, Mom slipped me an extra fifty dollars. Little did Mom know Dad slipped me money as well. There was an ample amount of money for whatever my best friend wanted for dinner. I told her anything on the menu...go figure...she ordered a salad and iced tea.

I wasn't going to let her off that easy. I ordered a Colossal Shrimp cocktail, Kona crab salad for her, as well as Bob's favorite dessert sampler at the end of the meal. She said she never tasted anything that good before and loved all the items I ordered for her. It made me feel good to see her eat with such enthusiasm.

I let Tish fly most of the way back while I worked the radios with air traffic control. The flight back was equally pleasant. The stars were shimmering, and the lights below got us in the mood for the dance. I can't say Tish was ready to dance cheek to cheek with me; nonetheless, I sensed she was starting to look forward to the evening instead of dreading it.

Arriving at the high school, I parked and went around the car to do my gentlemanly duty. Tish, ever independent, opened the door and was out without my assistance. She was cursing under her breath about being all tangled up in her dress. I took her by the arm and escorted her to the gym.

Entering the Senior Ball's 'Under the Sea' theme decorated gym, I noticed I was right. Every guy's eyes in the gym were locked on Tish. I suspect half of them did not recognize her. The ones who did immediately recognize her knew enough to close their mouths and avert their eyes. Luckily, Tish seemed oblivious to the commotion she caused by entering the room.

We found a table with several of my pals and settled down to chat before dancing. I noticed Jack and Heather were seated at the table occupied mainly with cheerleaders and their dates. We were greeted amicably by my football pals and their dates. The girls almost immediately started to compliment Tish on her gorgeous dress, and I was fascinated to see her join in the girl-talk. I never heard her quite as chatty before with other girls. It gave me a chance to talk about football with the guys.

Chuck Landers, my male best friend, said, "Coach says he is going to miss us. We were the best football team he ever coached. I guess it isn't every year he gets to brag about being the State Champions. How could we miss, with you as our quarterback?"

The rest joined in talking about the win over Orange Town and how close the game was with a score of 14-12. They seemed to want to flatter me with how great I was. It appeared to me it was a low scoring game, and I reminded them close is not a great win.

"Hey, you guys are the ones who make the touchdowns. I just handoff and throw the ball." I could be modest when I needed to be. It seemed this was not the time to honk my own horn.

"St. Anthony was a shutout. Who expected us to have such a large win over them in the semifinals?" one of the guys added.

Football talk would have continued for most of the night except we were interrupted as Meredith, the dog-crazy girl, came up to our table with Seth, her date. Meredith is always trying to get us to take a stray dog home. I guess she and her mother rescue them from the pound just before they are going to be destroyed. We know her heart is in the right place; nevertheless, none of us really wanted more dogs. Most of us already have family pets, and we don't need more. She can get a bit pushy about it. Therefore we usually try to avoid her. There was no avoiding her this time.

"Hi, guys," came her lead-in. "Doesn't the gym look great? I was on the decorating committee. I really want to know if you like it or not?"

I admitted silently, I hadn't really given the decorations much of a look. I checked it out. I had to admit, it did look good. The theme was something under the sea. I don't know how I missed all the fish, seahorses, and seaweed dangling from the ceiling. I thought to myself, 'what dumb butt would climb up on a ladder just to hang that stuff.' Then I looked at Meredith, and the answer came to me…Meredith, of course.

"It looks great, Meredith." I felt this was a safe thing to say. After all, how could she bring up dog adoption from an undersea theme?

"Did you know an experienced sailor is called a sea dog?" Meredith started to say more when I interrupted her. I found it hard to believe she could steer the conversation to dogs from the theme of oceans...sure enough, she did.

"Excuse us for a moment, Meredith. I must get Tish and myself something to drink. Why don't you sit down in my chair and chat with the rest of the group?" I pulled Tish up from her chair and hurried her away.

The team gave me a mean look as I left them saddled with Meredith and her campaign to find dogs homes. Meredith's focus was now on them, and they knew I gave them a bum's rush.

"What was that all about?" asked Tish.

"Meredith was about to start hounding us to take some of her rescue dogs. Hey, did you hear me trying to be witty? Hounding us, ha...ha...ha?" I chuckled at my joke. Tish wasn't laughing.

"Don't be mean, Scott. Meredith is passionate, and I admire her tenacity. She really cares about those dogs getting good homes." Tish was bristling a bit.

"Don't bite my head off, okay? I know Meredith means well; I get tired of her constantly pushing me to take a dog. She knows we plan to go to Chicago to start studying criminal law. How are we supposed to take a dog with us? We will live in a tiny apartment or house, and the only dog that would fit would be some small yappy thing. If we are going to have a dog, we are going to get a big dog that can help us in our private investigation business. Until we can afford a big place, there is no room for a dog." I was looking to the future as I talked to Tish about our plans to become partners after high school and working towards opening our private investigation office as *Evers and McFarlan*.

Tish is a natural candidate as my partner. She has a calm head on her shoulders…smart as a whip and all that, she also has a 3rd Dan Black Belt in Taekwondo, Combat Hapkido, and she is learning Ground Survival and Savate. She is fearless, which pushes me to be braver as well.

Don't get me wrong. There is no question my 6' 3" stature and 220 pounds is both threatening and a target. I get off on the sheer courage to hang in the pocket and take a brutal hit as much as I enjoy the cleverness and technical skill needed to play football at a high level. The one thing I am not is a trained fighter, like Tish. I really don't like to fight; nonetheless, I can throw a mean punch when I need to.

We found the soft drinks and the typical strawberry punch table. Tish wanted the punch drink, and I need a cold Coke. No one spiked the punch bowl yet. I guess ole Miss Sourpuss standing guard over the punch bowl deterred the pranksters, like Jack, the ass.

Speaking of Jack, the ass, I looked over and saw him groping Heather. I suspect he shared a bit of his dad's whiskey in the car with her before they came in, judging by how relaxed Heather seemed to be acting. It was out of her character to allow public displays of whatever. I can't call it affection since it was inappropriate, at best, and lewd at the worst.

I was totally disgusted and asked Tish if she would excuse me for a moment. I could not stand watching that Jack-ass touch Heather for another moment. She said she would stay put by the drink table if I would not take too long. I pretended to need to use the head and went towards the men's room.

I came out a few minutes later to find Lucy Loose on the ground and her jerk of a date, Jesse, in a guillotine choke by yours truly, Tish, my date. I saw Jesse slump to the floor, obviously unconscious. I rushed to get Tish out of the gym before the principal knew what was happening.

"Come on! Now!" I said to Tish as I grabbed her by her arm. She flicked her arm free of me in an instant. She smiled when she saw it was me and allowed me to retake her hand and lead her out a side door. We ran for the car, and I drove away like a maniac.

Getting a mile or two away, I slowed down and asked her what in the hell happened while I was in the bathroom. I turned right onto the road leading to the county park and stopped the engine. I turned to give her my full attention.

"I minded my own business when Lucy, that slut came slithering over to me. I was disgusted by what she said to me. I slapped her because it made me mad! Immediately Jesse came and grabbed me from behind. Well..." I interrupted Tish and said.

"Wait, back up. What did Lucy say to make you slap her?" I wasn't following the events very well.

"OK, as I was saying," Tish continued, "Lucy came up to me right after you left. She made some comment about how I would not have a date at all if she had not broken up Heather and you. I asked Lucy how she managed to break the two of you up. I knew Lucy and Jack sabotaged your relationship with Heather...I just wanted to hear it from her own lips."

"What else did Lucy say?" I asked.

"She told me you were crap in bed, and I boiled over. I knew they got you ripped that night...and for her to lie about you...was more than I could stand...so I slapped her." Tish muttered under her breath, "As if you would ever sleep with a walking disease bag."

"And right after you slapped her is when Jesse came up behind you?" I was touched Tish would go to such lengths to defend my honor.

"Yep, you are right. Jesse came up and grabbed me from behind. He intended to hold me while Lucy took a punch at me. Before Jesse could secure me, I flipped around behind him and caught him in a chokehold. He didn't even know what was happening. Lucy rushed up to break my chokehold, so I side-kicked her to the ground." Tish chuckled.

I chuckled…no…I belly laughed. It was great seeing Jesse turning purple. It was even more fun to see his lights go out.

We both laughed for most of five minutes before we could settle down. "You know the principal is most likely going to call your folks, don't you?"

"I doubt it. I suspect neither Lucy or Jesse are going to declare I got the best of both of them. More likely, they will come up with some other excuse for Jesse and Lucy being on the ground. Oops, they must have slipped on the spilled punch." And our laughter started all over again.

I looked out the driver's side truck window and saw the swings. I remembered how many times Tish and I played at this park when we were small. The old memory made me feel young again.

"Come with me, and I will swing you. It has been years since we played on this playground. It will be fun." I wasn't ready for the evening to end, and I could not think what else we could do at that moment.

I opened the car door for Tish, and we walked hand in hand to the swings. The evening was warm, and the end of our senior year was fast approaching. We listened to the crickets as I pushed the swing and watched Tish's gown float in the gentle air.

As she leaned back, she could watch the stars blur past with the movement of the swing. No words were spoken for several minutes.

I took the swing next to her and pumped my legs back and forth to get the swing started. I noted I did not fit in the swing seat like I once did. Finally, I let the swing come to a stop and waited for Tish to stop also. As her swing gently slowed to a halt, I held out my hand to assist her out of the swing seat. I noted, she did still fit in the seat.

We walked along the path leading to the pond. Frogs were croaking until we got too close, and then they became quiet.

Tish spoke first. "You know it is going to be expensive for us to attend Daley College. We both are going to need a part-time job at least on weekends. We will need to charge high fees when we get our P.I. License to pay for college."

"For sure. Too bad neither one of us was born with a silver spoon in our mouths. I envy Chuck. His mama is rich enough, so he will be able to attend law school and never have any debts. He said he might visit us in Chicago. I know that won't happen. He is such a mama's boy. He will return here and set up his law practice. Just watch." I did not mean for this to sound as derogatory as it did. After all, Chuck is my best friend. I know him like a book. He and his mother got very close when Chuck's dad died.

Tish continued the thought. "Yeah, he is a mama's boy. It would be fun to have a lawyer in town with us. You are right, though; he will never leave his mom home alone. I guess we will need to find another lawyer in Chicago to keep us out of jail." Tish winked, and I smiled.

I figured she wasn't far off the mark. We had enough trouble staying out of jail here in our small town, and we hadn't even graduated yet. Heaven knows what kind of problems we will be in when we are on the streets of Chicago, considering some dicey situations. Good thing, Tish can fend for herself. Chances are, I will need her to keep me from getting my block knocked off.

The walk around the pond was comfortable. Being friends for many years has made it pleasant to be in each other's company. Tish makes me feel contented. I don't need to worry about her feelings or to coddle her. She is rarely ever moody, or maybe I just never noticed when she was. Tish was just Tish.

Thinking about Tish taking down Lucy and Jesse this evening, I realized I had no knowledge of why Tish became obsessed with martial arts. It prompted me to ask the next question. I wasn't really prepared for her answer.

"Tish, I know you well, yet, I never understood why you got into martial arts in such a big way. You were always tough even as a little

Carole Walker Carter

girl. Why did you decide you needed to be even tougher?" I guess Tish didn't much want to tell me since she did not reply.

I decided she wasn't going to answer. Letting her off the hook since it was none of my business, I said. "You don't need to answer. It was a silly question, anyway."

I suddenly became aware Tish was sniffling. Was she crying? Tish doesn't cry. I was with her once when she broke her arm, and she did not cry.

I stopped and turned Tish by the shoulders to face me. She was crying. "What the hell? What's wrong? Did I say something I shouldn't have said? You know I am a big dope. Don't cry. I'm sorry. I didn't mean whatever I said." I stumbled all over myself, trying to apologize because I was at a loss for what else to do.

Tish took my hand and led me to a bench. "It is nothing you did, you dope. It was my uncle…." She let the words drop and said nothing else. I was not sure if she wanted me to hug her or ask more questions. Therefore, I did nothing more than to continue holding her hand.

Tish started to whisper between sobs. "I never told anyone this before, and you need to promise you won't tell a soul. Do you promise?"

"Of course, Tish, I would never repeat a secret you told me. I have your back, and you have mine. Remember?" I tried to be reassuring. I never know if I am succeeding or not. Sometimes I feel inadequate. This was new to me. Tish never acted like a girl before.

"When I was ten, my parents needed to go away for a weekend. I don't remember why they needed to go. They left me with my Uncle Joe." Tish paused and took a deep breath before she continued her story. I sat still as a statue and waited…afraid of what she might say next.

"At any rate, the weekend started out fine. My uncle took me to see a Disney movie, and we had popcorn and candy. It was nice, and he was funny. When we got home, he said I needed to take a bath. I told

38

him I was a big girl and I could take a bath by myself. He said he was in charge, and he needed to make sure I was safe in the bathtub. He also said he needed to make sure I was very clean down there." Tish looked down into her lap.

"Tish, it's me, your best friend. You don't need to be ashamed of anything with me." I was starting to feel upset. I remembered her Uncle Joe, and I thought he was a nice guy. Now I wanted to kill him. I was too late. He was already dead. A strange thought was starting to surface, and I didn't like it. Uncle Joe was murdered, and his murderer was never caught. His neck was broken.... Naw, Tish was not a murderer, she had every right to want to kill him. Especially if what she was about to say was what I thought she would say.

"Tish, you don't need to say anymore if you don't want to. I have a good idea of what happened. I completely understand why you got into martial arts now." I wanted to spare her any more shame or pain. Whatever she was feeling was really messing with my mind.

Tish said, "No one is ever going to take advantage of me again. No one!"

The ferocity in Tish's voice did not really surprise me. I wanted to scream obscenities; I was that mad. Tish was good and decent. What her uncle did to her should never have happened.

"Tish, I don't know what to say except you were a victim. It was wrong on many levels. If your Uncle Joe were alive, I think I would kill him!" I meant every word of it. I hated to hear myself saying such things. I hated to think I could kill anyone. I knew deep down inside, under the right circumstances, I could.

Tish sighed again. She wasn't crying any longer. I put my arm around her, and we sat in silence for a long time. What a way to end our prom night.

CHAPTER FIVE

We both agreed we did not want to go to the after-prom party. I suggested we both go home and get some sleep, and I would pick her up and take her out for breakfast in the morning. There is a truck stop just at the edge of town, and the cook makes pancakes that are out of this world. I told Tish I had money in my pocket, just begging to be spent. She agreed it sounded like fun.

I picked her up early the next morning. She washed off all the glitter and sparkles from the night before. She was Tish again, black jeans and a black tank top, and since it was a bit chilly, she put on her leather jacket.

I was driving my truck this morning. It seemed fitting to pick up Tish in my dad's car for the dance, then again, he wasn't going to let me drive it whenever I wanted. Truth be known, I would rather drive my truck.

It may be old, but it is a 1978 Ford F150 Stepside with new Candy Apple Red paint, compliments of my dad's auto body shop. It has a Ford factory crate 351 Windsor motor with a 3-inch dual exhaust system and a 4-speed transmission. Tish's father helped me install a 4-inch Rancho lift kit with 35" Dunlap mud rovers on American Racing rims at his tire shop in town. It is one sweet ride. Around town, it is known as 'Big Red.'

That's another thing about smaller towns. If one has a distinctive ride, everyone knows whose vehicle it is. It can be useful in some ways, but not-so-good in other ways. One can't get away with much when everyone knows your ride.

We both have saved up as much money as we could by working weekends and summer jobs. Tish bought a motorcycle. I keep telling her winters are too cold and windy in Chicago for a bike. I think she would be better off selling it and getting one of those economy cars. She makes a sour face at me every time we talk about it. I decided to drop the matter for now.

Tish jumped into my truck and buckled on her seatbelt. She rides a sweet Harley. I laughed, thinking how odd, in a car, she wears a belt. Tish is hard to figure sometimes. She is a daredevil on her Harley and a safety nut in my truck. Could it be…just my driving?

"I sure got the 5th-degree last night from Mom". Tish mimicked her mother. "Why are you home early? Did something happen? Why aren't you going to the after-prom party? Did Scotty get fresh with you?'"

I just chuckled at her imitation of her mother. Tish has mimicked her mother for years, and she is good at it. Sometimes to fool me, she acts like she is her mother when I call her on the phone. She gets me every time.

"Well, Moms are like that," I added. "Ready for the best pancakes in town?"

Tish said, "Let's Roll!" I stepped on the loud pedal a bit too much when I let the clutch out…squealing tires and fishtailing. Tish reprimanded me.

"Stop! You will wake the neighbors up, dumb ass. It is still early, and some of my neighbors are probably asleep…or were. My folks won't be happy if you make it difficult for them in this neighborhood. Remember, we are black. We are always under scrutiny."

I never think about the Evers being different from anyone else. They have been friends of my family for years. Our dads served together as Navy Seals. The reason the Evers moved here in the first place was that my dad told her dad what a lovely, quiet town it was. I guess he painted such a beautiful picture, that Cliff brought his bride, Dorothy, here shortly after they got married. Our families have been tight ever since.

I never gave it much thought that the Evers wasn't accepted by everyone. I was raised with them and knew what great people they were. Tish said from time to time, her dad got nasty comments just like she had on the playground when she was little.

I found it hard to believe that some people could dislike the Evers' family just because they were black. Small towns are no different than anyplace else. There are bigots and small-minded people here, just like in the big cities. It is just that everyone knows who the creeps are in the small towns.

Getting to the truck stop, I let my mind return to the reason we were out at such an early hour. My stomach. It was grumbling. I suppose just thinking of food was enough for my stomach to start producing acid.

We found a table at the truck stop, and Patsy took our order. I was content with the tall stack, eggs, hash-browns, and bacon, whereas Tish ordered the short stack, ham, and the fruit plate. The astounding thing is Tish will say that I can eat every bite and not gain an ounce.

I pulled out the Chicago newspaper, and Tish immediately said, "So you are going to read while we eat and not talk to me? We aren't married, you know."

I knew she was teasing me; I just chatted her up. "I found some small houses in Chicago that are affordable. They are not in the best neighborhood, then again, we should think about our monthly expenditures. Here is a two-bedroom house that is only $550.00 a month. They pay the water and garbage, which would leave us the electric bill. What do you think? Maybe we could make a run to Chicago and check it out next weekend. If we like it, we could put a down payment to hold it."

Tish took the newspaper and was looking at the ads. When our pancakes arrived, she set the paper on the chair next to her and grabbed the syrup. I guess she needed food on her stomach to make the right decision.

I found myself excited about the prospect of moving and finding jobs. I wasn't as polite as my mom would have liked. I talked non-stop while chewing, telling her the house was close to the college and not far from a shopping mall.

Tish finally said she thought it was a good idea and we should drive up the next weekend. I was elated. I felt like we were finally on our way to opening our own P.I. Office and starting our future lives.

Funny thing is Tish and I became junior private eyes back when we were in 5th grade. There was a rash of small dogs missing from our neighborhood, and the two of us decided we were going to find out why the dogs were missing. We spent a lot of time on the streets playing in those days, and when we saw a man grab a small dog right out of its owner's fenced yard, we followed him on our bikes. We discovered a dogfighting ring out in the countryside, and sadly, they were using the small dogs to bait the fighting pit bulls. We did manage to save some of the little dogs by rushing to a phone and calling the police. After that, we had people calling us to find missing pets and other items. It got us excited about helping people; we made a pact to become partners. Even then, we worked well together.

Tish interrupted my trip down memory lane by pushing her chair back and telling me she was heading for the ladies' room. I was a bit surprised Tish did not call it the head. I suppose Tish felt she should not be crude in public places. I watched her as she walked down the narrow hallway to where a sign indicated the toilets were located.

A few minutes later, I looked up to see Tish was being blocked from returning by two truck drivers I did not recognize. Obviously, they were not locals, or they would know not to hassle Tish.

I knew Tish could handle herself. To be on the safe side, I moved towards the location just in case it became a situation. I overheard one of the truckers saying, "Look at those knockers, Gus."

Gus replied, "Hey honey, why don't you give us a little Brown Sugar?"

My first thought, 'Oh No. You dumb jerks…you are in for it now', and just as I was thinking that, Tish put her hands into fists, leaving her thumbs out and jammed her thumbs into the sides of the closest trucker's jaw just below his ears. He dropped like a ton of bricks.

The other trucker started name-calling and was closing the distance between himself and Tish when I reached out and grabbed his arm from behind, spinning him away from Tish and causing him to face me. I calmly said, "You don't really want to do that, do you, Mister?"

He sized me up and decided I was just a wet-behind-the-ears kid…big and not very bright. I suddenly saw in his eyes, he changed his mind, and I was feeling pretty confident when I followed the trucker's stare. Behind me stood Mack and Harry, local truckers.

The two big truckers stepped past me, and Mack took the trucker on the ground and pulled him to his feet. Harry grabbed the standing trucker by the arm and said menacingly, "Let's help you two guys, to your truck. You have overstayed your welcome in our town. Good idea if you drive through next time and don't stop. Got it?"

Mack winked at us as the two of them pushed the truckers out the door. Tish started to become incensed when I stopped her with a couple of words. "No feminist crap right now, Tish. Those truckers are our friends, and in our business, we will need friends to watch our back. We won't always be able to work together. Don't alienate them, OK? It's good to have people you know watching your back when I am not with you."

Softening, Tish said she would thank them for their help and be kind. I knew she would. She did have common sense when she wasn't ready to fight the world.

We went back to our table, and when Gus and Harry came back inside, Tish was good as her word. She was friendly and sweet; Gus and Harry would have eaten out of her hand. If she wasn't planning on being a P.I., Tish could go into politics.

The rest of the week was uneventful, except when Tish said she walked in on a bunch of cheerleaders in the locker room who were grilling Heather to see what happened with Jack after the prom. I guess they did not go to the after-prom party like the rest of the crowd. Tish said the moment she entered; the room became totally silent. I guess I won't be finding out anything from her. I will need to wait and see what Jack tells the football players. If anything happened, he would be crowing about it. He's such a jerk.

The week ended without me hearing any gossip. I concentrated on Tish and my trip to Chicago to check out the apartments and smaller houses available to rent. Tish promised she would be up and ready early on Saturday. I swung by her home at 7 a.m., and we headed to the big city of Chicago.

Traffic was sparse early in the morning all the way to Chicago. Tish held the map on her lap and acted as a navigator; that way, we would not lose time getting lost on city streets. Neither of us knew our way around the city very well.

We came across a small house we both liked. The bedrooms were small; the kitchen was tiny, and the living room was narrow. Even so, there was a small-sized finished basement. I think you get the idea. It is small. On the plus side, there is side and rear parking areas. I won't need to pay to store my truck when not in use. That is worth a lot to me. There is an oversized one car garage for Tish to use when she gets a car. In the meantime, the garage will be used as storage. Even over-sized, it is too small for 'Big Red'. Tish said it would suit her Harley just perfectly. Egad, I was hoping she would leave her bike at home.

Most of the week, we will be using public transit. The bus stop is close, and the mall is only about a mile away. The campus is close, too.

The truck will only be used when we make trips home or want to go someplace further away, like downtown.

All in all, we decided this house would work just perfectly for us. We left a deposit for the first month's rent, a cleaning deposit, and signed a contract agreeing not to have a pet. That will make Meredith mad. It is the perfect excuse to say no when she tries to push one of her rescue dogs on us again.

We decided since we were here in Chicago, we would check out the college we would be attending in the fall. It is a two-year program at Richard J. Dailey City College in criminal justice. The curriculum will be intense for the whole two years. I am not worried since Tish is a brain, and she will be tutoring me.

The campus seemed imposing after coming from a small-town high school. Chances are most of our classes would be in one building. Once we find that building, we will be fine.

I was just really pleased we agreed to find a place to live and move up earlier than September. We both needed to find part-time jobs if we were going to be able to go to college anyway. I found myself envious of the kids who have wealthy parents and would not need to work.

We wanted to spend more time exploring the area. However, a two-and-a-half-hour drive was still ahead of us. I promised to try to find a good burger restaurant before heading out. I sure don't want Tish to be hungry for the ride home. She isn't moody until she is hungry and then look out!

We drove past Ford City Mall to see if there would be an excellent place to eat. I saw the IHOP and thought about pancakes for lunch. Tish nixed that idea immediately. I did make a mental note to myself; the mall might be an excellent choice for finding a part-time job. Starting courses in criminal justice might be impressive enough to get a security job there. It would be worth a try once we got settled in our new home.

I saw a postman delivering mail and stopped him to ask where the best place is to get a burger. The postman laughed and said, "You must not be from here. The best burger in the world is *Top Notch Burgers* on 95th Street.

The restaurant was a bit north and east of where we started. It was easy enough to find. Parking 'Big Red' was a bit more complicated. Wow! The postman was not wrong! *Top-Notch Burgers* make a fantastic burger.

The drive home was uneventful, especially since Tish's stomach was full, and she was not grumpy. We put on the radio. We kept singing, seat dancing and laughing about songs we both knew. Oh, how the time flew by, and before I knew it, we were back at our houses in Stanton.

It was strange to think about having a home with Tish. She isn't my life partner or even my girlfriend. She is my best friend and like a sister to me. I think it will be comfortable living with her.

.

CHAPTER SIX

The senior picnic was scheduled for Friday the week before graduation. There are one hundred and twenty-six students in our graduating class. We were going back to the lake just as we had two years earlier for our sophomore outing.

It was this sophomore outing where I was one of forty students, with a little help from the spiked watermelon, that got peer pressured into pooling our money. Tran Tam gave us a persuasive money-making talk. Tran is such an excellent public speaker; he could definitely be a politician.

Tran has an older brother, Riley, who works for a Texas-based computer company. Tran overheard his brother telling their father about his computer company, the importance of personal computers, their exponential growth, and something about Moore's Law that predicts a doubling of transistors in an integrated circuit every two years. This means electronics can be made smaller and cheaper with more features over time.

He told us his father asked his brother if the company was worth an investment. Riley's reply was, like all investments, it is a risk–but–it could be worth a look. Tran explained he investigated the opportunity and felt if we all invested in the computer company, as a group, we could be multi-millionaires within ten years. Everyone's eyes and smiles grew large at the thought.

I can't remember if it was Jack, Tran, or Douglas who said we ought to make this more exciting and come up with a contract where we pool our money, and the Final Alumni standing gets it all. It really did not matter who brought up the Final Alumni idea since the excitement in the group surrounding Tran was at a fever pitch.

Besides, it sounded like a fun enough scheme, especially since someone spiked the watermelon with vodka, and none of us were feeling any pain or thinking straight for that matter. We made a pact then and there, not to let our parents know about the small print, just the investment in a growing computer company.

Not everyone was invited into this scheme. For instance, Tish was not at the sophomore picnic that year. I think she got pulled out for some martial arts competition in Joliette.

The other 80 students just weren't part of our crowd. They would not be included. Basically, it was the football team, the cheerleaders, and a few of our close friends. Of course, they needed to have their parents' co-signature and come up with the $750.00 in the first place, and most of the other kids could not pull together that amount.

I knew Tish would want to be in on this deal. I committed $750.00 for her. Heather jerked my hand and gave me a dirty look when I made this commitment.

I discussed the opportunity with Tish that evening. As usual, she had a million and one questions. It took all that I knew to answer her questions. After thirty minutes of her grilling me, I promised to pay her back the $750.00 if it ended up being a bad deal. With that assurance and some trepidation, Tish finally agreed to participate. She had one final question. "How is everyone going to get their parents to co-sign?"

I shrugged. "I know $750.00 sounds like a lot of money, but in the big picture, it really isn't. Most parents will sign, thinking this is a good learning experience for us. Some parents may believe it will teach us not to gamble with our hard-earned money."

Riley's lawyer drafted a legal agreement for each of us to sign. Riley also agreed to make the computer company stock purchase through a

Texas-based investment company in the name of Stanton '92' Alumni Group. Before the end of our sophomore year, all of us and our parents signed the investment agreement. We provided the $750.00 required for the stock purchase. Each of the investors received a copy of the contract and a receipt for the investment.

It may seem surprising that we all forgot anything about the investment until we found ourselves back at the lake for our senior picnic.

CHAPTER SEVEN

The school provided buses for us to attend the senior picnic. I suspect they know from past years some students will no doubt bring booze, and they don't want any of us driving home from the picnic drunk. Our principal isn't stupid.

I was ready for the day. I even wore my swimming trunks under my jeans. The lake is pleasant, and the park provides grills for cooking the hamburgers or hot dogs the school will provide. I am sure there will be potato chips, potato salad, soft drinks, and brownies or cookies…standard fare when there isn't pizza around.

Tish was already waiting with a bunch of other girls. The buses were pulling up. I hurried. I wanted to sit with Tish. I noticed Heather in another line with Jack. Something about her seemed a bit off to me. I looked away before Heather caught me staring at her. I was concerned about what could be wrong with her.

"Hey, Scott, get your butt over here," yelled Tish from the line. She was saving me a spot in the line, like the buddy she is.

I sidled up to her with jeers from the girls behind us saying things like 'no cuts, end of the line' and some other crap. I just smiled my award-winning smile and knew they would let me into the line. I also knew they were just teasing to get my attention. Therefore, I played along with them.

Tish punched me in the arm and said, "Get moving. You are holding up the line." She pushed me from behind to get me onto the bus.

I noticed most of the girls were carrying large canvas bags. I asked them what they had in their canvas bags.

Carrie, a strawberry blond cheerleader, said coyly, "That's for us to know and you to find out."

Tish punched me again and told me to knock it off. "They have their swimsuits and towels, fart-knocker. What did you think they would bring to the lake?"

Tish could be a kill-sport. "Whatever...I was just teasing them, spoilsport."

There was lots of girl talk from behind us. I found myself eavesdropping when I heard the name Heather come up. I could just make out something about her going all the way the night of the Senior Ball or some such thing.

Knowing Heather, I felt it was a lie. Girls can be catty and petty. I was sure they were making things up, trying to impress each other with what they knew. Heather was a decent and respectable girl. All those years we dated, she kept me at arms distance because she was saving herself for marriage. Why would she bend her rule now...with Jack, for that matter?

As I continued to listen, I heard things I did not want to hear. Too drunk to know what Heather was doing was one thing said over and over. It made me sick to think Jack would get Heather drunk and then take advantage of her.

Tish noticed I was quiet and trying to hear everything said from the seats a row or two behind us. She touched my arm and whispered, "You aren't involved any longer. Let it go."

I guess she could tell I was starting to get angry. She was right, Heather was no longer my girlfriend. I needed to let it go. I wondered if I really could.

Getting off the bus, I saw the football team had taken over several tables as usual. We headed towards them. We always did. They were my buddies, and they accepted Tish as one of the guys. It made it much more fun to have her by my side.

I noticed Jack and Heather were staying with the cheerleaders and their little clique. Don't get me wrong. It isn't that I dislike cheerleaders because I don't. It is just annoying how they can be elitist and snobby at times. I never enjoyed being around Heather when she hung out with them when we dated.

We had a bit of time before the sun would be hot enough to swim. We decided a hike might be fun. Not everyone was up for the walk. Tran, James, and Doug said they would join Tish and me.

I played football with all three of these guys. They aren't the stereotypical dumb jocks. All of them will go on to the university in the fall. That means Tish and I should be able to hook up with them from time to time in Chicago. We told them where we would be living, and they are always welcome if they bring the pizza.

Tran pulled me aside on the trail and told me he had good news for the bunch of us who contributed towards the computer stock we purchased. Evidently, in two short years, the company's stock skyrocketed. The present value of our initial $750.00 purchase was over $3,000.00. That would make the Final Alumni fund worth $120,000.00!

Now, Tran was saying he wished we never agreed to the Final Alumni standing contract. He said we could all be rich in no time. Now only one of us would be filthy rich.

I asked him why we could not all just agree to end the contract, and Tran said several in the group refused. They still thought it was a game and wanted it to stay in effect.

I asked who the jerks were who would not agree to end the contract, and he named Jack, James, Douglas, as well as Jesse. I turned to James and Douglas, who was hiking with us at that very moment.

"Hey, you two. Why don't you want to end the contract and just let each of us own our own stocks? We could all be rich enough and not need to wait until everyone else dies."

Douglas spoke up first. "For one thing, Chuck says it isn't easy to end these types of contracts, and he is going to be a lawyer. He should know about this stuff. The other thing is we got into this for the fun of it, and what fun would it be to end it before it really got started?"

"Oh, come on, Scott. You agreed to do this. Buck up." This was my pal James talking.

"You guys all have enough money to go to a university. Tish and I could use the extra money to get through school ourselves. We aren't going to get scholarships, and neither of our parents can afford to send us to college. We are doing this all on our own dime. These stocks could make a real difference to us." I felt like I was whining when I said this to them. It made me look cheap. It was the truth, though.

Tish pushed me from behind again. "Get the lead out. I want to finish this trail before they start cooking the burgers."

I knew she thought it was a dead-end topic, and I may as well bite the bullet and move on. Tish is very pragmatic about life in general. She feels we should play the cards we are dealt and make the best out of our lives.

I moved on at a faster pace than any of them expected. I was partly working off the anger I was feeling at hearing about Jack doing Heather. Adding to this anger was the fact we had money we could not access.

By the time we made the loop back to the park, I could smell the burgers and hot dogs cooking. The food smelled great, and it helped to put me back into a better mood.

The chaperones set the tables and laid out all the food for us. Paper plates, cups, etc. were at one end, and the idea was to grab a plate, fill it up with buns, condiments, salads, chips, fruit, cookies and then go and get either a hot dog or a hamburger or both in my case. The drinks were in a cooler near the grills. It was easy to grab a drink and sit down. I already decided to go back for a second hamburger if there were any left once the whole class went through the line.

Oddly enough, I was quite full when I finished my plate. The sun was high in the sky, and it was getting hot. I passed on a second hamburger. I did not want to be too full to swim. A group of us were planning to play water polo. It would not be good to get a cramp while treading water.

Most of the girls were sunbathing or swimming in the shallows. Not Tish, she was swimming the distance to the float in the center of the lake. I watched her dive into the water like a sleek otter and gracefully stretch her arms out to stroke the water. One could barely see her splash as she kicked. She was as natural in the water as she was in her dobok at a Taekwondo competition. There was no question in my mind that Tish could replace me as the quarterback if she were born a guy. It is a good thing she wasn't born a guy...for more than one reason.

We divided into teams, Jack was the captain of one side, and I was the captain of the other. I knew this was going to be a good old 'no holds barred' game. It turned out to be as rough as I expected.

Our teams were evenly matched. Even though there were several rough kill shots, we were having fun. That is until someone noticed Wally, the fullback from our team, was floating face down in the water. Chuck and I swam to him and pulled him onto the beach.

He wasn't breathing. I started rolling him over to force out the water in his lungs as someone else ran to get the chaperones. When they arrived, they pushed me out of the way and continued the attempt to get him breathing again.

With my hands on my head, I just sat there in shock. How could this have happened? One minute we were all playing water polo, and the next thing Wally is dead. I could tell he was dead. No matter how much effort the adults made to save his life and to get him to breathe, he just wasn't.

I don't know how long they kept at it. I know someone drove to the ranger's station at the entrance to the park to send for an ambulance. The whole senior class formed a circle around him except, I noted,

Jesse quietly walking away. Girls were crying, and the guys were staring in disbelief.

When the ambulance arrived, the attendants gently placed Wally's body on a stretcher, covered him entirely, and took him away. Wow...Wally was gone...just like that.

The chaperones asked us all to gather our stuff and head back to the buses. Not a word was said. It wasn't silent...crying could still be heard.

CHAPTER EIGHT

The bus ride back to school was solemn. There were some hushed whispers about what happened. Girls who were sunbathing or watching the game on the beach did not seem to see much.

One girl said she was sure Wally was jerked under the water. When asked, she said she could not see who did it. There was lots of speculation. It seemed each girl kept her eye on this guy or another and was only willing to state they were nowhere near Wally when he drowned.

Tish's advantage from the float in the middle of the lake, while still a fair distance, was directly in line with the incident. She told me quietly Wally was one of the players on the outer edge of the group. He was treading water when he seemed to be jerked downward by something under the water. She didn't see who or what jerked his body underwater. Tish said she saw Wally try to resurface. Tish commented she thought she saw an arm surface from underwater, grabbing his head and pulling him back under. Tish said the moment she saw him go back under the water; she dove off the float to see if she could reach Wally in time. It was a long swim...she was too late...Scotty already had him out of the water.

It made me feel sick to think there was a possibility someone intentionally murdered one of our schoolmates. I decided that it was possible some rough fun just got out of hand. After all, why would anyone want to kill Wally? It was more likely someone was trying to keep Wally from getting the ball.

Grief counselors were at the school the next day. Anyone who needed to talk to them could leave class without asking and go to the room set up for that reason. I found myself watching as students left the classroom. I could not help wondering how many students went to the grief room versus how many used it as an excuse to get out of class.

Strangely, a morbid thought popped into my mind. Now there were only thirty-nine investors….

Later at home, Tish phoned. "Hey Scott, I have been thinking. I know Wally's drowning was not an accident. The more I replay the scene in my head, the more I am sure and not just suspicious someone meant to kill Wally."

I was curious and asked, "Why do you say that, Tish?"

Tish answered. "I was watching the water polo game from the float. I never saw anyone guarding Wally ever. Suddenly, he just sank from sight. When his head popped back above the water, I saw a hand push his head back under. I dove into the lake; I kept watching while I swam towards him, and I saw Wally finally pop up in a dead-man's float. I scanned the water, and no one was out of place from the game. I kept scanning the water, and I finally saw a boy appear from under the water next to a log. He was near the shore some distance from where the water polo game was being played. He did not come out of the water. He just stayed behind the floating log.

Pretty soon, there was much so commotion on the shore surrounding Wally; I lost sight of the boy by the log. Whoever that boy was, got out of the water while I was still swimming towards the beach. Everyone else must have been distracted by the resuscitation attempt and did not see the guy."

I tried to make light of what Tish was saying for her sake. I had my suspicions, too. Why did Jesse leave the group while everyone circled Wally? Was it because he already knew Wally was dead? Did he kill him? If so, why?

Jesse is a jerk, and he is mean. He is like a mean dog at the end of his master's leash. He isn't going to do anything without his master telling him to do it. Right now, his master is Jack. Seemingly, Jack was too busy being captain of his team. When would Jack have the chance to tell Jesse to drown Wally?

"Tish, the only suspicious person I saw the whole time was Jesse, who slinked away from the group when they were working on Wally. I don't think he would drown Wally without Jack telling him to do it. You know Jack was too busy showing off to give Jesse the sign to take down Wally. Besides, why would he?"

"Okay Scotty, but Jack paid Jesse to try to take you out, remember? Oh, I don't mean he paid Jesse to try to kill you. Jack did pay Jessie to injure your knees. He wanted you incapacitated. That way, you would not be the quarterback any longer. I am just saying he is someone to watch." Tish was really getting into being a real detective. She had me thinking, too.

"Okay, let's say Jack did put Jesse up to drowning Wally. Why? I know what Jack's motive was for paying Jesse to try to hurt me. He wanted my position and Heather. Why would he motivated be to kill Wally?" I was thinking out loud as much as talking to Tish.

Tish acted as if she was having an *ah-ha* moment. "The money! They just found out how much the stocks are worth today. I can think of one hundred and twenty thousand reasons. Why not start to eliminate the competition now?"

I disclosed the thought crept into my mind earlier. I passed it off as absurd and morbid. There are thirty-nine of us left. There is no way Jack and Jesse are going to kill thirty-seven people. Even if they did, one of them would need to kill the other one to claim the money. Just too crazy to think about.

"Tish, think about what you are saying and what the two of them would need to do to kill thirty-seven other people, well, thirty-eight other people. It is just insane. Except for maybe...if it gets down to just the two of them...they will change the contract and split the money."

The voice of reason came flooding back to my head. "These theories are just too crazy."

Leaving the subject, I asked her if she was going to the funeral? I knew I needed to be there. All the football team would assemble. I suspected some of us would be asked to be the pallbearers. I rather hoped I would not be one of them. Wally and I weren't very close.

It was going to put a damper on our graduation ceremony. Graduation was only five days away. Three days from now a funeral, five days I would graduate; ten days, Tish and I would pack up and move to our new house. I was looking forward to ten days from now when I could leave all the rest behind.

Somehow, we made it through the funeral and graduation. Tish and I were packing boxes. Tish would come to my house and help me decide what to take, or I should say, she would help me decide what not to take. I told her I could not live without my beer stein collection or my football banners. She vetoed both none-the-less.

I retaliated at her house by not allowing her to bring her boxing gloves or her motorcycle leather pants. If she wasn't going to take her Harley to the city, why would she bring her leather pants? I really vetoed them out of spite. I was hurting myself more than her since I love the way she looks in those tight pants. Dang...I must always remind myself I can look but not touch when she has them on. Being best friends with such a hot girl can be difficult.

Tish became solemn while we packed boxes. I could tell something was bugging her. I asked, "Tish, what is bothering you?"

She answered. "Scotty, you have a chance to play football at any top-level university. If I am not wrong, you were offered scholarships at several schools. I think you may be making a big mistake by not accepting it. We can postpone becoming private investigators until after you play college football."

I answered, frankly. "Tish, you have scholarships as well. Are you reconsidering our decision? I will understand if you want to take advantage of your scholarships. Is that what you want to do?"

"Scotty, you know I am interested in my martial arts and helping people. I decided a long time ago that being a private investigator was what I wanted to do with my life. You are a five-star quarterback. You can play college football and then go on to play professionally. I don't want our agreement to stand in your way," Tish said honestly.

"Tish, the most important thing in the world to me is working side-by-side with you. We have been best friends and partners since fourth grade. Football has been an ego boost. Honestly, my knees are hurting, and I don't want to be one of those broken down forty-year-old ex-athletes. If I am going to break down, it is going to be for a good cause...helping someone who needs my help. At least, I will feel good about my disability." I laughed as I said this to Tish.

I continued, "Now what about you? You are a straight-A student. You could go on to law school or something equally as good. Do you really want to be stuck with a broken-down jock wearing out your shoes pounding the sidewalks?"

Now Tish had to laugh. "Yes, that is what I want to do, as long as that broken-down jock is you. Come on, let's finish packing our boxes. Our new life is just waiting for us to get started."

The boxes were full of what we could not live without, and both our mom's donated dishes, pans, bedding, and what they felt we needed to set up our house. We did not want them to make the trip to help us settle in. Tish and I both knew there would be no stopping them. A mother's touch would mean frilly curtains on the windows, if nothing else.

Moving day finally arrived, and I woke up bright and early. I was eager about this new adventure; I could hardly sleep. We loaded my truck, went to Tish's house, and packed more boxes. We added Tish's grappling mat. The moms rode together in a small rental vehicle with our beds, dressers, dining room table and chairs that we purchased and stored over the last year, and we pulled away caravan style. Not wanting to alarm Tish's mother, I drove slower than I wanted. She did not realize I drove slower than her own daughter. Good thing Tish wasn't driving my truck, or her mother would have insisted Tish return home immediately.

Unloading took a bit longer than loading. The mothers wanted to check out the house first and decide where everything should go. Tish and I knew once they left, we would put things where we wanted, in the meantime, we would do things their way. We did not want to alarm them too much, or they might just decide to stay with us. That wasn't something either of us wanted.

It seemed like hours before our mothers were satisfied where each item was placed. The towels were folded precisely in thirds and placed neatly in the small linen closet along with a change of bedding for each bed. Curtains were hung at each window as I feared with no respect for our likes or dislikes. Cheerful flowers could be seen staring at us from each window. Tish and I looked at each other, knowing the curtains would go.

Tish, like me, preferred masculine colors. Black, gray, red, or maroon would dominate the house. An old sofa was left from the previous tenants, and it fits us just fine. The color was spot on; it was black. However, it sagged in the middle.

After stocking our cupboards with food and cooking us a meal or two to put in the refrigerator, the moms made their tearful goodbyes. They tried to make us promise we would come home every weekend. We said every weekend was not going to work since we needed to find jobs, and most likely, our employers would expect us to work most weekends. We promised to come home as often as possible. That did not really sit as well with our moms as we hoped. I think they knew we would do the best we could.

Both of our moms turned to us. Dorothy said, "At first, we thought you were both making a mistake by not using your scholarships and going on to a four-year university. We have great faith in both of you.

You both showed us you are mature beyond your age, and we trust you totally. You are making the right decision. Your fathers feel the same way, and we all will be there to support you in any way we can. Just whistle if you need us, and we will be here in a flash." Our mothers handed each of us an expensive-looking gold pendant whistle on a gold chain.

We both let our mothers put them around our neck. We knew this was the stamp of approval Tish and I needed from our parents. Now, we really felt good about our decision.

After they left, we decided to go for take-out pizza. Neither of us was quite ready for a home-cooked meal. It was just too exciting to be on our own. We may as well get used to how things are going to be from the start. Our home-cooked meals will be okay in the refrigerator for a day or two.

Full of pizza, feet up and watching TV seemed to be what the doctor ordered now. Everything was great until Tish spoke up. "We need to find jobs starting tomorrow, you know."

I really wanted a few days to explore Chicago and get a feel for the city. I certainly didn't want to start job hunting the moment we got moved in.

"Can't we put it off for a week and just see the sights. I have never spent much time in Chicago, even though we live in this state. When our family vacationed, we always went to Kentucky to visit my grandparents. I would love to kick around for a few days." I spoke, not really looking over at Tish. I was finishing off the last piece of pizza and was watching some inane commercial about bad breath. I was thinking about my breath and the pizza loaded with onions.

Tish kicked my legs off the coffee table to unsettle me. "Look, roomie, we paid for this month's rent and the last month's rent. If we don't find jobs, next month will be our last month. Do you want to go back to your room at your parent's house or live here with me?"

I was getting the idea Tish was trying for a reality check. I knew she was right. We came early to get a jump on the part-time jobs before the rest of the college students arrived.

"Got the message. Tomorrow it is." We chatted for a bit about what possible jobs there may be for us. I knew I would start my search at the mall and hope there would be an opening for a mall cop. I suggested Tish join me.

"No way! The only jobs at the mall for a girl would be selling clothes, cosmetics, or orange juice at the Orange Julius. I am not doing any of those jobs unless there is nothing else, I could do. I was thinking more about checking out the martial arts dojang seven blocks east on 79th Street. Just maybe they would hire me to teach the younger students. I am pretty good with kids."

I agreed it made sense to me. "You may as well capitalize on what you have going for you. If you don't want to model, then teaching karate seems like a second choice to me."

I knew I was in for a punch when I mentioned modeling, and sure enough, I wasn't disappointed. "It isn't karate anyway, stupid."

I found myself yawning and stretching. It was earlier than I usually go to bed; I was flat exhausted. Carrying boxes all day was a chore, even for a big muscular guy like me. I was not going to see if a moving company could use my help.

"I'm going to shower and go to bed. Okay, with that, or do you want the shower first?" I was not used to having a roommate. I thought I should check out her schedule and be accommodating as best as I could.

She replied, "If you let me wash my face and brush my teeth first, you can take a shower. I like to shower in the mornings. It helps me to wake up."

With that comment, she jumped up and headed for the bathroom. I barely got up off the sofa when she announced the bathroom was all mine. So far, so good…it seemed our bath rituals were not going to be a problem.

"Night, buddy. See you in the morning." She added just before she closed her bedroom door, "Oh, if you get scared being in a new place, just holler. I will protect you." Laughing, she closed the door.

Trouble is, she could protect me. Believe me, if I get scared in the middle of the night, she will be the one I give a holler.

CHAPTER NINE

I woke up bright and early. Tish was already up drinking a cup of coffee. I never acquired a taste for coffee; I passed whenever she offered it. We ate cereal with toast and drank a glass of orange juice, which our mothers packed away for us. Before long, I realized Tish, and I needed to decide who would buy groceries or if we would do those things together. There sure were a lot of things we needed to talk about if living together was not going to become a problem.

"You look nice." I meant what I said. Tish could clean up real good. She wore tailor-fitted black slacks, a white blouse with a lavender-blue blazer. It seemed appropriate for job hunting.

"Thanks. You aren't going job hunting looking like that, are you?" Tish was giving me a once over when she said those words.

A fleeting thought was that maybe Tish and I could enjoy our first day, living alone as adults…not under our parents' roofs. After all, shouldn't a fella be able to relax and enjoy the thrill?

"You mean I can't wear jeans to get a job? I always wore jeans when I got jobs back home. What's wrong with what I am wearing?" I was feeling a bit defensive. I always wore jeans and boots.

"Scott, you need to put on a nice long-sleeved blue shirt and a pair of khakis if you want anyone to take you seriously. You do have something other than jeans, don't you?" Tish was still giving me the once-over.

I finished my toast and pushed the chair away from our little dining room table. I begrudgingly went to change. I think my mom insisted I pack something better for church or going out to dinner. I was sure I would find something that would meet Tish's approval.

When I came back wearing what she suggested I wear, Tish gave a low whistle. "Now, you are cooking. I am sure you will get hired looking that sharp." She winked and grabbed her bag.

"I'm heading out now. It isn't far to walk. I will see you for lunch, right?" With those words, Tish was out the door.

I fiddled around for about an hour before I walked out the door. I locked the door and hoped Tish remembered her keys. I decided Tish had a good idea about taking a walk. The mall wasn't far from our house, and I needed to stay in shape. Walking past the campus on the way to the mall got me thinking about whether the college would have a gym I could use. I made a mental note to go by and check it out later.

Entering the mall, I looked for the offices where mall security would be located. It was tucked back away from the stores. There were several other offices as well. I guess there is more to managing a mall than just leasing stores.

I left my name with a woman at the front desk. She said she would be with me in a minute. Shortly, she came over and handed me a clipboard, pen, and application. I wasn't excited about having to fill out the application form. In a small town, a man either hires you, or he doesn't. I looked at the application and settled down to fill it out.

It took a bit longer to fill out the application than I thought it should. One of the problems was not having any local references. I put down the names of people from my home town who I worked for in one capacity or another and hoped that would be good enough. Then I just sat and waited.

I looked at the clock. I realized it was getting close to lunchtime. I hoped Tish would not be worried if I was not home by noon. Again, I worried whether Tish kept her keys with her.

Just then, a man walked out from behind a door and called my name. I stood up and nodded. I walked closer to him, and he held out his hand and offered his name as well.

"Hi Scott, my name is Mr. Clarkson. I am the head of Mall Security. I see you are looking for a part-time job. Come into my office and let's talk a little to find out if you would be right for a position with us."

I followed Mr. Clarkson into his office and sat in a chair that he indicated was for me. I tried to seem relaxed. I was nervous and hoped my shirt was not showing sweat stains. Giving a quick check, I relaxed.

Mr. Clarkson started the interview. "Scott, why would you like to work in security at the mall?"

It seemed a straight forward enough question. I answered as best as I could. I told Mr. Clarkson about starting college and wanting to get my private investigator's license eventually. Talking a bit about Tish as a partner, I told him a little about her. Most of the time, I talked more about myself.

"You seem to be in good shape. I am assuming you played sports in high school. Am I right?" A second question I could answer quickly.

"Yes, sir. I was the quarterback for my high school football team. We won state this year. I also played some baseball before my coach made me make a choice between the two sports. I like contact sports. Therefore, football won out. I also lift weights and jog to keep fit." It seemed impressive to me. I was hoping he would like my answer.

"I can see that you are fit. I am assuming your high school demanded that your grades were acceptable to stay on the team. What were your strongest subjects?" Mr. Clarkson continued to grill.

"My best subjects were math and science. I was also the president of the computer club. I will admit my weakest subject was Senior Literature. It wasn't that I did not enjoy reading; it was just that I was not excited about reading Dostoyevsky's short stories on unconscious and conscious thought," Scott said, realizing belatedly, he should have left out his weakness.

Mr. Clarkson hesitated a moment. "Good. You seem like a smart young man, and that is necessary for this job since one needs to think quickly on one's feet. By the way, are you trained in any self-defense?"

His question caught me by surprise. I came back as quickly as I could with this answer. "Presently, my roommate is teaching me self-defense. She is trained in multiple disciplines and has black belts in two I know of." I was stretching the truth a bit. I decided maybe it would be a good idea if Tish did teach me some stuff.

Mr. Clarkson looked at me carefully. "Scott, this job is not usually dangerous. There are times it can be. If you would catch a shoplifter who is packing a gun, would you know how to protect the shoppers as well as yourself?" I guess I stammered a bit. Mr. Clarkson saved me from embarrassment with another quick question.

"Would you be willing to start as the night watchman? After you get more training at your college and from your roommate, we could talk about giving you shift duty in the mall when it is open for business. What do you say? I do have an opening if you are interested."

I asked a few questions about hours, how many days, and the pay. After Mr. Clarkson told me it would be Friday through Sunday night to start with and what I would make for those 24 hours, I agreed to the job.

Mr. Clarkson smiled and told me to go fill out more papers with his secretary. He said she would give me a uniform as well. I would be starting this coming Friday night. We shook hands again, and I thanked him as he escorted me out of his office door.

I was not sure if I was relieved to have a job or disappointed. I would only be working 24 hours a week. Once I thought about my school schedule, I realized the situation could be perfect. Of course, I would be tired on Monday mornings when I faced my first class in the fall. The rest of my week would not be too bad once I caught up on sleep.

I rushed home to find Tish sitting at the table, eating a sandwich, and drinking a glass of milk. I wondered how our mothers managed to get that many groceries put away without my noticing.

"Hey, I got a job. How about you?" I said this as I went to the counter to make myself a sandwich.

Tish chewed the food that was in her mouth before answering. "It seems the Grandmaster feels I am qualified to teach self-defense to children as well as to women who want to learn to protect themselves. I am scheduled to teach three different classes. He even said that once school starts, he will try to create classes around my schedule. He suggested I start this Saturday with two different levels. I will have a white belt class followed by a yellow belt class. My women's self-defense class will be in the early afternoon. If I work out well, he may try an evening class as well. How about you?"

I told her I would be working the night shift Friday through Sunday until I am trained in self-defense. "Do you think you can take on a private class for me? I bragged about my roommate's abilities, and Mr. Clarkson seemed impressed." I gave her my best-friend forever smile.

She laughed and said she would be glad to show me some moves that would include disarming a suspect and fighting off more than one opponent. I smiled at Tish. I never waste one of my flashy smiles on her. She knows me too well. They don't work on her.

We did not order pizza as I hoped we would. Tish reminded me that our mothers took the time to make us some home-cooked meals, and we should eat them first. After that, she explained we would be taking turns cooking. Only when one or the other could not fulfill the agreement to prepare meals, would we order out. She explained our budget to me as best as she could, exaggerating and slowing her words as if I was a slow learner.

"Look, dumb butt, you will be making enough to cover the rent, and I will be making enough to cover the food bills…if and that is a big if…we cook at home. We will have just enough left over for tuition, books, insurance and our utilities. As much as I would love to eat pizza and drink cola every night, it isn't going to happen...got it?"

I did get it. We needed to make a budget and live on it. I knew Tish was right. I had to get a smart-ass remark in, making sure she would know it was still me she was living with. I knew she expected it, and I did not want to disappoint her. I said, "Well, I guess you know about money and stuff. I think we could live on pizza and probably be ahead on our food budget. After all, if we bought a cheap large pizza, we could eat a couple of pieces for dinner and still have leftovers for breakfast." I smiled to let her know I was kidding. She scowled anyway, knowing I wasn't taking the talk seriously.

I laughed at the funny face she made. She realized I was kidding and joined me in joking. "Yes, and we can have chocolate bars for lunch, and on the weekends, we will eat ice cream for breakfast, lunch, and dinner."

"Now you're cooking. We are on our own, and we can do what we want, right?" I was still laughing at the idea of two young adults eating like children just because we could.

She stopped laughing. I could see she was thinking about what I just said. I guess it just hit me as well, we were really adults and living on our own. We weren't just kids playing grown-up any longer. This was serious stuff.

Tish pulled out the college course catalog from under a stack of papers. "Look, Scott, there is a firearm training course starting in just a week. It is a mandatory forty-hour course for private investigators. We may as well take it this summer and get the requirement out of the way. What do you say?"

"Would this allow us to conceal and carry a pistol?" I asked.

Then Tish read, "We could conceal and carry a pistol only during work hours to and from home. However, we won't be allowed to carry a firearm until we were 21 years old."

She continued my education with, "This course is 20 hours in the classroom for firearm laws and the use of force and reporting. It also has 20 hours at the range in combat shooting, double-action shooting, and positioning."

I was starting to get excited at the prospect of combat shooting. "By all means, let's sign up for the class tomorrow. I think this should be fun. By the way, you know I am a crack shot already with a rifle. Dad and I spent time together hunting for years, and I have completed the required safety classes. I should ace the test. You may be able to defeat me in hand-to-hand combat, but honey, you are going to be on my playing field now."

"Don't get too cocky, bud. I know you will be amazed at how good I will be." Tish was confident as she said this to me with a challenge in her voice.

"You just wait and see who is the sharpshooter of this partnership." I could be just as confident as Tish when I wanted to be. Besides, I really am a good shot.

We watched a little TV. We both felt good about the day. We found jobs that will provide enough means to pay for our small house. It looked as if we would be staying the summer for sure, and if all went as we planned, we would be set for the duration of our college careers.

CHAPTER TEN

The next morning, we went to college and registered for the firearms course. We were fortunate; the class was not filled. I guess most people have other things to do in the summer.

We finally found the time to explore Chicago. Our jobs would be starting soon, and the course was next week. I convinced Tish this was our chance to be tourists and have some fun. I was glad when she agreed.

Over coffee, we planned what we would do for the next two days. There were many options, and Chicago is a big city. Some of the places were just too expensive for us to do at this point. We knew from time to time we would be able to squeeze in some of the more expensive sights.

Tish wants to go to all the museums. I told her I would pass on the Art Institute. I would go to the Museum of Science. She said if she went to the Museum of Science with me that I needed to go to the Art Institute with her. We passed on both for now.

I said we should see the Cubs play. Tish is a Sammy Sosa fan. Since Tish loved him when he played for the White Sox, she said she would go to see him play for the Cubs. Whether we can get tickets these next two days are still to be seen.

We finally decided to hop on and off buses to tour the city as cheaply as possible. Lincoln Park is a must, according to Tish. As tough as she acts, she has a soft spot for animals and knows an awful lot about them. It's a small park. It won't take all day unless she decides to tell me about each animal.

I wanted to take the river cruise. One thing I insist we do is to stop by the Chicago River and see where they turn the river green between Wabash Avenue and Columbus Drive. This way, we will know exactly where to be during the Saturday before St. Patrick's Day. Tish agreed to go since it seemed to mean that much to me. She said since I was going to Lincoln Park for her, she would go to the river with me.

I love the fact Tish is willing to do things I like to do without complaining. Finding the exact spot where the river will start to turn green for St. Patrick's Day is stupid. She agreed to go with me anyway. She is a good sport, or just maybe she loves me, I joked to myself.

The hard part of planning was deciding whether to take the truck part of the way and then use the bus system or just take the bus from our house. We decided to save time and take the truck to a better starting point. Pulling out a map and deciding where to go, where to park the truck, and how much parking would cost made us reconsider that option. Maybe taking the bus from our house-made more sense.

Public transit was always interesting. We sat on the bus and people watched. Neither of us spoke to each other. At one point, Tish nudged me and cocked her head slightly, indicating I should observe a creepy looking man who sat down next to a young woman.

The young woman seemed uncomfortable with the guy plunking down next to her. There were several seats he could have chosen; nonetheless, he deliberately picked the open space next to her.

We watched the young woman looking out of the window, trying hard to ignore the man. When the woman pulled the cord indicating she wanted to get off the bus, the creepy man stood to let her out.

I thought that was going to be the last of our entertainment until the man followed the young woman to the bus door. Tish immediately pushed me to my feet.

"Come on. We are getting off here. Something is not right about this guy." Tish grabbed my hand and pulled me along behind her as she said this. There was no time to object.

Tish's instincts were right. As soon as the woman started walking down the quiet street, the creepy man ran up behind her. He pushed her down as he snatched her purse. Tish rushed to the woman and yelled at me. "Get him!"

The creepy guy was faster than I thought he would be. He led me on a merry goose chase down an alley and through a backyard. I don't think he counted on my determination or my tackling abilities. All 220 pounds of me slammed into the creepy man's back, knocking him off his feet and hitting his head, disorienting him enough that I could get the purse and subdue him with a thumb lock Tish taught me.

Pulling him to his feet, I marched him back in the direction where the ladies were last seen. I knew Tish would have the situation well under control, and I was right. She screamed for someone to phone the police, and they were already on the scene.

As I got close enough to be seen, the woman pointed and yelled, "That's the man who stole my purse and pushed me down."

It was apparent she was not hurt seriously. Her nylon stockings were ripped with holes and runs, and her knees were bloody. Tish offered her a handkerchief to stop the bleeding.

The police officers rushed towards me and took the man into custody. "Nice collar, kid," said one of the officers. "Stick around. We need your statement."

I was willing to stick around. I knew our first day of seeing the sights was in jeopardy at this point. Maybe we could still get to Lincoln Park if the buses ran on schedule.

The young woman said her name was Callie. She was talking to Tish as I approached. She turned to me and said, "I really want to thank you for what you did for me. I don't know what I would have done if you two were not around. Your young lady friend told me how the two of you were suspicious of the man, and that is why you got off at the same stop.

What you don't know is I just came from the bank to withdraw my money to pay the rent. My landlord increased my lease payment, and he is also demanding I pay all the utilities. Until I can find a new place to live, I must use money from my savings account to make up the difference. If that man succeeded in getting away with my money, I would be in a world of hurt."

I felt terrible for the woman. I knew many people in poorer sections of the city were often preyed upon by the slumlords. It seemed this young woman was indeed being preyed upon. There wasn't anything Tish or I could do about her situation. I was glad we could help her a bit. Somehow seeing the sights did not seem relevant any longer.

It took more time than we expected for the police to take our statements. They wanted to make sure Callie was not severely hurt. Suggesting that she should be checked out by a doctor, Callie insisted she was okay. I suspect money played a big deal in making that decision. If she were having trouble paying rent, she sure would not be able to pay a doctor.

A crowd gathered. Curiosity and boredom often cause people to snoop into things that aren't their business. I noticed one man with a camera and a notepad. He was snapping pictures while scribbling rapidly in between shots. It turned out he was a beat print reporter for one of the newspapers in town and often followed police cars to scenes of accidents or crimes. A purse snatching was not big news. He seemed interested in writing an article about how two recent graduates from high school happened to stop the crime. Human interest articles still sold.

Tish wasn't interested in talking to him. I, on the other hand, had plenty of time with reporters wanting to speak to me about one big football game or another. I was willing to tell him the story from our point of view, even as Tish glared at me.

I grabbed her quickly as the reporter snapped his camera at us. I whispered to Tish, "This could be good for our P.I. business once we get it up and running. If the article gets printed in the newspaper, we could have the article framed and hung on the wall of our office." I guess she could see the benefits and gave a pretty smile for the next picture.

The reporter seemed content with the information and was now talking to Callie. After the purse snatcher was loaded into a patrol car, and it left the scene, another officer approached us.

"What are you two doing in this area in the first place?" He acted as if the area was out of bounds, and we did not fit in.

Explaining once again, we were on our way to Lincoln Park. We got off at this stop when we saw how suspicious the creepy man was acting.

"What if I give you a ride to Lincoln Park. You have already wasted a good share of your day by giving your statement. Who is riding shotgun?"

Tish immediately stepped forward. She quickly replied, "I've got shotgun."

The officer winked at me and said, "I was hoping that would be the way it would turn out."

His partner left the scene in the other car to assist with the arrested man, that left Officer Wilson at odds for a while. He explained he would return to the station. It was getting close to the end of his shift. There was no rush to go and pick up his partner anyway.

Getting settled into his patrol car, Officer Wilson pulled out into traffic and headed in the direction of the park. Light conversation followed. He told us his name is Anthony, but most people called him Tony. He also indicated he had been a patrol officer on this beat for three years. Clearly, Tony loves his job.

When we told Tony, we were enrolled at Daily College in the criminal justice program, he just laughed and said, "I should have guessed. Are you right out of high school?" Glancing at me in the rear-view mirror, he said, "I bet you played football, didn't you? With your build and with the way you tackled the perp, I knew immediately you were a football player. Tackle, right?"

I told him I was the quarterback. He was right about us being fresh out of high school. I guess that was obvious enough if one was good at telling ages. When I told him that we were from Stanton, he immediately said, "Ah-Ha! You are the quarterback that won the State Championship. Well, nice to meet you. I was really impressed with your team. I saw you play at Durand in the first round of the playoffs. My nephew plays tight-end for Durand. If I remember distinctly, you destroyed their team 43-0, and you rushed for three touchdowns that game."

He turned and glanced at Tish. "You two live together? How long have you been dating?"

Tish did not blush. She was matter-of-fact when she said, "We are friends…just friends."

"So, if I called you up some time, you might be free to have dinner and see a movie?" Tony asked.

I casually observed Tish, to see if she would show any sign of interest in Tony. Tony is a good-looking man as far as I can tell. I just don't know Tish's taste. She never dated in high school except for our prom date, if that could be considered a date.

Tish looked over at Tony. "I won't have much free time… I suppose I could squeeze in dinner and movie."

Tony smiled and said, "Give me your phone number, and I will call you."

"That is going to be a problem. We just moved in, and we don't have a phone yet." Tish wasn't making this easy for the poor guy.

"OK, give me your address, and I will swing by and find out when would be a good time to set up a date," Tony said persistently.

Tish continued her coy game. "It is on the statement we gave. You can get it from there. That will save you having to carry my address around with you now. Besides, we are in the park, and we have lots to see before we take the bus all the way back home." With that last remark, Tish opened the door, bent over and smiled at Tony as she closed the door.

Before getting out of the back seat, I added, "Hey, it was great of you to give us a ride. I look forward to you popping in some time." Giving him a friendly smile, I also departed the patrol car.

As Officer Tony Wilson drove away, I looked at Tish and asked, "You really interested in that guy, or were you just having some fun with him?"

Tish replied, "When have you known me to have fun with any guy? Of course, I would go out with him if he pursues it. I am just not going to make it easy for him. Come on; we don't have much time left to see the zoo."

I added as we walked to the entrance, "It is a good thing that you are pretty, or we would have walked all this way."

I thought it could be interesting to have a policeman as a friend. It could even be good for our business in the future. Now, I just hoped Tish did not make a mess of things with him. It would not be good to have a police officer as an enemy either. I had a strange thought of everything going south if she did.

We were in and out of the zoo before we knew it. Fortunately, the next bus that would take us back home arrived on schedule. I looked forward to a relaxing evening watching TV.

Our first day of sight-seeing hadn't gone as planned. Only seeing the zoo, we decided today was going to be different. I already spent time planning our route to the river, which was silly. I know we will have plenty of time until March to decide where we will stand when they dye the river green. Tish was a good sport and said she was up to it. I finally came to my senses and nixed that plan.

"I guess the Cub's baseball game is out tonight. I think they are playing again next week. The White Socks are playing today. It would be nearer anyway. What do you say?" I asked.

"The weather is nice, and the wind isn't all that bad. I think it would be fun to sit out and watch the White Sox play. Do you know who the Sox are playing?" Tish asked.

"The Angels, I think. What does it matter? Win or lose, it will just be nice to have the experience, and we could eat hot dogs and all the junk food that goes along with games. You know peanuts and Cracker Jacks; I don't care if I never get back...So it's off to Comiskey Park." I sang part of the verse just to annoy Tish.

We were dressed. Tish went back to her room for one last thing before we would be heading out when there was a knock at the door. I raced to answer it. As I opened the door, a clean-cut, young black man was standing with a smile on his face. It took me a second to recognize Tony without his uniform.

A smile crossed my lips, as well. "Hey Tony, come on in. I did not recognize you for a second without your uniform. I guess you are looking for Tish, right?"

I think I saw a blush come over his face. I acted as if I did not notice.

"Yes, is Tish here?" Tony asked as he stepped into the room. At that moment, Tish came out of her bedroom and entered the small living room. She was dressed, as she always was, in tight black jeans, a white snug-fitting top and a jean vest. I forgot Tony was not immune to the effect she had on men. His jaw dropped open.

I could tell our plans would probably change again. I was hoping the baseball game was not out. Oh well...another shot day...I suppose there would be plenty of games in the summer.

"Hi, Tish. I found your address on the statement, as you suggested. I was just wondering if you would like to go to see "The Patriot Games" tomorrow at the mall cinema and then go out to dinner afterward?" Glancing at me, he added, "You are invited, too."

I laughed. "Two is company, and I would be a crowd. No, really, I thank you for the invitation. I will start my job tomorrow night as mall security. They asked me to come a bit early to meet my training partner. I will need to pass this time.

I could see a sigh of relief as Tony said, "Oh, maybe next time then."

Tish interrupted to say she would love to go and asked what time to be ready. The usual chit-chat happened next with the time decided.

"You two look like you are heading out, I am sorry if I interrupted your day. I 'm heading back to my apartment, I will see you tomorrow." Tony smiled again at Tish and closed the door behind him.

"I like that guy. You could do worse." I commented as I watched Tony walk back to his midnight blue Dodge Stealth. I was lusting after his ride when I received a punch in the arm.

"What do you mean I could do worse? I could do a lot better too, and don't you forget it." Tish was bristling again--I soothed her temper fast, or the day could be ruined.

"I was just using a figure of speech. I did not mean anything by it. Of course, you could get any man you wanted." I hoped that would appease her and apparently it did because her face and body relaxed and she was smiling again.

"Let's go. I hear the game might sell out by game time. If we get there early enough, we will have a nice choice of seats. It would be fun to watch them warm-up. I am also looking forward to hot dogs and cold beer...oops, root beer." Tish said, and I could tell she was back in a good mood. The day was going to be fun.

It turned out to be a boring game with the White Socks losing. Alex Fernandez usually pitches a good game. Not this game, he was off.

Maybe it was just Angel's pitcher, Bert Blyleven was really hot that game. The usual ground outs, fly outs, and a couple good double plays. No home run to make it exciting. The typical pitcher's game. Hey, I occasionally like to watch a good pitcher's game. However, I prefer seeing lots of hits, base running, base stealing, and home runs. We both overate on junk food. I had a stomach ache by the time we got home. I knew it would pass. No sense in complaining. I did not want to hear Tish calling me a big baby.

We watched a little TV and talked about how we needed to get hold of the phone company to set up a time for the technician to install the phone service. We flipped a coin to see who would be the one to run down to the payphone to call the telephone company tomorrow. I lost, as usual. One more thing for me to think about tomorrow, I needed to get a nap. I wanted to be alert for my first night's work.

I hear it is hard to adjust to working night shifts. Luckily, I only have three nights. My body will probably complain until I get into the schedule. It's alright, I got this. I can handle it.

We were tired from all the sunlight and over-eating. We decided to head to bed by ten. Tomorrow was going to be a big day for both of us.

CHAPTER ELEVEN

Friday morning came early enough, and again Tish was up drinking her cup of coffee. I told Tish I make a mean blueberry and chocolate chip pancake, and she responded quickly with, "Good, I am starved. I will make the bacon."

Even though the kitchen was small, we worked well together. It was almost as if we cooked many times before with each other. Tish, being slightly built, did not hurt the cause. My bulk took up most of the space in the small kitchen. Tish seemed to be able to squeeze in, under and around me whenever she needed to do so.

Before long, we were sitting down to my delicious pancakes. They are Chicago's best; I can honk my own horn. Tish could make her bacon perfectly flat, something I have never been able to do. It was what my tummy wanted after the binge of junk food the day before. When breakfast finished, I collected plates.

"I will wash if you will dry." I offered.

Tish said she would be glad to wash the dishes. I told her I did not like to see her get dishpan hands before her big date. That got me another annoyed glance.

Tish lightened up quickly when I mentioned we could do some yard work. She told me she wanted to plant all kinds of flowers around the house to make it seem less stark. She doesn't appear to be entirely a softy. One of Tish's many attributes is her great feminine ideas.

"My mom gave me $100.00 before she left. I know she would love it if I used some of it towards flowers. It will make her first visit much more welcoming; don't you think?" Tish asked.

I can't say I was thinking about either of our mother's first visits. Somehow, I was hoping they would not come too frequently. On the other hand, maybe Tish had other ideas.

"Ahh," was all that I managed to get out of my mouth.

Tish looked at my face and laughed out loud. "Where is a mirror when you need one. Scotty, you should see the look on your face. You did not really believe we would escape parental visits, did you? You know darn well; our parents are going to want to make sure we are okay."

"I suppose you are right. If I had a daughter that just moved to Chicago on her own, I think I would buy the house right next door." Maybe an occasional visit from Mom or Dad would not be the worst thing. Having them live next door would be the worst.

I sort of remembered a garden center when we were on the bus starting our tour. We would need to take the truck to get the plants back home. I had a feeling Tish was not talking about just a couple of plants. I assumed I would be doing a bit of digging, which reminded me I needed a hand trowel. Luckily, the landlord left a push mower and garden tools in the garage. He said he expected us to keep the property looking beautiful.

We headed to the nursery to get a few plants and some dirt. I wondered if Chicago needed different types of plants than we planted back home. I thought we were in the same growing zone. I glanced at homes along the way to see what plants were growing. Unfortunately, I did not know the names of the plants I was seeing. I suspect Tish would know precisely what she wanted…anyway.

Getting to the garden center was easy enough. Tish was out of the truck in a flash and heading towards the flowering plants. I followed along, feeling like an obedient husband.

Tish was loading up a cart with Azaleas, Salvia, Knock-out Roses, Columbine, Daylily, Jacob's Ladder, and Sundrops. I grabbed the other items she said she needed and met her at the checkout.

We bought some bags of garden soil, fertilizer, vitamin B-1 starter, and the flowers, and after loading them in the truck bed, we headed back to our little abode. I was fearful Tish was getting too domesticated, and she would want her mom's cutesy flowery curtains after all.

I lucked out. While Tish planted the flowers, I mowed the small yard. I took longer than usual to avoid helping with the planting. I am not sure why I did not want to help. It just did not seem manly.

We cleaned up, had lunch, and I asked to be excused to make a run to a payphone to call the phone company for the install appointment. I was anticipating the all-nighter and needed a power nap.

Tish said she had plenty of things to do to keep her occupied. I suspected she wanted to try on multiple outfits to see which one would be the best for her date tonight. For all I knew, Tish would paint her toenails to match her lipstick. She might end up wearing those outrageous wedged sandals I saw her wear to graduation.

My nap was longer than I expected. When I woke up, I felt disoriented. I guess we have not lived in this house long enough for it to feel familiar when my mind is foggy.

I stumbled out to the living room to find Tish dressed and ready to be picked up. She wasn't wearing those crazy sandals. She was decked out in all black from head to toe. Her toenails, if painted, were not visible under her kick-ass boots.

"Wow! I can't believe I napped that long," I said casually.

"Oh, thanks. I thought your 'Wow' was going to be for how I look. Don't you like what I have on? Should I change my clothes? Do I need more color or what?" Tish was obviously nervous about her date.

"You look great! I was too foggy to notice whether she needed more color. No, don't bother to change. You will knock Tony's sock's off." I meant what I said. She looked wonderful. I always think she looks terrific.

Tish has the most beautiful, caramel-colored skin. Any color she wore looked good on her. Her body structure is slight but powerful. Clothes just naturally hang right on her. She doesn't have any fat pads she needs to hide, like some of the girls from high school.

A knock at the door announced Tony's arrival. I thought I saw a moment of panic pass over Tish's face. She covered it up immediately with her usual composure. I realized she was not as confident as I once thought she was. I remember now she did not date much in high school. Most of the guys were either afraid of her or intimidated by her beauty. At any rate, only a few guys were ever brave enough to ask her out, and then she was very picky and turned them all down. It was a good thing she and I were fast friends, or we would never have spent time together. There is no way she would date me, except as a friend.

I answered the door to allow Tish to compose herself. Tony looked nice enough for me. He wore black slacks with a light yellow shirt. Seeing them standing next to each other, I confessed grudgingly; they made a striking couple.

Tony said something about Tish looking great and asked if she was ready to head out. "I think there will be a line to see the movie. It is getting great reviews, and Harrison Ford and James Earl Jones are always good. We should get a move on."

Tish slid out the door with a backward comment to me that she hopes my first night on my new job will be fun. I appreciated that she was thinking of me even as she was going off on a hot date. "See you in the morning and enjoy," I replied.

I still had a bit of time to waste before I needed to head to the mall. My choices were TV or read a book. I did not pack any books, and we have not applied for a library card yet. Guess TV, it is. I was rarely home on Friday nights most of my high school years. Most of those were spent playing football or with Heather. That thought made me sad. I switched on the TV to get her out of my head.

Flipping through the channels, I found *America's Most Wanted* and settled down to watch it. The *Carol Burnett Show* would be on later. My parents always sit glued to it and roar at the antics of some strange little guy. His name escapes me. Watching a comedy would keep my mind off thoughts of Heather and Jack and what they might be doing at this very moment

Looking up, I noticed it was time for me to head out. Since I was supposed to hook up with my pre-assigned trainer; I needed to be in early. There is a requirement for a full eight-hour training before working solo. I was told Herb would be my trainer.

I entered the mall entrance that was unlocked near the security office. Once I entered the building, they would give me a set of keys to lock up behind myself. In the future, I would let myself in and out. The mall would be totally locked up during my shift.

Herb was an older man. He was short, probably about 5'7" and stocky like a bull. I could tell he kept in shape. Some mall cops let themselves go to fat...not Herb. I suspected he was ex-military by his demeanor.

We exchanged greetings, and he said he would show me around and tell me my duties as we walked. He told me it was essential to change the route I frequently took in case someone was casing a specific store. This way, the burglars would not be able to predict when I would pass one of the stores.

"Banks, jewelry stores, electronic stores, and high-end department stores were the most likely stores to be broken into at night. All the stores leave on some security lights to make it easier for us to detect movement," Herb told me.

"Basically, the job entails a lot of walking and watching. You need to be aware always, of telltale signs of break-ins or indigents hiding and trying to find a place to sleep at night. We check all the restrooms before the mall closes. Some of these guys are pretty clever about hiding." Herb was giving me the basics.

He went on to say, "You will carry a walkie-talkie, a baton, and your keys. There will always be someone back at the office that will phone the police if you see something suspicious. I will be making the rounds as well. Know that you will never be totally alone. I should be able to get to your location quickly if something should seem strange to you. I caution you not to ever go into a store that is unlocked without back-up. That is why we have walkie-talkies."

Trespassing laws, policies, and procedures were on the agenda for the night training. Herb seemed to know his stuff. I asked him how he came about security work.

His answer was he was military police most of his life. It seemed easy enough to fall into the security business once in the public sector. He explained there is also the private sector if I would be interested in protecting individuals, their families, and property.

I told him I was planning on becoming a private investigator with my partner. He did not laugh at two kids wanting to be P.I.s, which I appreciated. He told me most of the work, though, ended up being surveillance for divorce situations. I guess I did not like hearing that might be the case. I was expecting more critical cases.

The night shift went faster than I expected with Herb telling me my duties and showing me the ropes. I knew once I was walking the routes by myself, I would get bored. I decided I could do things that would help me keep in shape by wearing wrist-weights and ankle-weights. I did not bother to ask Herb if it was allowed. I could not think of any reason why it would not…why ask.

I was surprised when Herb took me back to the office and handed me a test. A test! I did not see that coming. Luckily, I don't have test anxiety. I just allowed my mind to go back to words Herb said and apply them to the test. It was a good strategy. I aced the test and was handed a certificate to prove I passed. I was now officially a Mall Cop.

The walk home was refreshing in the crisp early morning air. Walking into the house, I was surprised to see Tish awake. At the table was a cup of coffee for her and a glass of juice set at my spot.

"Why aren't you still asleep?" I asked. I thought Tish would be sleeping in after a late-night date. Instead, she was up early. I was a bit suspicious that her time with Tony did not go well, and Tish ended the evening early. If she went to bed early, that would explain why she was up early. I had a strange feeling that something was amiss.

"My night was quite eventful," Tish said with a long yawn. Her yawn gave away the fact she did not go to bed early last night.

"Tony and I were standing in line to see the movie. We started asking each other questions about each other and our families. Tony was asking me about how you and I met...when I heard a couple of guys yelling and swearing at each other just in front of us. I noticed one of the guys near me reached into his coat pocket and pulled out a switchblade knife. When I saw the glint of the blade, I reacted quickly and reached for his forearm, squeezing the pressure points with the fingers on my left hand, hoping he would drop the blade. With my right hand, I pulled his wrist around and behind his back into a wrist and arm lock that dropped him screaming in pain to his knees. At the same time, his friend lurched toward me to aid his buddy. I side-kicked his friend in the liver with my boot heel, knocking him unconscious to the ground in the fetal position. Once the two were no longer a problem, I turned toward a stunned Tony and asked him, "Well, are you going to stand there gawking like all the others, or are you going to help me?"

Scott asked, "What the hell, what was Tony thinking? Why didn't he get in there and help? Some date if you ask me."

Tish tried to respond in Tony's defense, "It all happened fast, I suppose it caught him completely off guard. One second, we are talking, and two seconds later, there are two bad guys on the ground. You know me...I don't mess around. What I can say is the rest of the night was interesting... I could tell Tony was quite embarrassed."

"He should have been embarrassed…okay, what happened next, Tish?" I asked.

Tish continued, "The theater manager came running toward us; Tony told him to phone the police. Tony came to my side and said he would take over holding the disarmed man to give me a rest. I let him take my place.

I went and asked the other two people who were being threatened what the beef was about. They made some lame excuse the other guys were trying to cut in line, and they would not allow it. They said the one guy pulled the knife on them when they told them to get to the back of the line.

I could tell by others in the vicinity they were not telling the truth. I asked a few more questions of the crowd and found most of the people averted their eyes when I looked at them for clarification. One person seemed especially uneasy. I targeted that person for more information just as the police came into the lobby."

Recognizing Tony, one officer said, "Nice work, Tony. We will take it from here. You know to stick around for a statement, right?"

Tish continued, "Tony was gallant enough to say that he did nothing; it was all me. The other officers just looked at me, and one whistled with amazement. Tony told them I disarmed and controlled the one while simultaneously taking the other out man completely. He told the officers the event took less than two seconds. Tony also said he was stunned by his date's quick reaction. There was no time to respond. It was over and under control before Tony knew what happened."

One officer remarked to Tony, "You sure know how to pick em!".

"You know I would be furious if I thought he was making some off-sided sexual comment. It really was a statement of awe. I was rather flattered." Tish beamed

"I bet you were," I said. I was in awe as well. I knew Tish was bad-ass, she continues to prove it time and again. Why I am surprised beats me.

My thoughts turned to Tony. I suspect Tony knew in the back of his mind this would be his only date with Tish. His only hope now is they would continue to be friends. I felt sorry for the guy. I know how hard it is to be 'just friends' with someone like Tish.

"Then what happened?" I asked, leaving thoughts of Tony in the rearview mirror. He needed to fight his own battles. Now, I just wanted to hear the rest of the story.

"We gave our statements, and I told one of the officers I did not believe the problems were cutting in line as was being reported, and I was sure the girl in pink knew more than she was letting on."

Tish continued, "The perpetrators were taken to the police car. Once they were out of sight, the officer pulled the girl in pink aside, and she said she was afraid to say anything because she knew the guys were drug dealers and they were from her neighborhood. If she said anything, she would be in trouble. The officer said he would not put her name in his report.

"Tony and I walked over to the officers by the squad car. Tony asked his fellow officers to search the pockets of the villains, and they found drugs. The two supposed victims who said the perpetrators were just cutting in line were searched and questioned further. The search did not reveal any drugs on their person, but they did have a sizeable amount of cash. It was looking like a drug buy gone bad. Unfortunately, there was little the police could do to prove they were about to buy the drugs. They were free to go to see the movie."

I said to Tish, "So now there will be two court cases you will need to make an appearance."

Tish dismissed my comment. She wasn't ready to be thinking about court cases.

"You know, Tony told me that I should think about helping to train rookies at the police force. When he saw how quickly I could take down two perps, Tony wanted to know more about my martial arts training. He did not realize I knew anything about martial arts on the day of the purse snatching. If you remember, Scott, you ran after the purse snatcher, and I stayed behind with the victim.

"We missed the movie, went to dinner, and spent the rest of the night talking about my martial arts credentials and training. He was impressed when he came home with me and saw the photos of all my trophies and awards in Taekwondo and Combat Hapkido. He came up with the idea of talking with the Police Academy self-defense instructor. At this point, the rookies learn tactical baton and psychomotor skills. Tony was saying the instructor might want to add some of my skills to the academy's curriculum. There are no guarantees. It would be an excellent second part-time job," Tish said excitedly.

"Oh! You haven't gone to bed?" I said lamely.

"Is that all you are going to say to me?" Tish said in an annoyed voice.

"Oh, my gosh, no! That was incredible what you did at the theater, and the fact it could turn into a job opportunity for you is a big bonus. If I were there, I would have carried you out on my shoulders to the cheering crowd.

"Stop it! Now you are just acting stupid!" said Tish.

"You want stupid. Look at my certificate. I am an official Mall Cop." I beamed sheepishly.

Tish laughed and gave me a big hug. She yawned, and we agreed we both needed some sleep. Then Tish remembered she needed to get prepared for her students at the dojang. I told her I felt sorry for her, and I would see her later in the day.

CHAPTER TWELVE

I felt terrible for Tish. She wasn't going to get to sleep until after her day of work was completed. I decided I would take a nap and walk down to watch her teach the Women's Self-Defense Class. I woke up in plenty of time to get there before the class started and was surprised to see Tony in the parking lot talking with a powerfully built black man who appeared to be in his fifties. I waved, and Tony signaled for me to come over.

"Hi, Scott. I want you to meet our department captain, who is also the firearms and martial arts instructor at the Police Academy, Captain Barry Jones. Captain Jones, this is Scott. Scott is Tish's roommate and best friend."

I shook hands with Captain Jones and looked towards Tony for some sort of explanation as to why they were here? Tony seemed to understand my puzzled look and continued.

"I was impressed with Tish last night at the movie theater. I asked Captain Jones to come and watch her teach a class. I was hoping he would be just as impressed as I am with her abilities." Tony seemed sincere.

I looked through the window of the dojang and realized Captain Jones was just in time to see Tish in action. It appeared the women had not arrived. Tish was in a defensive stance and was about ready to kick someone's butt. I nodded my head in the direction of the window, and their eyes followed.

Like bullets, all three of us dashed to the entrance. We did not want to miss a single thing. Quietly, we entered the building. Captain Jones reached up and silenced the bell that would announce our arrival upon the door opening as if he had been there before. A young man stepped around the corner of the office door to see if he could be of some assistance to us. I just gave him the 'hush' sign and waved him off. I indicated we were here to watch Tish. He nodded his understanding and went back out of sight.

Tish was dressed in her loose-fitting dobok. I was unaccustomed to seeing her in all white. Oh my…as always, she looked great. How someone can look sexy in canvas pajamas is beyond me.

I never had the opportunity to meet Tish's Grandmaster. I decided the man with Tish must be Grandmaster Kim Yong-Sool. He was average height for a Korean man, with long, thick muscles. It was apparent they were getting set up for the women's self-defense class. The Grandmaster came towards Tish's throat with his arms outstretched. He was not holding back as he rushed towards her.

Tish did not hesitate. Immediately she pushed both his arms aside and grabbed the Grandmaster's forearm with her left hand applying an elbow lock, as her right hand grabbed and pulled his wrist backward.

Simultaneously, her right shin struck the Grandmaster in his groin, knocking him to the ground. Even with the Grandmaster's body dropping to the ground, Tish kept the wrist lock even tighter, keeping the excruciating pressure on his wrist.

Releasing her hold, the man regained his feet and bowed to her, and she bowed back. Looking up, Grandmaster Kim Yong-Sool saw Captain Barry Jones, and a smile crossed his face. "Welcome, Grandmaster Jones. What do I owe this honor?"

I walked over to Tish as her Grandmaster approached the two police officers. "Wow! Wow! Wow! Tell me you are going to teach me that move. Oh, by the way, did you see who I ran into out in the parking lot?"

Tish's eyes never met mine. She was watching intently as the three men walked across the floor to the office. They were talking low and amicably when they closed the door.

Within a minute or two, the entrance door to the office reopened, and Tony appeared. He came across the dojang floor to where I was standing with Tish. He had a broad smile on his face and seemed rather pleased with himself.

"Why are you here?" Tish asked Tony.

I would say she was not pleased to see Tony. She seemed worried or something like that. I did not interrupt like I usually would. I stayed as quiet as possible, not wanting to miss anything that was said.

Tony answered her question. "I couldn't sleep last night. I was excited about how you handled those two guys at the cinema. I stayed awake intentionally. I wanted to be in the office the first thing this morning. I knew the captain would be coming in early. I was at the precinct even before he entered. I asked him if I could have a word with him before he got busy, and I told him the whole story while he glanced at the case folder in front of him. He was impressed, to say the least, and said he would not mind seeing you in action. I remembered you scheduled a women's self-defense class this afternoon, and the captain said he would come and watch you teach.

"We arrived early enough to watch you and Grandmaster Yong-Sool sparring. Captain Jones was favorably impressed. The Grandmaster and Captain Jones are old friends. They are talking now. I suspect they will talk about you and your potential to assist with the rookie training program if you are still interested."

Several women entered the front door. Tish noticed them and excused herself. It was part of her job to greet the women and make them feel comfortable.

I tapped Tony on his shoulder and suggested we find a seat that was out of the way. Tish would be starting her class soon. Tish took the center of the floor, and the ladies followed. They were all clothed in comfortable, loose-fitting garments except a few of the women who wore sport-bras and tight leggings. I suspected they might need the training the most.

Tish was talking about some of the more conventional approaches men might use to subdue a woman. She was painting scenarios that were entirely plausible and scary. Tish asked for a volunteer and looked right at me.

"Scott, would you mind being a perpetrator for a moment?" she said with such a sweet smile on her face. I had no idea what was coming next.

I agreed to help her out. What was a best friend for if not to help a buddy when needed? I got up and went to the center of the floor next to Tish and smiled at the women present. I could tell by the surprised expressions on their faces that Tish would call on me, given my height and mass.

"Ok, Scott, I want you to come up behind me…grab my left hand with your left hand as if you are trying to steal my purse while trying to choke me around the neck with your right hand…don't go easy on me." She directed.

I did exactly as she asked. Tish was in her awareness stance…as soon as she felt my hands near her, she grabbed my left thumb with her left hand, pulling my thumb back into a thumb lock, and at the same time, she grabbed my right wrist, which was coming around her neck, into a wrist lock. I was in horrible pain…I felt my feet dancing up and down entirely out of control. Then…if that was not enough, she ducked straight down and turned under my right arm, still holding me in the wrist lock…it hurt badly…. Tony told me later I cried, 'Mama.'

As I walked back to my seat, rubbing my wrist, I decided I would not volunteer ever again. Tony stifled a laugh as I sat next to him.

"Next time she asks for a volunteer, I want to see you step up!" I must admit, I said those words in a bit of a pout.

Tish continued her class, asking the ladies to pair up. They went through each movement slowly until everyone grasped what they were to do under that scenario. Before long, each woman felt rather pleased with what she could do.

Tish looked at the clock and told them she would see them again next Saturday. She asked them to practice with a boyfriend, husband, or another willing person until the movement became second nature. Next week, she would teach them a different defense technique.

The ladies bowed to Tish and then filed out the door talking animatedly. Obviously, they were excited about what they just learned and the feeling of some empowerment that accompanied the lesson.

Unbeknownst to Tish, the two Grandmasters watched the entire class from the window in the office. Exiting the office, I noticed the captain giving Tony some strange signal. Without warning, Tony rushed Tish from behind her left side, taking her down. Before I could even decide what happened, Tish was on top of Tony with him crying like a baby.

The Captain stood and applauded while Tish's Grandmaster smiled.

Tish said to Tony, "What the …?" Remembering where she was, Tish let the last word drop. Keeping him in a tight arm lock and chokehold, she looked up to her Grandmaster, who gave her a signal to release.

"You certainly passed the assault test with flying colors, young lady," Captain Jones said as he continued to clap.

As Tish helped Tony to his feet, she looked at Captain Jones.

"Let me introduce myself, Tish. I am Captain Barry Jones. Thank you for allowing me to watch your demonstration. You are quite accomplished for such a young woman. How long have you been training?"

I could tell Tish had no idea she was putting on a demonstration. All she knew was she was defending herself from Tony's onslaught. She graciously answered, "It was my pleasure, Captain Jones. I am glad I did not disappoint."

"Grandmaster Yong-Sool, it is always a pleasure to be in your dojang. Thank you for allowing the visit." Signaling Tony to follow, they both turned and bowed before exiting the dojang.

Grandmaster Yong-Sool said to Tish, "You made me proud today. I have not met your friend. Will you honor me with his name?"

Tish blushed in embarrassment. "Excuse me, Grandmaster Yong-Sool, for the oversight. This is my friend and roommate, Scott McFarlan. Scotty, this is Grandmaster Yong-Sool."

"It is my honor to meet you, Scott. You are welcome anytime Tish needs a punching bag." The Master smiled and told Tish he would like to talk to her about a proposal submitted by Captain Jones. "Would you excuse us, Scott?"

I knew when it was time for me to leave. I still needed dinner, a shower, and maybe another cat nap before I went to my night job.

It was my turn to cook dinner. I plated the spaghetti and salad for Tish after she showered and was ready to eat. We sat at the table, and I asked, "So what happened with Master Kim after I left?"

"First, KimYong-Sool is my Kwan Jung Nim. Refer to him as Grandmaster Yong-Sool, please, and never use his first name. It is not respectful, Scotty. Captain Barry Jones is a 9th dan black belt in Ninjutsu and Taekwondo, he will be my sensei. They are both Grandmasters in their fields. At the appropriate time, I will refer to Captain Jones as Grandmaster Jones." Tish corrected my mistake.

I was not offended and said, "So that means you...will be working for Captain Jones?"

Tish was slurping a strand of spaghetti into her mouth. Chewing, she made me wait for an answer.

"No, not exactly, I will not be getting paid by the Police Academy. I will be Grandmaster Jones's student. He will train me in Ninjutsu for free, and in return, I will help with training rookies in Combat Hapkido. When I complete my training and pass the various tests, I will be called Master Evers. What do you think about that?"

"You will be one hell of a busy gal, Tish. When are you going to get a chance to train me?" I was starting to feel left out.

"We have plans for you…." Tish said with a wicked smile.

"Maybe I should just leave well enough alone," I said with some trepidation.

"No, don't be silly. Both Grandmasters extended an invitation to you to train for free. I think they realize since you are my partner, it would be in my best interest to have someone at my side who could defend himself as well." Tish continued, "I think Grandmaster Jones is thinking, in the future, we could be invaluable to him as non-police investigators. He said we could go places and do things the police could not do without a lot of red tape."

I had some questions. "How is it you know what Grandmaster Jones has in mind for you? He wasn't there, was he? I saw him leave the dojang with Tony. Did he come back?"

"Apparently, Grandmaster Jones did not leave. He left the dojang for the parking lot to talk to Tony; then, he returned to talk with myself and Grandmaster Yong-Sool."

I said, "Wow, I never saw him when I left.

"Wait, there is more. Grandmaster Yong-Sool awarded me with the 4th Dan, Sa Dan, Black Belt."

"Tish, that is great! I am really proud of you," I said with a big smile."

With a blush growing on her face, Tish continued, "Both Grandmasters said they saw something special in me. They said they want to develop my sixth sense. It seems I use my subconscious mind to gain an advantage over opponents. However, they feel they can teach me much more and develop all the dimensions that go along with the sixth sense.

The Grandmasters told me our subconscious mind works quicker than our conscious mind. Some people think the sixth sense is supernatural, but it isn't like that at all. When the sixth sense is developed, things happen in the subconscious mind faster. One doesn't even register it consciously. All our different receptors can be formed on a much higher level allowing our conscious minds to perceive and react faster," Tish explained.

I was puzzled, and my head was spinning. "So, what you are saying is that we can detect body heat, vibrations, sounds, and the likes, but our conscious mind doesn't register them because it happens fast?"

"Yes, for example, you are about to step into the street, when your subconscious mind halts you abruptly in your spot as a bus speeds past where you would have been standing. I am sure your initial thoughts are a guardian angel just saved your life, right?

What happened was your subconscious mind registered the rumble or felt the vibration of the bus, at least two seconds before your conscious mind registered the danger. The unconscious mind had time to say halt and nothing more. The sixth sense never registers with your conscious mind. Therefore, you have no memory of the sound or vibration…you think it never happened." Tish was excited about her new information. It seemed to explain everything to her.

While I am not stupid, I hadn't thought of this before. It was kind of exciting for me as well. "No more ghosts! Just things happening tremendously fast, subconsciously, in our bodies that we have no memory, is what you are saying?"

"However, my Grandmasters both feel I can develop receptors for the things happening quickly. With that ability, I will be able to defend myself purely from reactions. They want me to be able to still my mind enough to conserve energy and not use any unnecessary movements to defend myself. I think I understand what they want to teach me. It isn't really something as easy as meditation. It will mean being in touch with all my senses and not just the five most people accept as senses. We have many other senses that we aren't aware of. Obviously, the sense of touch encompasses things like pressure, temperature, pain, itch, and all that. Our bodies also have chemoreceptors, proprioceptors, muscle tension, equilibrioception for balance and gravity, time receptors, and even magnetoception for our sense of direction." Tish was in teacher mode.

"If I learn one-fourth of what you know, I will be happy. Hey, are you planning on opening your own dojang someday?" I was starting to feel insecure again.

Tish smiled at me patiently. She still had the 'teacher mode' look on her face. "You know I am completely committed to our future. I told both Grandmasters I had no intention of ever being only an instructor in the future. My working as an instructor was just a means to an end. They both understand completely and are just happy to use me as an assistant in this time and place. Grandmaster Jones knows we will be of service to the police department in multiple ways in the future. He already thinks of us as silent partners."

Relieved, I settled down to enjoy my spaghetti for the first time. I ate half of the plate without even tasting it. I guess that was the subconscious element Tish was referring to in reverse. Once I allowed myself to think about the food, I self-proclaimed I made a mean spaghetti sauce. My salad wasn't all that bad either.

"What this meal is lacking is garlic bread," Tish added.

Tish could eat garlic and never smell like it. I wasn't blessed with her metabolism. If I eat garlic, my whole-body smells like it for days. I guess Tish did not realize I did not add garlic to the sauce either. I have found ways around particular tastes. Garlic and onions are two foods I leave out of my cooking entirely for everyone else's sake. Just imagine walking around with a 6'3", 220-pound garlic/onion sandwich, and that is what I would be if I ate the stuff.

Dishes were done, and a little TV, and I was ready to head out for my job. I did not mind the night shift. I had a feeling it might get old when I have classes and studies in the fall. For the summer, it was great.

CHAPTER THIRTEEN

I arrived home shortly after 7 a.m. It was an uneventful shift at work. Tish was still asleep. I thought I would surprise her with French toast, coffee, and fruit for breakfast. I figured the smell of coffee would wake her up, and I was right.

Stumbled out of her bedroom with a sleepy greeting, Tish plunked down in her chair. I served her coffee and continued to cook as she woke up. We were enjoying our breakfast when there was a knock at the door.

Opening the door, I found Mr. and Mrs. Evers standing there with a newspaper in hand. I invited them inside with an anticipatory glance at Tish.

"Mom, Dad, what are you doing here?" Tish asked as she stood and hugged each in turn.

I interrupted with an offer of coffee and breakfast, which they accepted with a smile.

Sitting down, Mr. Evers opened the newspaper and asked Tish to explain herself.

Tish read the article and relaxed. "It was nothing. You did not need to drive all this way over just for this."

Mrs. Evers responded, "If you had a phone, we could call to find out if you were okay or not. You left us with no choice. You are our little girl, and when we read things like this in the newspaper, we get worried."

Mr. Evers added, "It says that you single-handedly disarmed and took down two drug lords! They had a knife! What were you thinking?"

"Drug lords, Dad," Tish said exasperatedly. "They were just punk low-life dealers. Besides, Dad, my cop friend was with me."

Mr. Evers thundered, "You were with a cop, and he did nothing?"

I interjected, "That's what I said, too."

Both Mr. and Mrs. Evers looked at me, and I knew I should eat and shut up.

Mrs. Evers asked, "Honey, just who is this cop friend of yours, and why did he let you handle the whole mess on your own? We were worried when we read that you were involved with drug dealers in a movie theater."

"It was no big deal, Mom. I met Tony when Scotty and I rescued a woman from a purse snatcher…,"

"YOU WHAT?" Both Mr. and Mrs. Evers said in unison.

"How many times have you been in the newspaper? We only read about this drug deal." Mrs. Evers was wringing her hands as she asked this question.

I decided to hop in again against my better judgment. "It really was harmless enough."

Mr. Evers boomed, "Harmless, you say. This is my baby girl; none of this was harmless!"

I stammered a bit too much. There was no way I could get out a quick explanation. "You see, Tish and I were on a city bus heading to the zoo when we saw this guy who was paying way too much attention to this young lady. When he followed her off the bus, we followed also. Suddenly, he grabbed the lady's purse and knocked her down. I sprinted after the man while Tish stayed with the lady to make sure she was not injured too severely. See, Tish was safe the whole time.

"At any rate, to make a long story short, Tony was one of the cops on the scene, and he was immediately smitten with Tish. You can understand that, right?"

"Go on," said Mr. Evers, who seemed unconvinced that Tish was safe at any time in my story.

"Well, Tony asked Tish out to the movies, and when Tish saw the guy pull a knife, she just reacted. Tony helped…a bit after it started." I said more meekly.

Mr. Evers said, "Oh, by the way, what were you doing while this was going on. We let Tish come to Chicago because we felt that you would protect her."

I jumped up and brought out my certificate of completion.

Mr. Evers remarked after reading it. "Seriously, you are a Mall Cop?" Everyone laughed, and some of the tension was dispelled.

"Without getting into a lot of detail, Tish will be taking advanced courses, and I will be taking beginning courses in martial arts here locally and with the police academy," I said more seriously. I wanted them to know that we would be able to handle ourselves just fine.

"Police Academy…have the two of you decided to become cops instead of pursuing a career in the private investigation?" Mrs. Evers asked. She did not miss a thing.

Tish dispelled this thought. "No, Mom. The police captain asked that I help with training the rookies. In exchange, he will train me in Ninjutsu. We will work closely with the police department when we are private investigators. We won't become police officers."

"This all sounds confusing to me. I just want my baby to be safe." Changing the subject, she added, "I saw all the lovely flowers in the front yard. It looks beautiful, dear. After breakfast, you can show me around the yard. Then I think we should go to the grocery store. We won't stay too long. Oh, one more question. When are you getting a phone?"

"It was already on the calendar for the install. We will have a phone number by the week's end, if not sooner. We promise to call you with the number as soon as we get it." I was trying hard to dispel any fears.

The Evers left, and our refrigerator and cupboards were stocked once again. I thought now that we have extra money to spend, we can take a few more tours of the Chicago sights. Parental visits could be a good thing, after all.

After another night's work, we were both ready for the firearm training course. I was excited about showing off to Tish. She never went hunting with my father and me. She only had my word on how good I am.

As expected, Tish was good at the book study part of the program, and she was very good at target practice as well. For a girl who never handled a gun before, she proved to be a natural at it as well as most things she put her mind to. Within two weeks, she narrowed her shots to the inner ten ring. I, on the other hand, was hitting the x-ring within the bullseye every time. I think Tish is genuinely impressed with my marksmanship. I told her I was good. Modesty aside, I am that good. At fifty yards, I can put ten rounds of .45cal into the 2.0-inch x-ring.

The range master approached me with my target in his hand and asked me to sign it. He said somebody would be getting back to me very soon. I was nervous that I did something wrong.

CHAPTER FOURTEEN

Our new phone is both a blessing and a curse. Letting our folks know our number, helped Tish's parents feel more secure. Talking to my mom, though, made me feel less so. She told me Jack and Heather were getting married. It seems Heather is pregnant. That news hit me like a donkey kick in the gut. I don't know if I thought that someday Heather would return to her right mind and hunt me down? Marrying Jack was never what I saw for her future.

To the blessing side of having a phone, I got a phone call from Captain Jones. It seems the range master was told to be on the lookout for expert marksmen. Captain Jones asked me to come to the department. He said he wanted me to demonstrate my shooting abilities. Captain Jones said something about a shooting team. I don't exactly know what he is talking about. I am still excited to go in and talk to him. My quarterbacking abilities are what I got most of my kudos in the past. It is exciting to have other skills recognized.

Tish receives way too many phone calls from Tony. Captain Jones told Tony he did not want him dating Tish. It would complicate things for him to fraternize with Tish now that she is considered an instructor. Tony isn't asking her out on dates anymore. One can tell he would be interested in dating Tish if the captain hadn't kyboshed that idea.

A couple of my buddies from football got my phone number from my parents. They bugged me about being a mall cop. Ha-ha. They also pushed for us to return for a visit, or they would descend on us. I guess a home visit is preferable to our little house getting trashed by those animals.

I talked to Tish about a quick trip back home. She looked at our calendar and said we could squeeze in a trip after our firearms training was completed. That would be in another two weeks. I hadn't thought about being homesick until we talked about going home.

The two weeks passed quickly; we were back for only hours when I decided I was missing Tish and our little house in Chicago. Strange, I initially thought I was homesick, and now 'home' is somewhere other than my old bedroom. More than missing Tish, I just heard some strange news about one of our schoolmates. I phoned the Evers house, and Mrs. Evers answered and laughed.

"Don't tell me you can't be away from Tish for even a couple of hours. I know when you are in Chicago, you don't see each other for many hours at a time. Why are you phoning this soon? This is our time with Tish." Mrs. Evers said this good-naturedly. I knew she meant what she was saying and did not really like the interruption of their time with their daughter.

"I promise not to keep Tish for long. I just wondered if she heard the news about Tommy Gillespie?" I asked.

"No, what news are you talking about? Wait, I will call Tish to the phone, and you can tell her." Mrs. Evers put the phone down on the table, and I heard her calling Tish from the living room where she was sitting with her dad.

Tish answered the phone within a few seconds. "What's new since I saw you a couple of hours ago?"

I sputtered. "Tish, did you hear Tommy was killed in a freak chainsaw accident. It seems he was cutting down a tree for his folks, and the saw slipped away from him, cutting an artery. I guess he bled out before anyone even got to him. I really cannot imagine this happening to Tommy. First, the drowning and now this. We are barely out of high school, and already we have lost two of our classmates. Strange...."

Tish gasped. "I can't believe it. That is just awful. I mean, I wasn't close to him or anything. What a horrible way to die. I know his parents are just sick. Can you believe how lost they must be feeling right now?"

We chatted a couple more minutes about both deaths. It brought back some of those old feelings that something wasn't right. Soon Tish was being called by her parents. They wanted to know what happened. We hung up.

An odd thought crossed my mind; we are down to thirty-eight alumni of the original forty who were in the stupid investment. It made me sick to think that we ever agreed to such a preposterous 'Final Alumni Standing' contract in the first place. It made me angrier that we could not get a few of the people to agree to change the agreement to individual stocks. Crazy thoughts...I was wondering how much our shares were worth now. That was damn stupid of me. I let the greedy thought go quickly.

Mom and Dad did not seem to mind when I told them I was going out to cruise around for a short time that evening. I knew nothing changed in the few weeks that I was away. Sometimes it is just nice to visit familiar haunts. I was in the mood for a good old ice cream soda. Tish and I dieted sensibly while at our home. Tish wasn't here to tell me it was not on our diet...while the cat is away and all that.

Marty's is the place to go if one wants a good burger and a shake, malt, soda, or just an ice cream cone. They have curbside service. I was contented just to leave the radio on and listen to music while waiting for my treat. I did not notice Jess and Lucy Loose pull in next to me.

I don't like Jess, and he doesn't like me. I try to be cordial when we meet even though Jesse did attempt to take out my kneecaps before the playoffs. He rolled down his window and hollered at me. "Hey, McFarlan, what the hell are you doing in town. Miss us already? I heard you moved to the Big City. I guess you can take the yokel from the town, but you can't take the yokel out of the boy, right?"

I answered with some disappointment my lovely evening had just been ruined with, "Yeah, something like that. Hi, Lucy."

She leaned over Jess to expose her bosoms to me. She is such a slut.

"Hi, Big Boy. How's life with your black bitch?"

That did it. I rolled up my window and ignored Jessie and Lucy until my soda came. I paid for it and left. Those two are just low-life in the purest form. Maybe pure is not the word I should use when talking about those two. I was really irritated at Lucy's comment. I tried to remain calm by reminding myself who was making that comment in the first place. She was white trash and nothing else. I could not blame her for being ignorant, I guess. Still, it made me mad. If Lucy was a man, I would have gotten out of the car and beat him, I mean her until she apologized.

I dropped in to see Chuck. He doesn't start college until fall. I figured he would be at home with his mother. I was right. The two were sitting in front of the TV watching *'Beverly Hills 90210'*. I was invited in and given a bowl of popcorn.

We whispered while Chuck's mom tried to listen to the show. Finally, Chuck said we should go to the porch swing and let his mom concentrate on her program.

We took our popcorn and relocated to the front porch. Our conversation immediately went to Tommy and his sad death. Chuck and Tommy were closer than I was with Tommy. He was rather upset Tommy was no longer with us. Chuck talked about how he and Tommy were fishing together at Apple Canyon Lake the past weekend.

"I can't believe that he is gone. He was just pulling in a Muskie, and now he's gone. Just like that…it really makes one think how fragile we humans really are, doesn't it?"

I did not respond. I knew Chuck just needed to talk. I could not empathize with Chuck. I knew very little about Tommy. He was an excellent halfback. Off the field, we did not socialize.

We sat in silence, and I felt I needed to say something, being the thoughtless brute that I can sometimes be. I asked, "What exactly happened?" Once I said those words, I regretted it. It made me sound like a ghoul wanting disgusting details.

Luckily, Chuck did not take it that way. He answered. "From what Tommy's dad said, the saw kicked back and severed his femoral artery. Tommy's dad said Tommy always wore his chaps, gloves, and eye protection. For some reason, he didn't this time."

"I'm sad for you, Chuck. I know he was a good friend. Do you know when the funeral is going to be?" I asked.

We small talked a bit, and I added that I worked and could not come back over for the funeral. I asked Chuck to convey my sympathies to the family, and I headed back to my folks' house.

When I got home, my mother told me Tish phoned while I was out. Tish just wanted to know what time I would pick her up tomorrow. She wanted to get back to Chicago before dark. She also wanted me to be ready to pack up the pickup with several more boxes. I guess her mom boxed up some kitchen items for us and more food. My mom boxed up care packages, too. I sure hope I can fit it all in the bed of the truck.

Returning Tish's call, I told her I would see her just after lunch the next day. Emotionally exhausted, I went to my old room.

Surrounding me were pictures of Heather and myself at one class dance or another. She was in her cheerleading outfit in one, and I was in my football uniform. I turned the lights off, so I could not see her picture. The darkness did nothing to get her image out of my mind.

I saw her belly swollen with Jack's baby, and I could not fall asleep. I could not understand why she would sleep with him when she was adamant about saving herself for marriage. All I could think was Jack got her drunk and took advantage of her. I sure did not want to think of the other option…that she wanted it.

I guess I must have finally fallen asleep because the next thing I was aware of was the sun coming through my bedroom window. It was a beautiful day. I was determined my mood would improve with this sunshiny day. Being a grump about Heather would not go over well with Tish. She never really liked Heather. I guess she thought she was a bubble-brain.

It was nice seeing Mom and Dad. All the same, I was ready to leave after lunch. I thanked Mom for the boxes full of food, cleaning supplies, and whatever else she felt our house might be lacking. I loaded up, gave them both a hug and jumped into the truck. The next stop was Tish's, where the routine was repeated.

My mood improved considerably as we left the city limits. I noted Jack's father's name on the sign of the sheriff's department and wondered whether Jack would join his father someday as deputy. It would not surprise me in the least bit. Jack was a bully and loved displaying his power over other people. His father was the same way.

Chuck mentioned he thought Jack was joining the armed forces. His father wanted him to be a marine and follow in his footsteps. I wondered how that would play out with Heather and the new baby? I did not verbalize any of my thoughts to Tish.

Once back home, we settled into our routines. I remembered my meeting with Captain Jones for Friday morning. Tish was willing to ride along, curious what precisely the captain had in mind for me.

Captain Jones greeted us both as if we were his children. He invited us into his office and asked his secretary to bring us sodas or whatever we would like to drink. Once settled with our beverages, the captain told Tish he was really pleased that she would be helping with the training of the rookies. He turned his attention to me next and asked if I would like to be on his National Police Shooting Championship Team.

I was flattered and thrilled to be asked. Captain Jones said the range master was impressed with my steadiness. He went on to say the range master tried to distract me from shooting several times, and I was never detoured. That was what they were looking for...steady nerves under fire.

I was wondering just how much time I would be obligated to practice if I agreed. My schedule would be tight this fall with studies, work, martial arts training, and now shooting. I kept thinking about how my mom would say, *if you want something done, give the job to a busy person*. I guess being organized is vital here. I decided to accept the challenge.

Tish seemed genuinely happy for me. She said something about the middle of September being here before I would know it. That was when the national competition would take place. I guess she realized we both needed to get more organized. We would have little time to goof off from here on out.

Captain Jones told me when and where to meet for the next practice. He said I would like the team. They are all good guys or something equally trite. I don't mean to imply Captain Jones is mundane or anything like that. He just uses a common language when he is...well, being common.

We said our goodbyes and headed out of the department. Tony zeroed in on Tish. He headed her off in a flash.

"Hi, Tony," I offered.

He shook my hand; his eyes never left Tish's face. I felt sorry for the guy. It must be hard to have a major crush on a girl and not be able to ask her out. I decided to take pity on him, and I suggested he come over for pizza before I left for work. He needed to bring his own beer since we didn't stock it.

Tish did not say anything one way or the other when we headed home. I thought for sure I would be creamed for inviting Tony over. I could not quite read Tish. I thought she was interested in Tony. She showed no excitement about him coming over. Maybe I was wrong.

I tried to start a conversation about the shooting team. Tish's thoughts were elsewhere. She just nodded and said yes, no, or nothing as I spoke. I couldn't believe she was jealous that I was asked to be on the team...given all her awards. Finally, I just asked. "Hey, your mind is a million miles away. What are you thinking about?"

She answered slowly, "I was just thinking about Wally and Tommy."

"Oh yeah, what exactly are you thinking?" I said in my usual blunt manner.

"Well," Tish hemmed and hawed. "I really don't think Wally's drowning at the lake was an accident. That got me thinking that no one saw Tommy die. What if his death wasn't an accident, either?"

I was not following her. "How could it be anything but an accident?"

"Tommy has cut trees and wood for years. He was known for being very cautious. His dad said he always wore his chaps, gloves, and eye protection. Why wasn't he wearing his protective gear this time?" Tish was speculating.

"Come on, Tish. Accidents happen. That is the problem. All it takes is being careless one time and snap! You're dead." I cracked my knuckles for effect as I said this to her.

Tish looked at me in the way that conveyed I was an idiot. She said, "What if Tommy wasn't cutting down a tree? What if he heard someone in his backyard with the chainsaw and went to investigate? What if that someone cut open his thigh before Tommy could even react? What if that someone placed the blade of the saw in such a way that made it look like Tommy lost control or it kicked back into his leg.? What if it was really another murder?"

"Tish, no one murdered Tommy. It was just a crazy chainsaw accident, plain and simple. Why are you sure he was murdered?" Tish could really gnaw on an ole' bone. I could see why she was suspicious of Wally's death. After all, she is convinced she saw someone push his head underwater and hold him down. But Tommy....

I dropped the subject, and Tish took the hint. I guess she knew I was not convinced that Tommy was killed, or maybe I gave her some other things to consider. Whatever, Tish became silent again.

CHAPTER FIFTEEN

That evening, Tony did bring beer and stopped by for pizza. He did not offer us any beer because he knew he could get in serious trouble buying alcohol for minors. Since I would be on the job that night, I was not offended. I was content with root beer. Tish is never interested in getting drunk. She wasn't offended either.

I left them watching TV and talking as I went on to work. My night shift responsibilities were repetitive and benign. I did not expect anything to happen that night. I was hoping for a little excitement, it is just that I doubted…well, I knew it wasn't going to happen.

Herb met me at the office as I clocked in. He told me he forgot to mention something important the previous weekend when we were training. He said if I was ever in a situation where I could not talk without being heard, and I needed his help. I should click three times on my walkie-talkie. He told me two clicks would be his signal for my assistance. Herb also said, if he ever clicked for me that I should immediately call the office and let them know I was heading to his known location

I did not need to click three times that weekend, and neither did Herb click twice. Not much happened for the rest of the summer.

Tish and I settled into our routines with firearms training completed, and each of us working our shifts. Tish found time to train me in basic combat deflections, holds and locks; we both worked out at the police department gym several times a week.

Other than Chuck coming to visit once for a short visit, the summer flew by. I even got familiar with shopping at the grocery store and cooking. When Chuck visited, I purchased a small barbecue grill and cooked out hamburgers.

Fall was approaching, and our class workload would complicate our lives even further. As excited as I was for classes to start, I was always reluctant to leave the summer behind. Tish and I knew we needed to make another mid-week trip back home to see our parents before we got totally entangled with classes and homework. Weekends were never available for us to drive home; mid-week was our only option. We will leave the last week of August. The next time we visit the folks would be Thanksgiving holiday.

We packed our overnight bags and headed to the truck early Tuesday morning. Having plenty of spare clothes at our parents' homes, toiletries were all we needed to pack. We figured we could stay until Friday morning if our parents really insisted on an extra day. Otherwise, we would leave Thursday afternoon. I knew we would not be going until Friday, or our mothers would cry.

I dropped Tish off at her parent's house and headed on to my folk's home. I parked in front since the driveway was occupied by Tish's father's van. I was curious why he was over at my house.

Dad and Mr. Evers were sitting at the table. They both smiled and greeted me as I came inside.

"Hi, Son," Dad said as he and Mr. Evers both got up to shake my hand as if I was a guest.

"What are you two doing here on a workday? Why aren't you both at your businesses? I said as I greeted their handshake.

"We have great news. We are now in business together." Dad smiled as he said this and patted Mr. Evers on his back.

"What?" Was the only words I managed to get out of my mouth. Sometimes I wonder if I am a bit slow.

Mr. Evers spoke next, "We decided if we work together, we could expand our business to include popular van conversions, sound systems, 30's-60's hot rod restorations, custom motorcycle builds, customized paint and pinstriping, as well as specialty truck suspensions."

"Wow, you must be kidding…it sounds great…I am excited for both of you." Pausing, I remarked, "You cannot call it Evers and McFarlan. Tish and I already have dibs on that name. What about your existing businesses?

Mr. Evers responded., "No problem, we are calling the new business, 'Stanton Performance Automotive.' We will keep our existing businesses. My tire shop will concentrate on truck and winter tires, and the towing company will get us through the winter. Your dad's body shop is always at its busiest in the winter, and his Ford F-350 snowplow will also help with the cash flow. We bought the old Speights Buick dealership, that existed between our shops. Now we own the whole block with a fenced car lot and a nice showroom."

I agreed the new name sounded very professional and something a grown-up would name a business. I keep forgetting how young our fathers really are.

My dad said, "We have barely started, and already we have new customers for van conversions and truck suspensions. We may be behind before we even get started." Both fathers laughed at that remark.

"I really am impressed," I said quickly.

Mom walked in just then. "I am not laughing. Both Mrs. Evers and I are being put to work in the new business at the dealership building. Mrs. Evers is going to oversee bookkeeping and purchasing. I need to be at the front desk and handle the parts department as well." She gave me a big hug as she told me this.

"Good job, Mom. You are a working woman now. I guess an empty nest syndrome is not going to be your problem." I gave my mom a big hug back just as I said this.

A knock at the door announced Mrs. Evers and Tish. They walked in beaming.

"Can you believe our parents are going to be partners?" Tish said to me.

"I wonder which one of these two we will be investigating first? Who do you think is most likely to take the money and run?" I winked at Tish as I said this.

Mom hit me. Mrs. Evers said it would most likely be her since she was the one in charge of the books, and she has her eyes on the Bahamas.

Mom and Mrs. Evers went off into the kitchen to make some lunch. Mrs. Evers said she could cook up some barbecue beef sandwiches in no time. Mom's world-famous potato salad was on the menu as well. I was thinking this partnership was going to be outstanding for my stomach.

As we ate, we were congratulated on our successes. Dad was pleased I was on the National Shooting Team with the police department. The Evers were equally pleased Tish was a star with her martial arts training classes. I would say our parents' shirts were bursting with pride until I remembered just how much we all had eaten. The bursting was probably due to the barbecue beef and potato salad.

Mr. Evers was sitting back, happy, and full. "Oh, we forgot to tell you that we hired some of your buddies. I know a couple of your football friends were in the school auto shop. Two of them came around looking for jobs just as your dad and I decided to combine forces. Now that we have customers lined up, we could use the help. What do you think of Erik and Chris?"

"They are both good guys. That is great you gave them jobs. They are honest and hard-working. I think you won't be sorry." I was happy to hear a few of my buddies would get the chance to work with our fathers. I knew they would be excellent employees.

We enjoyed chatting and laughing, and soon it was getting late. We finished the dessert, and then the Evers bid us a good night and left. I really enjoyed the day.

The next day, I was not happy. I watched Heather walk past, and even though she was not huge or anything, I could see a slight baby-bump. It took two glances to notice the bump, sure enough, it was there. She saw me looking out the window, and she waved. I hate to confess that I pretended not to see her. I know that was cowardly of me. I just could not bear to go out and talk to her. I was determined not to let her ruin the rest of my visit.

I went into my room and took down every picture that Heather was in. Soon my walls looked bare. I found a box and stored them out in the garage. If the moisture got into the boxes and ruined them, so be it. We would never be a couple again; why torture myself with thoughts of it.

My mother watched as I stored the box away. She stood quietly behind me and said, "They are getting married next weekend. She is over three months pregnant. Before long, she will be noticeably showing. I guess they do need to hurry the wedding along. From what I hear, it will be a small wedding and not at the church. I guess the judge will perform it at the courthouse."

I looked at my mother and shrugged. "She made her choice. I hope she is happy, but I can't imagine anyone being happy with Jack. He is bad news." I said nothing more, and neither did my mom.

I wondered why Heather and Jack ruined every visit that I made back home. I made a conscious choice not to think about either of them. That was the one thing I had some control over...my thoughts. Instead, I called Tish.

Tish seemed to know me well enough. She knew I was feeling a bit down. She also knew me well enough to know Heather was most likely the reason why.

"Scotty, I thought we should roll my Harley into the back of your pickup. I won't drive it in winter when there is snow and ice or when it is too cold. It sure would be handy to ride it to the police department when I am training rookies. I know there will be times you need to stay home and cram for tests. I won't need to do much cramming with my photographic memory, Ha-ha!" Tish said this to get my mind off Heather.

"Tish, you can use my truck anytime you want. Why risk your life on your Harley in the city?" I replied.

"I won't be risking my life. I am safe on my bike, and I don't like driving your truck. Don't get me wrong," she added quickly, "I really appreciate you letting me drive it whenever I need it." I could tell she had more to add. "I hate parking it. My Harley can be parked just about anywhere, and I can park closer to the police department, and then I don't need to walk very far in the dark."

I knew she was making an argument that I should consider her safety. In a way, she had a point. I knew the captain would let her bring the Harley into his office if it meant she would be available to train the rookies. Tish had him wrapped around her little finger.

"Okay, I will find some lumber we can use as a ramp. I know my dad has tie-downs that he will lend us for the trip home." The up-side to Tish having her Harley along was that she would be wearing those leather pants more often.

It was time to pack up and say goodbye to our moms. I hugged my mom and went to pick up Tish as she was hugging her mom goodbye. We already received word we needed to stop at the old Buick dealership to pick up Tish's motorcycle. Tish's dad said he needed to make a few modifications before she could ride it in Chicago. I wasn't sure what that meant. I suspected he wanted to put on an alarm system.

As we drove up, we could see a canary yellow '55 2-door Chevy and a '55 navy blue Ford Fairlane in the showroom. They looked cool.

"Hey, didn't your dad have an old junked out '55 Chevy?" I asked Tish.

"Yeah, and didn't your dad have a rusted-out Ford sitting in the back lot of his shop?" Tish answered.

"Wow! If this is any indication of the amazing work that our dads can do together, we can count on having some cool rides in the future." My laugh didn't disguise just how impressed I really was.

We parked the pickup truck and went inside the old dealership showroom, hollering for our dad's as we walked in. It wasn't long before they both came in from the garage with big grins on their faces.

"What do you think of these ole' hotrods?" Mr. Evers asked.

Tish gave her father a big hug and said, "Wow! Just Wow!"

"I second that!" I said with enthusiasm as I walked around each vehicle, giving them my full attention.

Cliff, Tish's father, said, "Gabe did all the body, paint and framework. He also installed the sound and alarm system.

"And Cliff did all the suspension, brake, engine, driveline, rims and tires. We'll leave these here in the showroom as a draw for new customers," Gabe finished the sentence.

Looking out of the showroom window, we saw Chris and Erik pushing an outrageously gorgeous chopper out of the garage and setting it on its kickstand next to 'Big Red'.

"We were going to have this number on display for the fall and winter months. It seems a certain young lady has her heart on having her Harley to ride in Chicago. Well, there it is, Tish," Cliff said.

For the first time, everyone witnessed Tish cry. "That is my Harley? It is insane! I can't believe my eyes!" Rushing out of the Showroom with everyone following, Tish circled the bike. "It is even in the paint scheme I've always wanted. How did you know what I liked?" Tish continued to blubber and jabber on and on about her Harley as if it was alive.

"You can thank Chris and Erik. They said that a Harley chopper drove through town with flames on the tank, and you just about burst a gasket trying to follow it down the street," Cliff said, giving the boys credit for the paint scheme.

Tish smiled at the guys and thanked them for remembering that day vividly. They both just gave her a wave and a nod. Neither could talk much around Tish.

Cliff, Tish's dad, had more to say. "Let me show you what we did. Gabe fitted a bypass dual exhaust system per cylinder. With the flip of this red paddle switch, you can put it in silent mode or straight pipes. He also added an alarm and interlock system for both the front and rear wheels. Gabe's hand sewed the leather seat. Check out the female kickboxer figure that he added. I installed the oversized tank and extended the forks about 4 inches. I hope you like the skinny tire in the front and the fat tire on the back. The Harley just did not look right with the factory tires. The most difficult part was fabricating custom front and rear fenders."

Tish was wiping the tears that refused to go away. "I am just beyond words. I absolutely love what all of you did to my ride. I love the look, especially the diagonal slant to the exhaust pipes, paint scheme, perfect seat, and custom fenders. The fat tire in the rear is righteous! It looks so intimidating that I want to show it off and ride it to Chicago. How about if I follow you home, Scott? Did you know about this?" Tish was already grabbing her leathers, gloves, boots, and helmet out of the box in the truck bed.

"No, I didn't know; how about if I follow you? I can keep the big trucks off your tail." I said with a smirk.

I could not be happier for Tish; I just hoped she would not get hurt, driving around the city.

"Oh, one more thing. Here Scott, a present for you, too." Gabe said, handing me a garage door opener and remote. "We want you to install this in your garage. Tish deserves a safe place to park her Harley."

"Gee, thanks," I said, realizing that I had some work ahead of me.

Cliff said, "Hey Gabe, with all the excitement around Tish's Harley, you forgot to tell Scott why we rebuilt your old double-nickel, Ford."

"Oh yeah, Scott, hope you won't mind leaving the '55 Ford here in the showroom until spring. I guess that is my way of saying, it is our gift to you," Gabe remarked.

"You have got to be kidding, Wow! I was fine with Tish's new ride. Seriously, the '55 Ford is mine?" I asked in an excited high pitch voice as I took another look at the hot rod.

Tish commented, "Finally, we'll have something better than that jacked-up truck of yours for our ride in the city this summer."

"You keep your hands off my ride, and I will keep my hands off yours…deal?" I tossed this remark to Tish, who just laughed and said, "Right!"

Tish grabbed both fathers in a group hug. "Our dads are the best! Don't you agree?"

I could not argue with that statement. With a nod and trying to hold back the tear forming in my eye, I joined the group hug.

Realizing that we still had a long ride ahead, I broke free and said that I hated to break up the hug-fest. We needed to get rolling. Tish said she had to go and change before leaving, and off she trotted. Before long, she emerged from the ladies' room wearing an eye-popping outfit. I knew I needed to drive my truck close to her tail to keep the truckers away from her. They could not miss the fact that she was a shapely female in that outfit.

The ride home was uneventful, luckily. I drove close enough to keep any trucker from sliding in between us. I was amused to watch Tish as she passed other motorcycles on the two-lane roads. She seemed to have some signals that I could only guess what she meant. I noted that when she passed another Harley, her left arm was down at a 45-degree angle, and her thumb was up. When she passed the crotch rocket, her fingers changed to shooting sign, and when she passed an old guy riding his motorcycle, her left hand made a peace sign. I knew I needed to ask her why she changed her hand signals with the different types of riders and their motorcycles.

Once we arrived home, I started to unload the pickup. Tish dashed past me to the house. I yelled, "Hey, grab a load!"

She yelled back, "I need to phone Dad to tell him what a fantastic ride I just had! I'll be back in a moment."

I unloaded all the boxes in what was supposed to be 'a moment.' When Tish finally did get off the phone, she apologized for taking a long time. I said, "Fine, you can come to help me install the garage door opener. I don't want to do it tomorrow and ruin my day off before going back to work."

She agreed, and we went out to the garage. It was nice to have someone hand me tools and equipment. I would not need to go up and down the ladder as often. It is hard enough to balance on a ladder while screwing in the brackets while also holding the garage door opener in place.

CHAPTER SIXTEEN

Tish spent quite a bit of time riding her Harley for the next several days. She was getting to know Chicago well from the seat of her ride. I was feeling a bit jealous. It must be nice to feel free. Driving the truck is fun, but not in the Chicago traffic. Tish is right, it isn't much fun to park 'Big Red'.

With Tish gone a lot, I had plenty of rest before my shifts each night. I also spent time studying the required reading for the courses we would start on Monday. We both had a full load with English 101, Business 111, Social Science 101, Criminal Justice 102, and Criminal Justice 114. Tish would read the chapter once, and it would be in her head. I needed to read, reread, and highlight before it would get into my head. Along with martial arts training, shooting practice, and work, I was swamped.

Tish and I scheduled our classes together. In that way, we would share the same courses. I knew she would take better notes, and studying together would give me a fighting chance. Tish is quite good at explaining concepts that seem strange or alien to me. This semester would give Tish the upper hand. I knew when we got to the math, forensic science, and micro-computers, I would excel. It isn't that we compete as much as we help each other with our weaknesses. At least, that was how it was in high school.

Our routine became just that…routine. We studied between classes and in the evenings when Tish was not instructing at the police academy. On Saturdays, Tish had her classes at the dojang, and I worked at night. I squeezed in my shooting practices at both the police shooting range and at the local shooting range.

The National Police Shooting Competition was in just two weeks. Captain Jones would come to the range often. He said I was doing great and he was sure I would make a good showing at the competition. At this point, I was not feeling any stress. It was just another thing to do on most days. However, the day of the competition might be a different story.

The day before the competition finally arrived. Tish was up and dressed and ready to go without my bugging her. In fact, she was up so early that she made breakfast for me. I appreciated how she was trying to make the day easier for me. We ate, packed our suitcases in the truck, and headed off to Indianapolis for the competition. We had reservations for the night and would stay overnight the day of the competition and then head back home in time for classes on Monday. Herb gave me the weekend off knowing how much this shooting competition meant to both Captain Jones and me. Herb said it was smart to keep the police on friendly terms.

Eagle Creek was our destination. Map in hand, truck gassed up, a picnic lunch packed, and we were off at an early start. Tish dozed off soon after we got onto the freeway. I knew she got up early just to cook breakfast and make lunch. I appreciate how she thinks ahead.

I kept the radio low not to wake Tish and just enjoyed the scenery along the way. Often freeways go through the least scenic parts of a state, however since the terrain doesn't vary much in the midwest, I could just enjoy seeing the farms, cattle grazing, and some of the neat cars passing me on either side.

The drive wasn't all that far. We wanted to get settled. I researched some restaurants with the idea of paying Tish back for being such a supportive partner and taking her out to dinner. It needed to be a casual place since we packed light. I vowed it would not be a pizza parlor. I wanted to take her someplace different. I heard 'Steer-In' was an excellent place to eat on 10th Street.

Once settled in at the motel, we found where Captain Jones would be staying. We told Captain Jones that we would be dining at Steer-In. Since his wife had to stay home with the children, we invited him to join us for dinner. He gladly accepted.

There were a ton of choices for dinner that we all had trouble making up our minds. Captain Jones wanted the blackened catfish. He said his wife refused to cook it at home since it made the house stink for days. I finally decided on a hand-cut rib-eye steak, and Tish ordered the Chicken Glorioso. Even though it was chicken covered in white cream sauce with mushrooms and cheese, Tish insisted it was light enough that she could have a decadent hot fudge brownie for dessert. I told her she could have it if I could have one bite. Captain Jones said he would have pie since his wife was not around to remind him of his waistline. I always want ice cream. I ordered the sundae.

When Captain Jones tried to filch the ticket, I beat him to it. I told him we had extra grocery money this month, thanks to our mothers being generous, and I wanted to pay the bill to thank him for all his support. He graciously agreed to let me pay if he could leave a tip.

Saturday morning came all too soon. It was time for my relay to begin matches 8 thru 12 for the open class sharpshooter/municipal semi-automatic pistol championship. Captain Jones's range master was my second. He would provide me with the appropriate number of 6 round magazines for each match and stage. Sargent Tomlinson is a fantastic armorer; he prepares the districts Colt MK IV/Series 70 Gold Cup National Match Semi-Automatic 45cal Pistol that I've been practicing with for weeks. This Colt 45 has never failed to fire or eject a round. Even the magazines are tuned perfectly, and I will go through 25 of them today. I was told that he meticulously hand loads every round to his exact specifications.

My first match, match 8, was 24 shots total from the unsupported standing position. The first stage is 12 shots at 7 yards, and the second stage is 12 shots at 15 yards. We are given a maximum of 20 seconds for each stage. Each shot in each match was worth a maximum of 10 points. I scored a third place with 239 points in 17 seconds and 17 rounds in the x-ring within the bullseye.

Match 9 was 18 shots kneeling and standing at 25 yards. The first stage is 6 shots kneeling. The second stage is 6 shots standing left-handed with support, and the last stage is 6 shots right-handed standing with support. There is a total of 90 seconds maximum for all stages. I was fortunate to have experience shooting with both hands. When I was 12 years old, I broke my right wrist and practiced shooting left-handed. I wanted to be able to go hunting with my dad.

I scored another 3rd place with 178 points in 68 seconds and 8 rounds in the X-ring. Not one of my left-handed shots were in the X-ring, and two of those shots were in the 9-ring. I'll need to work on this going forward.

Captain Jones and Tish were in the safety of the bleachers cheering me on. I know Tish would have something sassy to say about the three missed points; I also knew she would be very proud of me.

Match 10 would be the most difficult for me. It is 24 shots, sitting, prone and standing at 50 yards. 6 shots sitting position, 6 shots prone, and 6 shots standing right and left-handed with support. We were given 2 minutes and 45 seconds to complete the three stages.

The Captain handed Tish a pair of binoculars and said, "You will need these for this match."

To my surprise, I scored the first-place ribbon for this match with 236 points in 2 minutes and 5 seconds with 12 rounds in the x-ring. I am lucky my distance vision is 20-15 in each eye, and I was at least 10 years younger than the other 28 competitors from around the country in my category.

Match 11 would level the playing field as there are two similar stages of 12 shots each at 25 yards fired standing right and left-handed unsupported. 35 seconds was allowed for each stage. I finished 4th place with a total score of 238 points in 56 seconds and 8 rounds in the x-ring. This was a really close match; the first-place winner scored 238 points in 52 seconds and 10 shots in the x-ring. I know I am going to hear from Tish about how I am a slowpoke.

The finals will be on the challenging National Police Course. Only the top shooters from the previous stages will compete in Match 12.

This match will comprise four separate stages with a total of 60 shots. Stage one is 12 shots at 7 yards in standing position without support. The time limit is 20 seconds, including the time to reload.

Stage two is 18 shots at 25 yards, 6 each kneeling, and standing right and left-handed with support. The time limit for this stage is 90 seconds. Stage three is 24 shots at 50 yards. 6 each sitting, prone, standing left and right-handed with support. The time limit for this stage is 2 minutes and 45 seconds. The fourth stage is 6 shots standing without support at 25 yards. The time limit is 12 seconds. All four of these stages are completed in one go.

I was a sweaty wreck when I finished this course...I probably smelled of gun powder and sweat. When the committee posted my score, I came in second with 584 points in a total of 3 minutes and 35 seconds and 28 rounds in the x-ring.

I finished 3rd place overall with a score of 1475 points and 73 rounds in the x-ring, nearly half of my shots were perfect. I missed out on a second place by a total of just 2 seconds and 1 less x-ring. I will need to work on my timing and perfecting more of my shots.

Wow! This event was even more exciting than winning the state championship. I guess because I did this on my own without a team behind me. I really did have a great coach and armorer. I will make sure I give them credit for my success.

Tish ran up and socked me in the shoulder and called me 'dead eye.' "Seriously, match 10 you shot at 150 feet and scored 236 points out of 240 with 12 of those shots in the x-ring and only 4 shots in the 9-ring. The target looked like you hit it with a shotgun at close range. Wow, first place in that match. I pity the deer, or whatever it is you and your dad hunt."

The Captain's grin was a mile wide. He told me my overall score would help the team tremendously. Captain Jones said I needed to check-in my firearm, holster, and magazines to his range officer and then take Tish to the canteen for lunch. The captain and his partner were going to get a few practice shots before his Master Level two-officer semi-automatic pistol relay began. The match would be the same as my final match 12 with the same four stages.

Even though I wore ear protection, my ears were ringing as I walked away with Tish. She had a huge smile and congratulated me on a spectacular showing. I was more than surprised. She did not razz me about being slow or not coming in first place. She was proud of me. It made me feel kinda warm inside.

"Come on, Tish. Let's go get something to eat and relax a while. I held out my arm and showed her how it was shaking. Even with all the practice, I put in daily, or almost daily, these matches were stressful and hard on me. Showing her how shaky my hands were, to get a little sympathy, was clearly a big mistake.

"All that means is you need to lift more weights. You can't let a little handgun make you shaky. That is pathetic. How much are you lifting now? We are going to double it by next year." Tish was in drill sergeant mode. I knew better than to make excuses.

"Yes, Mam! I will work on it." I responded as quickly as any private would have in the military.

The canteen had a wide variety of food. I guess police officers demand more than just hamburgers. I laughed to see donuts as an option for a snack.

Grabbing our food, we decided to eat under a tree where there was a picnic bench unoccupied. We both decided the pulled pork sandwich looked good. Adding potato chips, a soft drink, and two chocolate chip cookies each, we were in heaven.

The temperature was perfect. It hadn't become humid or windy yet, and the sky was clear. It was a sweet spot except for the constant gunfire. I was trying to decide whether to put my earplugs back in when Tish spoke.

"Maybe Captain Jones will let me join the shooting team next year. I hear there is a special award for the lady who shoots the highest score. It may as well be me next year, right?"

"Tish, you have more irons in the fire than you can handle now. You aren't serious about starting shooting as well, are you?" I don't know if I was feeling threatened that Tish might become obsessed with beating me or if I was really concerned about how much she had going on in her life.

"Relax, hot-shot. I am kidding. I do have more than enough on my plate right now. You know darn well if I wanted that trophy, it would be mine." Tish wasn't smiling. I could only believe she meant what she was saying. The trouble is Tish was right. If she wanted that trophy, it would be hers.

Stuffing the last bite of the cookie into my mouth, I said with my mouth full, "Let's put in our earplugs and go cheer the captain and his partner on. It is almost time for their relay to start."

Tish still had both of her cookies to eat, but she followed me to where we could sit and watch from a safe distance. I kept looking at her cookies and wished I had one more.

The match went fast. The Captain scored 592 points in three minutes and fifteen seconds with forty rounds in the x-ring, and his teammate scored 591 points in three minutes and twenty-two seconds and thirty-one shots in the x-ring. They came in first overall with 1183 points and seventy-one total rounds in the x-ring.

We need to stick around to find out the final scores. However, we need to wait until everyone completed their relays. It was going to be another hour or more. The captain and his partner were starved. They passed on breakfast to catch my relay. So, we decided to join them for another go-around of food and drinks. I did not really eat a second pulled pork sandwich. Although I was tempted. Instead, I ate two more chocolate chip cookies. Tish just had some lemonade.

We chatted cordially under the same tree. The time went by quickly, with many funny stories told about past events. Captain Jones laughed about the time his partner pressed the magazine release button while he was shooting. The magazine fell to the ground, and he had to scramble to find it in the dirt. Blowing the dust off, he shoved the magazine in place and continued shooting...losing only 4 seconds in the transition. Amazingly, the captain's partner still shot a perfect score.

Detective Dan Franklin added, "He will never let me live that one down. However, I have a story on Barry as well. There was this one time when Barry went from the sitting position to the prone position. He farted so loud that everyone on the range stopped shooting. He probably won for that reason alone."

Laughing hysterically, Barry said it was not factual. Everyone did not stop shooting on the range.

The bullhorn called the competitors over to assemble for the results of the Saturday Open-Class National Championship. Trophies were handed out, and I was glad Tish came along. I would have trouble carrying all my trophies by myself. I received a 1st, 2nd, two 3rd places, and an overall 3rd place trophy. The captain and Detective Franklin won a mammoth cup for 1st place team and a 2nd place trophy for the overall Municipal Open-Class Semi-Automatic Pistol National Police Championship.

The day had been a long, hard day. It was also loads of fun. Well, maybe Tish did not have as much fun as I did. Being a good sport, she would never let on that she was bored out of her mind.

I decided I would treat her to a nice dinner and a movie. We needed to leave in the morning since I would be working my shift on Sunday night. Herb had let me off for two nights to participate. I was going to take advantage of the second night free to do what I wanted to do.

Captain Jones decided he would drive home. His wife had been alone with the children and needed a break. He shook my hand and said how proud he was of me and what a great day it was when he got the phone call from the range master telling him about his new-found talent. "You know you will not be able to shoot as a sharpshooter next year. I will fill out the paperwork and approve moving you up to expert marksman when we get back. You guys have some fun…do not stay up too late." Captain Jones was a father and a good one at that, I could tell. He even fathered us as if we were his children.

Tish and I left for our night of relaxation and fun. I was still in the mood for lots of gunfire and suggested we see 'Lethal Weapons 3'.

"You know, Scotty. I never did get to see 'Patriot Games' that night with Tony. I would really love to see it," Tish purred.

I knew the minute Tish called me Scotty that she would get her way. Scott means business; Scotty means she wants something, and she is going to get it. I know better than to argue. We will see 'Patriot Games.'

We would have time to go and eat seafood before the movie. We sure did not need more pulled pork. A seafood salad sounded great after the heavy food I ate earlier. Tish, on the other hand, would probably eat the whole tank of lobsters.

CHAPTER SEVENTEEN

The drive home was quiet and uneventful. Except for when Tish asked me how I can remain accurate over the 150 shots in various positions and distances. I told her that I visualize the shot picture in my mind until I can imagine the bullet leaving the barrel and traveling its trajectory to the x-ring in the bullseye. I don't even realize when I pull the trigger.

Tish said, "Bullshit, you're telling me it's all mental? Are you saying there is no technique involved?"

I responded, "I am sure it is not the same for every shooter. For me, creating a mental picture first that coordinates my senses with my hand, ok, my finger, and my laser-focused eye is what helps."

"You're something else," Tish said a bit exasperated. "I don't get it. I have a photographic memory. Even with that, I can't visualize the connected senses required in the way you are describing."

I answered, "I am not saying the technique isn't important. I am saying, like you said to me before, that visualizing and imagining what is going to happen before it happens subconsciously makes me more successful. I believe your sensei was right, that our subconscious decision making can act, at a minimum, a fraction of a second faster than if we rely on our conscious efforts."

Tish thought about what I was saying. "OK, I think I understand what you are saying now. When I use my photographic memory, I see things static. If I could use my memory and let it imagine everything going on around me, I could visualize like you are describing."

"I am going to use your example with what Captain Jones is teaching me. Ninjutsu is more difficult than I imagined it would be. If I can visualize what happens before, during, and after each movement, I will be able to anticipate and react quickly and more efficiently. Since using less motion is better, I really think this will help." Tish was almost talking more to herself than she was to me.

She became silent for most of the ride home. I could only imagine that she was trying her new visualization techniques in her mind. I used the time to replay my own victories at the competition. Being part of a team, my individual accomplishments made me feel proud. This was all new to me.

I knew it would be less than an hour after we got home, and Tish would be riding around on her Harley. I asked her to please be back a couple of hours before my shift started. We could order a pizza and watch *Murder She Wrote*.

Tish responded, "I won't be gone long. I'm just going for a short ride."

I felt like a mother duck. I always worried when Tish was off riding her motorcycle. There was too much traffic, and one never knows how well car drivers are watching for motorcycles. Accidents happen quickly, and there isn't much protection when on a Harley. Leathers and a helmet only help minimally. Tish says I worry too much, and she is an excellent rider. Even excellent riders get hit….

Nearly asleep on the sofa, I was awakened by a low rumbling noise. I was greatly relieved when I heard Tish's Harley enter the driveway.

Tish walked into the door and immediately said, "Scott, did you phone your parents to tell them how well you did yesterday?"

Ashamed, I realized it never occurred to me to phone them. "I forgot …and please flip the switch that turns on your Harley's exhausts silent mode. You don't want to piss-off the neighbors," I said weakly.

136

"Thanks for reminding me, I will remember from now on. I am going to take a shower. You should call your parents right now. When will the pizza arrive?" Tish was already closing the door to the bathroom before I could answer.

I phoned my parents and apologized for not calling the minute I arrived home. I gave some lame excuse about taking a nap on the sofa since I had to work tonight. Dad was excited to hear I earned that many trophies.

"Scott, what an accomplishment. I understand you were up against the best marksmen in the country. I am proud of you."

I answered, "You taught me well. If you hadn't taken the time to teach me to shoot, I wouldn't be where I am today." I was starting to feel sentimental; I was glad when the doorbell rang.

"Gotta run, Dad. The doorbell is ringing. I will talk to you and Mom again next week." I hung up before my dad could hear the softness that was creeping into my voice. I guess when one is away from home, one really realizes how much ones' parents have done for a person.

I paid for the pizza, and Tish walked into the room in sweats and an oversized T-shirt. Geez, she would even look great in a burlap bag.

Crap, how my ears were still ringing. When I go to work, the white noise playing at the mall during the night will help.

Tish was ready for pizza, a TV show, and a relaxed night at home. I knew she would only watch the one show with me, and then she would hit the books and be ready for class in the morning. I needed her tutoring skills tomorrow, for sure.

Classes weren't exactly difficult, that is, for Tish. She was acing every class. With her help, I was holding my own. She kept me up to speed. I could take the tests with no anxiety. I envied Tish's ability to search her mind and find the answers to any question just by picturing her notes or the book text she read for the answers. We both were good at applying what we learned and using deductive reasoning. It was memorizing the details of the various laws that frustrated me. I would need to read and reread many times before it would stick in my brain.

It was heading towards the middle of November. Soon classes would be over in the middle of December, and we would not resume until the Spring term starting January 18th. I thought it was generous of colleges to allow a long enough break so that students could get holiday jobs to help pay for tuition for the next term. I wasn't sure whether Herb would add on a couple more night shifts once I was on break or not.

My job was comfortable now. I didn't anticipate bad men hiding behind every pole or in every corner as I had on the first weekend. Usually, Herb and I would meet in the middle of the mall two or three times a night. We would exchange greetings and observations, and then declare which route we would take the next time around. Knowing where the other might be in the case of an emergency could be life-saving.

It was my turn to take the stores on the connection level, and Herb would circle the Grand Mall. The parking garage doors to the mall remained locked, and unless one of us spotted a strange vehicle parked in a lot, we did not venture out into it. I checked the mall door to each store, making sure they were locked and found nothing amiss. I was just about ready to test the opposite side of the connection level when my walkie-talkie clicked twice. For a second, I froze.

Herb sent me the two clicks signaling he needed assistance. I knew it was urgent because he was unable to speak on the walkie-talkie to let me know exactly where he was in the mall. I called the security office while on the move and told the dispatcher that Herb signaled me for immediate assistance.

"Where was Herb heading the last time the two of you made contact?" the dispatcher asked calmly.

"I am on the far end of the connection level by the administrative offices, and Herb said he would be checking the west end of the Grand Mall," I answered as I ran up the escalator to the Grand Mall.

The dispatcher assured me he would be calling the police. I should proceed towards the location where Herb could be with caution.

Caution?... I was running at full speed, knowing Herb could be in serious trouble. For all I knew, he may be lying on the ground injured or dead.

I rounded the corner off the escalator and headed to the west end of the Grand Mall when I saw Herb being accosted by two masked men. One held a bat over his head and was about to club Herb when I realized I would not reach him in time to stop Herb from being bludgeoned.

I pulled off my wrist weight as I continued running at full speed and threw it like a football, spiraling straight at the man's head. It made a loud, crunching sound as it contacted the top side of the masked man's forehead.

In full stride, I removed my other wrist weight and spiraled the second weight at the second man's chest. I am sure it broke his sternum and his ribs as he dropped and started gasping for air.

Herb was still on his feet, when I reached him, holding his wrist gingerly in his other hand. Herb told me that both of my wrist-weights barely missed him. He said he could feel the wind as they whooshed by. He smiled as he said this to me. However, I could see Herb was in pain.

"What happened to your arm?" I asked.

"When I saw them coming out of the jewelry store, I yelled for them to halt. One of them ran up to me and smacked the baton out of my hand...I think the perp broke my wrist. The other one was getting ready to put my lights out when your excellent throw took the perp down," Herb responded.

I bent over and picked up his baton. "Cuff that one, will you, Scott?" Herb handed me his cuffs and said, "You will need to cuff the other one, too. I hope you called the dispatcher? Right? I suspect you didn't tell them to send an ambulance as well, did you?" Herb asked.

"I will contact the office and tell them we need medical assistance as well as the police." I offered.

Just then, the lights from the police cars could be seen coming towards us at the south entrance. Herb went to the door to let them in while I stayed behind to mind our two robbers. It was apparent Herb stopped a robbery in progress, judging by a big bag of jewelry lying beside the man with a throbbing headache.

The police led the two robbery suspects to the police car. They told me to follow one of them to retrieve our cuffs as the police would use their own. Before leaving, the ambulance pulled in beside the police car, and two attendants walked to the squad car.

Giving each suspect a good look over, they declared the man with the broken sternum and ribs should travel by ambulance as he was having extreme difficulty breathing. A ruptured lung was always a possibility. They requested one of the officers to ride along in the ambulance as well. Before the attendants left, they placed a brace on Herb and gave him a sling. They told him to go see a doctor as soon as possible.

The officer waited for Herb to be treated and then suggested cuffing the suspect to the gurney since the second suspect also needed to be seen by a physician. The officers would follow close behind the ambulance. The attendant seemed to be okay with the police just following once they promised they would be at the emergency room when the ambulance arrived.

Another officer stayed behind to take Herb's and my statements. This wasn't Herb's first rodeo. He knew just what to say and what not to say. He told me to state the facts and nothing more. He said to give them my first name only but not my address. All other questions needed to be directed to Ford City Mall Security Administration.

I knew I would be answering a lot more questions to my employer than I would be to the police department. I hoped it would not be a factor that I used equipment that was not issued.

Once the excitement was over for the evening, Herb told me I made a right judgment call under stressful conditions. "I like the fact that you used what you had on you to save my butt, well, head, in this case. If you waited until you were close enough to use the baton or your fists, I would be dead right now. I am certain their bat would have cracked my skull open like a pumpkin. For that, I thank you, my wife thanks you and my kids thank you." Herb was not smiling as he said this to me. I knew he genuinely was grateful I saved his life.

Herb stayed just long enough to make sure I was alright and then said since our shift was almost over, he would leave a little early to get his wrist x-rayed. "I am pretty sure it is broken. I am certain I will be back to work next weekend. A cast is not going to stop me from doing my rounds. Hey, thank you, truly." With one more thank you, Herb left the mall.

Getting home to Tish was what I was craving more than anything else. I wanted to tell her what happened at the mall and tell her how scared I was. I wondered if she would think less of me if I acknowledged that I was afraid. Tish only knows me as a big, muscular guy. I decided not to tell her I was scared…just the facts.

Tish listened over coffee and breakfast. "That is incredible, Scott. What if you weren't wearing the ankle and wrist-weights to build up muscles while at work? Herb could be dead right now. Just think about how probabilities work in life. You want to keep your muscles strong…you wear weights while you walk around the mall and boom! The weights are the weapon of choice."

I wasn't sure whether Tish was teasing me or being philosophical. I wasn't sure how to respond. Luckily, the phone rang, and I did not need to say anything to her remark.

Tish answered the phone, "Scott, it's Captain Jones. He wants to talk to you."

I went to the phone and wondered why the captain would be calling this early. It was only 7:45 a.m.

"Hi, Scott. I heard about your trouble at the mall last night. It is never boring around you two. Tell me what happened," Captain Jones asked.

I told Captain Jones the whole story, including using the wrist-weights to take them down. I could hear him laughing hysterically on the other side of the phone.

"That is a great story, Scott. It is better than my fart story. Now, we will have a story to tell on you. The Mall Cop, who brought down two robbers with wrist-weights. It is a good thing you were a quarterback in high school. I guess you deserved the state championship after all."

No longer laughing, Captain Jones said, "You won't need to worry about those two guys for a long time. They stole over $30,000 worth of jewelry. The heist will put them away for up to fifteen years in the state prison."

I was trying to think of something funny to say when Captain Jones said he would let me get back to breakfast and hung up. I turned to look at Tish and saw she was holding back a laugh.

"What?" I asked.

"You are my hero," Tish said as she gave me a big hug. "My Mall Cop hero."

CHAPTER EIGHTEEN

When I received a phone call from the boss to come in mid-week to talk about the crime, I wasn't surprised to see Herb there as well. What did surprise me was the boss telling Herb and me, we needed to go to the jewelry store after providing details for the report. The boss handed us each an envelope. Opening it, I found a check for $1,500. It was half of the reward fee from the jewelry store for saving them from a $30,000 loss. The note inside said for us to come to the store directly after receiving the check.

As we walked to the jewelry store, Herb tried to give me his reward check. He said he would not be here to spend the money if I had not saved his life. I told him there would not be any checks if he had not stopped the burglary from happening in the first place.

Herb and I went to the jewelry store and were greeted by applause from the store owner and his salespeople. Feeling embarrassed, I realized that being applauded on the football field was very different than this. I found I couldn't quite get in touch with my feelings.

Hands were shaken and many pats on the back with spoken words of 'good job' and all that. The owner told us he would like to discount any one item of jewelry from his store if we would be interested. My immediate thought was hmm…that is a shrewd businessman. But…

My eyes lit up when I realized I could get Tish a beautiful Christmas gift right here and now. I asked what he might suggest as a friendship ring for a special lady, and he brought out an exquisite gold ring with two giant diamonds. The diamonds were diagonally spaced, each connected to the endpoints of the split gold band. Amazing, the diamonds sparkled…just like Tish's beautiful green eyes.

I agreed it was perfect, and the owner personally wrapped the ring in a velvet box. With the discount, the ring was more than affordable, especially since I held a $1,500 check in my hand. The owner said to send a check whenever it was handy or come in another day to pay it off.

Herb said he would take a raincheck on the discount offer. As we left, Herb said with many children, he had other plans for the money. His wife would understand that Christmas gifts for the children would be more important than a new ring on her finger or a necklace around her neck.

Leaving the mall right on time, I headed straight for the bank. I deposited the check and headed for home. Tish was excited when I told her we could afford the answering machine for the telephone. She begged me to take her to the electronics store immediately.

"Okay, but let me change my shirt first," I said. I still had on my dress shirt and wanted to change into something more casual. Using the excuse to change my clothes would allow me to hide the box with Tish's ring. I knew she would never look inside my dress shoes. That would be the perfect place to stash it quickly.

The store had a large selection of electronic gadgets. I saw a police scanner as we walked in and was side-tracked by it. Tish went to check out the answering machines. After finding the one she wanted, she found me still investigating the different scanners.

"Are you serious about a scanner?" Tish asked casually.

"Sure. It would really be beneficial to our business. Why not get it now and get a feel for the language used by the police dispatcher and beat officers. The general codes are right here in the book that comes with the scanner. It would be fun. Wouldn't you like to know if something is going on in our neighborhood?" I said with my usual stammering and bumbling.

Tish must have felt sorry for me. She said it was alright with her if we got the scanner. "It could be fun. Sure, let's get it."

We decided on the programmable mobile scanner. It would be used in the truck as well as at home. With both a power charger for the truck's cigarette lighter and another charger for the house, the scanner was perfect. I was more excited about it than Tish, but she was a good sport about it.

Getting home, I made the mistake of phoning Captain Jones to find out what frequency he would recommend for our district.

"Oh no! I am not giving you any damn frequencies. You two are trouble enough without the help of a scanner," Captain Jones said sarcastically.

We talked a few minutes more about my practice schedule at the range and how I was coming along with Tish's Combat Hapkido training. I mentioned we also bought a voice answering machine, and if he wished to leave us a message, all he needed to do was press 327 (his badge number) when the recording started, then we said our goodbye's.

I wasn't offended that he would not give me a scanning frequency. I knew he was feeling fatherly and just wanted us to stay out of trouble. Besides, I knew Tish could get the information we needed from Tony with a bat of an eye.

Conflicted, I suggested asking Tony over for pizza. I knew he would know how to program the scanner. Tish seemed happy enough with the suggestion. I still wasn't sure how she felt about Tony. I just knew they were not supposed to date...for that, I was glad.

Friday the 13th was a work night. I sure wasn't superstitious, but I was careful driving to work. I usually walked. The weather was turning colder. It was drizzling and foggy as I left for work. Nothing terrible happened during the midnight hour that I worked on Friday the 13th. The rest of the shift went well. I left work Saturday morning at 7 a.m. as usual.

Arriving home, I noticed Tish was not up. She was in the habit of getting up early to have breakfast for me on the nights that I worked. I quietly went to her bedroom door and saw it was slightly open. Tish was not in her bed. I suddenly became alarmed.

Rushing out to the garage, I noticed that Tish's Harley was not parked inside. We talked numerous times about the weather, no longer being suitable for riding her Harley.

I rushed into the house and turned on the scanner. I sat and listened, not sure what I expected to hear. I just did not have any other ideas. There was the usual chatter, and my gut turned to water when a dispatcher told a squad car to go to the scene of a motorcycle/delivery truck accident at the intersection of South-Central Park Avenue and West 71st Street. That was only a handful of blocks away.

Frantically, I grabbed my keys to the truck. I felt my sweaty face as it went red. I could hear my mournful cries welling up again and again in my chest and throat. I was wiping tears from my eyes as I headed to the door…when…suddenly it opened.

It was Tish unlocking the door and walking in with her backpack loaded with groceries.

"Scott, what is wrong? Are you OK? Is it your father? What in the world has happened?" Tish said as she saw my face.

I rushed towards her and grabbed her in my arms. Hugging her as tight as I could, I felt fear draining from my body. I was relieved to see her.

"Scott, you are hurting me and your dripping tears all over my head." Tish managed to choke out.

I loosened my bear hug. Not letting Tish go, I said, "I am glad to see you alive. I just heard on the scanner there was a motorcycle accident and I thought it was you. Why were you out on your Harley? I thought we decided it wasn't safe to ride it anymore." I was scolding her. Letting go, I was still shaking out of fear for her safety.

Tish was making light of the situation, "I am glad that is all it was." Tish returned my hug, with her arms around my shoulders. She said, "I was afraid this was going to be the way you greeted me from now on. My ribs weren't going to be able to take too many bear hugs."

She gave me a second look. "You really were afraid, weren't you? I'm sorry. I thought I would be back before you got home. I just went to the store for eggs, French bread, and juice. I wanted to make you French toast, and I discovered we are out of the ingredients I needed."

Tish did not push away. She allowed our hug to go on for another minute. Gently, Tish pulled away and went into the kitchen. She looked at my face once more to see if my tears were gone. I could tell she was touched that I cared that much for her. However, she would not say anything to that effect. That just wasn't Tish.

Wanting to change the subject, "Tish, our dads said they wanted to have your Harley in the display window for the winter. I think that is a good idea. We can bring the '55 Ford for the winter. I can't get away for both Thanksgiving and Christmas. What do you think about having our folks here for Thanksgiving? They could bring down the Ford and haul your Harley in a trailer behind one of their custom vans," I volunteered.

"If you promised to help cook the turkey, I will be glad to cook the rest of the items for dinner." Tish agreed.

I laughed. "You know darn well, our mothers will bring all the side items and the turkey as well. We won't need to do a thing but set the table and offer them something to drink."

I was relieved that it was settled. I knew our folks would be just as relieved to hear Tish would not be driving the Harley during the winter. With Tish's next question, I could tell that not everything was settled.

"Scotty, does that mean you are going to let me drive the Double-Nickel?" Tish asked. "You know how much I dislike driving 'Big Red.'"

What was I going to say now? I was trapped by her charm once again. All I could get out was, "Yeah, I guess." Tish danced around the kitchen with glee as she plated our breakfasts.

Thanksgiving arrived faster than expected with classes, tests, jobs, shooting practice, and martial arts practices. I was relieved when our mothers did as we predicted. They volunteered to cook everything and bring it down. That left us with drinks, table settings, and decorating.

I hadn't thought about decorating. The day before Thanksgiving, Tish was in a panic. "We need to go and get some decorations to make the house more festive. Come on, Scotty. Drive me to the store. I want some small pumpkins or gourds, Thanksgiving napkins, napkin holders, and maybe we will get Thanksgiving paper plates. We have nothing to put the turkey on. We will need to get a platter. I am not sure if we have enough serving bowls, either."

Grabbing Tish by the shoulders, I said, "Hold on a minute and breathe. You know our mothers will think to bring a turkey platter and serving bowls…relax. If you want a few festive items for the table, we can do that, but only a few things."

Tish seemed to calm down. I rarely see her in a panic, and I wasn't sure why she was reacting the way she was. I thought about asking her why she was acting crazy, then I thought better of it. The word crazy would be a poor choice. I knew Tish would be reactive to that word.

We got into the truck, and I let Tish give me directions. She navigated us to the store that she wanted to go to without an argument. Tish is pretty good about letting me know what lane to be in and what turn to make long in advance, which allowed me to be relaxed when we arrived.

"Scott, grab a cart, please," Tish said as she marched ahead of me into the store. I followed her along like a Great Dane puppy pushing the cart as she threw in this item or that.

When it was time to check out, we had several small pumpkins, gourds, napkins with orange flowers on them, with plates to match.

Tish also placed two giant pumpkins pies and one apple pie in the cart. Whipping cream was added next. I was about to object when she found a Thanksgiving wreath for the front door. I shut my mouth quickly before I got in trouble. The last thing Tish added was cut flowers and a vase. She said something about the table being company ready if there were flowers in the center.

"Oh, I forgot something," Tish said as she dashed off, leaving me wondering whether to stay put or follow. I decided to follow. I had to move quickly to keep her in my sight.

I found Tish in the aisle with candles. "What do we need candles for?" I asked stupidly.

Tish looked at me as if I was as stupid as I sounded. "The candles are for the table and for the bathroom. It is nice to have both scented."

I guessed it was a girl thing. I was unaccustomed to Tish, acting like a girl. I suddenly got a mental picture of her pregnant and nesting. Her poor husband would be run-ragged with 'do this and do that.' The thought left quickly when Tish interrupted. "Scott, why are you just standing there blocking the aisle? That lady needs to get past you."

I excused myself and moved out of the way. It is always a bit awkward when Tish catches me daydreaming. She'd be furious if she knew I pictured her pregnant.

Finally, Tish was ready to check out. We loaded everything into the truck bed, making sure nothing would blow out on the drive home and headed in that direction.

I tried to think of something I needed to do. I wanted to be out of the way for decorating. Tish had other ideas. "Grab the vacuum, please, and give the rugs a quick once over. After that, would you make sure the tub and toilet are clean? Oh, and after that, it would be nice if you dusted the end tables. It would not hurt to make sure your bedroom is neat and clean. After all, we want to impress our mothers with how well we are doing on our own, don't we?"

So that was it. The source of Tish's panic was now evident. Tish wanted our parents' approval that we were doing well on our own. I decided if it was important to Tish to impress our parents, I could vacuum, dust, clean the toilet and tub as well as pick up my room.

I acknowledged that our home looked very cute and festive on Thanksgiving morning before our parents arrived. We even had two bottles of wine for our parents, thanks to Tony. He declined our offer to join us because of his own family gathering. He still brought over bottles of Gewurztraminer, Pinot Noir, and four wine glasses, excluding us on purpose.

The unmistakable rumbling sound of the '55 Ford announced the arrival of our parents. As we went to the door, I could see my father driving the Double Nickel into the drive and Tish's father backing the van with the trailer behind him into the driveway. I stepped out, and my father hollered, "Hi Scott, we want to load the Harley first thing. Get the keys and meet us at the garage."

Grabbing the remote control for the garage door and the keys, I headed at a lope to the garage. Tish rushed out to meet the mothers and to help them carry the food items. Tish glanced at the '55 Ford and smiled. I managed to catch the look on her face and knew I would not get to drive my new ride very often.

With the Harley loaded, covered and ready to be taken back to the showroom, and the Ford safe in the garage, the fathers were prepared to enter the house. I told them the TV was on the right channel for the afternoon football game between the New York Giants and the Dallas Cowboys. The kickoff would be at 3 p.m. The men were hoping for an early dinner.

"The house looks and smells really nice," my father said as we entered.

Dorothy, Tish's mom, said, "Yes, Gabe, the kids have gone to a lot of trouble to make the house look festive for us. Aren't they adorable?"

"Mom, adorable is for children. Scott and I aren't adorable. We are responsible adults," Tish whined.

Cliff added, "Speaking of responsible adults, we transferred the insurance from the Harley to the Ford, that way, both you and Scott will be covered when you drive."

Tish came over and hugged her father. "Thank you, Papa. You always think of everything. You are the best."

"Tish, you will give your dad a big head if you talk to him like that." Dorothy laughed.

Alice, quietly working in the kitchen until just then, added. "We will be eating in 30 minutes. All we need to do is heat up the food and bake the dinner rolls. I hope you are hungry. I sure am glad you have a double oven."

Dorothy and Tish took the cue and went back into the kitchen while Cliff and Gabe made a beeline for the police scanner. "Scotty, show us how this works. I thought maybe your father and I should have one for the tow truck. We could double our towing business by beating the competition to the accident scenes," Cliff said as he looked the scanner over.

"This would be a good model for you to consider if you are serious. It is a mobile unit, or it can be set up in your home or office, as we have it now. It was a little expensive...not for you working men." I winked as I said this.

"How is it that you could afford one?" my father asked.

"I received a reward fee when Herb and I stopped a jewelry heist in progress," I said casually.

From the kitchen, Alice screamed, "WHAT! What do you mean you stopped a jewelry heist in progress? Were their guns? Was anyone hurt?"

Tish came to my defense. "Let's just say there were bats and wrist-weights involved, and the bad guys were carried out on stretchers."

Dorothy said, "Wrist-weights?"

"Okay, I will tell you the whole story. Do any of you want a glass of wine before I begin?" Tish said.

Alice answered, "I think I might need a glass of wine. Hey, how is it you have wine?"

"Our Mall Cop Hero…." Tish recounted the rest of the story, adding that Tony brought the wine over for guys.

As the group settled around the table, my father made one last crack, "Still got the arm, hey, kid, or is it Mall Cop Hero now?"

"Let's eat," I said in response.

Alice cleared her throat. "Let's pray first. It sounds as if you need it."

After pizza for dinner several times a week, it was great to have a home-cooked meal by our mothers. I love Thanksgiving dinner. Mrs. Evers' sweet potato pie was something to die for. It was a shame that Tish even bothered to buy the store pies. No one wanted a piece of either of the other pies when one could eat sweet potato pie. I guess I will be eating pumpkin pie or apple pie for breakfast for the next several days.

The big game between the New York Giants and the Dallas Cowboys was scheduled to start. Tish and I told our moms to leave the dishes. We would have time to do them later.

"Anyone want another glass of wine while watching the game?" Tish asked like a true little hostess.

I heard my mother as she leaned over to Mrs. Evers and asked, "Do you think something is going on between Tish and Tony?"

Mrs. Evers responded, "I don't think so. She doesn't act like a girl in love. I suspect she is just flattered to have him pay attention to her. Besides, he is a cop." Fortunately, I eavesdropped on their conversation.

My dad called me over to the sofa to talk about football. Unfortunately, I did not hear what her last statement meant. 'Besides, he is a cop' kept turning over in my brain. Did Mrs. Evers mean Tish would not be interested in a cop, or did she say she can't fraternize with him because he is a cop or what?

"Son, you could have taken a pointer or two from Troy Aikman. He just made a 26-yard pass to Emmitt Smith. Touchdown!" Dad yelled excitedly.

The game continued with Tish asking if anyone would like a turkey sandwich or another piece of the pie. Looking down at his watch, Mr. Evers said, "The weather is supposed to change rapidly, and we still have a long drive. How about if you make a few sandwiches for us to eat on the drive home, Honey?"

Everyone started to get up and move around. The mothers were getting a weepy look on their faces, and the dads were moving slowly towards the door while keeping their eyes glued to the TV set. I just went to the kitchen to help Tish wrap the last of the sandwiches. I knew the goodbyes were going to be gut-wrenching.

Tears started flowing, and hugs were exchanged. My mom said something about feeling guilty about leaving all the dishes. Tish said she would be careful with the bowls and platter and have them packed up nice to bring back at Christmas.

The knowledge that we would be home for Christmas seemed to pacify our parents enough that they were able to leave without too many tissues being used. It was both sad and a relief to see them pull away except for Tish.

Seeing her Harley wrapped and strapped on to the trailer seemed to put her over the edge. She cried for a second. I gave her a hug and said, "It is only for a couple of months…and you get to drive my Ford. You will love it."

Tish hit me on the shoulder and said, "Let's go watch the rest of the game before we tackle the dishes."

CHAPTER NINETEEN

Now that Thanksgiving was over, we had final tests to get through before Christmas. I knew Tish would do well, and I figured I would pass all the tests. Tish was like a drill sergeant and pushed me to study. She quizzed me often, and I felt as though I had a good grasp on most of the subjects. I wasn't too afraid of failing. There are always those instructors who like to make the final exam hard enough that only the top 10% can pass it. I sure hope none of our instructors is that mean.

I hadn't gone down to watch Tish with her self-defense class for quite some time. I usually tell her I need a nap before I go to work. She is often nice and lets me off the hook. The real reason I stayed away is that I hated being a punching bag. If I walked through the door, Tish would say, "Good, a volunteer," and the fun would begin. That is fun for them, …not for me. However, I was feeling benevolent and decided to stop in.

"Good, a volunteer," Tish said with a wicked grin. The next thing I knew, I was on the mat with some woman's foot on my neck.

With class over and the women gone, I said. "You know I only came down today to pay you back for helping me study for the final exams. I felt I owed you that much." I was physically rubbing my backside when I said those words to her. Even with a wrestling mat, it hurts when one falls.

Tish laughed at me. Grandmaster Yong-Sool entered grinning as well. "It is an honor to have you revisit my dojang, Scott. I see my apprentice has used you wisely. She is doing very well with her self-defense classes."

I agreed with his statement. He did not stay long. I was grateful for his warm welcome, even if it came with a grin that humiliated me.

As we walked home, Tish confided to me that one of her self-defense students was taking the course because her husband is abusive. "Scott, I don't know if I should tell her to leave before she gets hurt or not. If she uses what I have taught her on her husband, it may make him furious enough that he would hurt her seriously or even kill her. What do you think? Should I mind my own business or tell her to run for her life?"

I did not feel equipped to give Tish advice. I figure the lady wanted to stay with her husband, and she thinks if she can defend herself, the chances are that he will stop his abuse. I had a feeling Tish's scenario of the husband getting furious and hurting his wife worse than before was probably accurate. I ended up saying, "I think you should tell her to run for it. Unfortunately, you know that she won't. Many of the women who are abused say they are afraid to leave for fear the husband will hunt them down and kill them. You will need to convince her that her chances of staying alive are better if she leaves. Maybe you can just take her to a shelter and let the experts talk to her."

"I think that is an excellent suggestion. Chances are Mrs. Blakey won't listen to me. Maybe she would listen to women who have been in her shoes. Next weekend, I will talk to her and see if she will go with me to a shelter. That means I have some homework this week to find a shelter and maybe stop by and see what they say."

We walked the rest of the way home, chatting mainly about the final exams coming up next week. I will be glad when the tests are over and done.

Final exams are scheduled Monday through Thursday with English, Social Science at the beginning of the week, and the two Criminal Justice exams at the end of the week. With eighteen credit hours, the exams will be more stressful than the workload of the actual classes.

Friday afternoon, we walked to the campus, where the grades were posted for each class. No surprise that Tish aced each final exam and ended up with a 4.0-grade point average.

What was more of a surprise is I ended up with a 3.5-grade point average. I indeed received three A's and three B's on my final exams. I guess Tish is a pretty good tutor. I would not have made the grades in a couple of classes without her.

We decided to celebrate with dinner out. I knew Tish would vote for the world's best hamburger joint. A nice juicy hamburger sounded good to me. I did not want to eat a salad on our night of celebration. I warned Tish ahead of time I was going to eat onion rings. Tish said since I would not be going to work until 11:00 p.m. that evening, she would join me for onion rings out of self-defense.

Tish said we needed to be home in time to watch *'Dinosaurs'* and *'Likely Suspects.'* I thought Dinosaurs was a funny TV series—especially the baby dino who called his father, 'Not the Mommy.'

Getting home, we found the telephone answering machine's light flashing indicating that there were messages. Listening, both our parents and Captain Jones left messages asking how we did on our final exams. It was too late to return the calls. We decided to call them when I returned from work and after breakfast. I knew our parents would be proud of us, and Captain Jones would be very impressed with Tish. He would be proud of me, too, but he would not show it as much as he would for Tish. Like I said before, she has him wrapped around her little finger.

The next morning, we made those phone calls. The reactions were pretty much as I suspected they would be. Lots of gushing from the parents. Captain Jones was pleased. He did not gush as much as I thought he might over Tish. I guess he has come to expect excellence from her.

Tish had classes to teach. Her white belts would be challenging for yellow belts soon. Tish wanted to make sure they knew their stuff. Her other level was due to complete their test soon as well. Tish said she would stay at the dojang until after her self-defense class was over, and then she would see me at home.

I planned to nap just as long as I could. Usually, in the afternoon, Tish and I took some time to relax. We often shopped for groceries. Today Tish said she needed to start Christmas shopping. That reminded me I had no idea what to get my parents for Christmas. I just hoped I would see something at the mall when we were shopping, or Tish would have a good suggestion. Until then, I would sleep.

I woke up after 3:00 p.m. I did not see Tish anywhere in the house. I decided to take a shower. I was sure she would be home sometime soon. When 4:00 p.m. rolled around, and Tish still wasn't back, I started to worry.

At 4:30 p.m., Tish entered the house. She looked rattled. That was unusual for Tish. Rarely have I seen her shaken.

"Hi Tish, why are you late?" I tried to sound unconcerned and casual. She already experienced me at my worst...a complete basket case when I thought she was in an accident on the Harley.

"Can you get me a cup of tea? I will tell you all about it after I take a quick shower," Tish said as she headed to the bathroom.

I went into the kitchen and put the kettle on the stove. I was feeling more worried than ever. I waited impatiently while looking for the tea Tish preferred. I had a cup of tea in hand when Tish came out of the bathroom in her robe, with a towel wrapped around her wet hair.

"Here is your tea. Now, what happened?" I said as I handed her the cup of tea.

"You know that lady I was telling you about last week who is taking self-defense classes because her husband is abusive?" Tish said.

I responded, "Yes, I remember. What about Mrs. Blakey?"

"Well, she did not show up for class. I had a strange feeling something was wrong. I looked up her address and went over to see how she was. When I arrived at her house, I could hear loud shouting and angry words. I rang the bell, and it became silent immediately. I rang the bell again, and a man pulled the door open forcibly and yelled, 'What do you want?'"

I sat quietly, waiting to hear what Tish would say next. I had a bad feeling about what was going to follow.

"And…" I said to prompt her to continue.

"He recognized me as the woman who was teaching the self-defense class to his wife. Obviously, he was following his wife. He said, 'So you are the bitch who is filling my wife's head with nonsense!' Then he jerked me into the house and slammed the door behind me."

Before I could get another word in, Tish continued quickly. "I could see Mrs. Blakey against a wall with a swollen lip and a black eye. She was bent over and holding her ribs. I knew she was badly hurt. Her husband raised his hand with his fist closed and started to hit me when I just reacted. I slammed him onto the floor faster than a blink of an eye, and I held him down with my foot and an arm lock. The next thing I knew, Mrs. Blakey was screaming for me to let him go and not hurt him. I let him up, and he stormed out of the house, obviously enraged and embarrassed."

"Tish…," I started to say, but she interrupted to finish her story.

"No, let me finish." She took a deep breath and continued. "Mrs. Blakey was shaking and crying. I knew she needed medical attention and could not stay in the house. Mr. Blakey would hurt her worse. That is for sure. I told her I would help her pack a bag, and I was taking her to the hospital first and then to a safe house. She continued to cry, not arguing. And that is what I did. I got her medical attention, and then I took her to the safe house I found this week. The other women at the safe house convinced her she could not return to her husband. I think she finally understands. As I was leaving, they were helping Mrs. Blakey fill out the papers for a protective order and a domestic abuse claim."

With those last words, Tish stopped talking and sipped her tea.

"Tish! Don't you realize how dangerous that was? Even police never go to a domestic violence call without back-up. I am your partner! Why didn't you call me? I would have gone with you. That is what a partner is for. Don't you ever do something like that again without letting me be there to have your back? Do you understand?" I was shaking with fear for Tish.

Tish bristled for a moment. I knew she was starting to feel defensive about how she could take care of herself and all that bullshit...suddenly, her shoulders relaxed, and she smiled.

"You are right, Scott. I did put myself in danger. I won't do it again. You are my partner. I would want to be there for you if you were in danger. I understand that you would want to be there for me. I promise. Never again."

CHAPTER TWENTY

Christmas shopping was next on the agenda. The week ahead would be the only week we could shop for our parents and whomever else might be on our lists. My list was short...my parents. Tish's present was safely tucked inside my dress shoes. The trick was to make sure I packed the ring when we were ready to go home for Christmas.

Tish probably had a more extensive list of people to buy gifts for. She was already trying to think about what would be a perfect gift for Grandmaster Yong-Sool and Captain Jones. I suggested that we go in together on a gift for Captain Jones. I hadn't even thought about buying him a gift until Tish added him to her list.

"After all, Scott, he has provided us with a lot of great opportunities. I think he deserves a present, don't you?" Tish's words came back to me as I sat and thought about what might be appropriate. He probably has most anything that he wanted already. It should be more of a token gift. I thought maybe a paperweight with his name on it that said something like 'Best Adopted Father in the World'. Tish laughed at the idea. I decided it was best to leave the gift buying up to her. I would just chip in whatever money she needed.

Mom was easy. I could buy her anything sentimental, and she would be happy. Dad, on the other hand, was not so easy. I thought about buying him specialty cigars. There was a tobacco shop not far with a cigar vault. Maybe a pipe and tobacco would be something he would enjoy. I remember my dad puffing on a pipe until a solution would pop into his head. A new pipe might be the perfect gift.

I knew Tish would drag me around various shopping malls and specialty shops most of the week. I was just resigned to the fact. My job would be to carry the packages and keep out of the way. Most likely, I could enlist her help in finding the perfect gift for my mom.

We did shop most of the week. Tish wore black jeans and a leather jacket most of the time. She broke with her official fashion statement Thursday when she came out wearing white winter pants, a red pullover sweater, and a fluffy white jacket. I asked her if the jacket was rabbit fur, and Tish hit me. Tish looked stunning in white, but I did not say so. I just told her that she looked Christmasy. She seemed to like my response.

The malls and shops were festive. Tiny lights were strung up in trees and around the frames of shop windows. Reindeers, stars, Santa's, and holly were everywhere. Christmas songs were played on the streets and in the stores. It really was beginning to look a lot like Christmas as the lyrics from one song suggested.

I enjoyed the week of shopping with Tish more than I ever imagined I would. She made it painless. I still carried all the packages. Thanks to the extra weights on my wrists and ankles, during work hours, I was up to the task.

We both laughed when a lady clerk said, "Shall I give the bag to your husband to carry?" We decided not to correct her, and I just took the bag along with all the others that I was carrying and left, saying, "Are you ready, Dear?"

I was sure that comment would land another punch in the arm, and I was braced to receive the hit, when Tish said, "Yes, Honey, I am ready to go to the next store."

Playing along, I said, "Ugh, not another store. The children are waiting with the sitter for us to come home."

Tish just laughed at me and said, "You, idiot," as she pulled me along to the next store.

Tish found a money clip that was perfect for Captain Jones. It was gold with two small diamond chips. Half of it was scored, and the other half was plain. The effect was elegant. I knew he would love it the moment she showed it to me.

She found a beautiful neck scarf for my mother. It was cashmere, and Tish knew the color would be perfect for my mother's winter coat.

I offered to buy her some hot chocolate. I really needed to sit down for a while to rest my feet. Even though I walk a lot, it is different to walk fast than it is to stroll, stop, and look at things and saunter again.

Tish was excited to have hot chocolate. Like most females, chocolate seemed to be the way to her heart.

"I am starved. Can I have a sandwich with my hot chocolate?" she asked nicely.

"You can have a steak if you want," I answered back. I knew I was hungry. When I looked at my watch, I realized why we were both hungry. We ate breakfast at 7:00 a.m., and it was now at half-past three.

We managed to get a booth in a window, and we both relaxed and watched other shoppers as we ate. I was fascinated to watch mothers with screaming children. The children either wanted to go see Santa, and they could not, or they did not want to see Santa, and they were being dragged there. I was glad our children were home with the sitter right now. I said as much to Tish, and she called me an idiot again.

With the shopping done, our stomachs full, we could really go home. Tish and I talked about getting a small tree to decorate. We decided that since we would be away for Christmas, it was an unnecessary expense.

Nevertheless, Tish wanted some decorations for the living room and kitchen. She ended up buying several large red bows to place here and there in the house. I suggested twinkle lights. She said 'fine,' but I must put them up and take them down. I decided it would wait until next year.

This weekend I had my regular working hours. Tish had her self-defense students as well. With Christmas on a Friday, as well as New Year's, Tish's classes would be canceled the following two weekends. I would have Christmas weekend off, working the New Year weekend instead.

Friday night came and went. Herb was there, and he gave me a small present. I felt stupid. I never thought about getting him anything. I thanked him and told him that I did not buy a gift for him. He said he hadn't expected anything from me. He said it was small. It was just another way to say thank you for saving his life. I was beginning to think he would feel beholding to me until he saved mine. I did not say as much. That would be rude.

I got home Saturday morning, and Tish had breakfast waiting for me. She was thinking about making sure I ate a big breakfast after working all night. Fried potatoes, eggs, toast with jam, and fruit juice was ready as I walked into the house.

"Wow, this smells delicious. I am starved." I looked at Tish, and I added, "You are really too good to me. I don't deserve such a great partner." I was serious as I said this to her.

"I don't deserve you either. Who else would have spent his whole week off from school, carrying my shopping bags and treating me to lunch and hot chocolate?" Tish said this with a twinkle in her eye. It appeared she wants to be playful. Taking her lighthearted lead, I stopped any attempts to engage her in a needed heart-to-heart talk.

Tish said after chewing a mouthful of potatoes, "What are you going to do today while I am working? Are you going to sneak out and get me a Christmas present?"

"I'm going to sleep like I always do on Saturdays after I get home from work. What makes you think that I am going to get you a Christmas present anyway?" I said teasingly.

"Scotty, I got you a present. Aren't you going to get me something?" Tish said, batting her eyelashes.

"I thought carrying all your shopping bags would be gift enough," I said, teasing her right back.

"Not funny!" Tish said with pouted lips.

I laughed. "I already have your gift. I got it weeks ago."

Tish became an excited little girl right before my eyes. "What did you get me? What did you get me? Come on, tell me. What did you get me?"'

I said sternly, "You need to wait until Christmas to open your present, young lady."

"If I find it…can I open it?" Tish asked coyly.

"No way! If you find it, you leave it alone. Don't even think about opening the present. I want to see your eyes the instant you realize what is inside; don't you dare cheat me out of that moment," I said this almost as a threat.

"Scotty, you are damn predictable. I knew you would say what you just said. You know I wouldn't open it without your permission. You must think I am sneaky." Again, Tish was acting playful.

I yawned. I was feeling tired. "I will help you with the dishes before I hit the sack. I will wash. You can dry."

"No, there aren't that many dishes. Just go get some sleep. I am fine. I have plenty of time to do dishes and wrap some presents before I must head to the dojang. I intend to give Grandmaster Yong-Sool his present today. I know he isn't Christian. I think he will accept my gift anyway. He will understand the meaning behind it," Tish said as she gathered our plates and took them to the sink.

I said, "Now I am curious. What did you get Grandmaster Yong-Sool"?

"There are a few things I could give him that would be appropriate. What I do know is that he has a sweet-tooth. I think he will enjoy a box of See's chocolate-covered cherries. If I present the gift to him with both hands outstretched, bow and act modestly, I think he will be happy to accept them. If I offend him, I will know immediately," Tish remarked.

"I will look forward to hearing how he accepted your gift when you get home. Right now, I am going to accept your gift of getting out of dishes." I said this with another yawn and headed for bed.

I was rudely awakened by the phone. I thought about letting the answering machine take the message. I decided it might be Tish. I got up to answer it.

"Hello, this is Scott," I said into the phone.

"Scott, this is Grandmaster Yong-Sool." I heard a concerned voice on the other end of the phone. My first thought was he was offended by Tish's gift of chocolate-covered cherries, but why would he call me if he was.

"Yes, Grandmaster Yong-Sool, what can I do for you?" I said, waiting to hear his response.

"Scott, I think you should come to my dojang right away. Tish needs you. She has had a terrible experience," the Grandmaster said in response to my question.

"Is she hurt? What happened?" I said with fear creeping into my voice.

"She is unhurt. We will tell you the details when you arrive. Drive carefully. As I said, she is unhurt." With those parting words, the Grandmaster hung up the phone.

A million thoughts raced through my mind. I pictured a thousand horrible things that could have happened as I grabbed the keys to the truck and ran out the door.

When I arrived at the dojang, the police car was just pulling away. My heart stopped. I parked as quickly as I could and ran into the dojang to find Tish sitting quietly in the Grandmaster's office.

"Tish, what happened? Are you okay? Grandmaster Yong-Sool said you've had a terrible experience. What happened?" I think my speech was rattling a mile a minute.

Tish took my hand and invited me to sit. "I am fine. It was just that Mr. Blakey decided he should kill me today."

"What!" The only word that came out of my mouth.

Tish patted my hand to calm me. I thought how strange that she is trying to calm me when I should be the one to calm her.

"I will explain as best as I can. Grandmaster Yong-Sool saw everything from the window. He can fill in the details that I leave out." Tish looked to her Grandmaster to see if that was agreeable. When he nodded, she continued.

"My self-defense class was over. I gathered the small gifts that some of the women bought for me and was heading to the car. Mr. Blakey was waiting for me in the alley. When he saw me heading for the car, he showed his knife and yelled at me. He said I ruined his life by stealing his wife from him. Mr. Blakey closed the distance, threatening to kill me.

I pulled the garbage can between us as he continued to call me names and brandished the knife toward me. He repeated that I stole his wife and how she belonged to him. I had no right to take her away, and all the while, the guy was circling me. When he finally lunged at me, I deflected his forearm away with my left hand and grabbed his wrist with my right hand. I twisted it until I hyperextended his elbow and dislocated his shoulder. Mr. Blakey dropped the knife and fell to the ground screaming. Grandmaster Yong-Sool was standing at my side by this time. He told me to go in and phone the police while he kept Mr. Blakey on the ground."

I looked to Grandmaster Yong-Sool to see if he was going to add anything to Tish's story. Grandmaster Yong-Sool added one statement. "Mr. Blakey underestimated me. He thought I was just an old man and that he could still use his knife on me with his other arm. I kicked him lightly in his solar plexus to keep him down. Mr. Blakey will never bother Tish again." With that comment, Master Yong-Sool excused himself.

I took Tish into my arms and hugged her. "Are you okay to drive home? If not, I can drive you home in the Double Nickel and walk back for 'Big Red.'"

"Don't be silly, Scott. I am fine. I can drive home," Tish said.

We went out to our cars, and I followed Tish back home. She drove the '55 Ford into the garage, and I held the back door open for her. As she entered the house, she turned to me and said, "Scott, will you hold me?"

We went to the sofa, and I held her tightly. She did not need to act brave any longer, and she knew it. She let herself sob as I held her in my arms. I felt angry and helpless. I should have been there to protect her. I started to say words to that effect when she put her fingers to my lips to stop me.

"There is no way you could have known that creep would be waiting for me. Don't you dare blame yourself? I took him down. I did a good job...I did a good job...." And she cried some more. Tish fell asleep in my arms, and I continued to hold her. She would be safe with me.

Grandmaster Yong-Sool's words came back to my mind. "Mr. Blakey will never bother Tish again." I wondered how the Grandmaster could be sure of that fact. I decided right then and there to phone Tony and see if he would find out where they took Mr. Blakey. Quietly, I told Tony all the details of the assault on Tish's life. Tony promised to get back to me with any news he found out.

Later, Tony phoned back to say that Mr. Blakey was in custody. He was taken to the hospital and was given a sling after the doctor reset his shoulder. Mr. Blakey's arraignment will be on Monday.

Tony asked if he should plan on staying overnight to make sure Tish was safe while I went to work. I saw Tish was awake and asked Tish if she would feel safer if Tony stayed the night here. She assured both of us that she was okay and not in danger. I suggested that Tony come over for pizza anyway. I thought maybe Tish would change her mind. I wasn't feeling right about Tish being alone after an attempt on her life. A part of me wondered whether Mr. Blakey had a brother or friends who might want Tish dead.

Tony came over with pizza in hand. I thought it was nice that he stopped for the pizza instead of us having to order it and have it delivered. I really like Tony even though a part of me does not want to like him. Mrs. Evers' words came to mind again about Tish, not acting like a woman in love. I liked Tony even better knowing that Tish wasn't in love with him, and I wondered why that mattered to me.

In the morning, I expected to find Tony asleep on the sofa or in my bedroom. He wasn't in either place. I surmised that Tish had sent him home. Tish was still asleep.

That meant I would make breakfast this morning. So, of course, pancakes were on the menu. I had the bacon frying, the coffee made, and the pancakes mixed and ready to go when Tish's bedroom door opened. I sincerely hoped she slept well. Judging by the dark circles under her eyes, I knew she did not.

Cheerfully, I greeted Tish, "Good morning, sleepyhead. How did you sleep?"

Tish stumbled towards the kitchen table and sat down. "I slept fine. How was work? I am sorry I overslept. I guess Tony stayed too late. Sorry…I should be making you breakfast."

I was confident bringing up yesterday's episode would make Tish upset again. It would be best to face it front on. I said, "after the horrible day you had yesterday, I think you deserve breakfast in bed." I was trying to make her feel loved.

"Don't be silly. Someone trying to kill me does not mean I need breakfast in bed," Tish grumbled.

"Oops, someone got up on the wrong side of the bed," I said, hoping to lighten up the situation. It did not seem to help. I got a glare instead.

"Okay, that wasn't funny. To tell you the truth, I don't know what to say to you. No one has ever tried to kill me before…Jesse only tried to take out my kneecaps. What do you need from me? Another hug?"

"Just shut up until I wake up and give me some coffee," Tish demanded.

Tish was going to be okay. I could tell by her rude response.

After a cup of coffee, Tish was perkier. We talked a bit more about when we would leave for our Christmas break with our folks. I still needed to work tonight, and I needed some sleep before driving. We agreed we would leave Monday afternoon. That should get us back home by the early evening. Christmas Eve would be Thursday, and Mom would expect me to go to mass at midnight. Christmas would be on Friday. I still would have the rest of the weekend free. We could stay another week if we really wanted to do so.

"So, Tish, how long do you want to stay at your folk's house. I don't need to be back to work until the following Friday. If you wanted to stay for an even longer visit, I could drive back up sometime after New Year's to get you. We don't have classes starting again until January 12th; I think you can have a nice long visit with your folks." I offered.

"No way, Scott. I am leaving when you leave. I have the rookies to train. I can't just lay around my parent's house like you seem to think I can," Tish said a bit surly.

Oh, Oh, I was thinking. Maybe Tish is not as fine as I hoped. It wasn't taking much to trigger her.

"I'm sorry. I forgot about the rookies. Of course, you need to be back for their training. Captain Jones depends on your help. Stupid me," I said contritely.

Tish sighed, "I'm sorry for being snappy. I'm just tired still. Maybe I will take a nap when you go lay down. Right now, some blueberry chocolate chip pancakes would hit the spot."

We ate in relative silence. Tish was mulling over the experience from yesterday. I was trying to think about how I could keep Tish protected from Mr. Blakey when he got out of jail. A restraining order doesn't really make much difference when a person wants to kill you."

The next morning, I got home from work. Tish had my breakfast on the table as usual. She seemed in a good mood. I supposed she was happy we would be leaving from Chicago, Mr. Blakey, and the whole mess for several days. Being with her parents would be healing for her. I was wrong about what had put her in a good mood.

"I missed a phone call early this morning from Captain Jones. He knew we were leaving to see our folks for Christmas. It sounded like he wanted to give me some news before we left; I called him back." Tish said as I came and sat down at the table.

"What was the news? He opened his Christmas present early and loved the gift?" I ventured.

"No. The captain did not open his gift early. He called to tell me Mr. Blakey had a sudden heart attack and died very early this morning. He said I would never need to look over my shoulder again and be concerned about Mr. Blakey." Tish hesitated a moment and continued. "I know it is awful for me to be glad that someone is dead. However, I am. He was a horrible person. Now two women are free from fear because he is gone. Mrs. Blakey can leave the safe house and start her life over, and I don't need to worry if he is going to come after me again."

I agreed it was tragic a person died. I was glad and relieved. "That is good news, Tish. You know, even if he would have lived, you and I would be able to handle him, right?"

Tish smiled and added, "Yes, Scott. You and I are capable enough to handle him or anyone else, for that matter. Isn't it great that you won't need to stay with me 24/7 to be my bodyguard?"

I said casually, "I was looking forward to 24/7."

"Don't be an idiot, Scott," Tish said like she usually did whenever I made a comment about having kids or being tied to her. I could tell secretly my comment pleased Tish.

CHAPTER TWENTY-ONE

Monday afternoon came quickly. After eating breakfast, finishing the dishes, and taking a nap, we were off in the '55 Ford for our parents' house. I knew it would be foolish to take the Double Nickel when the weather can be iffy around Christmas time. However, I hadn't had much chance to drive the Ford since Tish needed wheels. I just wanted to drive the Double Nickel and was willing to take the risk. I am sure Tish's dad would have chains for the rear tires if we needed.

Getting to the Evers house meant having to carry in suitcases and all the presents. I started to wonder if I should have bought her parents a Christmas present. It isn't like we are married or anything. I guess they won't be expecting anything from me. I should ask my mother whether I need to find a little something for Mr. and Mrs. Evers.

Reaching my folk's house, carrying one suitcase and the small bag of gifts in my other hand, I used my key and entered the house. I hollered as I cross the threshold, but received no answer.

Mom and Dad were both gone. Settling into my old room before my folks got home from work, I found it comforting to see them when they entered the house, even though it was less than a month since I saw them last.

They were chatty talking about the business. Mom was saying how much fun she was having being a working woman. Dad talked about the next project he and Cliff would be working on. I could tell Dad was nervous because he does not usually chatter. They chatted on and on until my Dad turned toward me and broke some bad news.

"Well, Scott, I have been dreading to break the news, but you have lost another classmate. Three in less than a year. Strange and sad…." Dad sat and sort of stared out the window.

I interrupted his serious mood. "What are you talking about? Who died?"

Dad woke back up from his daydream and filled me in on the details. "It seems that Lucy Delucci died in a car accident." Dad hesitated again. "But if you ask me, she was murdered."

I said with more annoyance than I wanted, "Dad! What are you talking about?"

My dad continued his story. "Well, Lucy was driving on slick roads when she lost control of her car on a left turn and ran the driver's door hard into a tree. She was killed instantly. When Cliff got the call to tow her car away, we took it to the garage. The insurance company asked us to give the car a once over. Cliff found the brake line was punctured by a pointed object, creating a leak each time the brakes would be depressed. The puncture mark was in the flexible line near the front of the rear housing, between the proportioning valve and the 'T-fitting' above the rear end. Cliff only found it because of the brake fluid puddle under the rear end of the car."

"Did you tell the sheriff, and what did he say?" I knew Jack's father was an ass, but he was a straight-shooter, most of the time.

With frustration in my dad's voice, he continued. "The sheriff said there was no way for him to know if the line was pierced before, during, or whether it got pierced after the accident."

I was baffled. "Why would anyone pierce the line after the accident. What in the world is the sheriff saying…you or Cliff punctured the line when you took it to the shop? That is crazy, and I am certain it could not get punctured in the same spot just by being towed to the garage." I was now feeling angry that the sheriff would even say such a thing.

"Naw, he isn't saying we punctured the line. He just doesn't want a murder investigation. I would say he is lazier than dishonest."

I shrugged and said, "If the sheriff doesn't investigate, I am sure the insurance company will get to the bottom of it."

Mom had been silent until now. "Well, poor girl. I know you weren't very fond of her. However, she was only nineteen, and she had her whole life in front of her. She was in cosmetology school, and she was looking forward to opening her own shop here in town."

"How do you know all this, Mom? You aren't friends with her mother or anything." I asked.

"Her mother went to our church. Emma knows her mother, and she told me everything Mrs. Delucci said. That is how I know these things." Mom said defensively. "I get around, too, you know."

"I need to phone Tish. I won't be too long," I said as I rushed to the phone. I wanted to get Tish's take on the news.

"Tish, are your folks' home from work, and did they tell you the news about Lucy Loose? I mean, Lucy Delucci." I felt sort of bad using her nickname now that she was dead.

"My folks just told me. Before we talk about Lucy, I want your promise that you won't say a word to your folks or mine about Mr. Blakey. Got it?"

"Sure, Tish. If you don't want them to know, my lips are sealed." I supposed Tish had a right to decide whether to worry her parents about a situation that is now a moot point.

"Back to Lucy," I said. "Dad said the flexible part of the brake line was pierced. He told the sheriff and the insurance company. It seems the sheriff isn't going to investigate. I know the insurance company will want to get to the details, so the sheriff isn't going to get off that easy."

Tish stopped me from saying more. "Scott, I know Mandy, Lucy's best friend. I want to talk to her today, and I will get back to you. I have a gut feeling there is more to this story than any of us know."

Our conversation was now on hold. I could hardly wait until later when Tish would get back to me with what she found out from Mandy.

I did not hear from Tish that evening. Later the next day, Tish called and said she was having lunch with Mandy. I wish I could be a fly on the wall. I could find out whether there was more to the story and not have to wait. In the meantime, I wanted to relax a bit. Instead, I ended up going to the garage with my father. He said there was a project or two that needed my brute strength. Now, how could I pass up that offer?

One thing he wanted it seemed, was for me to look at Lucy's car. My dad said the insurance company suggested that we needed some standard routines when dealing with vehicles that we tow. My father decided that since Tish and I would be private investigators, I might have some suggestions. I did several.

Wear gloves. Don't add your fingerprints to compromise the situation. I suggested they needed an excellent camera. They should take pictures of the vehicle and the scene before even getting close to the vehicle. That would include any damage, bloodstains, tire tracks, footprints, the inside of the vehicle, including what gear the vehicle was left in.

I decided I would enlist Tish's help with her photographic memory and write down what she recalled from our criminal justice class. There was a section this past term dealing with precisely what my dad was asking. I told my dad I would get back to him once I talked to Tish about the particulars, and I returned home.

Tish phoned just moments after I entered the house. She was talking fast and excitedly. "Do you want me to come over to your house, or are you going to tell me over the phone?" I asked. I really wanted to see her expressions as she told me what she learned.

I got in my car and was at Tish's house in less than five minutes. She had a soda waiting for me, and we sat on the sofa.

"Go ahead and guess what Mandy told me," Tish asked with a short pause that cut me off. "Forget it; I won't try to make you guess. I will just tell you what she told me." I guess she saw me rolling my eyes.

"Go ahead. Don't keep me in suspense." I encouraged.

Tish got comfortable if sitting on the edge of one's seat is comfortable. "Okay, Mandy told me Lucy broke up with Jesse. Evidentially, Lucy got wind that Jesse was muleing drugs. He wanted Lucy to mule drugs for him as well. Lucy wanted nothing to do with the idea. She told Jesse she was breaking up with him. Well...according to Mandy, Jesse got uptight. Mandy said Jesse was really nervous about what Lucy might say or do."

I started to say something. Tish cut me off. "Wait, there is more. Mandy said Lucy told her Jesse bragged about killing Wally and Tommy. Lucy told her in detail how Jesse drowned Wally and how he staged the chainsaw killing. What Lucy did not say was what Jessie's motive for these supposed murders. She had no firsthand knowledge."

Tish stopped talking and just stared at me. "Well, what do you think?" she finally said when I just sat and said nothing.

"That is incredible! If any of this is true, and I am beginning to believe it is, it would be the motive for Jesse to kill Lucy," I said.

"And if Jesse finds out Mandy knows, he might come after her. I told Mandy not to tell anyone else but to go straight to the sheriff. Mandy isn't as stupid as Lucy, saying that Jack is most likely involved, and the sheriff won't do anything. She understands she is already in danger, so she is fleeing to Florida to live with her grandmother," Tish told me.

"Well, someone needs to turn in Jesse if Mandy won't be around to give a deposition," I said.

"There is one problem with the assumption that Jesse killed Lucy. Mandy knows for certain that Jesse is down in Texas, and he's been there this whole week. According to Mandy, Jesse is lining up some drug run with the cartel down near the border of Mexico." Tish continued to fill me in, and I was stumped.

"If Jesse did not kill Lucy, who else would? Your dad and my dad insist the brake line was pierced, and Lucy's death was no accident. Someone had to have done it." I looked at Tish as I said this, asking for some ideas and saw no revelation in her eyes.

"I don't know...." Tish sighed. "There is something we are missing. Why would Jesse want to kill Wally and Tommy, first off? It just doesn't make any sense. At the same point, why would he brag about killing our classmates if he did not really do it? Unfortunately, there is no first-hand witness to what Jesse said since Lucy is dead." Tish was thinking out loud.

I had an idea. "What if Jessie wanted to scare Lucy to make sure she told no one about his being involved with the cartel? What if he made up the idea of killing Tommy and Wally just to scare Lucy and let her know he would kill her without a second thought if she betrayed him?"

"Well, someone killed Wally, Tommy, and Lucy. If it wasn't Jesse, then who was it? I still think Jesse is as good a suspect as anyone. The problem is Jesse is stupid. He could not come up with a plan if it hit him over the head. If Jesse killed anyone, someone told him to do it. Now, the question is, who would tell Jesse to kill anyone?" Tish was on a roll.

"Wait! You are surmising too much. First, we don't know if Jesse did kill anyone. All we have is Mandy's word that says Lucy told her. Lucy says Jesse was bragging. You know as well as I do that Jesse likes to brag about anything that will make him look like a tough guy. Can we really believe any of this? This is all hearsay." I was trying to be logical.

I thought a moment and said to Tish, "Let's treat your interview with Mandy as a deposition and start documenting everything else we know, including who, what, where, when, and how."

Tish smiled and said, "Look at you. You did learn something from our classes. I am going to start three case files right now...one on Tommy, one on Wally, and one on Lucy. I will go ahead and put whatever evidence we have, depositions, suspects that have motive and opportunity, and photos. When we get back to Chicago, I want to show Captain Jones the files to see what he says. I know he will say it is hearsay and lacks evidence. I am sure he will have an idea of the next step. Which brings me to another thought."

Tish continued. "I bought you a Yashica T3 35mm camera for Christmas. What if we give our fathers the camera to take crime scene photos of the accidents? I will buy you a miniature tape recorder and a similar camera when we get back to our house."

"Crime scene photos…aww, come on…. Hmm, maybe you are right. I think it is a great idea!" I affirmed.

I was excited. "That is a great idea. I was just in the garage, and our dads want us to help them set up evidence recovery protocols they can use when they go to an accident scene. The camera will be invaluable to them. You are always one step ahead of me."

Giving their new business a camera was like giving all our parents an extra Christmas gift. I knew everyone would use it from time to time. I was sure there would be before and after pictures of the projects as well. Tish thinks things through.

I wasn't very excited about getting dressed up for Christmas Eve service. I knew it meant a lot to my parents, especially my mom. I brought along my suit and dress shoes to impress the families. Thank goodness, Mom reminded me before we left Chicago, to bring my dress clothes. Phew! I might have forgotten Tish's ring at home. Otherwise, I would be driving back to Chicago on Christmas Eve.

CHAPTER TWENTY-TWO

Christmas Eve is a candlelight service at our parish. I suppose it is in most churches if they can get around the Fire Marshal rules for a fire in a building. I remember one year the marshal tried to nix the candles saying the candles could catch the altar linens on fire. Our priest told him the Catholic Church has been using candles for thousands of years, and his parish would not stop using them on Christmas Eve this year or any other year. I guess the Fire Marshal knew when he was licked.

The church looked beautiful, and we sat in the same pew my family sat in week after week after week. Something was comforting about traditions. The cantor sang like an angel, the choir sounded better than ever, and the priest was eloquent. At least, I assume he was. My mind was in any place but on his sermon.

Before entering the church building, my mother and I was stopped by Mollie McReynolds, our town's busy-body. Mollie knew I dated Heather and wanted to be the first one to tell us the news.

"It seems Jack is home on leave from the military. You probably knew Heather was pregnant. Unfortunately, she fell down the stairs and was hospitalized yesterday. I learned this morning she lost the baby." Molly was almost gloating.

I was shocked at what happened to Heather and horrified that Molly McReynolds seem to get such joy out of relaying Heather's misfortune. I was about to blast Mrs. McReynolds when my mother jabbed me in the ribs. I guess she sensed I was stiffening up and knew what would most likely happen next. I excused myself and went ahead to find my Dad.

I found myself mulling things over in my head during midnight mass. It was still a mystery why Heather would allow Jack to get her pregnant in the first place. I could only imagine how unhappy Heather must be in the hospital, knowing she lost her baby. Part of me wanted to go and visit her. I knew that would be a big mistake.

The service was over, and Dad got a jab in his ribs. He had dozed off, and Mom was afraid what people would think if they got up to leave and saw Dad asleep. I figured most people would think it is past midnight, and the man works hard to make a living. I doubt Mom would agree. At least, the jab in the ribs indicated something other than that.

With a bit of a snort, Dad woke up quickly. He had just dozed off and stood up hurriedly as if nothing happened, joking with men around him and wishing everyone a Merry Christmas. I chuckled at him and wondered if I would be the same at his age.

We drove home, and Mom suggested we each open one gift. She always wanted to open a gift before Christmas. Mom is a curious woman and claims to hate surprises. I know she is just an excited little girl in a woman's body. I suggested we each open our stocking. Mom wasn't happy about my suggestion since she filled each stocking and knew what was inside her own stocking. Part of the reason I suggested the Christmas stockings was to watch her try to figure out another angle to get to open a real present.

Finally, Dad felt sorry for her, forgiving the jab in the ribs, and presented Mom with a small box, neatly wrapped. I knew Dad did not wrap the present. The package was perfect; it looked like it came from a department store. Mom carefully unwrapped it and was excited to find a bottle of perfume. Smelling it, she kissed Dad and said, "It smells expensive. I hope you did not spend too much money on me."

I knew she was pleased he took the time to find a present for her and that he spent a lot of money. I also knew it would not be the only present under the tree with her name on it.

We said our goodnights and headed to bed. Happily, the Evers would be joining us for Christmas. I wondered what kind of pie Dorothy would bake this time. Her pies were to die for. I knew the sooner I got to sleep, the sooner I would find out, with visions of Dorothy's pies dancing in my head.

We opened a few more gifts in the morning. We decided to wait for the significant presents until the Evers arrived. Mom prepared a Christmas brunch. Dinner would be served late afternoon. Mom was up early, getting the prime rib ready to put into the oven. She found a recipe where one cooks the prime rib on low heat in a large damp paper bag. She assured me the bag would not catch fire, and the meat would melt in our mouths.

The Evers arrived, and I grabbed Tish aside to tell her about Heather before we were called to the table for brunch. I knew she would not really care to hear about Heather. I also knew she would still listen to me, knowing Heather had once been the love of my life. There wasn't much to tell her since I only had the few details Mrs. McReynolds could not keep to herself.

While drifting to the table for brunch, the conversation stopped abruptly when we all spied the table settings. As usual, the table looked great. Mom said she wanted to keep brunch light. That was just Mom saying she wasn't going to serve cooked meat. Instead, she made two different kinds of quiche, a fruit plate, shrimp with cocktail sauce, sweet rolls, and crepes for those who felt like making one for themselves. Mom had the crepe maker plugged in. The crepe batter was made. All a person needed to do was cook a crepe, fill it with fruit, whipped cream or cream cheese and smoked salmon. Champagne cocktails were also poured for those who were old enough to drink. Orange juice and coffee were available for those who did not drink.

When no one was looking, I poured champagne into two glasses, half-filled with orange juice. I doubted anyone would notice if I gave the second glass to Tish. Dad noticed, raised an eyebrow, but looked away. He knew I would not pour a second drink for either of us now that I knew he knew. I probably would not pour another anyway, but having one's dad notice, made it guaranteed.

Everyone was feeling full and relaxed. Mom announced that we should open gifts. I noticed Mom wrapped a few extra presents for the Evers, probably knowing that I would forget to buy them each a gift. I suspected the Evers did the same to keep Tish from embarrassment as well.

Mom loved the scarf, and Dad said he could not wait to go out and smoke his pipe. He was no longer allowed to smoke in the house. The Evers bought Mom and Dad a Traeger grill. Cliff promised to show Dad how to use it on the first sunny day of spring. My folks gave the Evers a fruit press and a stainless-steel vat to make blackberry wine and apple cider. It seemed summer was going to be a fun time for this partnership.

When Tish opened my gift to her, she let out a squeal. She ran up to me and stopped short of a hug when she saw our parents smiling as they watched both of us. Tish grabbed me tightly, stepping on my feet as she reached up to whisper in my ear. "I love...Love...your present! Putting it on her right hand, she held it out at arm's length to admire it.

I noted that my mom and Tish's mom quickly had their heads together. I was sure they were wondering if the ring meant more than it did. I felt I needed to interject something at this point.

"There are two diamonds on the ring, one is for Tish, and the other represents me...friends, forever. Our partnership may end someday; our friendship will endure forever, right, partner?" I looked at Tish and sort of indicated our mothers with their heads still together.

She figured out exactly what I was doing. "You are right, buddy. Thank you again. It is a beautiful ring, and I love what it represents."

I already knew Tish purchased a camera for me. It was going to go to our fathers. I was pleasantly surprised when Tish handed me an actual present to open. I did not expect anything until we returned to Chicago, where Tish promised a mini tape recorder and camera to replace the one given to our dads.

Opening the box, I found a pewter metal yin yang martial arts circular necklace. Flipping it over, I saw engraved, 'You are my rock. Luv, Tish'. I winked at Tish and signed 'thank you.' I would put the pendant on the same chain with the whistle our moms gave us.

Once again, I noticed our mothers had their heads together. I could only guess what was going on in their minds. I suspected we both would get the fifth degree when we were alone with them.

Dad and Cliff were excited about the camera. Tish was busy telling them how to use it and when to use it for the business. I could overhear Tish telling the fathers that she would write up a protocol before leaving to return to Chicago. She also said she would like them to take pictures of the brake line puncture and the damage to the car. Tish told our dads that it might make sense to get photos of the skid marks before the car hit the tree. She wanted these pictures to add to her case files.

We played Yahtzee until it was time for dinner. We all seemed to win a game or two. Having the luck of the Irish, even if she did not have an ounce of Irish in her, Dorothy won every other game.

The dinner was excellent. When I saw Mrs. Evers' chocolate mousse pie brought into the house, I knew I needed to save room for a large piece. I still indulged in a massive slice of prime rib. I passed on most of the side dishes to make up for it. Mom commented on how my eating habits deteriorated since leaving home. She made some remark about needing to come to visit us more often just to make sure we were eating well. I about choked on the piece of prime rib I was chewing when she said that.

Tish graciously said, "Anytime…you are always welcome. I am sure Scott won't mind sleeping on the sofa for a few nights." She smiled sweetly as she said this, and I gave her a look telling her to stifle it.

As the evening was winding down, and Mom and Dorothy were in the kitchen doing the dishes, I had an opportunity to talk to Tish more about Heather.

"Come on, Scott. Give it a rest. Heather isn't your concern anymore. You need to get over her."

I could tell Tish was tired of the subject of Heather. I was about to say something in my defense when the Evers assembled near the door, indicating it was time to go home.

A big thank you said, and some hugging at the door and the Evers were gone. Mom said she was tired and would be heading for bed. Dad agreed it was time to go up, too. I told my folks I would make sure the tree lights were unplugged, and I would be up shortly myself. I could not sleep knowing Heather was lying in the hospital.

It would be nice to have a few more days at home with my parents. Tish wanted to be back early the next week. The captain told her the rookies were planning on coming in on Wednesday to practice, and he would love to have her help if she was available. I also knew Tish was using the captain as an excuse to return to Chicago. She said once before she loved being on her own and found it hard to be back at her parents' house as their little girl.

In my bedroom, I looked through my closet and dresser drawers to see if there was anything, I really needed to take with me to Chicago. I found a load of sweaters and decided to pack them for the cold winter days. Layers seemed to work better than a shirt and a coat. It also gave me something to do other than toss and turn in bed.

I came across my keepsake box under the bed. I lost track of time as I browsed through pictures of myself playing different sports as a child. There were lots of photos of Tish and myself fishing, playing peewee golf, and other fun things we did together. Most of the pictures had one or both of us making funny faces. I watched our aging, sort of like a growth chart, from photo to photo. I also noticed for the first time in one of the pictures that Tish lost her happy, silly smile at about age 10. It never occurred to me before that the silly Tish died about that time, and the serious, street smart Tish emerged. I was feeling anger again at her uncle and wished he was alive. I wanted to put a major hurt on him. Sadly, I wondered, what would Tish be like if she had not been abused.

I did not phone Tish for the next two days. I did not want her mother to complain about not having uninterrupted time with her daughter. I hung out with my parents. We stayed at home most of the time due to the cold weather. We talked some and watched TV more than I liked. Mom cornered me alone in the kitchen, as I suspected she would, on Sunday afternoon.

"Dorothy and I were wondering about the ring you gave Tish. Does it mean something special…like a promise ring or anything like that? We love Tish. It would be great if the two of you got together. Is there a reason why you two aren't engaged? Don't you like her as more than a friend? She is a beautiful girl and smart. Scott, for certain, someone will snatch her up before you know it."

I could tell she wasn't really looking for me to answer. She was trying to supply support in case things worked out for Tish and me. I was glad when Dad walked into the room.

"Alice, give him a break! Scott and Tish have their own lives to lead, and you and Dorothy aren't going to help matters by badgering them," Dad scolded.

"Gabe, you know you like Tish as much as I do, and you would love to have her for a daughter-in-law. Admit it," Mom snapped back.

Dad laughed. "There you go again. You aren't putting words in my mouth. I will repeat…Scott and Tish have their own lives to live. Give him a break." With those words, he left the room with me quickly tagging along behind him.

Monday morning came with Mom and Dad heading off to work. I thought it was adorable to see Mom pack two lunches. Tish's parents would be going into work as well. Tish wanted to stay for a while longer. There were two things on her agenda. She would type the protocol for our dads, and she wanted to talk to Mandy one more time.

I loaded up the '55 Ford with the items I planned on taking back and found that I had a headache coming on. I decided to stop at the drug store before picking up Tish. Driving all the way to Chicago with piercing head pain was not something I wanted to do.

I drove downtown to the drug store and went inside. I looked down the aisle to where the pharmacist's counter was at and saw Heather standing there paying for a prescription. I was about to walk out when she spotted me.

"Scotty, Scotty McFarlan!" She called from the back of the store.

I could not pretend that I did not hear her. I did pretend; however, I did not see her before she called my name.

"Hi, Heather," I said casually. I noted she looked horrible. I can't say most people look great when they get out of a hospital, but I had never seen Heather look that bad.

I walked back to where she was standing. "How are you doing?" I asked with nothing better to say.

"Obviously, I am not doing well, as you can see by my appearance," she said bitterly while trying to smooth her hair, which had not been washed in several days.

"I heard you lost your baby. I am truly sorry." I knew there was no way to pretend I was unaware. "I heard you tripped and fell down the stairs." I felt stupid standing there saying such obvious things.

Heather looked extremely nervous. "I did not trip. I was tripped," Heather said in a hushed tone.

At the same moment, she looked up at the door as the bell announced another person entering the store.

In a panic, she whispered to me, "Please, leave quietly, and don't let Jack see you. Please, hurry before he knows that we spoke."

Heather picked up her bag with her prescription inside and hurried towards Jack, hoping to stop him before he saw me. I did as she asked and ducked down another aisle.

Once outside and back inside the Ford, my head throbbed more than it had before seeing Heather. I knew I was angry. There was a part of me that wanted to rip Jack's head off. What did Heather mean when she said she was tripped? Had Jack tripped her? What was Heather saying, and why was she acting nervous about Jack seeing her talking to me? All these questions flooded into my head, and I had no answers.

When I stopped to pick up Tish, I asked her if her parents had any aspirins or anything for a headache. I loaded her suitcases as she went to the bathroom to get a couple of aspirins and some water for me.

"Thanks, Tish. Are you ready to roll? Did you get the protocol typed, and did you get a chance to talk to Mandy again?" I asked as we went to the car.

"I'll drive if your head is hurting that badly," Tish offered.

"No, I can drive. Besides, I would rather have something to do than just sit in the seat and stew."

Tish looked at me as she got into the passenger seat. "Okay, what is the matter?"

I told her that I had a headache before running into Heather. The incident made my head hurt even worse. I relayed the bizarre incident to Tish as we drove through town to get to the highway.

"You are telling me that Heather implied Jack deliberately tripped her, causing her to fall down the stairs?" Tish continued to look hard and long at me as she said these words.

"I am only telling you what Heather said to me. She did not say who tripped her. All I know is she was a nervous wreck, and she was afraid…I mean, really afraid that Jack would see her talking to me." I recounted.

"Jack is an ass, I admit. Do you think he would intentionally trip his wife, hoping she would fall and kill his child?" Tish was doing the same thing to me as I had done to her when she theorized who killed Wally and Tommy. She was trying to be completely logical and let me hear how silly the whole idea of Jack tripping Heather sounded to her.

"I don't know anything but what Heather said and what I saw. She is living at Jack's parents' house ever since her mother left her stepfather and ran off with her new boyfriend. Heather only has Jack's family now. I can't imagine any reason Jack's mom or dad would trip her either. Who else could she be talking about?" I tried using logic back on Tish. "It had to be Jack she was talking about."

Tish went on, "Does Jack's family have a dog or cat? Maybe she meant a pet tripped her."

"Why would she be nervous around Jack if it was a pet that tripped her. Besides, they don't own a pet." I was starting to feel annoyed at Tish's questioning.

"She could be feeling guilty around Jack. She might feel he thinks she was careless, and now his baby is dead. How is that for a reason why she is nervous around Jack?" Tish said a bit sarcastically.

I was finished talking to Tish about Heather and Jack. I decided to try to change the subject.

"What more did you learn from Mandy?" I asked.

"It appears that Mandy left town immediately. She is on her way to her grandmother's house. I do have my three files along. I intend to show them to Captain Jones to get his opinion," Tish said, patting her briefcase.

I sighed. "You know the Captain is going to say it is all circumstantial evidence and there is no case, don't you?

"No, I don't know that is what he will say. Maybe he will give me an idea of how to find evidence that is not circumstantial," Tish said with a bite to her words.

We both were getting a bit angry. I turned on the radio to let our tempers calm. It seemed to be what we both needed. We listened to Mariah Carey sing *I'll Be There*, Michael Jackson's *Black or White*, and by the time Tom Cochran's *Life's a Highway* came on the radio, we were even singing along in good moods.

"Hey, I have a question. Did your mother say anything to you about her and my mother talking about us?" I asked as I turned the radio down.

"As a matter of fact, I thought it was kind of funny. My mom said they were talking about us getting together," Tish answered.

"That is interesting. My mom said the same. Why do you suppose they would be pushing us to get together?"

Tish said, "I don't know. I do know one thing, your mommy loves me more than you, Scotty." Tish laughed her wicked little laugh. "No, really, it is only natural they would want us together. They like each other enough to be partners in business. I think they want to keep everything in the family, and that includes us."

Pulling into Chicago, I got a strange sensation that I was home. Tish was back to herself; my headache was gone, and I was happy. I touched my pewter necklace and noticed Tish glancing down at her ring. I knew a little spat would not hurt our partnership.

CHAPTER TWENTY-THREE

The school was back in session. This term's classes included Psychology 201, Biology, English 107, Criminal Justice 202, and Criminal Justice 211. I was glad we had a break before heading back into studies, work, and competitive shooting practice.

Tish was back in full swing as well. She was adding another defense class at the dojang, and Captain Jones asked her to train a few female cadets one-on-one to further their training. He felt they were a bit behind the male counterparts. The extra training meant Tish would be out two other evenings.

Tish talked to Captain Jones about the odd coincidental deaths surrounding our sleepy hometown. The captain told her what I said he would say…circumstantial. However, Captain Jones did tell her it looked suspicious. Our fathers notifying the insurance companies was a good move. Captain Jones applauded Tish for setting up an evidence protocol for our dads and for giving them a camera to document all accidents from here on out. He was especially interested in the fact that the brake line was punctured high in the rear end tunnel. Intrigued by all the details surrounding the drowning from Tish's point of view, the captain suspected foul play again. The chainsaw incident was genuinely odd…hard to prove. The only one that might be provable at this point was the suspicious brake line death. The insurance company and local law enforcement should not let that one drop.

Tish would stay on top of all the happening in our hometown. I would help her any way I could. Right now, I was more concerned about starting our own private investigation business to be too worried about the strange things happening at home. I suppose I should be more involved.

The end of February was almost a heatwave. Our instructor for our Criminal Justice Course-Introduction to Investigation told us to plan to attend the Thursday lecture. Guest speakers were coming, and he wanted us all to be at the lecture.

Tish and I were particularly excited about the guests. They are a husband/wife team of private investigators whose careers in Chicago spanned the last forty years.

The class was introduced to Mr. and Mrs. Jamieson. The instructor turned the podium over to the team of private investigators.

Tish and I sat glued to our seats as the detective team talked about their experiences in the world of investigation. At the end of the lecture, the class was open to questions and discussion. Mr. Jamieson found Tish's inquiries to be direct and insightful. As the students filed out at the end of the lecture, Patrick Jamieson found an opportunity to address Tish and me alone.

"We have heard remarkable things about you two from Captain Jones," Mr. Jamieson started his conversation.

Tish surprised by the comment said, "Do you know Captain Jones?"

Aileen, Patrick's wife, said, "Know Captain Jones…he is our children's Godfather. We have known the good captain and his wife for many years. He told us to be on the look-out for you two. He speaks highly of both of you. I almost feel as if I already know you." A sincere smile broke out across Aileen's freckled face.

Tish responded well to her positive comments. "I am pleased Captain Jones speaks highly of us. He has been a special mentor since we came to Chicago."

Patrick interjected, "Yes, we have heard what a splash the two of you made almost immediately upon coming to the city. Believe it or not, Captain Jones shared a few of your newspaper clippings."

I finally felt comfortable enough to speak. "You are kidding. The captain kept the newspaper clippings of us?" I was feeling incredulous.

"Yes, we saw the articles about the purse snatching, the assault, and the theft-gone-wrong at the mall. You are true celebrities in the captain's eyes." Again, a chuckle from Aileen.

Mr. Jamieson did not let the conversation lag. "Captain Jones has also told us about your marksmanship, Scott, and your skills in martial arts, Tish. He brags about you as if you are his own children. He even showed us the money clip you gave him for Christmas."

Aileen rubbed her stomach. "Look, I am starved. Would you join us for lunch? We have something we want to discuss with both of you."

I confessed I was also hungry. Tish agreed more from curiosity than from hunger.

We walked down to the campus cafeteria. After going through the line, Patrick's treat, we each carried our tray to a table away from the crowd and sat down to eat and talk.

"Just so you know…our lecture today wasn't pre-planned by the faculty. We requested the opportunity to speak so that we could meet face-to-face. We have a proposition we hope you will find appealing. We know you have part-time jobs. We are wondering whether you would be interested in working for us part-time?" Mr. Jamieson opened the conversation.

Tish and I looked at each other curiously. We could read each other's minds that this is all happening a bit too fast.

Tish responded, "You don't really know anything about us, and we don't know anything about you. Why would you want us to work for your company?"

Aileen smiled. "Tish, we know more about you and Scott than you realize, and if we were your parents, we would be incredibly proud. We also know that you and Scott have plans to start your own private investigation business. We can not only help with that desire; we can provide you with all you will need to get started.

"You are kidding, right? What? Help us start our own detective business? Wow!" I looked at Tish and said that we should at least listen to their proposition. Tish nodded approval. Therefore, I asked Mr. and Mrs. Jamieson to continue.

Mr. Jamieson spoke first, "Like Tish and you, Scott, we realized at an early age, we had a unique knack for discovering and solving other people's problems. We have been in business for more than 40 years. During those 40 years, we investigated more than 1,600 cases. While we have a great track record at solving these cases, many remain unsolved. These cases are dated and numerically coded and are kept in our metal file cabinets...in paper form. We believe that given new computer and database technologies, we may be able to solve the more intractable and weighty cases."

Aileen, interrupted, "Tish when you brought your case files to Captain Jones to review, he realized it was time for us to meet. He believes, as does Patrick and I, there is a mutual benefit for the police department, yourselves, and our company, to work together. Captain Jones believes you would gain knowledge on how to maintain a low-profile while gaining the confidence of those involved in the cases that you will be investigating."

Patrick, kindly looking at his wife, continued, "This past Christmas, our daughter and son-in-law gave us two Apple II Mac's, several software applications and a printer. Our son-in-law is an engineer at Apple Computers in California. Their thought is these computers and software will help us to create a database for our case files. Unfortunately, neither Aileen or I know anything about computers."

Tish gave me a nudge, then she spoke up, "Scott is a natural when it comes to electronics or anything to do with computers."

"We learned from Scott's high school transcripts and your college instructors that you have an aptitude for computers and software. We believe with your help using computer forensics in our database that we can solve more of our cases," Patrick finished.

My excitement for using one of my passions in a job caused me to shout, "When do we start!"

Tish said, "Hold on, Scott. How many hours per week do you want us to work? How much are you willing to pay? How long will the job last? And do you have a description of the work you wish us to complete?"

"We knew you would be a no-nonsense person, Tish. We can pay each of you $15.00 per hour for 20 hours of work per week. We believe your position at our company will be long and productive. The description of the work we wish completed is in this letter." Aileen handed Tish and me a formal letter describing the position, salary, and job description.

Patrick said, "If you agree with the offer, you may start today. We have a computer in our car and a few of our files. We can drive you to your house. That way, you can get started right away."

Tish was still unconvinced, wondering when the other shoe was going to drop. Suspiciously, she asked, "What is in it for you or the Captain for that matter? Why do you think we can start today?"

Aileen responded without any hint of annoyance at Tish's tone, "Tish, Patrick, and I are nearing retirement age. We provided a great service to our community. We have solved many difficult cases. It is time for us to consider how we will spend the rest of our lives. If all goes well with you and Scott, we will have left our life's work in your good hands. As far as Captain Jones is concerned, we have a good working relationship and he wants the same with you. He is convinced, the two of you will be top-notch private investigators."

I could see Tish's face showed she was having an *ah-ha* moment. Tish smiled, and her face softened as she thanked Aileen for her openness.

On the ride to our house, I started to go into the technical details about Apple's HyperCard application and how it could be used to create a searchable database, and with some programming using HyperTalk, I could....

All three looked at each other, a bit overwhelmed, then at the same time said, "Scott...please, not now."

I could not wait to get started. Mr. Jamieson helped me set up the computers. After we finished, we moved upstairs and listened to Mrs. Jamieson and Tish talking at the kitchen table.

Mrs. Jamieson said, "Tish, I know you have some apprehension and more questions. If I may, I'd like to put some of your feeling at ease. Our company provides an excellent service to our local community. The relationship we have with Captain Jones and the district police is invaluable.

Patrick and I are getting older, and the times are changing rapidly. The type of cases that we solve is moving from the street to computers and something called the internet. Many more of our younger people are involved in criminal activities and scams than ever before. That is not to say our typical street cases are going away; they will still need to be solved the old-fashioned ways.

We believe we can teach you and Scott our tried and proven, old fashioned, private investigation techniques. We also think Patrick and I will benefit from your youth and experience in the newer technologies. Together we will build a new investigative team. I hope I have helped?" Aileen Jamieson concluded.

"You have, I feel much more at ease, and I am fascinated by the opportunity," Tish responded.

Both Patrick and Aileen gave us a big hug and said they would be talking with us again the next day. Mr. Jamieson placed an envelope in my hand, saying it was for expenses. Once they were away, I opened the envelope to find a check for $500.00.

Tish said, "Oh my gosh, our first check. Let's get a copy for our wall by the computer! Oh, Oh, we'll need to open a business account at our bank."

We both sat on our sofa with the adrenalin rushing out of our system. I told Tish I needed her help even if she did not feel competent on the computer. I knew once the applications up and running, there would be plenty of work for her to do with data entry. I assured her she would not need to be a computer genius to do the job. Besides, she acts like she knows very little about computers. She used computers for classwork all through high school. I really think it is more likely that Tish doesn't like sitting that long.

Wow! We just fell into an invaluable situation. The extra money would not hurt either. The more we could put away into savings, the more we would have when we opened our own business. I was intrigued by the thought the Jamiesons were possibly grooming us to take over their workload.

The files were totally fascinating; they were formatted and organized in a uniform way to tell the unique story for each of their cases. The basement was turning out to be an excellent quiet area for reading the files and entering the data into the templates stacks I created for the HyperCard application. I was almost at a point where I would be able to create street maps using my HyperTalk script to show areas of the city where the crime was committed. Intrigued was maybe too mild of a word to use. I was becoming obsessed with the project.

Tish came down to the basement at 3:00 a.m. on a Tuesday and wanted to know why I wasn't in bed. She reminded me that we had a class in six hours, and I needed to sleep if I wanted to be able to comprehend the subject matter.

I just told her to come over to the screen. Excitedly, I showed her something interesting that had arisen from the entered case file data.

"Look, Tish. Remember that unsolved case Aileen and Patrick were talking about?" I asked.

"There were several if I recall correctly. Which one are you talking about?" Tish asked sleepily.

I answered, "The one where a business burned down and an insurance company paid off the owner for a commercial building. I just made some interesting correlations. Several commercial businesses burned down every other year in the same district.

"Each business was paid off by a different insurance company. Right? I discovered additional documents the Jamiesons requested from the insurance companies. These documents contained information about contractor bids, contractor work completed, and fund disbursement. Each of the materials also indicated that the separate businesses eventually went bankrupt for one reason or another.

It seems every two years or so, another building burned, and another bankruptcy was filed. This appears to be a pattern in this one area of Chicago. I think we need to do some snooping into public records to see if there is any connection between these buildings burning and the ensuing bankruptcies. Something just seems odd to me at this point.

The Jamiesons might never have caught this since they were all separate cases, different years, independent insurance companies, and separate bankruptcies. Oddly the addresses given for the owners were different post boxes…all at the same Oak Lawn post office." I stopped talking to look at Tish to see if she was following me.

"Are you up to spending a few afternoons down at the Federal Record Center next door to our Daley College and the Secretary of State office on Martin Luther King?" I asked Tish.

"Are you coming with me to help research, or are you just going to crawl back into your bat cave and play with the computer? If you are going to put in leg work, I am game," Tish said, "but right now, I am going back to bed, and I suggest that you go to bed. I am not going to let you sleep in and miss class. You are going to write your own notes this term."

Tish headed up the stairs, stopped and hollered down. "Now, Scott!

"I grudgingly got up the next morning. My head was a bit foggy. That didn't hamper my excitement about the research data we may find after classes. Tish and I headed to the Federal Record Center. It was an easy walk from the campus.

We provided the Admin clerks with the business cards the Jamiesons gave us. They were happy to help us with our research. To our surprise, the clerks returned with an enormous stack of papers related to the different cases. Luckily, we had cashed the check for $500 and had working capital. We paid for the paperwork files. The cost was exactly $80.00 for all copies. At this rate, the $500 would not last very long.

There was no reason to stay at the federal offices to pour over the information in the 800 total pages. I offered to buy Tish lunch, and we could go down into our 'bat cave' and start perusing all the information while eating. I was starved. Tish let me sleep in a bit this morning, which meant I missed my breakfast.

On the walk home, Tish commented, "I noticed one thing already. Each of the bankruptcies was filed by the same law firm. It may just be a coincidence. I think that is odd. It isn't the only bankruptcy law firm in that area."

When we got home, and I went down to the basement while Tish ran for the phone book. She said she would be right down to eat. When she came down, she said, "I checked the telephone book, and you wanna take a guess? I phoned the law firm's number in the book, and it is not in service any longer. I don't think we will get much information from them."

I was still chewing, but I managed to say, "We can get information on them through the State Bar Association. They will know if the firm is still around. That is for another day. Right now, let's see what we can make of all these papers."

Tish raised her eyebrow and remarked, "You are actually learning something from our classes. Good for you."

Snarling my upper lip in defiance, I didn't have a retort for her. I wasn't sure if it was sarcasm or praise. I will pretend it was praise.

Tish was scanning each of the cases quickly when she said, "Here is something strange. Many of the contractors declared as claimants in the first bankruptcy are the same contractors that provided bids in the next set of insurance claim documents." Tish looked at me and repeated the information, making sure I was getting every word. "Oh my, they are the same companies as claimants in the bankruptcies and the bids in the insurance claims. I wonder if any of these companies are still around?"

I pondered what Tish said. "Let's write down the company names. We will check them out along with the commercial building business owners when we head over to the Secretary of State Office."

Tish agreed, "This problem we are solving could be big.... I am really cautiously excited. This is getting interesting, isn't it?"

My head swimming with new data, I decided to program a few more HyperCard's into my program to organize the information. I wrote an additional linkage program to connect this new data to our mapping system.

Tish was busy writing down the names of the different companies the insurance companies paid off and the companies that went bankrupt. A list of the contractors paid for services rendered in the restoration and reconstruction of the burned companies was added. She also added the law firm and real estate agency to the list. "I may as well be thorough with the investigation," she muttered more to herself than to me.

The list of names was long. Johnny Roscetti owned Fire Damage, Clean up, and Repair Company. The construction company was owned by Vince Ceroni, and the real estate agency was Aldero Realty Company. Tish did not find the sales agent's names. Also, the list included Rosa Palmer, owner of Palmer Electrical Supply Company, the first building to burn down. Cara Zurich, owner of Best Plumbing Supplies; Pia Jeffers, owner of Acme Industrial Cleaning Supply Company and Anita Barber, owner of Kleen Janitorial Supplies, were added to the list. The law firm of Tucker and Rossetti made Tish immediately suspicious. "Scott, do you think it is interesting that Rossetti, the lawyer, is a very similar name to Johnny Roscetti, who owns the fire repair and clean up company?"

I looked over at Tish from my computer screen, "Could be a coincidence, or maybe they are related. It isn't a crime to be related to a lawyer, you know." I smiled, thinking I had said something witty.

Tish did not laugh. She looked back down at her list and underlined the two names in red. "Maybe not illegal, but still suspicious in my estimation," she mumbled.

The next morning after class, Tish was armed with her list and a red pen. I had a print out from the computer. Together we knew we would be putting in another long afternoon at the state records office. We will probably spend more of the money the Jamiesons gave to us for expenses on more copied documents.

After a long and tiring day, Tish drove the Double Nickel back home. She said as she maneuvered around the traffic. "I did not find anything that was out of order. All the companies were legit as far as I can tell. The thing is, there is just something off that I have not put my finger on. I feel like I need to come at this from a different angle."

I could sense Tish's frustration, and her driving habits made me a bit nervous. I had my own frustrations from hitting dead ends. "After a good meal and some relaxation, we will feel better. Tonight, no computer. We are just going to sit and watch T.V. and let our minds work out some of the kinks."

Tish nodded. "Right. Sometimes my mind works better in neutral. I have pork chops out for dinner. I thought we could share a baked potato and have fried apples," Tish said.

I objected, "I want my own potato. I don't want to share."

"Okay, Scott. If you are eating a whole baked potato, you and I are going down to the basement to work out and get a bit more practice in for you. You are a long way from getting your black belt. You need to buckle down and take your practice more seriously."

I knew better than to argue. If I did, Tish would burn my pork chop. Besides, I have a good reason for being lazy lately about hitting the mats. I just hated being flipped around that easily by a girl....

We sat quietly on the sofa watching *'Law and Order'* when Tish caught something Detectives Mike Logan and Phil Cerreta were saying in the episode called *'Severance.'* Detective Logan said, *"These guys sound like boy scouts,"* Detective Cerreta said, *"or shadow lives. Somebody paid good money...you peer long enough something emerges from the shadows."* Then Detective Logan said something about, *"A law degree is a license to lie."*

Bouncing up and down on the couch, Tish declared, "That's it! The lawyer is lying. He changed his name, and they are all in on the scam. We need to go to the Oak Lawn Village Clerks office to check on name changes, birth, and marriage certificates."

"Wait a minute," I said. "How did you come to that conclusion?"

"When Paul Sorvino said they sound like boy scouts and Chris North said a law degree is a license to lie. I knew they weren't boy scouts; they are all Roscetti's, and the lawyer is lying for them all," Tish replied.

"I always wondered how you could make two plus two equals five. However, I have a lot of respect for how you are always right," I teased.

Tish could not wait to drag me home to get the car and head out to the clerk's office after school the next day. It took us a little more than two hours. Finally, we found all the documents. I am completely blown away; these guys were all related.

When we arrived home, we spread out all the documents in chronological order. The actual time frame for the scam was a little less than ten years from 1981 to 1989.

"Can you imagine what Patrick and Aileen will say when we show all of this to them?" I said both proudly and with awe at the amount of money scammed.

Tish rushed to the phone. "I'm going to phone them to come over tomorrow. That way, we can spread this out and show them the paper trail…and the computer trail," she added.

It was arranged. The couple would be over after we got home from our classes. They even said they would bring lunch. I was hoping they would bring Rueben sandwiches. Patrick took us to a deli not long ago that had the best-corned beef.

It is incredible how long a morning can drag by when a person is anticipating something. For me, I was looking forward to lunch as much as showing our investigative work to the Jamiesons. When I am hungry, I can't think about much else.

Tish elbowed me. She could tell I wasn't listening to the instructor. She also heard my stomach growl, and that was the reason she looked at me in the first place. I hate it when my stomach gives me away.

Pointing to her notes, she tapped her pencil. That was her way of indicating I should be taking notes. I got my mind back on the subject at hand, relieved when the instructor stated we could leave.

Rushing home, we got to the door just as Patrick and Aileen drove into our driveway. Tish opened the door as I went out to greet them. I also wanted to sniff the lunch to see if I was going to be disappointed. I could smell the corned beef. I was in heaven.

We went down into the basement, where we had most of the papers spread out already in anticipation of their arrival. Aileen was passing out sandwiches and drinks as we huddled around the documents.

I said as I pointed out the papers on the top row, "The first thing we did was to plot on the map where the companies were located that burned. After that, we inputted all the information the files provided by the different insurance companies. Tish noticed the lawyer's name, and one of the contractor's names were very similar. We decided more time was needed at the records department. It wasn't long before we established all the different names involved in the bankruptcies and insurance claims. Tish was still suspicious of the similarities in the two names, and so we went to the Oak Lawn Village clerk's office to get marriage certificates and any name changes from that time."

Taking a deep breath, Tish continued with my explanation, "It took some time. Finally, a pattern started to surface. Each of the businesses that filed insurance claims and then also went bankrupt used the same contractors as Scott mentioned. We found the business owners of each company had the maiden name of Roscetti. Further research gave us a name change of a lawyer from Roscetti to Rossetti. It was the same law firm representing each of the bankruptcies for all the businesses. One last thing we found interesting was one of the real estate agent's maiden name was also Roscetti." Tish stood back and waited for the Jamiesons to respond.

Aileen was the first to speak. "How did we miss that connection, Pat?"

Patrick said, shaking his head, "I have no idea how we missed it."

I needed to add my comments. "Wait before you come down on yourselves too hard. You were looking at a period of ten years, with each seeming like an isolated incident. Tish and I had all ten years right in front of us after we inputted the data into the computer program. Of course, it was Tish's suspicious mind that gave us the first lead to work on."

Patrick whistled. "If your data is correct, and I have no reason to think that it isn't, this family received $10,130,000 in fraud monies from the insurance companies, and that doesn't include what they made legitimately."

Aileen commented after hesitating to take it all in. "Would the two of you be willing to come into our office when we meet with representatives of the four insurance companies named? I think they will have sufficient evidence to re-open their own investigations collectively and take down this family operation before another business is torched. One thing that bothers me is the fire investigation. It seems he was the same fire investigator on each of the fires. Did you check him out?"

We both admitted we missed checking him out. Now that it is evident all four fires were scams, it was likely we would find out he was a cousin or a brother-in-law. We offered to chase down the lead while the Jamiesons put together a conference with the four insurance companies. It would not take all that long to find out his connection to the Roscetti family now that we know our way around the clerk's office.

After finishing our lunch and talking for another hour, Aileen and Patrick left, but not before mentioning they had another couple of boxes for us to pick up from their office. "Maybe you will find another case to reopen when you enter all the data from the next set of files," Patrick said with a wink.

Tish and I sat down and relaxed for most of the rest of the afternoon. "Why don't you come down to the rookie training tonight with me?" Tish asked.

I answered, "Sure, why not? The only other thing I would be doing would be going over your notes. I don't suppose you remember that I wasn't listening to the lecture."

"Come on. I will tutor you right now, and you won't need to study tonight. I really want you to come and participate. It is a sort of graduation for this group of rookies. I am very proud of how well they learned what Grandmaster Jones and I have taught them," Tish said as she led me back down the basement stairs where our study desks were set up next to the computer. When we walked across the sparring mat, Tish flipped me onto my backside. I knew I was in for another Combat Hapkido lesson before being tutored.

CHAPTER TWENTY-FOUR

Silently I watched the rookies practice hoping Tish would not decide to bring me in as a punching bag. I did not need to worry about Tish; it was good ole' Captain Jones, who pulled me from my nice seat to participate.

"Scott is a student of Ms. Evers, just like you. He has a bit more practice with her. I think it would be interesting to see if the top rookie can take down this hulking specimen. Ms. Evers, who has the distinguished honor of being first in this class in your estimation?"

Tish sized up the rookie class and pulled one from the line of young officers. Of course, he was bigger than me. "I would say Officer Ruiz is your man, Grandmaster."

Dressed in official sweatpants and sweatshirts, Officer Ruiz looked relaxed and unrestrained. I, on the other hand, was wearing tight jeans and a flannel shirt. I also had on cowboy boots. I did not feel like there was much room to move. I started to object when a bull came at me. There was no time to do anything but react.

Tish taught us both well, and we found each of us on the ground from time to time. I wasn't sure if I was allowed to punch the rookie when a fist from my opponent landed on my jaw.

Staggering back for a moment, I decided everything was fair in this match. I feinted to the left and caught Officer Ruiz with my right fist. He went down on the mat, and I followed him down by landing on top of him. I thought I had him pinned when he twisted his legs up and under my belly and lifted me over his head where I landed on my back.

Even though his move caught me by surprise, it did not knock the wind out of me. Subsequently, I rolled quickly and regained my feet. A quick glance at Tish reminded me I wasn't using my Combat Hapkido training. I had resorted to street fighting.

Centering my stance, I slowed my movements to only necessary ones. Officer Ruiz was well trained. He matched my actions, and we established our ground rules as he lunged at me. I maneuvered backward, grabbing his wrist and forearm while using his own weight to pull and twist his arm downward and then behind his back. I knew it was excruciatingly painful as the rookie bent forward, trying to relieve the pressure.

Officer Ruiz promptly spun around to his right, breaking my hold with his right arm, he grabbed my right thumb into a thumb lock. I cartwheeled to the left to unlock his grasp while clutching his left wrist in a wrist lock. I swept his legs out from under him, tossing him to the ground on his stomach. Still holding him in a very painful wrist and shoulder lock, I finished him off with multiple snappy fake head and lateral rib kicks.

When I let go of the holds, Officer Ruiz stood up and bowed before me and then Tish and the Captain. I smiled and said, "I hope you won't hold that against me and give me a ticket the next time we might meet."

Officer Ruiz smiled and responded, "I will make sure it doesn't hurt as bad as the beating you just gave me." I laughed.

The captain had words of encouragement and praise for the rookies, and Tish congratulated each one reminding them she would be willing to work with any who wanted a refresher at any point. The evening ended for the rookies. As the rookies left the room, Captain Jones suggested that we join him for coffee in his office.

"First, Scott, I want to tell you how impressed I was with your technique and skill. Tish has taught you well to this point. Tish says you will be ready for the test for your next belt in a couple of weeks.

"I also want to let you know Patrick phoned today to tell me about the wonderful investigative work the two of you did for the insurance fraud. Again, I am impressed." Captain Jones was beaming as he said this.

We chatted for a bit longer, but before we parted company, Captain Jones invited me to the next rookie graduation. I declined quickly. I almost had my thumb broken this graduation. It made me nervous to think about what might be broken the next time around.

As we drove home, Tish asked, "I did not teach you cartwheels. Where in the world did you learn that maneuver?"

"Probably been watching Bruce Lee too much," I said flippantly.

Tish looked serious. "Listen, Scott. That cartwheel maneuver could have gotten your thumb broken if you hadn't been sparring with a rookie. The cartwheel is just too big of a maneuver. I will show you how to get out of a thumb lock next time we practice. It will be a short, simple maneuver that doesn't waste energy or put you off balance, which could be deadly for you. No, showboating!"

"Yes, Mam!" I said, standing at attention and adding a quick salute. Joking aside, I knew she was right. She was concerned I might be hurt or killed because I was not taking a fight seriously. I patted her hand to let her know I understood her lecture was for my own good.

Back to our regular routine with classes, studying and jobs was a bit boring after the investigative work Aileen and Patrick had given us. We had boxes of data to enter. Most of the cases were resolved and not unusual, except for the knowledge we could take away from them.

Sitting in with Aileen and Patrick as they showed our investigative work to the four insurance company investigators was an eye-opener. I had no idea the insurance companies would pay rewards to anyone who helped them to catch their thieves. One of the insurance investigators said they would take the case over. We should expect a check at some point. I made a mental note to take on more insurance fraud cases when Tish and I had our own company. It sounded profitable.

Spring break was a week away, and we were planning to head to our folks' homes for a short break. When spring break started, we left after my night shift on Monday morning. We needed to be back for my night shift by Friday. It didn't seem like much of a break. It would need to do.

Tish was talking about bringing her Harley back now that winter was almost over. I secretly was wishing she would leave it until summer. I knew better than that. The thought of giving up the Double Nickel made me sad. Happily, Dad said he had a converted sports van to put in the showroom; I could keep the old Ford all summer. We would just drive the truck down and bring back the Harley.

We got to our folks' houses Monday. Luckily, Tish drove. I got a short nap in after being up all night. I dropped her off and promised to talk to her the next day. I knew her mom would want her all to herself the first day, as was usual.

The next day Tish said she was going shopping with her mom. She would call later in the evening. It always seemed strange not to have Tish in the next room where I could just holler at her if I needed to talk to her. Having to phone her was a pain.

We chatted that evening, and Tish casually remarked she ran into Heather while shopping. Tish said they stopped for a coke and chatted for a few minutes. That was all she was willing to share. I did not push the subject since I knew I was supposed to be over Heather. It wasn't right to think about a married woman too much.

I spent a good share of the mini-break at the shop with my parents. I was excited by the projects they had going on. The custom van business was really taking off, and it seemed Tish's Harley staged in the showroom helped their business. Both Cliff and my dad seemed to have plenty of jobs for me to do for them.

I got a chance to talk to Chris and Erik during work breaks to catch up on the local gossip. What I learned was not much changed. Chris was seeing a new lady who moved into town. She was divorced and had a little boy.

Erik was shy and wasn't seeing anyone. He never dated much in high school. Erik was only a fair athlete and did not excel very well with book work either. However, He managed to catch on quickly in the auto mechanics class and was a shining star at the shop.

Chris was a heck of an athlete but only a fair worker. He was not quite as good a mechanic as Erik, according to my dad. Chris made a comment to me that he had seen Heather with some bad bruises on her arms one time when Jack was at home. Chris did not say anything more about that when I asked him to be more specific.

"Can't say what I don't know." Is all Chris said when I questioned him further. Erik just looked out the window as Chris said these words.

I was not sure if the implication was that Jack caused the bruising or not. I was pretty sure Chris did not bring it up just because black and blue looked good on Heather. I wanted to ask Tish if Heather said anything. Deciding there was no way Heather would talk to Tish, I let it drop. It was amazing they even stopped for a coke together, knowing how Tish felt about Heather.

Dad helped me load Tish's Harley in the truck. With both of our mothers working full time, this was the first trip back to our Chicago house without care packages. That gave us plenty of room in the truck for the Harley for once.

Tish had said goodbye to her parents in the morning as they scurried out the door to work. I said my goodbyes at the shop. This was a tearless goodbye for once since my mother needed to answer the phone. I picked up Tish, and we were off on the long drive home.

Tish did say on the drive back to Chicago that Heather said Jack was getting an early out from the military. I asked what would be the reason for him to get an early out, and Tish said, "Jack's mother is dying, and Jack is getting a hardship discharge. Jack's father intends to hire Jack as one of his Deputy Sheriffs when he returns home. Apparently, this will allow Sheriff Johnson to spend more time with his dying wife. If you ask me, hiring Jack as the Deputy Sheriff, is like letting the fox guard the henhouse."

I could not have agreed more with Tish's statement, but I let it ride. I felt enough animosity towards Jack the way it was. There was no sense in making my negative opinion even more pronounced by jumping in on a Jack-bash. However, Jack, with power, was going to be dreadful for this town.

Back to Chicago was settling for Tish and myself. Our regular routine made me feel as if all was right with the world. Because everything was going well with classes and work, I was not prepared when my mother phoned to say there had been a double homicide. She said I knew both people who were killed.

"What in the world happened?" I asked.

My mom told me the whole story. "You know that cute couple from high school, Rose Lee, and Ray? Well, they were parked at Lover's Lane, and somebody shot them both in the head."

I was in shock. Rose Lee and Ray were going to get married in the summer. They were voted 'cutest couple' and were inseparable and in love since our sophomore year. I could not think of anyone who would have wanted to murder them. "Why would anyone want to murder them, Mom?"

Mom replied. "No one knows. No one saw anything. The only reason they were found quickly was another couple down the lane heard the gunshots. They said they saw no one, no car, or anything that could help the police.

"It is just a horrible crime. Our town doesn't feel safe anymore when a sweet couple like Rose Lee and Ray can be killed. I am locking our doors at night. I don't want some crazy person to come into our house and kill your dad and myself in our sleep."

"Get a dog," I said. I wasn't really flippant. It was just the first thought that came into my head. "Or maybe get a security system. Even though security systems are a bit expensive, if you sleep better at night, it might be worth it."

My mind was swimming…my rambling on about dogs and security systems was just a way for my brain to stall while I thought through the hideous crime. I was sick at heart! Ray was a football buddy….and Rose Lee was a truly good person.

My mind hit a wall and stopped. 'Two more alumni dead. That stupid contract. Could this have anything to do with that?' I pondered.

I finished my conversation with Mom, learning absolutely nothing more about the murders. I needed to talk to Tish. Unfortunately, she was teaching a self-defense class, and would not be home for a couple of hours. With nothing else pressing to do, I went down to the basement and entered more data into the computer from the files.

When I heard the Harley enter the driveway, I flew up the stairs to greet Tish. As she walked into the door, I grabbed her by the hand and pulled her to the table.

"Whoa, cowboy! Let a girl get into the door before you try to hogtie her." Tish brushed off my hand and set down a few items on the table. "Now, what is so pressing?"

Not knowing where to begin, I just jumped right in. "Ray and Rose Lee were murdered!"

Tish sat down. She looked at me in disbelief. "Murdered? What are you talking about?"

I told her about the conversation I had with my mom. "There are no suspects. No one saw it. I have this nagging feeling that it has something to do with that stupid Final Alumni contract we all made."

Tish put out her hand. "Stop. You aren't making any sense. There must be some reason why they were killed. How about jealousy for a motive? Maybe someone wanted to stop Rose Lee from marrying Ray."

"Aww, come on, Tish. Rose Lee and Ray dated for almost five years. They haven't dated anyone else ever. Everyone in school knew they were meant for each other. No, jealousy was not the motive.

"Stop and think. You said yourself that the other three deaths were not accidents. Now, this is out-and-out murder. That makes five of our classmate's dead. We both know the stocks have sky-rocketed and are worth, well, I don't know exactly how much the Final Alumni would get. A small fortune is what I am thinking. That is motive enough for someone to kill."

Tish sat back in her chair and said, "Exactly, Scott. The first three deaths were made to look like accidents. Why would the killer suddenly change his MO to an apparent murder? Why wouldn't he continue to set up accidents to kill the next alumni?"

Tish had a point. Killers usually stick with one style, I thought. A light went off in my head. "What if there is more than one killer?"

"Scott," Tish said with some strain in her voice, "if the motive is the money from the contract, only one person can get it. That means the final or last alumni standing gets the money. There is no sharing. It makes no sense that there would be two killers. Unless…"

Tish ran to the phone. I heard her talking to her dad. "Dad, when you went to the scene of the murder to get Ray's car, did you remember to photograph the area? Did you find any evidence?"

Tish became silent as her father talked on the other end of the phone. I was trying to be patient, but I could not wait to hear what all her dad said.

Before hanging up the phone, Tish reminded her dad to start a file and keep a copy for themselves before handing it over to the sheriff.

She asked her father to send copies of the file and photos of any footprints in the area to us.

When Tish finally hung up the phone, she turned and looked at me.

"Well? What did your father say? What file? What footprints?" I asked anxiously.

Tish came back to the table and sat down. "They found footprints, and they photographed them. They also found 45cal casings in the bushes on the right-front side of the car, which means the killer shot Rose Lee and Ray from the passenger's side of the car. Since the casings were ejected, it means the weapon is an automatic pistol. If someone from town did the killing, it could suggest the perp is a law enforcement or ex-military."

I added, "or it could be a killer from a big city out of state."

Why out of state, Scott?" Tish asked.

"Gun laws here in Illinois would make it nearly impossible for a local person to register an automatic pistol."

My comment could have opened a whole new line of questions. She let it ride.

Both of our minds would be working out the kinks. I wanted to run this past the captain. He would have some insights from his years on the force. I was anxiously waiting for the copies of the footprints to arrive. I was going to ask the captain to see if his guys could identify what shoes the killer might be wearing. It was a long-shot; there wasn't much else to go on at this point.

Tish did not reference the killings until the copy of the shoe prints arrived. She was ready to go immediately to the police station to see if the lab could give us a lead. The captain was encouraging when we told him about the murders. He said it was amazing what his tech guys could tell from shoe prints. The problem would be if the shoe were a common type of shoe. We crossed our fingers for something exotic. Chances were the shoe tread would prove to be Dexter,

Rockport, or even Nike. The shoe size would help some, we hoped. Again, if it were a size 10, that would not narrow down many suspects, especially since there were no real suspects.

Days later, the captain told us we were in luck. "The shoe size was an 8. That means the killer was slightly built. He also said even more lucky was the fact that the shoe was expensive. The lab techs matched it up with an expensive Italian shoe company called Salvatore Ferragamo. The tread matched the Sardegna Driving Shoe style. There are only a couple places in the USA that carry this shoe. The stores are SAKS Fifth Avenue and Nordstrom."

I turned to Tish. "It looks like our killer is a small hit-man with expensive taste."

Tish rolled her eyes at me. To Captain Jones, she smiled and thanked him for his help. "I know you are doing us a big favor to have your men take time out to research this for us. We both really thank you and owe you big time."

I could tell Captain Jones would have done the work himself for Tish. He was obviously very taken with her. Hey, who wouldn't be? Well, several women from high school came to mind. I would not say that Tish is a man's woman, but then again, maybe I would. She is undoubtedly intimidating to women.

When Captain Jones declined our offer to treat him to lunch, saying he would take a raincheck, Tish and I left his office with pictures of the Sardegna driving shoe and the lab information in hand.

"Okay, what are you thinking now?" I asked Tish as we walked to the car.

"It doesn't make any sense to me. Why would a guy who can afford to wear expensive shoes be out at night killing young lovers?" Tish said out loud. I could tell she was still thinking things through.

"I'm telling you; it was a hit job. Someone wanted Rose Lee and Ray dead bad enough to pay some expensive hit-man to take them out. It must be a local who would know Rose Lee, and Ray often ended up parked at Lover's Lane. The only thing that makes sense to me is it was a way to kill two birds with one stone. I'm telling you it is connected to the Final Alumni contract we made in high school."

Tish sighed. "Okay, Scott, let's say your theory is right. Who do you think would mastermind a plot like this?"

I needed to let my mind wander through the facts. Someone in our class drowned Wally. So, it should be someone in our class. It also must be someone who would gain by everyone, except for themselves, in the crazy contract, dying. It is someone without morals or compassion. That would narrow it down a bit, except for the methods for each murder is different. It still seems there is possibly more than one independent murderer.

I looked at Tish straight in the face and said, "There are a few people in our class that I would never trust. I could make a list starting with Jack and Jesse. However, there are several more guys that I could add to the list. I wish Lucy were around. We needed to question her further. She definitely indicated Jesse was not to be trusted."

"Yes, both Jack and Jesse were at the picnic. Jack has an alibi. He was in the midst of the water polo game, and I could see him clearly when Wally was killed. I have no idea where Jesse was when the drowning happened. Jesse could be a suspect.

"I don't think Jack was in town when Tommy or Lucy died. That would be easy enough to check out," Tish said.

I looked down. "First off, neither Jack or Jessie could afford an expensive hitman. Also, Jesse is stupid. He can carry out orders, but he can't put an original thought together if his life depended on it. I won't count Jesse out as the murderer of Tommy and Wally. He obviously did not kill Ray and Rose Lee. Even though he is small, he would never be able to afford expensive shoes."

Tish said. "Scott, we don't have enough information to solve these cases. We are going to need to let the town police do their work. We can let them know what Captain Jones found out. I hope it would help in their search, that is all we can do for now."

I hated to hear Tish say she was giving up. I knew she was right. There wasn't much we could do from Chicago.

CHAPTER TWENTY-FIVE

The phone rang. Tish beat me to the punch. I heard her say we would be right there, and then she hung up the receiver. I looked at her to confirm that it was Captain Barry Jones on the other end of the line.

Tish confirmed my suspicions. "What was that all about?" I asked.

Tish looked pensive and slightly unnerved. "Ah, Captain Jones said someone took a shot at Patrick when he pulled into his driveway last night. The bullet missed him by an inch. No one saw a thing. Captain Jones said he thinks it might be someone from the Roscetti-Ceroni family that was indicted for the insurance fraud."

I let all that Tish told me sink in. "And Captain Jones phoned you for what reason?"

"Come on, Scott. He knows we are friends with Aileen and Patrick. He also knows whoever shot at Patrick will try again. Captain Jones said he doesn't have the manpower to watch the Jamiesons 24/7. Basically, he wanted us to do a little surveillance when we could."

I replied quickly as not to look too much like an ass. "Of course, we will watch the Jamiesons' house as much as we can. I think we should watch every night. We need to take turns sleeping. We don't want to be too tired for classes in the morning. Of course, I can't take a watch on Friday through Sunday. Maybe the police force could spare some men for those three nights."

Tish just shrugged her shoulders. "I think we should go over to their office and see what they can tell us."

I shook my head. "No, I disagree. If they think we are getting involved, they will dissuade us. You know they would be too concerned for our well-being to agree to our surveillance. We need to do this totally unbeknownst to them."

Tish laughed. "Unbeknownst?" Where did that word come from? You usually don't speak in polysyllabic words." In a sing-song verse, Tish continued her teasing. "Someone's been to college."

"Okay, make fun of me. I don't care." I said with a pout on my face. "But I think I am right, and we shouldn't let them know we are watching their house."

Tish reluctantly acknowledged that I had a point. "We will do as you suggest. I will contact Captain Jones to let him know we are willing to watch their home from Monday through Thursday and see if a patrol car can make a swing past their house every half hour on Friday, Saturday, and Sunday. I suspect he will agree since we are taking the lion's share of the nights."

"Our shift starts tonight. I suggest we both get a nap after we finish our homework. We need to let some of the computer work slide until we know for sure Aileen and Patrick are safe. It sure would be nice if there were not that many cousins in the Roscetti-Ceroni crime family." I added.

We took a ride over to the Jamiesons' office, after stopping at the police department. We wanted to see if they would tell us on their own about the attempt on Patrick's life. They clammed up and did not say a word. I noticed Patrick's car was missing. I assumed he took it to a shop to replace the glass in his windshield. I was amazed at how casual both he and Aileen acted after such a horrible incident.

I took the time to mention to the Jamiesons that we would let our computer entry work slide for a week while we study for finals. I felt I needed to explain why we would not be working on the database. I certainly did not want them to know we would be setting up surveillance all week in their neighborhood.

I hated to lose the income. There was no way we could do the computer work as well as watch their house. If we could afford a portable MAC computer, I could do some entries at the same time.

Aileen said, "You two must be really busy with your studies right now. I can understand that. Time really has gone by quickly."

I let her think that was the case. "Yeah, it is getting intense. It is just a good thing I have a brilliant study partner."

Tish blushed when I said those words. Tish's blush warmed my heart. The hard-ass act is just that. Deep down, Tish is a modest woman. I gave Tish my best flirting smile in return. Predictably, she socked me on the shoulder.

"Don't let him fool you. Scotty is doing quite well in his academic studies without me. There are times that I copy his notes," Tish said.

'Scotty, she called me Scotty,' I thought with some alarm. I wasn't sure why that should melt my heart, but it did. I liked the sound of Scotty when Tish said it. It felt different when my mother said the same name.

Patrick interjected a thought and brought me out of my reverie. "If you too aren't too busy this summer, do you think you would be willing to help us out on a couple of cases. I promise it won't be divorce cases."

We both nodded our heads in agreement. Tish spoke first, "We would love to have actual cases this summer. It won't be long before we turn twenty-one and will be able to apply for our P.I. License. Any field experience will benefit us to no end."

"Good," Patrick said. "We are getting inundated with new cases. We are trying to pull back and slow down. It seems our reputation proceeds us too well. You two will be a great addition in the field to this team."

We small talked for a bit longer. When it became evident that neither of the Jamiesons was going to mention the attack, we decided to leave and catch a nap.

The evening came too soon. We buckled down and got as much done as possible. Tish packed a snack for us along with a thermos of coffee. I grabbed a pillow and blanket for whichever one of us got to sleep first. I really wished we could afford night binoculars. We were going to need to rely on our youthful eyes. Thank goodness, both of us have excellent night vision.

It turned out our naps made it impossible for either of us to sleep until after midnight. We spent the night watching diligently. By midnight, I was feeling drifty. I asked Tish if she would be alright if I took a quick nap. Leaning the seat back, I grabbed the pillow and blanket and was soon fast asleep.

Tish nudged me at about 3:30 and said she was getting too sleepy to be useful. I yawned, stretched, and passed the pillow and blanket over to her.

I learned that I saw more if I did not stare directly at an object. I found myself using my peripheral vision more and more at night. The window was down, and I strained my ears for any sounds out of the ordinary. A car approached slowly with its lights off, and I ducked down in my seat while pulling Tish down.

She startled awake and had the sense to whisper. "What the heck?"

I signaled for her to keep low and watch the approaching vehicle. At 6'3", it isn't easy to curl up in the front seat of a car without being seen. I knew peeking out a window at my size would be too obvious to the passing vehicle.

"Tish, see if you can see what kind of vehicle it is. Also, if you can see how many people are in the car. Oh, and yes, and if you recognize them. And while you are at it, get the license plate number."

Before I could add anything else, Tish shushed me. I could see her slide into a position that allowed her to stay curled up. Even in that compact form, she could peek out the window. Her flexibility was undoubtedly an asset during surveillance. I was grateful for her training.

"There are two men in the front seat and one in the back. I don't recognize either one. I don't think they are undercover cops. They look very ethnic to me," Tish whispered.

"What do you mean by ethnic?" I whispered back.

"My guess would be Italian. I won't rule out the crime family that holds the Jamiesons responsible for getting the insurance companies involved," Tish continued in a hushed voice.

I wondered if Tish had been watching too many old movies to come to that conclusion. *The Godfather* came to mind. My momentary lapse was interrupted by Tish.

"The vehicle is black. It might be a Caddy. I am not sure about that. I don't want to peek too long for fear of being seen. I doubt I will be able to get the license number," Tish said as she ducked back down.

The car was too close to our vehicle for either of us to try to watch further. We both tucked ourselves down as far as possible. I bashed my dang knee into the edge of the dash. I turned bright red and sucked up the pain; I gritted my teeth. Fortunately, no one heard.

As the black vehicle passed the Jamiesons' house, the driver turned on their lights and stepped on the gas. We both popped up, hoping to see the license plate number as they drove away. All we came up with was the Letter A and the numbers 2 and 8. We could not agree if the license were A2 8__ __ __ __ or A something 2 8 __ __ __.

Rubbing my knees as I sat up straight in the seat, I added a comment. "Remind me…you saw three men, possibly of Italian descent driving a black vehicle that may or may not be a Cadillac, right?"

"That's about it," Tish replied. "That doesn't give us much to turn into Captain Jones, …but it is something. However, all we can say for sure is a suspicious vehicle drove by with its lights off until after it passed the Jamiesons' house, and then once past, it turned on its lights and drove away quickly."

"I think that is a good start, really," I added with encouragement. It would soon be light, and I suggested that Tish try to get a bit more sleep while I continued to watch. I would wake her up at the first light, and we would go home, eat breakfast, and go to class.

We both were sleepier than we cared to be during our classes. We took turns poking each other to keep us from falling asleep. It was decided after classes that a nap was more important than our studies. With Tish's photographic memory, I knew she would be fine. I convinced her to tutor me while we sat and watched the house that night. She would be able to repeat the lectures verbatim, and that should help me a lot more than re-reading the chapters.

Captain Jones said he would have someone check vehicle plates with the DMV with the A 2 8_or A _ 2 8 etc. The make and color would be listed at the DMV, but it may take some time to find all the possibilities.

The second night of surveillance went about the same as the first night except for no black vehicle. We snacked while Tish quizzed me on relevant material from our studies. We took turns napping and spent a rather dull night outside the Jamiesons' home.

The third night of surveillance was exactly like the second night. Uneventful and boring. I was having second thoughts about becoming a private investigator if this was an indicator of what life would be like.

By Thursday night, I was not expecting much action. I was tired and found it easy to fall asleep. Tish sat vigilantly as I dozed off. I was suddenly awake when I heard a car idling nearby. I instinctively skootched down in my seat. That was when I realized Tish was not sitting in the seat next to me.

My mind filled with panic. What could have become of Tish? Why didn't she wake me if she was getting out of the car? I found that I was out of choices, I needed to raise up and look outside.

I saw the black vehicle. Indeed a Cadillac idling with lights off across the street from me. Parked in the opposite direction as our parked truck, the driver was visible behind the wheel. His head was turned towards the Jamiesons' house.

I turned my attention towards the Jamiesons' residence and caught the movement of two men running down the long driveway towards the back of their home. I did not see Tish anywhere, and my anxiety drove me to open the car door.

Being on the passenger side gave me some cover from the driver of the Cadillac. I was thankful I had the foresight to remove the light bulb from the dome light. If I had not done so, the dome light would catch the driver's attention and make my stealthy exit impossible without being detected. Hmm, now that I think about it…that is why Tish could get out of the car without waking me.

I wondered where she was as I peered around the front of the car. I could sneak across the street to the Cadillac if I were quick and quiet. I knew the only way I would be able to get to the back of the house would be to eliminate the driver as a threat.

I duck walked along the side of the car until I was even with the driver's side door. Jerking it open, I grabbed the unsuspecting man and pulled him out of the caddy while putting his neck in a half-nelson. I pressed harder and harder until the man stopped struggling.

Checking his pulse, I was relieved that I had not killed him. I was unsure how long he would remain unconscious. I knew I needed to move fast.

I sprinted across the lawn and stopped at the edge of the house, where I could peer down the driveway before making another sprint towards the back of the house. Keeping close to the home, I managed to stay concealed. I peeked around the corner of the house siding; my heart skipped a beat.

Tish was crumbled on the ground with the two men whispering.

"We can't shoot her, or the whole neighborhood will be alerted." One of the men whispered to the other.

"Stupid! You have a silencer on your gun. Just shoot her and be done with it." The smaller guy hissed back.

As the larger man pointed his gun towards Tish's head, I moved like a bull charging a red cape. I was furious, and all reason was gone. I hit the larger man full force and knocked him off his feet, the gun falling from his grasp. I rolled on top of him and let my fists rain down on his face with such force that my knuckles cracked open and bled freely.

The smaller man flung himself on my back. That did not phase me; I continued slamming my fists into the assailant's face. Blood streamed from his mouth, nose, and cuts above his eyes. I kept punching his face into a bloody pulp.

The smaller man returned for the fallen gun, and just as he pointed it at my head, I heard a shot. Standing in the back door was Patrick with his smoking gun aimed at the smaller man. The slighter man fell to the ground bleeding from a gunshot wound to his chest.

Aileen rushed past Patrick to see if Tish was alive. Bending down beside her, with her fingers to Tish's throat to feel for a pulse, she looked up at Patrick and smiled. "She's alive."

At that moment, Tish started to move. Mumbling, she opened her eyes and looked at Aileen. "What happened?"

"That is what I was going to ask you? Are you alright?" Aileen said as she assisted Tish into a sitting position.

Tish looked around at the scene, and for the first time, she saw me hovering over a bloodied pulp of a man. Blood was splattered across my face and down my shirt.

Tish jumped to her feet. "Scotty, are you okay?" She rushed to my side and wiped the blood from my face with her T-Shirt.

Rising to my feet, I embraced Tish. "Thank God, you are alright! I was scared to death when I saw that man pointing his gun at your head."

Patrick returned after placing a call to the police. "The police will be here in just a few minutes. Would you care to fill us in on what happened and why you are here before they arrive?"

Tossing handcuffs to me, Patrick came over to assist me as I put them on the unconscious man. "I doubt he will need these, but better safe than sorry is what I always say."

I asked Patrick for another pair of handcuffs. The driver would get away if he were not secured too. "Patrick, the driver of the car, is lying unconscious, but he won't be for long. Can you take care of him?"

Patrick looked at the man lying in a pool of blood and said, "I know he won't need them. He's dead. I'll go secure the other guy out front. Then will you tell us what is going on?"

When Patrick returned with the driver of the black Cadillac, Tish started. "We were keeping surveillance on your house over these past four nights. Captain Jones told us about the attempt on your life, and we volunteered to keep watch during the night."

Aileen smiled. "So that is why you let the computer entry work lapse for a while. Go on. I did not mean to interrupt."

Tish continued. "We saw a suspicious black vehicle slowly passing your house with its lights off a couple of nights ago. We got a partial license plate number and asked Captain Jones to check it out. In the meantime, we sat and waited, knowing it was likely that whoever fired the gun at you would try again.

Tonight, I just had this eerie feeling this would be the night. I decided to watch from the bushes along your driveway. I did not wake Scotty just in case I was wrong. He needed some sleep," Tish said this as she glanced lovingly towards me. I knew I could not be mad at her for not waking me.

"Anyway," Tish continued, "The next thing I knew, two men were busy trying to break into your back door. I thought I could sneak up on them and disarm them. I wasn't as quiet as I hoped to be.

"I was closest to the smaller man, and I grabbed him and put his arm in an arm lock behind his back when the larger man sucker-punched me in the side of my face, over the smaller man's head. I hadn't anticipated the big man thinking so quickly. He seemed rather dumb."

I added, "I guess that is when I came on the scene. I saw Tish on the ground and heard the smaller man telling the larger man to kill Tish, and I just went berserk. I guess the rest you can surmise."

The sirens could be heard, and neighbors were stirring in their houses. We all knew the scene would be chaos soon.

The Jamiesons came and hugged us both. "We owe our lives to you."

"And I owe my life to you, Scott," Tish said as tears welled up in her eyes.

The following hours were spent with the police, being questioned at the scene and then at the police department. Captain Jones was pulled from his bed and met us at the department.

Indeed, the gangsters were members of the Roscetti family. Brothers, Nico, Francesco, and Antonio, were cousins of Johnny Roscetti and very involved in the family business. Wanting revenge for their family, Nico planned the assassination and ended up dead. Francesco and Antonio were willing to confess their involvement with hopes for a suspended sentence.

Captain Jones demanded that both Tish and I be seen in the emergency room. A police officer was assigned to take us to the hospital and then return us to our own car if the doctor was willing to release us.

The sun was coming up when we got to our own car. My hands were swollen. Not swollen enough that I could not drive. Tish was to take it easy for fear that she may have a mild concussion. We both decided to take the day off from school and slept the whole day.

I was feeling very reluctant to leave Tish Friday evening to work my shift at the mall. Checking her pupils and with her solemn promise to stay in bed and call the Jamiesons if she felt the least bit nauseated, was the only reason I did not call in sick.

The night was long, and I had a lot on my mind. I replayed the sight of Tish lying on the ground with a gun pointed at her head. I could not stand the thought of losing her. I knew right then and there that I loved her. Now, I needed to try to work side by side with her and not let her know. I won't let anything get in the way of our partnership. Even if she did not return my love, I could, at least, be with her day and night.

CHAPTER TWENTY-SIX

With the long night of questioning behind us. Tish and I were relaxing on the sofa. We were both exhausted. Tish rested her head on my shoulder, and I suddenly felt invigorated. All I could think was, 'so this is how it feels to be in love.' I only wish Tish felt the same way.

Tish startled me as she spoke. I was lost in my own thoughts and daydreams. "You were wonderful tonight, Scotty. I would be dead right now if it weren't for you."

I started to say something, and Tish cut me off. "I would like to finish before you say anything, okay?"

I nodded my head that I understood. She could feel my head nodding in agreement since her head was still on my shoulder.

Tish shared her concerns. "The thought that I almost died has given me a new perspective on everything. I still want to be your partner, and I still want us to be private investigators. Two things concern me now."

Tish hesitated, and I could tell something was bothering her. I found myself feeling apprehensive. There was a large pit growing in my stomach. I waited for her to say what was on her mind.

"First, you put yourself in danger. You remembered your training when you confronted the driver, and I was impressed with how you handled him. Then, you totally forgot everything I taught you when you saw I was in trouble. You reverted to your football training, and that can't happen again. From now on, you and I will train two hours every night, no matter what. Got it?"

I figured she wanted me to talk at this moment. I said, "Yes, I got it."

Tish continued with her second concern. "Secondly, and this is harder for me to say. When I realized that I almost died, it flashed through my mind that I have never told you how I feel about you. This may ruin our partnership. I hope it won't…what I mean to say is, I love you. I don't want to die without ever letting you know how much you mean to me."

I could not resist; I let Tish's head fall from my shoulder into my arms, and I kissed her deeply and passionately. She responded immediately and melted into my embrace.

When I came up for air, the words exploded from my heart. "I love you, Tish. When I thought I might never see you again, I realized I love you deeply. I was afraid to say anything for fear you did not feel the same way, and our partnership would be ruined."

Tish said nothing. She just pulled my head down for another long, fervent kiss.

"I guess this means we will be missing class again," I said.

Peering deeper into my eyes, she said, "I think you will understand that I need to take this slow. I want us to continue to hold each other tightly and express our love. I am just not ready for a more intimate relationship. There are things I must work out…. Before we get carried away, we should go to class. Scotty, we are committed to a lifetime together as partners and now, as lovers. We will have plenty of time to talk about where we go from here."

"You know what? I am okay with that. I just want to be near you. So, class, it is. We both need a shower; let's get our butts in gear," I said as I realized Tish would be the voice of reason in our partnership even romantically.

After classes, we dropped past Aileen and Patrick's office. We wanted to see how they were doing after the attempt on their lives last night.

"Are we ever glad to see both of you." Aileen greeted us. "I have some lox, cream cheese, and fresh bagels, as well as some grapes. Join us for a light lunch."

We accepted gladly. Both of us felt as if the Jamiesons were family, and it fitted to have a celebratory lunch with them after the night we all shared.

Patrick asked Tish to join him outside for a moment, and I helped Aileen set the small table in their office for our lunch. All the time I was helping, I wondered what Patrick needed to say to Tish in private. These thoughts were interrupted by Aileen.

"Scott, do I sense a change in your relationship with Tish?" Aileen asked with a knowing smile.

"Nothing really has changed. We finally have admitted to each other what we both knew all along."

"Patrick and I are happy for you. We have often talked about how we felt you two belonged together as more than just business partners. This revelation will bring you closer together. Nothing has been more wonderful for Patrick and me than to love each other and to work together. Hey, don't get me wrong. There will be times when you want to strangle each other. But you won't," Aileen winked at me as she said these last words.

When Patrick and Tish entered the room, I noted that Tish seemed sullen. I wanted to know what was said. I could see now was not the time. Obviously, it was private, or Patrick would have included me in the conversation.

Tish seemed to become more animated and chipper as lunch proceeded. I decided there was nothing to be concerned about as we talked and laughed.

The Jamiesons reiterated how nice it was going to be for us all to be working closely together this summer. Patrick made the comment the insurance companies were coming close to ending the complicated review of the Ceroni-Roscetti fraud cases. He mentioned there would be a very fat check for all of us after the insurance companies concluded the investigation.

I was about to say something when Tish got the jump on me. "It was a pleasure to help you find the evidence to put these criminals behind bars. We look forward to whatever we can do in the future to assist in other cases."

She did not mention money at all. So, I decided not to either. I figured there was a reason she chose not to.

As we got up to leave, Patrick gave Tish a big bear-hug. I could sense a father-daughter relationship emerging. Tish could use all the fathers in her life she could gather. Her strong-willed personality needed more than one father to temper her.

When we left and were driving home, I knew we would both need a long nap. I still had the night shift ahead for me. Tish would be tired out from our long night of surveillance.

I hesitated to ask. I blundered on with my question. "Why did Patrick pull you outside, or shouldn't I ask?"

Tish smiled at me and told me what Patrick said. "Basically, I got scolded. Patrick told me I used poor judgment to leave you in the car asleep while I went off to scout on my own. He was right, of course. That was stupid on my part. Not only did I leave you vulnerable, I almost got myself killed. Patrick said we are both young, and we will make mistakes. We must learn from them quickly and never repeat them again."

When we got home, Tish asked, "Scotty, would you mind if I take my nap with you. I feel the need to be close to you right now.

I wasn't about to object. I knew it was going to be near impossible to sleep with Tish's exotic body next to mine.

She undressed down to her tank top and underwear. Stripped down to my boxers, we cuddled together in Tish's bed, face to face. I could feel her soft, warm skin next to my chest. I pulled her even closer.

I was finding it difficult not to be aroused as she gently rubbed my chest. "You have a gorgeous body, Scotty. I always knew you were strong. I never realized how wonderful it would be to lie next to you," Tish said lazily.

Her hand and fingers continued to caress my chest and abdomen. I wished she would let her hand explore a bit further. Rats! Double Rats! I knew she would not, since she said she wanted to take our relationship slower.

In the meantime, I let my fingers run up and down her soft arm. She almost purred as I gently slid them along the long, smooth lines of her muscles. I found it astonishing someone as strong and muscular as Tish could feel like velvet. I figured she was made of stone. No way was that the case. I found myself drifting off as I turned onto my back. I let my arm draw Tish even closer, and Tish put her head on my chest with eyes closed.

I was annoyed when I woke up and knew I needed to get out of bed. I wanted to stay warm and curled up next to the woman I loved. However, it was time to get dressed for work. I was hoping our relationship would allow for us to sleep together every night and not just occasionally for naps. I was wondering how to broach the subject when I received a smack on my butt.

"Get up, sleepyhead. I will make us some dinner while you get dressed," Tish said, once more being the voice of reason.

I groaned and pulled Tish back down into the bed as she tried to get out. "Couldn't we snuggle for another ten minutes?" I offered.

"You can stay in bed for another ten minutes. I need to get up now if you are going to get dinner before you leave. Have you looked at the clock? It is 10:00 p.m., and you need to be at work in one hour."

I released Tish, and she scooted out of bed, grabbing a robe on her way out. I rolled out of bed and sat up. I had never been inside Tish's room other than to grab something or another that she asked me to get for her.

Tish's room was Spartan in most ways, I noted. I spied three photos on her dressing table. There was one of her mother and father, one of her best friends, Michele, and one of me.

I could not place that particular photo of me. I was wearing my football jersey with a big smile on my face. It was obviously a candid photo taken from the sidelines of one of my games. My helmet was off, and I could see the satisfaction of winning in my eyes. Which game, which year, I could not possibly know. Tish had taken the photo and kept it as one of her most valued people in life. I was touched and warmed by the knowledge she truly cared for me even back then. I wondered how long Tish considered me as something other than a friend. Did she love me while I was with Heather? I knew better than to ask. I was curious, though. Probably just my ego talking, I told myself.

When I returned home from work, I noted my pillows were gone as well as several of my personal things. My state championship trophy was missing, and I noticed several of my drawers were open and empty. I looked towards the door and saw Tish standing in the opening.

"I moved you into my room. Are you willing to move in with me? If not, I will move everything back into your room," Tish said as she stood suggestively in the doorway…one arm reaching up to the door frame while her other hand rested on her hip.

I wasn't sure if she changed her mind about taking things slowly or not. I knew for sure I wanted to move into her room even if it meant no sex.

"So, what you are saying is we have a guest room now?" I was hoping she would say yes.

"Yes," Tish said, "but I can still kick you out of my room if you make me mad. Seriously, I hope we won't be having any company right away. I would rather our parents not know we are taking our relationship a step further, or our mothers will start planning our wedding."

"What would be wrong with that? I would love to marry you and have children with you," I said eagerly.

"Hold on, Cowboy. We are trying to establish ourselves as private investigators. What do you think children would do to those plans? I don't mind having our sign say, McFarlan and McFarlan...but not McFarlan, McFarlan, and Sons." Tish laughed out loud at the absurdity of it all.

"Hey, I kind of like the sound of that," I said, laughing with her.

"How about McFarlan, McFarlan, and Daughters?" Tish added without a smile.

That got my attention. I hadn't thought about having daughters join us in our business. I wondered why risking Tish's life did not seem odd. Then again, risking our daughters' lives seemed somehow wrong. Was I going to be a chauvinistic father?

"Wow! You have a point. Maybe putting off children for a while is a good idea. We would need to decide how they would fit into the family business if they wanted to be part of it," I said maturely. Nothing more sobering than the thought of raising children and having to be responsible for them.

As Tish took me by my hand and pulled me back into the living area, she said she had something more relevant to talk about. 'Oh, oh,' I thought. 'What now?'

Tish proceeded once we were sitting on the sofa. "Scotty, I think you should consider terminating your night job. We are almost at term's end, and we will be working full time for the Jamiesons this summer. We are already working several hours a week for them entering cases into the computer. I think trying to hold down your part-time job would not be beneficial to you or us. What do you say?"

I thought about it for a few seconds. Tish had a point. Already, my night shift job at the mall made it more difficult for us to do surveillance when the Jamiesons needed us. Luckily, we hadn't needed to continue surveillance during my night shift. It would be unfair to Tish if we were in a real case, and she needed to do the work alone. My security job was an entry-level into law enforcement. It served its purpose. It was time to give notice. Frankly, I would love to have three more nights at home to sleep next to the sexiest woman in the world. Yep! That decided it for me.

"Yes, you are right. It is time for me to give notice. Are you going to continue classes and training the rookies?" I knew Tish's classes would not interfere with our work. I wanted to find out upfront what she was going to do.

"I don't think it will hurt our job for the Jamiesons if I continue to work; if I find that it does, I will quit," Tish answered.

"Sounds fair to me." I agreed.

"Besides, teaching self-defense to women makes the streets safer for them. Teaching rookies made the streets safer for everyone," Tish added.

"Speaking of making the streets safer, we should go down and practice my moves before I shower. I said knowing Tish would be pleased I was taking her suggestion to heart to become more proficient at martial arts.

Down to the basement and two hours later, my body was aching and ready for a shower. Tish said she would make me a delicious breakfast. I knew part of the day would be spent in studies since our finals were just around the corner. It was incredible to realize we were over halfway finished with our program. This summer would be an eye-opener into the real world of the private investigator. I was genuinely excited about our future. Life was great.

CHAPTER TWENTY-SEVEN

Things were all set. When I gave my notice to the security company, they were visibly sad to lose me. They were willing to provide me with a recommendation and let me know I could return at any time. I worked another weekend as they found a replacement sooner than they expected.

Tish and I studied hard for our exams…me, more than Tish. It paid off for both of us. Grades were in, and we aced our classes. Summer was upon us, and we were ready for our first assignment. It came sooner than we expected.

The Jamiesons asked us to join them for lunch. We excitedly agreed and met them at our favorite burger joint.

"We have an assignment for you if you are ready and willing," Patrick said as he ate a French fry, dipping the next one into a ketchup-mayo-horseradish mix. Patrick proceeded to tell us what we were about to undertake.

"A prestigious magazine company has called us. They need us to investigate without any notoriety. It seems some expensive clothing and jewelry items were taken some time during or after photoshoots. These items were on loan from famous designers, and they cost an immense amount of money. Even though this magazine is insured, they can't afford to have this continue. Insurance companies will not insure them if it does," Patrick said

Aileen took up the explanation as Patrick shoved a large bite of mushroom burger into his mouth. "If you are willing, we are going to send you and Scott undercover. Tish, you would pose as a model and Scott, we would get you a job as the photographer's assistant. The head of the magazine will be expecting you on Monday. He will be the only one who knows you are undercover. Are you interested and willing?"

My heart was pounding. I was thrilled; I could hardly eat.... Well, okay, I could eat. After all, this was my favorite hamburger joint, and it has the best double cheeseburger in the world. The red onion rings were out of this world.

Tish wasn't caught off guard. "Yes, we will accept this assignment. I can hardly wait to start. What do we need to do? As you can tell, I am not a model. I don't even know how-to put-on eyeliner."

"Don't worry about any of that. The magazine company has make-up artists, stylists, and anything else you could ask for. All you need to do is be personable and do what the photographer tells you to do. You will be perfect."

I almost choked. "You said, 'personable.' I guess you haven't noticed Tish doesn't go out of her way to make friends and influence people. Well, she does influence people if busting noses and dislocating shoulders counts."

My arm got punched for that remark as Tish said, "Scotty has a point. I will have a bit of trouble, NOT speaking my mind. You know I can be a bit, um, what's the word?"

"Assertive?" I interjected.

"Yes, strong, confident, determined..." Patrick enumerated.

Aileen came to Tish's defense. "You are also sweet, kind, and compassionate. These are the traits you need to show for the next couple of weeks as you interact with everyone at the magazine. Remember, any one of the people could be our thief. It is up to you to get to know as many as you can in a personal way.

Scott, you are there to watch everyone and to have Tish's back. You will be less involved with getting to know individuals."

"I don't know much about photography. I do own a camera, thanks to Tish. I will need a crash course if I am going to look as if I am knowledgeable about photography at all," I said with some trepidation.

Patrick said. "Don't worry about that, Scott. Aileen is quite good with a camera. She knows more than most professionals. We would send her undercover. However, everyone knows her. She can teach you quite a bit this weekend before you go on the job on Monday."

I was feeling a bit relieved. A weekend wasn't a lot of time to learn all that I needed to know to pull this job off. If anyone could teach me, it was Aileen. She is probably the most patient woman on this earth and talented. Looking at her work as she tutored me, I was wondering how she got so good.

"Practice and a good eye helped quite a bit," Aileen said as she adjusted the camera. "Now, watch the light meter..." and our lesson continued.

The weekend was spent with Aileen and Patrick. While Aileen was teaching me the inside-outs of photography, Patrick was working with Tish to help her soften her personality. I guess the interactive role-play was hilarious. I would have loved to have been involved. I knew I would get a first-hand look at what the results of their time spent together would bring at the photoshoots.

We entered the magazine offices at different times as to avoid suspicion. It was decided we were not to appear as if we knew each other while on the job. I was sent directly to the photographer's office. It seems there are several photographers. One is more of an outdoor photographer, another sets his platform indoors, and yet another is for close-ups, etc. I was to report to Victor.

In the meantime, Tish was meeting with the agency that supplies models for the magazine. The head of the magazine, Mr. Walsh, had already requested a model type that fitted Tish to a tee. There was little chance she would not be directed to the magazine. The shoot would involve settings for several weeks. This provided Tish with the time to find the culprit…with my help.

The first time I saw Tish at the magazine company, was the very next day. I had to turn my head. I did not want anyone to realize I had intimate knowledge of this lovely lady.

Tish was being introduced around to various people. When I was introduced to her, I just nodded my head and moved back into the background. Victor, on the other hand, gushed all over her.

"You are lovely. I will enjoy capturing your exquisite features on the camera. I already know how I want to set the stage. I don't know for sure which designer yet, maybe Perry Ellis. I do know the feature is Gypsy Grunge. You will be dripping in jewelry. I suspect the magazine will borrow large gold earrings and plenty of gold necklaces as well as rings on every finger and maybe even on your toes. It is going to be glorious." Victor continued gushing over Tish, and I was starting to become a bit jealous.

Tish just blushed. She was playing her part well. In real life, Tish would never have stood for anyone dressing her up like a doll or even a gypsy. I remembered how foolish she felt at our Senior Ball and smiled at the memory. Tish was gorgeous that night; she was a shining star. She would look beautiful no matter what she wore.

She caught my eye and narrowed hers. I took that as a reminder to keep my mind on business. Somehow, I felt as though she knew what I was thinking.

Fidgeting with the camera, I needed to act as if I had only one thing on my mind…my job. It was sure going to be hard with Tish distracting me.

The first day went well enough. Over dinner that night at home, Tish said she met several people, including her make-up artist, hairdresser, stylist, and several other models. She was great at remembering names. There was Alyssa, Myra, Chelsea, Alexandria, Charity, and Max.

"Is Max a gal or guy?" I asked puzzled.

"Max is really a gal. I think her name is Maxine. Everyone calls her Max. She is one of the models, and her claim to fame is her butt. I guess she is one of their top jeans models. She used to be a Tommy girl."

Now I was really puzzled. "What in the world is a Tommy girl?"

"Tommy Hilfiger, you, silly goose," was Tish's goofy response back at me.

It seems several of the models would work for one designer or another. Now, most of them are free-lancing as their contracts ran out. It is more dog-eat-dog when that happens, according to Tish.

"It is a good thing you aren't a model for real. It wouldn't be much fun to scramble for every job, would it?" I asked. I was hoping she would not want to join the fashion world once she experienced it and ruin our future careers.

"No way! You could not pay me enough to do this full time. I hate all the fussing. It isn't me, that is for sure," Tish said, relieving my fears.

"By the way, you are making quite a hit yourself. You should hear the girls talking about you. 'Hubba-hubba' or something like that. I heard one of the models say, '*Yummy.*' Not only do you need to watch out for the girls, but you also need to watch out for some of the photographers. I know Victor is gay; however, you won't be hit on by him. He is in an exclusive relationship. He still looks; I saw him," Tish said with a giggle.

Now I was blushing. I know many girls think I am good looking. I rarely let it go to my head. Well, sometimes, I let it go to my head. I can be flattered by women's attention. I will never let it interfere with my relationship with Tish.

"You know I only have eyes for you," I said.

Tish just about choked as I said these words of love to her.

"You better only have eyes for me, or you may be missing some valued body parts," Tish retorted with some vehemence.

"Got it!" I quickly said.

The week went by quickly. Tish had several fashion shoots. She was dripping in gold with rings on her fingers and toes as well as multiple bracelets. The gypsy look became her. None of the jewelry was terribly expensive or from well-known designers. Tish said whatever clothes she dressed in would not tempt the thief. However, she heard one model say that Alyssa was going to be wearing a necklace borrowed from Neil Lane, and it was worth a small fortune.

"We will need to be on guard when that piece of jewelry arrives," I said.

"Duh!" Tish's come back sounded sarcastic.

"What happened to the sweet, compassionate, shy darling from the day job?" I countered.

"Oh, okay, I am sorry, Scotty. I guess I forgot myself. Will you forgive my rather rude response? I am sorry for acting like such a prig. I don't know what came over me. All I can say in my defense is that the devil made me do it." Tish laughed at her ending sentence.

"You are a prig!" I said and pulled her towards me and kissed her hard. That ended most of our discussion for the rest of the evening.

Victor's boyfriend, Mark, was in the building when I arrived for work. Victor introduced me to Mark, and I was bewildered when Mark started a tirade towards Victor. "Why didn't you tell me your new assistant was a hunk? Didn't you think I would find out? You had better keep your hands to yourself!"

I interrupted Mark to stop the jealous talk. "Look, don't worry about me. I only have eyes for one woman."

Seeing Tish glaring at me, I stopped that train of thought and continued without glancing at Tish. "Besides, Victor talks about you all the time. He is crazy about you."

I was going to go on and on trying to diffuse Mark's petty jealousy. I must have been convincing since Mark took Victor by the arm and lovingly gazed into his eyes as he guided him away. I could hear him saying, "That is sweet. You do love me."

I dodged a bullet, is what I was thinking when Tish glided over to me and under her breath, reminded me to be careful. "No more talk about being in an exclusive relationship. Do you hear me? It is better if the models think they have a chance with you. Got it?" And she walked away as if she had said nothing to me at all.

This was getting a bit hard for me, having never taken an acting class in my life. I didn't even take public speaking. Now, to be an investigator, I was finding I also needed to be an actor. I got back into character as best as I could.

Jackson, the outdoor photographer, was going to do a shoot at the lake and needed me to come along. Victor, as the lead photographer, found it was to his advantage to have Mark hear him say I was available for Jackson all day. That wasn't good for our investigation. That would leave Tish here on her own. There was nothing I could do without causing suspicion. I knew I needed to go.

That evening, I was excited to get home to find out what happened with Tish. When I walked into the house, Tish was cooking dinner.

"Well, what happened today? I was worried sick all day that something might happen, and I would be out of commission." I guess I should have said, "Lucy, I'm home." I might have been greeted with a kiss.

Instead, Tish started on the day's events without a kiss. "Alyssa said the shoot is going to be tomorrow. She will be wearing an evening gown. I guess the fashion industry is trying to get women out of jeans and hip-hop clothing.

"It seems the shoot will be outside on a yacht. That means I won't be able to go, but you could. You need to get Jackson to take you once more."

"Just how am I supposed to get him to do that?" I asked. "I was on loan to Jackson today because Victor wanted to impress on Mark that he was not the least bit interested in me. I intentionally didn't make myself valuable to Jackson today, because I was worried that he will drag me off again to another outdoor shoot away from you. Now I am feeling beaten that you want me to go with him to the shoot, and I have sort of burned my bridges."

Tish thought a moment. "Come on in and sit down. Dinner is almost ready. We will think of something together." She kissed me, and I felt as if she was right. We could do this together.

Between bites, Tish said, "We need to phone the Jamiesons. They will phone Mr. Walsh and let him know it is important that both of us go on the shoot tomorrow. I know Patrick can make it happen."

I did not see any other solution. After dinner, the phone call was made, and Patrick said it would be arranged.

The next day, Victor told me Jackson required me again today. That was great.

Tish and several other models gathered to go on the yacht. Mr. Walsh told the group he wanted bikini models as a background for Alyssa in her flowing gown.

It all seemed odd to me. Why would one model be in a flowing gown with a fortune in jewels on her neck while others were posing in different positions around the yacht with bare legs and bare bellies, and then it hit me. What did I care if it was odd? I was going to be in heaven. That is if I could be a good enough actor so Tish did not catch on to what I would be looking at from behind the photographer. The thought made me chuckle. 'I may be taken, but I ain't dead.'

We loaded up everything and headed out to the yacht. Tish edged up to me and reminded me that I was to be watching one thing and one thing only…the necklace. Now, I was sure Tish read my mind, and I was feeling a bit uncomfortable about that. However, she was right. We were here to do a job, and we wanted to make the Jamiesons proud of us.

In the early morning, the lighting was perfect in my estimation. I used the light meter, as Aileen taught me in my crash course. I preset the lenses on the cameras and handed one to Jackson. He made a few minor adjustments, very few, I must add. I felt like I was holding my own as his assistant.

Alyssa came out in her expensive gown. The bikini models all arrived, and Jackson placed them strategically around the yacht forming a semi-circle around Alyssa. I noted Tish looked as good as any of the other models, and I felt my heart swell with pride.

I was lost for a moment in that thought when the security personnel brought out the black velvet box with the necklace that would be used for the shoot. I wondered why we were needed when there was a security team in place to guard the priceless jewelry.

The necklace was placed on the model, and the camera started to click. The central model, Alyssa, maneuvered into various positions, flowing gracefully from stance to stance, while the other models amplified Alyssa's movements. Tish seemed to join in casually as if she had been modeling all her life.

I kept my eye on the necklace. I just could not imagine how anyone could get it off the model's neck without being seen. I decided if it were going to be stolen, it would not be during the shoot. Of course, after the shoot, the security men would have it safely back in the lockbox.

Maybe this was not going to be the target. Perhaps it was the dress. It was a designer dress and worth over $10,000 itself. I wondered why the Jamiesons thought it was going to be this particular necklace.

The wind was picking up, and the yacht was rolling with the waves. I noticed it was getting harder for the models to balance themselves for the various directions given by Jackson. He wanted several more shots with different lighting and suggested everyone take a half-hour break while the sun changed positions in the sky.

The security men quickly arrived to take the necklace off Alyssa's neck. The models were told to go below for a touch up of makeup and hair. As all the lovely ladies left the deck, all that was left were the men.

The security guards talked together in one group. Jackson told me what he would be doing next. I repositioned the light stands, and reflectors changed the lens filters and recalibrated the cameras needed for the next shoot. Deckhands were making sure all the necessary gear was in its proper place on the yacht. I could see nothing amiss.

The sun was setting, and Jackson said it was time to resume the session. The ladies were called back into place. This time Jackson wanted more action. The models in bikinis were to be in more precarious positions.

The yacht was a sailing ship, and I don't pretend to know a thing about them. There were lines everywhere and rails to keep people from falling overboard. Some of the ladies were holding onto ropes, and others were hanging onto the rails. Alyssa was up in the front, where the wind would cause her gown to stream furiously behind her. Jackson was contented with what he saw in the camera lens and was snapping pictures continuously.

It seemed to happen quickly. One-minute, Alyssa was on the deck, and the next, she was overboard. Tish reacted immediately, as did Max. They both dived into the water, knowing that Alyssa could drown with the weight of the dress dragging her down.

I rushed to the side of the yacht, as did everyone else. The two women were doing a sidestroke and dragging Alyssa towards the dock. Each of them was stroking as hard as they could to keep the model afloat with her saturated gown.

We all rushed from our point of view towards the dock. Hairdressers and stylists found towels, and they were rushing through us to get to the sopping wet ladies.

"Move aside and let us get these cold, wet ladies back to the yacht," one of the stylists commanded.

Large towels were draped over the three wet models, and there was a gaggle of ladies pawing at them to help them dry off. I was making sure Tish was safe and was glad to see she was okay.

Several minutes later, a few of the ladies came back on deck, saying that everything was fine. The shoot was canceled for the rest of the day. Many of the stylists, hairdressers, and makeup artists were halfway down the dock when Tish rushed up from below, yelling for us to stop all of them.

"Stop them! The necklace is missing!" Tish yelled again as she ran for the boarding ramp.

As the security detail realized what was being said, they joined the chase as did I. Most of the women stopped when they saw all of us in pursuit. Apparently not understanding what was happening, one of the hairdressers headed towards a waiting car.

Tish's long legs moved instinctively as she pursued the woman. I followed close behind with the security team on my heels. We were almost upon the getaway car when it sped away.

"Darn! Someone quick, call the police. Did anyone get the license number of that car?" Tish yelled to everyone.

One of the security officers ran off to make the phone call. I yelled to the officer that the license number was A782 641. The car is a gold 1993 Plymouth Duster.

I learned my lesson; the night we missed the plate numbers on the black caddy. This time, as I ran, I memorized the license number. I wasn't going to make that mistake again.

Tish was visibly frustrated. She had been within an inch of grabbing Hilda before she got in the car.

"I almost had her," Tish mumbled.

"You did great. You noticed the necklace was gone and reacted quickly. There is no way Hilda won't get caught," I said soothingly. "The police will be placing roadblocks on every street."

I knew there was a possibility that Hilda and whoever was driving the car could get through a street that was not blocked. However, the police knew who the suspects were, and it would just be a matter of time before Hilda was caught along with her accomplice.

Tish sighed. "I suppose... I would love to catch her red-handed. If the police don't catch up to her with the necklace, she will probably say she did not take it."

The thought struck me like a hammer. "Maybe Hilda did not take it. Maybe it is still here, and Hilda is just the red herring."

Tish immediately understood what I was implying. She raced down the stairs below deck to catch Alyssa, taking the necklace out from her bodice.

"You can hand that over right now," Tish said to Alyssa. "You thought you were pretty clever to have Hilda take off like a bat out of Hades while you casually strolled away with a fortune in diamonds."

Alyssa feigned ignorance. "What are you talking about. I just found the necklace tucked in the bodice of my dress. It must have fallen off when I fell into the water."

"Right," Tish said. "I think Hilda and her accomplice will spill the beans when the police take them into custody. It would be in your best interest to confess now rather than face your partners' accusation in court. Maybe it was Hilda's idea and not yours." Tish was trying to give Alyssa a way out, and she took the bait.

"It was all Hilda's idea. She stole the other items and sold them on the black market. She came up with this whole idea because she knew the security team would be tight. There was no way they would let the necklace out of their sight unless they thought someone had stolen it. I was just supposed to pass it off to Jackson, who would smuggle it off the yacht. Hilda said we would be let loose when the police did not find the necklace on her or Victor."

Tish continued to press. "So, Victor was driving the getaway car?"

"No, Victor told Mark to pick up Hilda at the dock. He told Mark that Hilda needed to get back pronto and not to let anyone detain them. Mark would do anything for Victor. He had no idea Victor, Jackson, and Hilda were stealing jewelry and fashion wear to sell to the black market."

I heard Alyssa's whole confession. The security team who followed us down the stairs listened to her confession. One of them walked forward and took the necklace back into custody while the second member of the security team put handcuffs on Alyssa.

The security team found Jackson quietly leaving the yacht with his camera bags. We were lucky to have solved this crime quickly. The security team thanked us while they place the cuffs on a dejected Jackson.

"Why did you get involved with Hilda, Jackson, and Victor?" I had to ask.

"Greed, I guess. I found out Hilda, Jackson, and Victor were the ones who were stealing the items. I told them I would tell if they did not cut me in on the deal. I thought it was a great scam. No one was getting hurt, and I was making a better salary with the scam then I was with modeling. My modeling career was coming to an end, and I knew it. This was a way to secure my future. I could live out my life on some gorgeous island until I found a rich man to take care of me. I figured, why not."

"One more question. What if Max and I had not jumped into the lake to save you. You could have drowned. Why risk it?"

Alyssa admitted. "It wasn't really a risk. The dress was a fake. It was in two pieces. I would have ripped the skirt away quickly if I had needed to. The real dress is in the dressing room. Hilda had another one made when she knew which dress was going to be used. Hilda has quite a few friends in the business. Hilda doesn't let them know why she needs things; she just pays them well to do the work when she needs it. She has made other fakes in the past. It has helped to smuggle the original items out to sell on the black market."

I was surprised Alyssa folded. I thought it would take time to pull out a confession. I wondered why she did not stay with her claim that the necklace had fallen in her bodice and let the courts decide if she was guilty. It did not make sense to me.

Later, Tish said she felt that Alyssa was basically honest, and she did not feel right about her part in the whole scam. I suppose Tish wants to think the best of people.... I just think Alyssa was stupid.

The Jamiesons were ecstatic that we could find the criminals in such a short time into our investigation. They told us all of the crooks involved were in custody, except Victor, who is still at large. They disclosed there was not much chance he will make a getaway. Now, they needed to find another case for us to work. In the meantime, we were entitled to a vacation.

Patrick said the trip was on them. We could go anywhere we wanted to go. I knew I wanted to go someplace warm and exotic. Precisely what place needed to be a decision Tish and I agreed on. I also did not want to pick someplace outrageously priced for the Jamiesons' sake.

As we sat on the sofa, cuddling, I asked Tish where she would like to go. Without hesitation, she said, "Hawaii!"

"Okay, Hawaii, it is," I said as I watched Tish's eyes light up. She could have said Antarctica, and I would have been just as happy if she showed as much excitement to go there.

I already knew Tish looked great in a bikini. I wondered if Mr. Walsh would loan Tish a few of those skimpy bikinis for the trip. I made a mental note to check that out.

Summer was barely starting. We already solved a crime and had a vacation to which to look forward. As I said before, life is great.

CHAPTER TWENTY-EIGHT

The thought of a vacation with Tish made me delirious. I was packed and ready to go. I could just imagine the white beaches and Tish in a bikini. The idea of walking hand in hand along the beaches was seriously what our relationship needed at this point.

Tish wanted to take things slowly. What could be slower than walking hand in hand? I must admit that I could not get hula skirts and coconut bras out of my head. I could imagine Tish doing the hula just for me. I didn't want to give this dream up. However, Tish was looking at brochures about scuba diving, surfing, and outrigger canoeing. She showed me another leaflet that told all about the volcano on the big island and how one could ski there in the winter.

So much for laying in the sand, spreading sunscreen all over Tish's tight body. I had a feeling she was going to run my body ragged. So much for hulas and coconut bras.

Our folks were excited for us. They were amazed that we were instrumental in catching a ring of thieves. Even when we explained there were only four thieves, they would not listen. They argued that the people who fenced the items were part of the ring. It was a vast ring.

It was better not to argue. In a way, they were right. They also demanded that we leave a few summer days available to visit them. After promising we would do our best to visit, we were heading for Hawaii.

We were greeted with countless billowy white clouds floating magically in the tropical blue skies when we departed the plane. It didn't take us long to find our hotel limo after we gathered our luggage.

The hotel was magnificent, and our room was beyond imagination. The crystal blue pool was so inviting we rushed to put on our swimming suits.

A four-star restaurant and every other amenity imaginable were included. Patrick and Aileen provided us with plenty of money for food and activities. The fact that they were still paying us a salary, while we were on vacation, made this trip a dream come true.

I wanted to play golf. Tish would only agree to my request to play golf once she knew I would agree to her list of activities. My chosen activity was totally safe. The worst is, I could get hit by a ball. Tish selected activities that were not safe. Simply stated, the worst is, I could be eaten by a shark, stung by a jellyfish or poisoned by a snake! I was beginning to wonder if my life was going to be wrapped in danger if I married this woman.

Tish was committed to taking things slowly even though we were still sharing a bed. Seeing her in a skimpy swimsuit all day and hardly wearing anything at bedtime, made me very frustrated. I was thinking of begging for a little help, except I knew real men did not do that. What I did know is, real men, go scuba diving, surfing, wind sailing, outrigger canoeing, snorkeling, and spearfishing. If there was another thing, I knew for sure…I would be in better shape, horny but in better shape when I returned from Hawaii.

To make matters worse, Tish insisted that we go to the hotel gym every morning and practice Combat Hapkido. Finally, the staff at the hotel asked us to 'take it down a notch.' They explained we were scaring the other guests. Tish took their advice and relented. Instead, she pushed me to work out on the gym equipment for an equal amount of time.

The next day after the usual work out had Tish and I laying on the beach, a rarity in my estimation. I noticed Tish wasn't relaxed as she should be. I was about to ask her why when she said...

"Hey Scotty, watch the man with the straw hat, standing near the lone palm tree about 75 feet away. A few minutes ago, a couple was lying on those towels. They went down to the water with another man, wearing a blue ballcap, to take what appears to be surfing lessons. They left all their valuables under the towels. That man by the palm tree has been watching them closely ever since they arrived."

As Tish was saying this to me, the man by the palm tree nonchalantly approached the towels and grabbed several items, including what looked like a hotel card key. Tish was on high alert and told me to follow the man.

We jumped to our feet, needing to move quickly as the man who stole the items was running away from the scene. He was unaware that we were following him. We acted like a couple jogging. He was moving out fast. As we pursued, we could tell he was heading towards our hotel on the beach.

We followed him into the hotel. He took the lobby elevator, it stopped on the ninth floor. Tish told me to go and get security and meet her on the ninth floor.

I tried to stop Tish from going up alone. She cut me off with a harsh command. "You are wasting time. Go now!" Without another sound, she took the next elevator and was out of sight.

I sprinted to the desk and told the clerk what was happening. He immediately called security and told them to go to the ninth floor. I did not wait for security to join me. I ran for the elevator and punched in the ninth-floor button.

I looked down the hall and found Tish standing against the wall at one of the rooms. As I approached, she put her finger to her lips to silence me.

The door to room 906 was cracked open. Inside we could hear rifling through drawers and items being tossed. The security team was not insight, and it is evident that the man inside was wrapping things up.

Tish whispered. "Stay here on the right side of the door. I am going to stand on the left side of the door." She slipped quickly to the other side. She continued to signal what she wanted me to do with exaggerated hand signs.

From what I could tell, Tish was going to catch the man's attention as he exited the door, and I was to grab him, subduing him from behind. There were several ways to reduce a person's means of escape. Tish taught many. At this point, I could only hope I would use the correct one. I was sure I would be in for a lesson from Tish if I picked the wrong one.

As the man came out of the room with his hands full of the couple's valuables, Tish smiled and said, "What are you doing?"

The man's attention was on Tish…I stepped quickly behind him, putting my left arm around his neck while grabbing his right arm behind his back with my right arm. He was effectively subdued in a fraction of a second. Most of the valuables he was holding were now on the hall floor.

The security team arrived and took custody of the man who was still holding the couple's passports and travel checks in his left hand. "How did you know he was intending on robbing Mr. and Mrs. Copley?" the hotel security officer asked.

Tish explained, "We were on the beach, and we saw the couple leave for surfing lessons. We watched as this man took the valuables from under the beach towel, including the hotel key. From that point, we quietly followed in pursuit."

The security officer said, "This is a pervasive crime on the island. Unfortunately, tourists are easy victims," he explained. "They think they are in paradise, and nothing bad could happen here. We believe this man did not act alone. Would you mind showing me where to find

Mr. and Mrs. Copley? I need to tell them about the robbery and find out if their surfing instructor is involved."

We agreed to take him to where the crime had begun. One security officer took the offender away and contacted the island police, while we accompanied the other security officer back to the beach.

When we arrived where the Copley's learning how to surf, the surfing instructor took one look at the security officer and paddled out to sea. The officer took his radio and called the hotel desk. He said he needed the Coast Guard to apprehend the fleeing surfing instructor.

Mr. and Mrs. Copley were astounded. Sadly, they did think they were in paradise. "How could this happen here? All of the hospitality people we meet are quite charming. Why that nice young man offered us a free hour of surfing lessons," Mrs. Copley said.

The hotel security officer remarked. "Yes, and why that nice young man had you away from your belongings, his nice young associate was taking all your valuables that you left on the beach, including your hotel key. The other nice young man had several of your valuables in his hands when he was caught. If it weren't for this young couple, you would be trying to figure out where you left your key and where you were going to get more money to replace what was stolen. You would also be trying to get a temporary passport to return back to England."

For the first time, Mr. and Mrs. Copley turned their attention towards Tish and me. Mrs. Copley said, "So you are the nice young couple who saved us from all the misery the officer described. How can we possibly thank you?"

"You don't need to thank us, Mam. Tish and I feel we have a duty to stop any crime that happens when we are watching," I said, sounding a bit like a boy scout.

"Captain America! You are both superheroes, in my opinion. We insist on doing something to show our appreciation. How about reward money? Young people can always use money," Mrs. Copley rambled on.

Tish held up her hand. "No, really. We don't want anything, especially money. If you really want to thank us, how about buying us lunch tomorrow?"

Mr. Copley expressed his opinion. "Would dinner tonight be an option? We need to catch a flight tomorrow to go island hopping."

We both laughed. "Dinner tonight will be great. That is more than enough thanks for either of us. Our room is 621 if you wish to call us to let us know what time to be ready."

With a bit more fuss, Tish and I were ready to fill out police reports. We followed the security officer back to the hotel. He advised the Copley's to return to make sure that everything was secure in their room.

The island police filled out the report. The thief was already booked, and his partner was picked up by the coast guard, still paddling out to sea. Exactly where he thought he was going to go was beyond me. It would be a long row back to the Mainland, that is for sure. At any rate, the crime is solved, and the hotel was handling all the details.

Speaking of details, when we returned to our room, there was a huge fruit basket sitting on our table with an envelope and a short note from the hotel manager thanking us for a job well done.

"Whoa! Tish, look at this. The hotel manager is changing our room to the penthouse on the top floor. I thought this room was incredible. I can't imagine what the penthouse will be like. We need to pack our stuff and move right now."

Tish stood, looking at the fruit basket. "I really thought the fruit basket was going over the top. The penthouse is a bit much if you ask me."

"I'm not going to argue. I want to stay in a penthouse once in my life. This may well be the only chance I ever get. Let's get a move on."

It did not take us long to pack our suitcases, grab the fruit basket, and move to the top story. We did not wait for a bellboy. We just packed and ran. We used the card key the manager provided and opened the door; Tish gasped.

I walked in and turned in circles, wanting to get everything into my head at once. There was a huge living room with massive curved domed skylights bringing in the natural light from the expansive skies. Off the living room, one could see a dining room furnished with a light rattan table and chairs fitting the island style. Beyond the dining room were several more rooms yet to be explored. Tish ignored the astounding furnishings in the living room and ran straight to the expansive windows.

"The view is incredible! Look," she said as she pulled the glass doors open, revealing a large tiled terrace with flourishing potted ferns and hanging baskets of flowers. Decorative cushioned bamboo furniture lined the outer side of the patio where one could lean back on the sofa and look out at the ocean.

"I intend to sleep right here on this sofa," Tish said as she reclined into a lounging position.

As beautiful as the terrace was, I ran back inside to check out the bedroom. I hollered to Tish, "You can do that. I get this king-sized bed all to myself."

Tish came in and found me lying spread-eagled on the bed, and there was still plenty of room. With a running leap, Tish landed across my body. "Maybe you will share the bed when I get cold from sleeping outside."

Recuperating quickly from having her body slam across mine, I took advantage of having her on top of me. Trapping her with my one arm, I turned us both over where I could look down into her eyes. "I could live here forever with you."

We kissed, and I slid off Tish, allowing her to breathe. She laid in the crook of my arm, and we talked about how we landed here. "I did not realize people could be so grateful when we were just doing the right thing," I said.

Tish did not answer immediately. She snuggled up under my chin. "You know most people just look the other way. Maybe we are different."

"Well, if we are different, I am glad. I would hate to be part of a complacent world. I want to know there are other people like us out there who watch each other's backs."

"There are," Tish said. "The Jamiesons are like us. They care about other people. Captain Jones wouldn't be where he is today if he did not spend his whole career helping people. There are lots of good people in this world. You, however, are the best of the best."

Tish nibbled on my chin and let her tongue lick up my neck. It tickled and sent chills through my upper body.

"That was supposed to be erotic," Tish said with pretend offense.

"It would have been if it hadn't tickled. Here, let me try it on you," I said as I held Tish down and let my tongue lap her face.

"Stop!" Tish said between giggles. "You are like having a big old St. Bernard dog on top of me. I get your point. It isn't erotic at all. Stop it!"

We just laid together, giggling. Before long, Tish was sound asleep, and I was on my elbow watching her breathe. I could not be happier.

The phone rang and woke us both. It was a call from the desk. The manager wanted us to know he had taken the liberty to book scuba diving lessons tomorrow here in our hotel pool and outrigger canoeing for the next day. He suggested that we take cameras instead of spears for some snorkeling one day of our stay.

I thanked him profusely. I was overwhelmed with the hotel's generosity. I also wondered how he knew what all Tish wanted to do on this trip until I remembered all the brochures she laid out on the table when we first arrived. No doubt, the bellboy told the manager when he delivered the fruit basket and our new key cards.

Slipping out of bed, I decided the bathroom should be my next stop. I yelled, "Tish, get your butt in here."

As she scrambled to see what had excited me so much, I noticed Tish stopping in her tracks. Not only was there a jacuzzi pool, but there was also an actual mini-swimming pool in our bathroom! Both of us stood dumbfounded.

Stripping, we plunged into the pool and swam around like sea otters, laughing almost hysterically at our good fortune. There was no way our parents would believe where we stayed while in Hawaii.

Dinner was pleasant. Mr. and Mrs. Copley told us about their lives in England. He was a college professor, and she owned a book store. They said they saved for this vacation all their lives, and it would have been spoiled if we hadn't stopped the crooks.

It was getting embarrassing with the amount of praise and gifts being bestowed on us. Even in the dining room, people stared and whispered about the cute couple who saved the day.

All Tish and I wanted to do after dinner, was take a walk alone. We thanked the lovely English couple and told them we hoped they enjoyed island hopping. They said to look them up if we were ever in England. It was a nice gesture. We doubted that would ever happen.

Strolling along the beach as the sun was setting, I took Tish's hand. It was barely light enough to see. Few people were on the beach. One could see the silhouettes of surfers sitting on their boards waiting for the last wave. The breeze was warm, and I could hear the rustle of the wind through the palm trees. I stopped and pulled Tish down to sit beside me in the sand.

"This is just too beautiful for words," I said. I wanted to say something poetic since Tish would be impressed. Beautiful was the only word that came to mind.

"It is beautiful," Tish said softly. "I can see why people forget they are in the real world when they are here. It is hard to remember that some people can be bad, ugly, and mean when a person sits here looking out at the vast ocean."

"Where did that come from? Are you talking about those two thieves from today?"

Tish did not respond immediately. "No, I was thinking more about my past. I guess I continue to be nauseated by what my uncle did to me. He stole my innocence when he molested me. Worse than that, he has made it difficult for me to be open with you."

I did not press. I just waited to see if Tish would say more.

"I love you, Scotty. I want to express my feelings for you in every way that is possible...but I'm afraid."

"You are afraid of me?" I asked, somewhat confused.

"I am afraid that when you finally do enter me, that all I will be able to think about is how horrible it was when my uncle held me down and violated me," Tish confessed.

I was at a loss for words. How could I possibly change the horrible images that were in Tish's head from those times when her uncle abused her? What could I do to make it enjoyable and not evil?

I ventured, "Tish, I love you with all my heart and soul. My body aches for you. You are my major concern, and I don't want to hurt you ever. We don't need to have sex, at least, not until you are ready." Reaching out, I wrapped my arms around her. I held her close.

"But that is it, Scott. I want to have sex with you. I want you as much as you want me. I just want it to be only you who touches me. I am trying to find a way to wipe out my uncle from my mind. I don't want him to ever come between us."

I said, "I suggest we take it really slow. The minute you are not enjoying sex with me, tell me immediately, and I will stop. We have a lifetime to wipe out your uncle from your mind. It doesn't need to happen in the first try. It may take many, many tries. But, Tish, know that you are worth as many tries as it takes."

We sat looking out to sea and leaning against each just to feel the closeness that we both wanted desperately. I reached down and took

Tish's hand in mine. We sat quietly in each other's company until the light faded to darkness. We silently walked back to our penthouse, hand in hand.

The rest of our vacation was packed with adventure and thrills. Tish proved to be an exhausting partner. She wanted to go from one thing to the next as if she needed to fill this vacation with as much fun as possible. One evening, we went to a luau with the traditional pig cooked in the ground with hot rocks and poi. I did not enjoy the poi except when Tish fed it to me with her fingers.

When the Polynesian dancing began, Tish pulled me to my feet and demanded I dance with her. Tish's hips vibrated with incredible speed, whereas mine just…vibrated. Tish wasn't the only one laughing at me. The couples who were not brave enough to get up and make fools of themselves seemed to enjoy my lack of hip gyrations as particularly funny.

I must have looked ridiculous, but I did not care. I was enjoying the twinkle in Tish's eyes and the flush on her face. It was worth it just to know she was having a great time…even if it was at my expense.

We only had one more day and night in Hawaii. We had accomplished everything on Tish's bucket list and a few things that were not. When she asked me what I still wanted to do that we had not done yet, I said I wanted to go fishing. I am not sure she was expecting that for an answer. I have been an outdoorsman all my life. I had never gone fishing out in the ocean. Tish said, "Fishing it is."

We took a chartered fishing boat and headed toward the island of Lanai. Tish sunbathed out on the deck while I wished I had taken Dramamine. The rolling vessel was causing some nervous stomach problems for me. I was wondering why I suggested deep sea fishing.

Motoring near an aquaculture buoy, we fished with spincast reels and poles for Aku Skipjack. The Captain directed the mates to place the Aku fish we caught in the live bait well. The mates hooked two of our Aku's to their larger fishing rigs and trolled them behind the boat in the hope we would catch a swordfish, mahi-mahi, or ono.

I was in the head when I heard the first mate yell, "Fish-On! Fish-On!" I slammed the door open from the head and ran up the stairs while pulling up my shorts. I leaped over the back of the fighting chair, grabbing the pole in both hands; I set the hook as we practiced. Tish came around the side of the boat from where she was sunbathing. She screamed, "Yee Ha, Cowboy! Hold on tight and don't lose our dinner."

Wow! It seems like the more I reeled in, the more line the fish took back out, as it ran for the deeper waters. Just when the strain was starting to burn my forearms, the fish showed itself to be a large wahoo or ono as the islanders call them. Jumping madly out of the water, the ono zig-zagged from my left to right across the horizon.

My adrenaline kicked in, and I no longer felt the fatigue. I was determined to get this fish to the boat. Tish all the while was yelling encouragement in my ears.

Once the fish came near the boat, the first mate gaffed the fish. The second mate assisted in pulling the large, beautiful, iridescent dark blue-green fish with silver stripes on the sides, into the boat. As I approached the fish, I was greeted with high-fives from the deck mates and a hug from Tish. The captain yelled to us from above that this was the largest ono caught this year. The first mate brought a pendant out of the cabin that represented the ono catch and raised it up the flagpole.

I smiled at Tish and told her, "There's your dinner."

"That is an awful lot of fish for us to try to eat tonight," Tish said with her eyes wide open in amazement as she realized the fish was almost as long as she was tall.

The first mate laughed. "I will make sure that two thick steaks are cut and sent to your hotel kitchen to be prepared for your dinner. The rest will be inspected, canned, boxed, and sent to your room before you leave. It can be shipped on your airlines when you leave tomorrow.

When we got back to the hotel room, I was exhausted. I needed a hot shower and a change of clothes before I would be presentable for dinner. Tish asked if there was room for two in the shower.

"Get your butt in here. The water is great," I said. There was plenty of room in the shower as it had two separate shower heads and room enough for a small army.

We took turns lathering each other. Tish pressed her body up next to mine and slowly rubbed herself up and down my body. If I wasn't excited enough from the day, I sure was now.

"Is this an invitation, or are we just practicing for later?" I asked.

"Let's call this practice," Tish answered as she stood on her tip-toes and kissed me passionately. "It is also your reward for providing us with dinner."

It was difficult getting to dinner on time afterward. We told the cook we would be down for dinner at 7:00 p.m. We made it down at 6:59 p.m., squeaky clean and refreshed.

The ono is known for both its texture as well as its flavor. Ono means delicious in Hawaiian. The chef told us he has a unique and secret grilled recipe for ono that he would prepare just for us. Tish said it was the best fish dinner she had ever tasted. I had to admit she was right. The fact the fish was fresh and cooked to perfection might have been the reason. I like to think it tasted great because of all the effort it took me to land it. I would remember landing that fish forever. I even had a picture with the fish to prove I caught it and how big it actually was. I would not need to tell a fish story. I could show it.

We both hated to leave Hawaii and the best vacation ever. We were loaded down with presents for the Jamiesons and our parents. Not only did we have canned fish for them, but we also found some wood carvings that we felt would be perfect for their home. Tish had a box of chocolate-covered macadamia nuts for Aileen and one for herself. She already told me to get my own if I wanted any because she wasn't sharing hers.

Tish slept most of the way home on my shoulder. I relived our vacation and our intimate talk. I wondered when Tish would be ready to take our involvement to the next level. I was ready last night. A promise is a promise, and I was not about to lose Tish by pushing. Tish was worth the wait, no matter how long.

The Jamiesons were waiting for us at the airport to take us home. They were surprised when we showed up with our luggage and boxes of canned ono. The surprise became joy when they found out several of the boxes of canned ono were for them. They assured us they would be able to get all of it into their van.

They could tell we had the time of our lives. We thanked them profusely. Patrick told us that seeing the pure joy on our faces was thanks enough. Tish and I knew he meant it.

CHAPTER TWENTY-NINE

We hadn't been home for more than a week or two when Tish announced her friend, Michele, needed her to come to our hometown for a mini-crisis. I offered to drive her. She said it was going to be a fast trip, and I should stay and get some work done for the Jamiesons. I hated for Tish to leave for even a couple of days, but she was right.

Tish was gone for only a day and a half. I told her it was hardly worth the drive home. She said it was a mini-crisis and no big thing.

It was a day later that Mom called to tell me Heather was missing. "Missing, what are you talking about?" I asked.

Mom said, "It is odd. She is just missing. None of her clothes, her car, or even her purse was gone...just Heather. Her disappearance is looking suspicious."

"Suspicious? What do you mean, suspicious?" I asked, knowing my mom could be dramatic.

"There was blood at the scene, but not a body!" Mom blurted out.

"Are you saying Heather was murdered?" I said with shock in my voice. It was difficult to believe what Mom was saying.

"No one knows anything except the blood is Heather's blood, and she is missing," Mom reported.

"Is Jack a suspect?" I found my words taking on a sour note as I asked this question.

"Of course, he is a suspect. With his dad as the sheriff, how far do you think the investigation will get?" Mom complained.

"Does he have an alibi?" I shot back.

Mom hesitated. "I don't know. I only know what I have told you thus far. The paper did not say whether Jack had an alibi. I can only tell you what I read and what the town gossip is."

With a million more questions forming in my head, I gave up since Mom had limited information. After hanging up the phone, I yelled to Tish.

"Tish, come here," I yelled down the stairs to the basement. Tish came up quickly to see what was wrong.

"What is it? You sound upset," Tish said as she took the last stair to the landing.

"Tish, Heather is missing, and there is talk she might have been murdered," I blurted out.

"Wait. Hold on. What are you saying? You are getting way ahead of yourself. Stop and start over," Tish directed.

"Mom just phoned and said Heather is missing. She did not take anything with her, and there was blood at the house. It was her blood. However, if there is nobody, there is no murder, right?" I asked, knowing Tish would know the legalities.

"Yes, officially, there is no murder without a body. So, Heather is considered missing. What exactly are you saying? What else do you know? How much blood? Where was the blood? You said nothing else was missing," Tish asked.

"I'm not saying anything. The newspaper reported Heather missing. It read no different than my mom reported to me...no clothes, purse or car were taken. Heather's body is gone. I guess the blood was in the bathroom. The newspaper said there was a large amount of blood. They do know it was Heather's blood.

I think Jack killed her and took her body far away. Maybe he buried her or dumped her body in the lake with weights to weigh it down." I was thinking about the worst-case scenario.

"Hold on, Scott. You are interjecting your personal feelings here and without any facts," Tish said with a calm voice.

"We do know Jack tripped Heather and killed her baby. We do know she sports bruises way too often. It is only a short hop to suspecting Jack as her killer," I said, getting angry.

"You don't even know that she is dead," Tish said as she walked into the kitchen and poured herself a glass of water. "Also, you don't even know for sure that he intentionally tripped her. Heather never filed a report with the police."

"She was living at Jack's parent's house at the time. Jack's father is the sheriff. He would never have believed Heather. Why would she even bother to file a report?" I was starting to get really riled up.

Tish took a sip from her glass. "Do you want to drive home and see if you can find out anything more?"

I said, "Maybe...."

Tish said she would hold down the fort if that was what I wanted to do. The subject was dropped.

I thought about whether it would be beneficial for me to go home and ask questions. I did not believe the sheriff would make much effort. He wasn't really a corrupt sheriff. He just wasn't motivated to make a case against his son, I suspected.

Would it help if I went and lit a fire under the sheriff? Would it help if I nosed around and found out whether Jack had an alibi? I wasn't sure where my questioning would lead. There was no timetable that I knew. How would anyone know if Jack had an excuse or alibi until death was confirmed and the time of death was known? I just knew that I felt as if I should do something. Maybe the first thing would be to find Heather.

I laid in bed next to Tish, unable to sleep, listening to her rhythmic breathing. She was sound asleep. I just kept trying to figure out where Heather might be if she was not dead. Then I would replay my suspicions that Jack killed her. It did not make sense. Why wouldn't Jack clean up the blood if he killed her? None of this made any sense at all. It was just before dawn when I finally dozed off.

Tish did not wake me. She let me sleep. A note was left saying she would be at the Jamiesons' office. I headed there myself after showering and having a quick breakfast of cereal and toast. I wanted to run all this past Patrick to see if he thought I should go down and nose around.

"Son, I think you are too close to the case. You are sure to make facts fit what you want and not see the situation through clear eyes. I think you should leave it alone.

You aren't still in love with this woman, are you? If you are, I might have a different opinion," Patrick advised.

I thought for a moment. "No, I am not in love with Heather. I know for certain I never was. She was just a high school crush."

I noticed Aileen and Tish stopped what they were doing and were listening. A smile crossed Aileen's lips. Tish's face was unreadable.

Patrick interrupted. "Then don't get involved with this case. I think you will just be hitting your head against a wall. It would be different if someone hired you to investigate Heather's disappearance. No one has, and no one will. Let it go."

Nodding my head in agreement, I thought, 'I wasn't being paid to chase this wild goose. I wasn't an avenging angel. In fact, there was no evidence that Jack killed Heather or that Heather was even dead. Patrick's advice made good sense to me. However, something still bothered me about the whole thing. I knew my mind was not going to give it a rest, at least for now.'

Aileen said at that moment, "We have another case we want you to focus on if you think you can give it your all."

Both Tish and I had our interest sparked. "What is it?" Tish asked before I could get anything out of my mouth.

"It is another insurance fraud case. You have proven to be tenacious enough to follow every lead even if it means hours spent at the courthouse. Are you interested?" Aileen asked.

"You bet we are." I beat Tish to the punch this time. I looked to her for an agreement.

"Well, it seems a lady has turned a claim into her insurance company. She told them a burglar broke into her house and stole a $500,000 diamond necklace. The police felt the scenario surrounding the break-in seemed contrived. The insurance company is paying the claim. Now it seems they would like to investigate this woman. They have their investigators on the case as well. Nevertheless, they need more surveillance time, and their current investigators are too busy to spend time sitting in a car or tailing this woman," Patrick added to what Aileen had started.

Tish asked, "So, they want us to sit and watch to see if a fence comes to her house or whether this lady leaves to fence the diamond herself, right?"

Patrick nodded his head, indicating the answer was yes to her question. "That is about the size of it. No going to the courthouse. It means going to all the pawn shops and finding out where else a woman might pawn such a valuable diamond necklace."

"Have you considered that this woman may have sold the necklace before she reported it stolen? It is also possible she has no desire to sell it at all, and it might be safely stored somewhere in her house forever. How would we investigate without breaking and entering her house to prove or disprove this possibility?" Tish again asked.

"Yes, breaking and entering would be unreasonable. As private investigators, it never pays to break the law, or the law enforcement will stop being of any assistance, and they may become a hindrance.

So, no breaking and entering…got it? That leaves getting close to this woman."

Tish again was first to ask the question. "Do you know anything about her that may be of any help to us and the investigation?"

Aileen answered this question. "Her name is Mrs. Latimer. She is a widow and inherited a large amount of money in a trust fund when her husband died. It seems she was a trophy wife. There was a significant difference in their ages. The necklace was a gift from him.

"What we do know for sure is she loves animals and gives to many charities that support them. She is particularly interested in African elephants and stopping poachers and the illegal ivory trade. We also know that she has kept her luxurious lifestyle even though she lives off her trust fund. We suspect she is spending more each month than she is getting paid and may need extra income.

This may be a case where you will need to divide and conquer. One of you needs to do surveillance while the other finds a way to get to know Mrs. Latimer personally."

Tish volunteered, "I think I should get to know her personally by plugging into the charities she supports, and Scott should do the surveillance."

"Wait," I said. "Why should I be the one sitting in the car or truck all the time?"

Tish answered, "I know more about animals than you do. You would need to bone up way too much to be convincing."

I had to agree that Tish was right, as usual. My family had a pet dog once, and that is about all I know about animals. My time was spent on sports, whereas Tish spent a lot of time at the zoo and even took horseback riding lessons for years. Now that I think about it, Tish would try to get me to go out to someone's farm during the summer to help do chores. There was no way I was giving up my summer to feed animals and clean out stalls.

"You have a point. I will do the surveillance, and you get to know the lovely, rich, Mrs. Latimer," I said a bit begrudgingly.

Patrick said at this point in the discussion, "We felt you two would come to this conclusion. We have already taken some steps to provide Tish with a plausible cover. Captain Jones is good friends with the Mayor, and the Mayor is also one who supports animal rights campaigns. He will be willing to make an introduction to Mrs. Latimer at a charity fundraising event that will be held this Friday evening. It is a black-tie event. Tish will need an evening gown. Aileen will shop with you to find one, Tish."

I could see Tish starting to regret her decision to be the one that would get close to Mrs. Latimer. Tish hates dressing up. I laughed out loud at her discomfort and got a nasty look in response. Rubbing it in a bit more was necessary to alleviate my annoyance at having to sit in a hot car all day.

"Make sure you find some really high heels to go with that gown," I said with a smirk.

Looking at me with disgust, Tish said to Aileen, "Maybe we can go shopping right now."

I knew she wanted to put some miles between me and my grinning face. I laughed harder as they left the room and headed for the car.

Patrick took all this in with a smile. "Scott, I suggest you start to nose around pawnshops. Remember, if Mrs. Latimer has fenced the necklace already, the necklace will not be obvious. There is no way it will be at a counter. You will need to ask some questions to see if the owner will give you some leads."

I nodded. I understood what Patrick meant. I knew it was not going to be easy to convince anyone that I would be able to buy a $500,000 necklace. I wasn't the least bit sure how I was going to get information from the pawnshop owners if they had any information to give.

After spending the entire day driving from pawnshop to pawnshop looking at diamond necklaces and asking questions as to whether the owner had anything more expensive, I gave up. There were some pretty diamond necklaces, but nothing as exquisite as Mrs. Latimer's necklace. Anytime I would ask leading questions, I got nowhere. None of the pawnshop owners acted as if they knew of something expensive being for sale. That did not mean they were unaware.

I returned to Patrick and Aileen's office to find Tish and Aileen sitting at the table. There were several boxes and one long plastic-covered dress on a clothes hanger, evidence that the shopping trip had been successful.

"Hey, let me see the dress and shoes," I said with the same annoying grin on my face.

Aileen immediately said, "Tish is going to be gorgeous. We found the most incredible evening gown and the perfect shoes and purse to go with the gown."

Aileen quickly went to the hanger and removed the plastic protective cover revealing a black sequined covered dress with a scooping neckline.

"Whoa! I can't wait to see that on you," I said to Tish, not taking my eyes off the dress.

Aileen turned the dress to reveal the back. I thought the front was daring. The backline of the dress scooped even lower than the front. I was trying to imagine how much it was going to expose of Tish's muscular back.

"Put it on. I really want to see you in it." I was almost salivating.

"You will need to wait until Friday evening," Tish said. "After all, I will need an escort. Patrick isn't available...that leaves you. We have an appointment for you to get fitted for a tux and dress shoes."

Now it was Tish laughing at my discomfort.

"No way! I am not going to wear a tux. Once was enough. This is not prom night all over."

Even Patrick was laughing at my discomfort. What a shock…men don't stick together like women always do.

CHAPTER THIRTY

Tish was gone all Friday afternoon. Aileen set up appointments for her hair, her fingernails, and even her toenails. I, on the other hand, sat outside Mrs. Latimer's house until she also went out to get her hair done. I followed along, like a puppy, to her appointment, hoping she would not notice the truck following her.

Finally, my surveillance was done for the moment, and I rushed home to get dressed. Patrick picked up the tux and dropped it off at the house. The formal wear was waiting for me to put on after my shower and shave.

Tish arrived home while I was showering. I came out wrapped in a towel to find Tish struggling to get into her tight, black gown.

"Here, let me help," I said as I advanced towards her to button the few buttons at the small of her back. She leaned over to adjust her bust into the gown.

"How are you going to keep those puppies inside that low neckline?" I asked with real curiosity.

"Oh, stop it. I am not going to be falling out, exposing myself. We, women, have a few secrets," Tish said with a wink.

"No, really, how are you going to keep your boobs inside that dress?" I was starting to worry every man at the fundraiser would get a look at the goods. It was bad enough they would be getting a peek.

"If you really need to know, Aileen has a special tape that will keep my boobs from flopping out," Tish said with some disgust. I couldn't tell if the disgust was from my question or that she needed to tape her boobs. I decided to drop the subject.

"You look fabulous!" I said as I stepped back to take in the full view. "You look even better than on our Senior Ball night, and you were a total knockout then. Now, you are better than a total knockout. Let me think of a word…"

I was racking my brain for the perfect word when Tish stepped over and snatched my towel. "Scotty, pick up your face. You look fly, too," she said, looking down at my tight end and winking. "But you had best get dressed. Our limo will be here in a few minutes."

"Limo!" I said with excitement. "We get to ride in a limo? That almost makes it worth having to wear this tux."

"Yes, you don't think I can arrive in 'Big Red', do you? And there is no way I could ride on my Harley in this dress," Tish said without humor.

I, on the other hand, found myself laughing as I pictured her on her Harley in her black gown, with her perfect hair-do coming undone in the wind.

We were both dressed and ready to go when the limo arrived. I was disappointed we were still too young to be allowed to take advantage of the bar. Just how often would I get a chance to ride in a limo anyway?

Arriving at the hotel where the fundraiser was taking place, we were met by the mayor. He introduced himself even though we both already knew who he was.

"Before going in, I need to put this necklace on you," he said.

He pulled out a sparkling sapphire and diamond necklace. "This is my wife's. I am entrusting you with something very special to her. If you lose it or if it is stolen, my goose will be cooked."

"It is beautiful…why are you loaning it to me?" Tish asked.

I was starting to think Tish was not as bright as I gave her credit. "It is for the trap, right?" I blurted out.

"Let's say it is bait." The mayor corrected my word. "There is a possibility, according to the police, that a jewelry 'fence' runs in these circles. My wife has never worn this necklace in public in Chicago. It won't be recognized. However, it is extremely valuable, and the jewelry 'fence' will realize that. It could also give you an opening into a conversation with Mrs. Latimer."

Tish was nodding her head that she fully understood. "Will I give it back to you after the fundraiser? I sure don't want to be held responsible for keeping this necklace safe beyond this evening."

"Yes, I will meet you at your limo again when the fundraiser is over. My wife will be keeping a close eye on it all night. She is already inside. If an attractive blond lady keeps edging up to you, it will just be Maddie making sure the necklace clasp is on tight."

I recognized Mrs. Latimer from our surveillance. Tish reviewed several newspaper clippings from other charitable gatherings at the office. She also knew what the target looked like. We entered with the mayor and mingled for a few minutes. The mayor guided us slowly toward Mrs. Latimer; we finally were in front of her.

"Wendi, I want you to meet Tish and Scott. Tish is visiting Scott from New York. She is also an activist for the African elephant. I thought the two of you should meet since you share a common passion," the mayor said as he stood around, making sure the introduction led to more conversation.

Mrs. Latimer shook hands with both of us. Giving me a once over, with approval, I might add, she turned her attention to Tish. "You are an animal lover, too? This whole room is jammed with animal lovers like us. The mayor must be impressed with your efforts to bring you to my attention."

My antennas went up. Why was Mrs. Latimer suspicious? Was the introduction too obvious? I was getting nervous.

"Come on, Scott. Let's let the women chat. I will show you where you can get Tish and yourself a drink." And with those words, the mayor pulled me away. Tish was now on her own.

I kept looking over to where I had left Tish and was relieved to see the two women chatting and laughing. Maybe Mrs. Latimer, Wendi, wasn't suspicious. Perhaps she just talks like that.

The mayor had told me to give them some space before taking Tish her drink. He told me they needed plenty of time to get to know each other. He was hoping Tish would be able to make a date for coffee or tea or something to continue their budding relationship.

I was just about to go over when Tish came to my side. "Is this drink for me?" she asked as she took the champagne glass from my hand. Sipping from the glass, Tish added, "this sparkling cider is delicious."

"So, how did it go?" I asked, barely concealing my curiosity.

"I will tell you later in the limo. I don't want anyone to overhear us here. Remember, this room is full of Mrs. Latimer's friends, and acquaintances and gossiping is one of their favorite past times." Tish cautioned.

We mingled with several other couples and finally sat down to dinner. A movie was presented while we ate, telling the plight of the African elephant. The speaker was a well-known elephant researcher from Nairobi, Kenya, that everyone knew except for me.

I was touched by the presentation. If I had any money, I would have pulled out my wallet right then and there. Mrs. Latimer took the podium.

"I have already made a pledge of $500,000 to this worthy cause. I challenge all of you to reach deep into your pockets and make a pledge. Together, all of us can make a difference." She talked on for several more minutes, and applause ended as the next speaker took the podium. Unfortunately, for me, the talks went on for what seemed like hours.

Tish jammed her elbow into my ribs when I started to doze off. I was immediately on alert. Finally, the evening ended.

The mayor was true to his word and met us at the limo. Discreetly, he removed the necklace and handed it to his wife. She seemed relieved to have it back in her possession.

"Thank you for loaning the necklace to me," Tish said with a gracious smile. "It worked like a charm." A few more words were spoken, and the mayor and his wife left for their own ride.

I was more than curious. When we got inside the limo, I asked. "What do you mean it worked like a charm?"

Tish explained that she told Mrs. Latimer after the researcher's compelling talk, she felt obligated to give money to the cause. Tish went on to say to me that she told Mrs. Latimer all her funds were tied up in other investments. The only item worth anything was a necklace that she could sell. The next thing that happened was Mrs. Latimer introduced Tish to a man named Maurice. It turns out he buys and sells jewelry and has contacts all over the world. A date was made for him to estimate a value and give an offer.

I was wondering how Tish was going to get her hands on the necklace again. The mayor's wife looked way too happy to get it back into her hands. I doubted whether the mayor's wife would allow the jewelry to be taken for the evaluation and appraisal meeting.

I was about to ask more questions when Tish said, "Wendi and I have a date to meet for tea. I believe she might tell me how to obtain the most money when selling the necklace. It is a long shot, but it is all I have at this moment. Obviously, I can't sell Maddi's necklace."

I agreed with Tish's assessment. I doubted she would ever get her hands on the necklace again. Tish needed to work fast if she was going to get anywhere with Mrs. Latimer before her appointment to have the jewelry appraised.

"When are you meeting for tea?" I asked.

"We agreed on, tomorrow. We won't be going out. I was invited to Mrs. Latimer's house for tea. That will be much better. We can talk more candidly.

"I just wish I had a better ride to take to her house. I guess I could ride my Harley, and maybe Wendi would just think I was adventurous and fun-loving."

"You are adventurous and well, maybe not fun-loving." I needed to poke some fun at Tish. It had been a long, boring night for me. I needed to lighten up the evening a bit.

"What do you mean I am not fun-loving. Didn't you have fun with me in Hawaii?" Tish said defensively.

"No, you tried to kill me in Hawaii," I said with fear in my voice. "I remembered too vividly all the dangerous stuff we did in the name of fun. Your idea of fun is out and out scary."

Tish laughed and gave me a kiss. It was a good thing the limo was pulling into our driveway, or the kiss may have become a necking session. I wished we had many miles left before reaching home. I would have enjoyed a necking session in the back seat of a limo. When will I ever be in a limo again?

The next morning, early, we got a phone call from our fathers. They are always early to work.

"Did we wake you kids?" Cliff asked.

"Tish said with a yawn. "Yes, Dad, you did. We were up really late last night at a fundraiser for the African elephant."

"My, my, my, aren't you getting all snooty on us po folks," Tish's father said with a laugh.

"It is a new case we are working on. Believe me, I did actually enjoy it," Tish added with a yawn.

"What is on your mind, Dad?" Tish asked.

"Gabe is here with me. He sends his love to you both as do the Moms." Cliff said with Gabe's voice being heard in the background.

"Give them our love, too. Now, what is going on? You sound as if you have something important on your mind," Tish continued.

"Gabe and I have a surprise for you guys. We will be driving it over today if anyone is going to be home," Tish's dad said with excitement in his voice.

"What do you mean, driving 'it' over?" Tish asked.

"We have a surveillance van for your work." Cliff could hardly contain himself.

In the background, Tish could hear Gabe saying, "Tell her more about the van."

Cliff said, slightly muffled as he held his hand over the phone piece. Cliff spoke to Gabe, "Hold on, Gabe. I was about to do that, but I did not want to spoil the surprise."

Back onto the phone, Cliff roared, obviously excited. "It is a 1976 Ford Econoline van. We researched what would be the best surveillance van and how it should be equipped. Anyhow, Gabe and I built a special engine and electrical system, surveillance video equipment, and computer system. We are very proud of this work, and it may lead to another market for our business. We will be at your place, mid-afternoon. To save on insurance costs, we will return home in either 'Big Red' or the '55 Ford; we'll let you decide."

Chatting a few more minutes, we hung up. Barely had the phone been put down when it rang again. Tish answered on the second ring.

I could hear Captain Jones's voice in the distance. I saw Tish's face blush and knew she was embarrassed about something. The phone conversation lasted about a minute. When she hung up, I asked what Captain Jones wanted.

"It seems the mayor phoned Captain Jones very early this morning. He told him about my meeting Maurice and asked the captain to check him out," Tish commented.

"So why were you blushing?" I asked.

"I just felt stupid," Tish admitted. "I should have thought to call Captain Jones first thing this morning myself."

"Duh, you were occupied with our fathers. You could not have called him any earlier. You have nothing to feel embarrassed about," I said, feeling a bit exasperated that Tish would put pressure on herself.

"We did not need to sleep in longer. I should have set the alarm and called Captain Jones by 8:00 a.m.," Tish said, not giving herself a break. I knew better than to keep this line of conversation running.

"What time is your meeting with Wendi?" I asked to change the subject and to plan the day.

"She asked me to come over for lunch at noon. I still intend to ride the Harley. I hope she isn't expecting me to arrive wearing a sundress or anything fancy. I intend to wear my usual attire," Tish said reflectively.

I could tell she was mentally planning this meeting with Wendi. I let her think for a few minutes as I got up and made coffee and started breakfast.

Over my shoulder, I asked, "Is anyone else invited to lunch, or are you a solo?"

Tish startled a bit. She was entirely lost in rehearsing how she would bring up the necklace and other details. "I think it is going to be just me. Do you think I should wear a sundress and ask Patrick to rent a sports car for me?"

I thought for a moment. "No, I think the Harley will give you a rather devil-may-care look. You can tell her you learned to ride a motorcycle while in Kenya. It was the best and cheapest way to get around the country, aside from riding a bicycle. You can also tell her a bike was out because you would not have been able to out-run wild animals or poachers for that matter. Make up some story about how we were going to tour part of Canada on motorcycles. What do you think of my cover story?"

Tish beamed and looked relieved. "Not bad, Scotty. I like the whole idea; it would explain my leathers. It makes me sound like a bad-ass."

"You are bad-ass," I said as I continued cooking our breakfast.

We ate our breakfast, and Tish took her shower. She was dressed in her usual all-black attire when she came out of the bedroom. It was several hours yet before she needed to leave. We sat down and talked about various scenarios. We figured the more angles we covered, the easier it would be to keep a conversation steered towards the necklace when Tish was in Mrs. Latimer's company.

"I really liked Wendi when I talked to her last night. She is passionate about her love for animals and keeping elephants safe for generations to come. I think she is the genuine article," Tish said after we stopped our role play.

"It is okay to like her. I think it is to your advantage since you won't need to pretend," I said, hoping to make her feel comfortable.

"I just hope that liking her does not cloud my investigation. What if I become too sympathetic to her?" Tish confided in me.

"Don't worry, Tish. It won't cloud your judgment. You have a job to do, and that is what you are doing. I would be out front watching the house except our dads are due to arrive, and someone needs to be at our home to greet them."

"And exactly, how would your sitting outside the house influence my judgment?" Tish said testily.

"I didn't mean that my sitting outside would help you to do the right thing. I am sorry if I implied that. I don't know what I meant. Just forget it, okay? I guess I was just trying to say I have your back." I found myself apologizing again. I wondered why Tish always put me on the defense. A guy would have known what I meant.

Tish left shortly after the discussion that got me in trouble. I heard the Harley take off into the street and wondered if Tish was going to stay in a bad mood while talking with Mrs. Latimer. I sure hope I did not screw things up too much.

I went downstairs and continued to work on some computer entries for the Jamiesons. I wondered if we would ever get all their cases entered into the computer. It made me realize how long the two of them had been in business together. They seemed happy and contented. Would Tish and I ever get to that point? I wondered.

I also found myself thinking about Heather even though I tried to block thoughts of her from my mind. I decided Jack would not have been stupid enough to kill Heather and not cover his tracks. Thinking this, I ruled out murder. It was more than likely Heather was on the run. What would have made her bolt so fast that she did not take anything? I started to think that maybe Heather planned this for a long time. Perhaps she had money and clothes stashed somewhere else. Heather would bolt when she decided it was time.

I wondered why I never asked Tish if she had heard anything about Heather when she made her quick trip to fix her best friend's dilemma. Of course, I knew why I had not asked her anything. Tish would be offended, and the last thing I ever wanted to do was anger, Tish. As much as I love her, she can be quite unfriendly when she is mad.

I did not realize time had passed until I heard the doorbell ring. Looking at my watch, it was already 3:00 p.m. It must be Dad and Cliff at the door. It is difficult to hear any street sounds from the basement. It was no wonder I was caught by surprise.

Rushing up the stairs, I opened the door to see Dad and Cliff grinning at me. "Is Tish here? We don't want to give the tour of the van until she is here," Dad said.

As curious as I was, Cliff blocked the door and said, "Not until Tish is here. Aren't you going to invite us in?"

I backed out of the doorway and opened the door wide enough for them to enter. "I'm hungry," I said. I forgot all about eating lunch. "How about if I order some pizzas?"

Cliff was the first to say, "Sounds good to me."

I went to the phone and ordered a couple of pizzas as my dad and Cliff made themselves at home. Dad was the first to use the toilet as Cliff sat on the sofa. I handed Cliff a soda and sat another one on the coffee table for when my dad made his exit from the bathroom.

"Hey, how come your bed is made, and Tish's bed is unmade? You are the sloppy one, not Tish. It should be the other way around," Dad said as he came down the hallway into the living area.

I turned every shade of red. Trying to think of how I was going to tell Cliff and my dad that Tish and I were sleeping together could be difficult. Just when I was about to put my foot into my mouth, I heard Tish's Harley coming into the drive.

"Saved by the Harley," I said out loud and kicked myself for being such an ass.

Cliff and my father got up, and we all went outside to meet Tish. Finally, I was going to get to see the van.

Tish was already looking the van over from the outside. The flat silver paint was beautiful.

"It is called 'Hot Rod Silver Matte' paint," Dad said.

Cliff added. "You notice that we did not make anything flashy on the outside. We know a surveillance van should not draw attention to itself. No chrome or showy hubcaps for this van. You can park it anywhere, and no one is going to notice unless they look closely."

"Come on, let's get a closer look," my dad said as he got the keys out of his pocket and opened the door. "We will look at the engine soon enough. I am sure Tish would like a tour of the inside, first."

The inside was incredible. Tish jumped in and noticed the swivel chairs were locked down. They would not roll around during transit. Cliff stepped into the farthest seat to show her how to unlatch it from the floor. Now, Tish could sit next to Cliff's position at the console.

Afterward, Cliff scooted aside and sat behind Tish on a bench seat to let me join Tish inside the surveillance van. My dad peering through the back doors pointed out the features on the console.

"If you will open the cabinet to your left Tish, you will find a Macintosh PowerBook. Take it out and plug its connectors into the back of the console. You will also find a Sony Handycam® video camera that fits into the fixture in the Bubble Window in front of Scott.

"Scott, plug it into the fixture and attach the cables. Tish, if you will power up the Mac, and select the camera application, you will be able to see what is being viewed by the Sony Handycam®. The buttons on the side of the Handycam® will allow you to zoom in and out and record. Cliff set up another camera on the rear-view mirror. This camera is adjustable using the little remote-control unit on the console."

Cliff added, "Actually, you can adjust either camera by turning the camera switch next to the remote control. We will be adding two additional cameras, one at the rear of the van and a roof bubble camera that will be hidden by a roof equipment rack."

"Hey, I don't need a camera to see the pizza delivery guy heading this way," Tish interrupted.

"We don't really want anyone to see the van," Cliff said. "Gabe, quick head him off."

"Why is it that I always get stuck with the bill?" my dad said as he pulled his wallet from his back-jean pocket.

Returning with the two boxes of pizza, he added, "Tish, reach into the refrigerator on your left and get out some sodas."

"Really! There is a refrigerator?" Tish said with awe.

"Not only is there a refrigerator, but there is also a sink and faucet under the top of the counter just above the refrigerator. You can access water when the faucet lever is turned on. The cabinet above the refrigerator contains paper supplies and food. You can thank your mothers later for the cups, napkins, plates, snacks, toiletries, and the other niceties like the curtains. Anything technical, we put in. Anything else the moms added," my dad said, giving credit where credit was due.

Both Tish and I were flabbergasted. The expense alone would be insurmountable for us. "This is all extremely expensive. How are we going to repay you for it all?" I said.

Gabe commented, "You haven't seen the half of it yet. Wait until we show you the engine."

We all jumped out of the van and walked to the front. Gabe opened the hood, and Cliff explained what was inside. "We custom-built a Ford 302 with a turbo and a special pre-oiler to allow the engine to be idled for long periods. The alternator produces 200 amps for recharging the engine battery and the two 70 amp/hour batteries for the surveillance equipment, toilet, and the pump for the sink."

"Toilet? How did I miss the toilet?" Tish asked as she ran around the van to the back doors and opened them wide, revealing the closet at the rear of the interior on the left. Opening a closet door, Tish found the RV toilet.

Laughing, Tish said, "You have to be kidding. You included everything...even the kitchen sink. This is wonderful. There is no reason for you to complain about surveillance anymore, Scott. And oh, by the way, you will need to sit to pee, just like me."

"No way. I can stand and pee from the console," I bragged.

Still laughing, Tish added, "No using this toilet for number twos. There is no way you could keep our surveillance a secret with that stink!"

Cliff, who was also laughing at his daughter's wit, said, "We can explain anything else while we eat that pizza before it gets soggy. I hate soggy pizza."

Locking up the van, we walked to the house where we broke open the box of pizza. As we each took a piece, I asked my dad about getting a loan to pay for the van.

He laughed, "This is a present from all four of us. We don't expect for you and Tish to pay us back. This is an investment in your future. It is our pleasure to do this for you and Tish."

Tish hugged both of our fathers. "You are the best fathers in the whole world. Someday, we will repay you in some way."

I just nodded my head in agreement. I was too choked up to try to utter words of thanks.

At that very moment, my dad decided to reopen the conversation that I hoped he would have forgotten. "What's the story on the bedroom situation?"

Tish looked from my dad to me. "What are you talking about?"

"We noticed Scott's bed was made, and yours was a mess. As I remember, you always made your bed first thing when you got up, and Gabe claims that Scott never made his bed unless he was forced," Cliff said, looking Tish in the eyes.

"Oh, is that all," Tish said nonchalantly. "I have been getting after Scott to make his bed immediately when he gets up. Today, he told me to leave my bed. He would change and wash the sheets since I needed to get ready for lunch with Mrs. Latimer, the person we are investigating."

I was taken aback by how quickly Tish came up with a cover story under pressure. I was flabbergasted how easily she lied to her father and with a straight face. There was no tells as far as I was concerned. She was a competent liar, and I was unnerved but impressed.

"We need to get going. Your moms are expecting us home this evening. Before we go, Tish, there is something I want to show you," Cliff said.

He reached into his pocket and pulled out a velvet pouch. "When you were telling us a bit about this new case you are working on over the phone this morning, I realized you might need this. You mentioned the expensive necklace loaned to you as bait, and you also said there was no way you would be able to use it to further this investigation.

I talked to your mother, and we both agreed to risk your inheritance if you want to risk it." With those words, Cliff pulled out the most fantastic cognac colored diamond I had ever seen.

"This is a ten-carat diamond that has been in our family since my great-grandfather brought it out of South Africa. When he came over to America in 1890, he passed it on to his son, who passed it on to your grandfather, and he passed it on to me. Now, we want to pass it on to you, especially if you can use it to catch the villains."

Tish was turning the diamond over and over in her hands. She seemed mesmerized by the color and clarity. "I never knew you had this diamond. Why didn't you ever show it to me before and tell the story behind it? This is family history…not just a diamond."

"It is yours now. Someday, if it isn't stolen from you during this investigation, you will hand it down to your son or daughter. That will be your decision. As I said, it is yours. You may do with it as you like. It is part of your inheritance. It is only right that you have it to further your career and business or…keep it for posterity."

"I can't accept this. You and Mom may need it in your old age," Tish started to say.

"We have you for our old age." Cliff laughed. "We plan to move in with you if things get too tough."

"I just don't know what to say. I am speechless," Tish said quietly.

"I guess we had better get out of here before she finds her tongue, Gabe," Cliff said, trying to lighten the moment.

Tish and her father embraced as my dad and Cliff exited the door. "Oh, which vehicle are we taking back with us?" Cliff asked.

"Big Red!" Tish said without hesitation.

"It looks like we weren't fast enough with our exit. Tish found her tongue," my dad said good-naturedly.

I tossed them the keys to the truck. I was going to miss 'Big Red'. I certainly was not going to give up the Double Nickel. I could not be too sad watching 'Big Red' pull away. The van was too incredible for words.

CHAPTER THIRTY-ONE

When we were alone, I asked Tish how things went with Mrs. Latimer. We were busy with touring the van; I had almost forgotten she had been gone all afternoon.

Tish started the conversation. "Wendi was great. We sat and talked for hours. She is so concerned about the African Elephant; she could talk of nothing else."

"So," I said, "you weren't able to broach the subject of the necklace at all?"

"Yes, I did get around to it in a backward way," Tish said.

I found it hard not to interrupt her to ask pertinent questions. I held my tongue and let her proceed at her own pace.

Tish continued her story. "I lied about being in Africa and told her how I was trying to chase and photograph poachers, with little results. She acted impressed. I suspect she would never have believed me if I did not arrive on the Harley.

Anyway, she said getting as much money as possible was imperative. I told her that I considered selling the necklace I wore to the charity fund event. I said I was feeling uncomfortable that I would not get enough money for it.

That is when she said something about getting double for her necklace." Tish paused.

This is crazy. I had to jump in, "You mean Mrs. Latimer admitted she committed insurance fraud?"

"Not exactly," Tish said, acting a little impatient that I interrupted her. "She said she knew of a way to get double the value for my necklace and asked if I wanted to pursue it. After all, it was for a good cause."

I did not interrupt this time. I just sat and waited for Tish to go on with the conversation she had with Mrs. Latimer. When she did not continue, I decided she was waiting for me to ask a question.

"And you said...?" Trying to get Tish to continue the story.

"I said I wanted to give as much as possible to save the elephants. I asked Mrs. Latimer what I could do. Her response was to tell me she would get back to me. That is how our lunch ended." Tish seemed exasperated.

"Good start, Tish. Mrs. Latimer sounds as if she is buying your story and seems to trust you. When she calls back, you can tell her you can't sell the necklace. Say you are too afraid that it will not bring the value that it is worth. Instead, tell her you own this fabulous pre-1900's cognac-colored diamond to sell. Pause for a few seconds, then tell her it is more valuable than the necklace; she should be interested enough to jump at the bait," I said, trying to sound both encouraging and supportive.

"I hope so. I really want to tell Wendi to come clean and help me set up the real criminal. She is such a nice lady, and all she wants to do is help save a magnificent creature. What is wrong with that?" Tish said.

"What is wrong? She is stealing money from the insurance company to fund her elephant campaign. Come on, Tish. I know you know she is doing something wrong. Don't go all soft on this case. Tish, Wendi is a criminal. She is the one that is being fraudulent even if it is for a good cause. She can't just walk."

I was starting to feel Tish was not going to make an outstanding private investigator if she was going to let her heart lead her head. I was puzzled by this new side to Tish. I have only known her to be practical, logical, and totally honest. How could loving animals cause her to rethink her values and morals?

"I know you are right, Scotty. I just wish there was a way I could keep Wendi from jail time." She stopped talking.

I was about to say something when she blurted out, "What if she turns herself in. I think she still has the necklace. If she comes clean to the insurance company, they may not press any charges against her."

"You will need to talk to Patrick and Aileen to see if they can intercede on her behalf with the insurance company, but first, you will need to find out if she has the necklace and whether she is willing to come clean."

Tish did not reply, she just sat quietly on the sofa and continued to think. I got up to make her a cup of tea to give her some space. I could tell she did not need to be crowded at this moment. She needed to do some soul-searching.

The next morning when Tish and I went to talk to Aileen and Patrick, I could tell Tish was still embarrassed about going soft on Wendi when we arrived in the office. It was fairly clear she wasn't sure how to proceed.

We sat down around the table in the office with cups of coffee and cinnamon rolls. Fortunately for Tish, Patrick was the first to ask how things were progressing with the case.

Tish explained what went on at lunch. She told the Jamiesons she did not feel Mrs. Latimer was an ordinary thief. Tish said she felt Wendi just wanted to do good for the animals, and she was using poor judgment.

"If Mrs. Latimer comes clean, do you think the insurance company would consider not pressing charges?" Tish asked pointedly.

"Are you saying she still has the necklace in her possession?" Aileen questioned.

"I really don't know. What I do know is it was not stolen. What I also know is Mrs. Latimer suggested I may be able to get double for the necklace I was wearing to the fundraiser. I told her I was interested. She is supposed to get in contact with me sometime soon," Tish told Aileen while avoiding eye to eye contact.

Patrick talked next, "Tish, this would be easier if you weren't too emotionally involved with Wendi Latimer and her cause. I know we told you to get to know her personally and to try to become friends. You must remember that you are not her friend. You are investigating her. You need to remain as neutral as you possibly can while acting as if you aren't neutral at all. It is a tall order, and I know, not everyone can do it."

Aileen tried to soften what Patrick had just said to Tish. "Both Patrick and I investigated cases that tugged at our hearts. It isn't easy to remain neutral. We understand from first-hand knowledge. This is going to be a learning experience for you. You may decide you aren't cut out to be an investigator, but we both feel you will be top-notch if you can become a good actress. Is this going to be too much for you? Patrick and I can take over the investigation if you want out."

"No," Tish said. "I can do it. I just wanted to ask you if you thought the insurance company would be willing to let her go or, at least, suggest clemency at her trial."

Patrick intervenes, "If you can get Mrs. Latimer to come clean and help us catch the jewelry fence, we will do everything in our power to help her, including asking the insurance company to plead on her behalf."

"Are you ready to try to get her on your side when she contacts you? Do you have a plan?" Aileen asked.

"I do have a plan, thanks to my parents," Tish said as she told the Jamiesons about the five-karat diamond given to her. "I plan to use it as bait. We all know Maddie is not about to let her necklace out of her sight again.

"I suspect Maurice, the gentleman Wendi introduced me to at the fundraiser, is the jewel thief and the fence. My theory is the women in this circle often want more money than their husbands are willing to give them. From what I surmise, they contact Maurice, and he breaks in and steals the jewelry. He gets a percentage of the jewelry value when he sells it to a buyer, and the women get their cut plus the insurance money," Tish confided.

"Did Wendi Latimer tell you this?" Patrick asked explicitly.

"Not in so many words. Mrs. Latimer told me some of her friends needed extra money. She later said their jewelry was stolen, and they got insurance money to cover the loss. Wendi went on to say her friends ended up with extra money, and Maurice's name was said in conjunction with the story. She never truly said Maurice stole the jewels, fenced them, or anything incriminating. It is just the way she said it that made me feel he is the culprit."

"I guess at this point, all you can do is wait for her phone call," Aileen said, offering more coffee. "I can't believe your parents gave you such an expensive stone to be used as bait. They must believe in you 100%, as do Patrick and myself. We know you can pull this off. We will do anything to help you."

Patrick said, "I think I know a way that will protect you and your diamond. We have a fully furnished, safe house that we have used for similar cases. I will give you the address and the combination to the safe. The safe has an alarm that will go off if the door is opened without the additional code. We will need some of your personal items, like magazines, a few pieces of clothing, and some pictures of you to place in the house to make it appear as if you live there.

Your job will be to lead Maurice into a discussion about how he can get you double your money on the sale of your diamond. Do you think you can do that?"

Tish agreed. "I know I can do it. I really want this to work out."

Tish and I declined the extra cup of coffee. We quickly told the Jamiesons about the surveillance van and asked them to come over and check it out. In the meantime, Tish needed to get back to the phone and see if Wendi Latimer called. If she had not phoned, I was going to put the van to use.

There was no phone message from Wendi Latimer when we got back home. It was decided that I should park the van nearby Mrs. Latimer's home. I will photograph anyone who arrives or departs.

I stayed watchful. The new technical surveillance system made it easy. I rotated cameras around and watched from as many different angles as possible to test and become familiar with the camera range.

The first day or two was exciting. By day number three, I was getting a bit bored. I ate all the snacks and even used the toilet a time or two. With Tish, not being in the van, I felt rebellious and did my duty. I was sorry I had. The fumes permeated the van, and I knew I was going to be in big trouble if I did not clean the toilet soon.

Returning home, Tish greeted me with excitement. Wendi Latimer phoned. She wanted Tish to meet with Maurice and suggested a meeting at her house the following day.

"That is great. Did Wendi say anything about her necklace?" I asked.

"No. What Wendi said, she is waiting for the insurance company to settle the claim. Once they do, she can give a big check to the *Nairobi Elephant Research* fundraiser. Wendi made a pledge, if you remember and challenged everyone else to do the same. She did say she hoped to get more money soon. I assumed she meant she would get more money once her necklace was sold by Maurice. You know what they say about people who assume…."

"Yes, I know. It makes an ass out of you and me," I ended the line for her. "Was there any mention of your necklace. I mean, the one you wore to the fundraiser?"

Tish said, "Yes, and I told her I was not ready to part with the necklace. I heard a long pause on the phone, and when Wendi did not say anything. I immediately told her about the diamond and how valuable it might be.

Wendi seemed relieved that I still had something of value to sell. I told her I would bring it along tomorrow for Maurice to see." Tish rubbed her hands together in a manner that suggested she was nervous.

"Tish, are you alright with all this? You could pull out, and we could let the Jamiesons take over the case. You have already provided some good leads," I said, trying to comfort her.

"No, I will see this one through all the way. I still have hopes I can convince Wendi to come clean on insurance fraud. The problem is, she has convinced herself she is doing the right thing by saving the elephants. Now I need to convince her she is doing the wrong thing for the right reason."

I knew this was difficult for Tish. I told her I would be sitting in the van the whole time watching her back. We came up with some signals if there was any funny business, and then we put the topic aside and watched T.V. to let our nerves calm.

The next morning very early, we phoned Aileen and Patrick. They said they would be over to discuss our plan and to see the new van. I suggested they come for breakfast, and I would make my world-famous blueberry pancakes.

Tish gave the tour of the van while I continued to watch the bacon frying and mixed up the pancake batter. I had the table set, and the syrup warmed by the time they came back inside.

"The van is great!" Patrick said with some envy in his voice. "Aileen and I could have used one all these past years. All the comforts of home, I see."

"Yes," said Tish. "And it seems someone is taking advantage of all the comforts of home. Scott, didn't we agree not to use the toilet for that purpose? It stinks in there."

"Oh, no. I thought it would air out, and I just had to go. I could not leave the surveillance to run down to the gas station. Something important might have happened while I was gone," I said rather sheepishly.

"You clean it, or I am not going into that van again!" Tish scolded.

Aileen laughed. "It wasn't that bad, Tish. I could hold my breath long enough for the tour. Thankfully, though, you cut it short. That was kind of you."

I needed to change the subject fast. "Breakfast is served." I was glad to see everyone still had an appetite. I did not dare mention that, or the haranguing would continue.

As we ate, we talked about the known details and the assumption that Maurice was the jewel thief and fence. Aileen and Patrick explained when assumptions could help the investigation and when it was detrimental. They both agreed being suspicious of Maurice was a good thing at this point.

"Everyone is a suspect until one proves they are not," Aileen said. "The fact that Wendi Latimer immediately introduced you to Maurice when you mentioned a contribution to the cause, especially since all you have is a necklace to sell, makes me mighty suspicious. However, he could just be a knowledgeable jeweler Wendi or her friends used in the past to appraise jewelry. Now it is time to see if you can push the envelope and find out who is the real Maurice."

Patrick said excitedly, "Tish, we have a way for you to prove everything. I can get a judge's warrant to record your meeting in less than two hours. We will wire you. Your conversations with Wendi and Maurice will be recorded. I can quickly set up the recording device in the van for Scott to use. Are you good with this?"

Tish nodded her approval for the plan. We talked about the details, and the Jamiesons said they needed to get going to put their part of the plan into action. They said they would be back with the recording device and the miniature transmitting microphone.

"I have my diamond with me. Do you want to see it?" Tish asked, excited like the schoolgirl she really was.

"Of course, I would love to see it. The history alone has me intrigued about this jewel. I think it is thrilling you have something that has been passed down for generations. I mean, wow! And the fact your parents never told you about it until just now is intriguing."

Tish brought the diamond out of its velvet pouch. After much exclamations of pleasure and both Patrick and Aileen turning it over in the light several times, it was back safely in the pouch to be used later in the day. I could hear some apprehension creeping into Tish's voice as the morning drew on.

The Jamiesons told us they needed to leave. We could get ready for the rest of the day, and they could do what they needed to do and be back to wire up Tish. Patrick and Aileen went to the front door. Before closing the door, Aileen had one more jab for Scott, "Clean out that toilet, Scott!"

I did not look at Tish. The last thing I wanted was to be reminded I ignored her toilet rule. I hurriedly gathered plates and glasses to take to the sink to wash. I did not really need to avoid Tish's eyes; she hadn't heard a thing Aileen said. She was lost in her own thoughts.

From the kitchen, I yelled, "Are you going to wear your motorcycle clothes again today?" I knew the answer. What else was she going to do? It was the only ride she had. I asked anyway to see if I could get through her shell.

"What did you say?" Tish asked distractedly. She walked into the kitchen and listened as I asked the stupid question again.

"What else would I do? Rent a car?" Tish said with sarcasm in her voice.

I should have left well enough alone. Tish was irritable and upset that Wendi might go to jail and her part in putting Wendi there. She was not going to be a happy camper unless she could convince Wendi to do the right thing.

Tish went to the bedroom to find her best riding outfit. I knew she would be wearing her expensive studded boots when she came back out.

"As much as I paid for these boots, they are still not as expensive as what Wendi wears to scuff around her house. She is going to know that I don't have money." Tish was getting herself upset.

"Tish, you never said you had money. You have only said you have a passion for stopping the illegal ivory trade. Why do you think you need to present yourself as a rich bitch?" I questioned.

I could see Tish relax. "You are right. I never said I was rich. I said I bummed around Africa trying to get footage of poachers. The fact that I am supposed to live in New York doesn't mean I am rich. You are right, Scotty. I don't need to act rich at all. I just need to continue to act as if I care for her cause as much as she does. I don't know why I got side-tracked."

I gave Tish a big hug. I could feel her melt into my arms. I guess I did the right thing for once.

CHAPTER THIRTY-TWO

The Jamiesons were good to their word. Aileen and Patrick returned within two hours with the mini-mic to wire Tish. A policeman accompanied the couple. Captain Jones felt it would make everything more legal to have an officer involved at this point in the case. Luckily, it was Tony.

"We are off on another adventure, are we?" Tony said as he entered the house. "I got the short straw. I am afraid I am stuck with you today."

I grasped Tony's hand. "Welcome aboard. Wait until you see the surveillance van our fathers put together for us. Oh, gosh, that reminds me. I will be right back."

I ran to the garage and got a bucket. I filled it with water and took it to the van to put down the toilet. I read in the manual our fathers left for us that diluting the poop with a bucket of water would help eliminate the odor. I ran back into the house and found a few candles Tish had bought for our own bathroom and ran back out the door to light them in the van.

I returned, not out of breath, but flushed. I entered to see Tony and Tish involved in a conversation. I was glad no one was looking at me as I returned. There was no way I wanted to explain to Tony why I was embarrassed.

"Don't worry, Scott," Tony remarked. "Tish explained your odd behavior. I appreciate your social graces. From what Tish said, I would have passed out within minutes if you did not try to air out the van." Both Tish and Tony started laughing, and unfortunately, my flush returned.

Aileen had the wire in place, and Tish was set to leave. She still had a half-hour before she was to be in place. That gave us time to go out to the van and to make sure the recording device was working. Patrick braved the van after seeing how much effort I was putting into making it smell like flowers.

Patrick showed Tony and me the dials to increase the sound. We both had headsets to listen in on the wire. Patrick assured us we would be able to hear fine. He warned us, when we parked, to always wear the headsets. He did not want anyone eavesdropping. Wendi's neighborhood was quiet and peaceful.

Patrick put a finger to his mouth to shush us. We were listening to Tish and Aileen speaking from the kitchen.

"Tony is such a nice young man," we heard Aileen saying to Tish.

"He is the best," Tish replied to Aileen.

Teasing, I nudged Tony in the ribs and whispered, "you're the best." We both laughed until we noticed Patrick giving us the evil eye.

"I hope the two of you are going to take this seriously. This is important to get the conversation between Maurice, Wendi, and Tish recorded. It is vital to the case," Patrick said firmly.

We both stopped laughing and sat up straight. "Yes, Sir!" I could not resist one more joke, and Patrick smiled. Patrick was straight and narrow, but not without a sense of humor.

We recorded the conversation between Tish and Aileen. Playing it back, we were convinced the recorder was working correctly. Patrick offered to come along in the van just in case we had trouble with the recording device. "Sure, the more, the merrier," I said, sensing Patrick was more likely coming along to make sure Tony and I did not goof around too much.

"We are all set. Your voices came through loud and clear," I said as I entered the house. "Are you ready to head out, Tish? Got your diamond tucked safely inside, ummm."

Looking Tish over, I could see lots of curves in all the right places. I did not observe any bulge where the diamond should have been. Believe me, as tight as Tish's motorcycle riding clothes were, one should be able to see anything.

"Turn around. I want to make sure your wire is not showing through those tight clothes," I said, just wanting a good look at Tish's behind.

Looking over her head as she turned, Tish said. "Scotty, the mic is not hidden in my crack if that is what you are looking for."

"Just admiring the view," I said. "I don't see the mic anywhere. Where did you put it?"

"If you must know, Aileen put it in my bra," Tish said with a wink. She knew that would drive me crazy...as well as Tony.

"Where is your diamond?" I said. "I don't see any bulges that aren't supposed to be there."

Tish picked up her leather jacket. She patted a zipped-up pocket in front. "Right here, dumbass."

"I love it when you talk dirty to me," I said.

"Got to run. Remember our signal if things get a bit hairy?" Tish said, reminding me.

For a second, I was stumped. "Oh, yes, you will say I have a headache. I think I need to leave. Is that right?"

"You got it," Tish said reassured that I remembered. "And if I say that, you come in with guns blazing."

I nodded my head, gave Tish a quick kiss, and she was out the door. I grabbed a bag of snacks and headed to the van with Patrick and Tony just ahead of me. We were determined to make this happen, was the thought going through my head.

We pulled up on the street, the opposite side of Mrs. Latimer's house and parked. I quickly and quietly made my way to the back of the van where Tony and Patrick were seated. Patrick was in the furthest control seat, and Tony was sitting on the bench, leaving me the left control seat. I powered up the computer and video cameras, aiming both cameras on Mrs. Latimer's house and driveway. Patrick turned the recorders on for both audio and video.

In the house, Tish was ready and waiting for Maurice, who had not yet arrived. Wendi and Tish were chatting like old friends. We heard Wendi say, "I hear Maurice's car arriving."

Sure enough, a loud engine from a costly sport's car could be heard coming down the street. It turned into Mrs. Latimer's driveway and parked right behind Tish's Harley.

"Look at those wheels," Tony said in a hushed voice. "That must have cost him a pretty penny."

I was pretty sure how he could afford to buy such a cool ride. I knew it was foreign made but wasn't exactly sure what it was. I was about to ask Tony when Patrick gave me a sign to keep very quiet.

I zoomed the side camera in on the person exiting the car to verify it was Maurice and to capture the license number. I recognized him from the fundraiser.

Maurice entered the house. Reintroductions were made in case Maurice did not remember meeting Tish at the fundraising event.

He got right to the point and wanted to see the diamond. As he examined it, we could hear him saying how near-perfect it was. The color, the clarity, and hardly any imperfections were words he was using to describe the diamond. He went on to say the value approximately $300,000. He added it could be worth more to an enthusiastic buyer.

Tish asked him how he found his buyers and what percentage of the selling price would Maurice exact. Maurice answered Tish's questions. He then added, "Do you just want the value of this diamond, or would you like double?"

We froze. Now, we were going to get the incriminating conversation on the recording device.

"As you know, Wendi and I are trying hard to stop the ivory poaching trade to save the African elephant, and we need every penny we can scrape up. So, how does this work?"

'Smart girl,' is what I thought as Tish said those words. Now, he needed to explain in detail, and we would have him.

Maurice said. "Simple. I break into your house and steal the diamond just like I did for Wendi. You make a police report and file a claim with your insurance company. In the meantime, I will find a buyer for the diamond and get the highest price I can. It may take a couple of weeks. Your patience will be rewarded with $540,000 to donate to the charity or to do with as you please.

"Do you want to take the double? If so, just give me your address and let me know when you will be out of the house for an evening."

Tish was silent. We were not sure what was happening. We were on pins and needles waiting to hear a voice saying something.

"Great," Maurice said. "I guess you have a safe. Write down the combination. I promise I will make it look like a break-in. The insurance company will never be suspicious.

"When will you be out of the house for an evening? The sooner, the better."

Tish was quiet again. I could only guess she was writing down the combination to the safe and the address to the safe house.

"I will be gone tomorrow evening if that works for you," Tish said.

Wendi Latimer had been silent through much of the exchange. When Maurice announced he needed to go, Wendi once again took the lead in the conversation, thanking Maurice for coming as she showed him to the door.

As Maurice fired up his car and drove away, we were listening to see what Wendi and Tish would say next. Instead, it was silent.

Patrick fiddled with the controls and turned to us and said, "Tish turned off the microphone. Why would she do that?"

I knew exactly why she turned it off. I did not say a word. It was not up to me to explain what Tish was doing.

We waited for another half hour, and finally, Tish came out, got on her Harley, and drove away. Discreetly, we followed. Arriving home, we went inside to find Tish and Aileen sitting down with iced tea.

"Why did you turn the mic off?" Patrick asked as we went through the front door.

"Dear, sit down and have a glass of iced tea with us," Aileen said to her husband.

All three of us came in and sat down while Aileen poured three more glasses of iced tea and passed them around to Tony, Patrick, and myself.

Patrick was staring straight at Tish and did not bother to pick up his glass of tea. Tony and I both gulped a big drink down, feeling uncomfortable for Tish.

"Stop glaring, Patrick. Tish has her reasons. Go ahead, Tish. Read in, Patrick and the boys," Aileen said calmly.

"I told you I like Wendi and don't feel she is a criminal. I turned the mic off. I wanted to talk frankly to her." Tish paused, taking a sip of tea to stall.

"And?" Patrick said impatiently.

"I told her I was undercover, and I did not want her to go to jail. I explained if she gave up Maurice and the other women who perpetrated fraud, she could get a reduced sentence or even probation.

Since Wendi hasn't taken any money, the insurance company may not press charges. I also mentioned that if she decides to discuss anything with Maurice, that I personally would walk her to the prison gates."

Again, Tish hesitated. Seeing none of us were going to interrupt her to ask questions, she continued, "Wendi started crying. She already pledged the money to save the elephants, and now she wasn't going to be able to make her pledge.

"I asked her what happened to the necklace, and she told me Maurice sold it. She should receive $400,000 from the sale of the jewelry soon. Unfortunately, that would not cover her pledge."

Tish stopped again. This time I needed to say something, "Wendi isn't upset about going to jail. She is upset because she is missing $100,000 for her pledge?"

Tish confirmed, "That is right. Mrs. Latimer hasn't received the insurance money yet, so…there is no giving it back. She is willing to admit the theft was an enactment and turn in Maurice. She is less willing to tell us which women in her group also used Maurice to steal their jewelry."

Tony jumped in, "I am not going to let her off that easy. Heck, even if Mrs. Latimer does not provide more names, once we pick up Maurice, he will probably squeal on the women himself. I should phone Captain Jones and tell him what we have on tape."

Tony jumped up and went to the phone. The rest of us sat around the table and quietly talked about the details of the case. When Tony came back from communicating with the captain, he said, "It is a go, from our end. We will have plain-clothed police in place to catch Maurice as soon as the alarm goes off. This will just be one more nail in his coffin, figuratively speaking."

Tony excused himself and left while the rest of us made a few more plans. Aileen asked Tish to gather a few personal items that could be placed strategically around the safe house. Patrick told me as Tish was doing as Aileen asked, that our part in the case was now over. "We will take things from here. You two have done an incredible job. We are really impressed and proud of both of you."

Tish and Aileen came back to the table. I said, "Patrick was just saying how proud he was of our efforts, but it is time for us to let them take it from here."

"But," Tish said. "I need to talk to Wendi to make sure she will do what I told her to do."

Aileen interrupted. "I've got this, Tish. I have a friend who is a lawyer, and I know she will be willing to go over with me and talk to Wendi. We will make sure she does the right thing and give her advice. I am sure Mrs. Latimer has her own lawyer, but for your sake, we will intercede and make her see reason.

"Patrick, do you have the Cub tickets on you? You said you would bring them along to give to Tish and Scott." Aileen finished her sentence, sounding upbeat to put Tish at ease.

"I've got them right here," Patrick said as he reached into his pocket to extract the pair of tickets to Friday night's game against the Los Angeles Dodgers.

"Wow!" I said. "That is nice of you. I wanted to go and see the game and now we can. Thanks a bunch."

"This is not payment for all your work. It isn't even the bonus you will be getting. It is just a way for us to make sure the two of you have some downtime," Patrick said as he handed over the tickets.

Patrick and Aileen left with the bag full of Tish's belongings to use at the safe house. I could tell Tish was not exactly happy with how things were ending.

"I know you want to be there to talk to Wendi, Tish. You need to have faith in the Jamiesons; they have been doing this for a long time. They will know what to do from here. They also know how much Wendi means to you. You can trust them to make sure she is in good hands."

Tish moaned. "I know. I just feel like I have come to the end of a good book and the last page was torn out."

"You will find out everything that happens. It isn't like you are now out of the loop. Aileen and Patrick will fill you in on everything. Can we just go to the game and relax? I really want to see Sosa play."

Tish came up to me and gave me a hug. "Yes, we can go. It is probably for the best. If we stayed home, I would want to be at the safe house to help catch Maurice. I know that would not go over well. Captain Jones would probably lock me up for interfering with police work."

I noticed the mailman walking down the street. Tish went to check to see what was in the mail. We have some utility bills coming soon.

Tish returned almost immediately with a letter. It was from Tran's brother in Texas. As she opened it, she read it out loud. It said Tran would be in Chicago for one evening only and was wanting all the investors to assemble. He wants to give us an update on how well the stocks are doing. He rented a meeting room at a hotel, address included. She went on to read that dinner would be served. It will be next Saturday.

"What the hey?" I exclaimed. "Sounds interesting. I wonder how many of our classmates will be able to attend. Do we need to RSVP or anything?"

Tish scanned the letter and said, "Yes, he wants a headcount. There is a telephone number we are to call and let his secretary know if we will be attending or not attending...either way, we are to telephone."

"We don't have anything else to do. I guess we may agree to go. We probably should phone now, or we may forget. I will phone Chuck to see how many of our classmates involved in this investment are planning to attend. I would think he should know something."

"I suppose these types of meetings are normal in the financial world. I thought we would be getting mailings from the company letting us know how much the stock is worth. Maybe they will send a representative to give us the news first hand. Is this normal?" Tish asked with some skepticism in her voice.

Tish is always suspicious. I wondered about her sometimes.

"Oh, Shoot! There was a stock statement that came about a month ago. I put it aside and forgot all about it. It probably shows the account value and investments...I suspect it also announced this meeting in advance. We did have more than one week's notice. I'm sorry. I guess I was not thinking," I apologized.

I rooted around to find the statement and felt rewarded when I could put my hands on it. It was under a pile of other mail, mainly junk that I hadn't gone through yet. "Here it is."

Tish tore it open, and her eyes got wide. "Oh my gosh. I had no idea our stocks had gone up sky-high in value. This gives my theory even more credence. Anyone would kill for this amount!"

I went and read over her shoulder. I was flabbergasted. The amount the remaining alumni would receive upon the death of the rest of us was astronomical. A person would be set for life with this amount of money.

"I guess we had best make the phone call now before we forget," I said as I picked up the phone.

I RSVP'd that we both would be attending. I phoned Chuck next. After a lengthy chat, I hung up.

Turning to Tish, I filled her in, "It seems the alumni investors have decided to take a bus to the dinner meeting. I think Chuck said it was arranged by Jack, who won't attend the dinner because he will be on duty. Chuck said everyone was going to be on the bus except Meredith, who is taking a rescue dog down to Tennessee that day and won't be back in time.

"Chuck also mentioned Jesse wouldn't be able to take the bus, but he will be at the dinner meeting. He said something about Jesse having personal business in Chicago that day. Tran won't be on the bus either.

He is leaving town early to pick up his brother from the Executive Terminal at Midway Airport. It seems Tran's brother has the company plane bringing him to Chicago."

"Okay, except for Meredith and Jack, it looks like everyone will be at the dinner meeting," was all Tish said at that moment.

"Well, everyone except the five of our classmates who have already been killed," I said without thinking.

"You did say killed, didn't you?" asked Tish. "I mean you used the word killed and not the word died. Are you starting to think my theory is right, and Wally and Tommy were murdered as well?"

I had to agree her theory was starting to make more sense. We already know two of our classmates were assassinated at close range. We know what kind of bullet was used and we know the killer was wearing expensive Italian driving shoes. We also know Lucy's brakes were deliberately punctured.

What we don't know is who killed Wally and Tommy. If they were killed. It doesn't seem likely anyone with expensive Italian shoes was at the lake the day Wally died. Of course, no one was looking for shoe prints when Tommy died. Everyone just thought it was a horrible chainsaw accident.

"There are still things that don't add up. I am saying, it seems like that amount of money is going to make a lot of people think about killing to get it."

Tish suddenly stiffened up. "What did you just say?"

I thought for a moment. "I guess I said that was a lot of money, and a lot of people might kill for it."

"That is it. Scotty, we talked about this before…what if it is not just one killer. What if it is several killers? What if a couple of our classmates are working together?" Tish looked at me with horror in her eyes.

Neither of us wanted to think our small hometown could have multiple killers. It was hard enough to fathom that there could be even one killer in our group.

"That is a horrible thought!" I said.

CHAPTER THIRTY-THREE

The game wasn't exactly relaxing as the Jamiesons hoped it would be for us. I kept thinking about what Tish had said about there being multiple killers in our graduating class. I kept mulling things over and over in my mind and was barely aware the game was over. Sosa was up to bat three times, and I did not remember if he got on base any of those times.

Tish and I talked about the possibilities all the way home. I said, "My money is on Jack and Jesse."

"Yes, Jesse was my suspect for the drowning. Jack was in plain sight. I know he did not drown Wally. If I remember correctly, Jack wasn't around when Tommy had his accident either. Jesse, however, was," Tish relayed, as she thought back to each killing.

"So, you aren't suspecting Jack?" I said.

"I know you want him to be one of the killers. I get that you dislike Jack intensely, and you think he had something to do with Heather's disappearance. It doesn't seem likely to me," Tish said.

"Jesse doesn't have the brains to pull off one murder, let alone two murders. He can't even wipe his nose without someone telling him to use a hanky and not his sleeve," I said with disgust.

"Yes, Jesse is as dumb as a rock. He would not hesitate to kill if someone ordered him to do so," Tish said without guilt. "He is a bad seed."

"We both suspect Jesse, okay! Question is who put him up to the killings?" I asked.

"There is also the killer with expensive shoes. Is he part of this, or is it a coincidence?" Tish asked out loud and not necessarily for my response. Like most women, she likes to talk things out, even if it is just for herself.

I answered, anyway, "I think the five deaths are tied in somehow. We just need to find out how. Who do we know who could afford expensive shoes, for one thing?"

Tish did not reply. I knew she was still thinking things out and did not trust I would be a good sounding board at this point. I let her think.

The week went by quickly. We both had things to do since we were preoccupied with the jewelry fraud case. There was data to be entered from the Jamiesons files, and I had not been to the shooting range to practice for two weeks. The captain would expect me to be at my best this fall when the police would be competing again.

Tish was at the dojang every day. She also insisted I work out with her for several hours a week. I was feeling sore and bruised and was ready to have an evening out, even if the evening out was just to watch our classmates for any suspicious actions.

The invitation did not say anything about formal wear. I came out wearing my jeans and a clean shirt. Tish came out in essentially the same attire as me, only her jeans were black, and mine was blue.

"You don't think we are dressed too casually, do you?" I asked.

"Look at who is suddenly Mr. GQ. Yes, I do think we are dressed too casually. I also think we need to be dressed sensibly. Even though I am not anticipating any trouble tonight, I want to be ready to deal with it, if trouble should arise. Besides, I will be riding my Harley tonight. If we need to be separated for any reason, we both will have wheels," Tish said, smoothing down her black vest.

"I suppose I could dress up these black jeans with a nicer blouse," I heard Tish say as she returned to the bedroom.

Now I was wondering whether I should dress up my jeans with my better belt. Nay. I decided I would leave my good belt for when I really needed to dress up.

"Are you almost ready?" I shouted out to Tish.

Tish came out with a low-cut blouse that sparkled in the lights. "Wow! Where have you been keeping that blouse? I think you should wear it more often," I said with an approving look.

Tish isn't full-figured like May West, but she sure fills out her top. There was a bit too much cleavage showing now that I thought about the other guys from our graduating class being at this dinner. I did not like the idea of them looking down Tish's low-cut blouse.

"I think the other top was fine. I can wait a minute if you want to change back," I said, hoping she would put on something more modest.

"I will have my leather jacket on a good share of the time. Just relax. No one is going to get a free peep show," Tish said, knowing primarily, what was bothering me.

"We need to get to the Magnificent Mile in downtown Chicago. Let's get going. I will lead the way, and you can keep drivers off my rear," Tish said as she grabbed her helmet and jacket.

I wanted to argue about her top, but there was no sense. Tish was right about the possibility of us needing to split up. I was not sure of what we might be walking into tonight. There was also the possibility that our theory was totally wrong.

CHAPTER THIRTY-FOUR

Tish was heading to the Hyatt with me on her tail. I don't know if I wanted our theory to be right or wrong. If we were right, there are people we know who are killers. If we are wrong, I guess I will just feel foolish.

We arrived and parked in the underground parking lot. Tish found a spot for her Harley in a hurry. I had to scout around a bit to find a parking space for the Double Nickel. Tish waited at the door to the stairs for me to escort her into the lobby.

We stopped at the lobby desk to ask directions to the meeting room. They sent us to the elevator to go up to the mezzanine floor where there would be signs to the Michigan Room. We were the first to arrive.

"I guess you can pick whatever table you want," I said as I looked around the room set up with multiple tables and a speaking podium at the front. Each table was set with service settings for dinner. It seemed apparent that most of our friends would be attending.

Just as Tish decided which table would give her the best advantage for watching most people, noise in the hallway announced the arrival of our school friends. The chatter was almost deafening.

"Oh my gosh! Look, there are Scott and Tish." I think it was Lauri that yelled, but I could not say for sure.

"Hey, you guys. How is life in the Big City?" I heard Marty shout out at us. I went over and greeted him.

For several minutes, we were surrounded by our classmates who were giddy from their trip to Chicago. Everyone agreed the bus ride down had been enjoyable. The party atmosphere which started on the bus continued in the meeting room.

Soon the chatter concentrated more on local gossip and catching up. We found out three of our classmates were engaged and due to get married in the fall. Another two were holding off for a spring wedding. I found it hard to believe that many were getting married this quickly after graduating.

Other gossip filled the air. There was talk of the murders and the disappearance of Heather. Unfortunately, no one said anything that we did not already hear. I strained my ears to hear more about Heather without asking questions and appearing too interested knowing Tish was within earshot.

Servers were entering and filling glasses with water. Some of our classmates took it as a signal to find a place to sit. Most of the gossip ended. Soon Tran entered with Jesse on his heels.

Tish and I both took notice of the two guys entering so close together. Knowing Tran and Jesse were never friendly at high school, my antennas were up

Leaning towards Tish, I asked, "What is your take on Jesse and Tran? Would you say it was a coincidence they entered together?"

Tish whispered, "I am not sure. I think we should keep an eye on both. We already suspect Jesse of the murders of Wally and Tommy. I just can't imagine Tran being involved."

Tran's brother entered the room with one of the Hyatt staff. They talked for a few seconds. Tran's brother stood behind the podium and whistled to get everyone's attention.

"Please, be seated. The Hyatt staff is eager to begin to serve your dinner. After dinner, I will once again take the podium to let you know the good news about your investments."

Everyone grabbed a chair, and chatter immediately began, and it didn't quiet down until the dinner was served. As was often typical of conferences and meetings at hotels, people were asked in advance whether they would like fish, chicken or beef. Tish ordered fish, and I, of course, ordered red meat.

We talked sociably to the others at our table. I was glad Chuck grabbed the seat next to mine. Tish took the place at the end of the table. I wasn't certain if it was to avoid having to engage in small talk with our classmates or if it was the best position to observe the happenings in the room.

Chuck talked about our parents' new business and how well they appeared to be doing. He also told me Jack moved his new girlfriend into his house. I was astounded to think Jack could be that brazen and asked a few leading questions.

According to Chuck, it seems Jack started an affair while in the military. His girlfriend moved into an apartment soon after Jack was discharged. It was only a matter of months after Heather's disappearance they shacked up together.

I was dumbfounded. I ran the scenario through my head. It was disgusting to view it as a choppy video.

Jack gets Heather pregnant…they marry…he joins the military service…he comes home on leave and trips Heather…she falls down the stairs and loses the baby…Jack gets a hardship discharge…Jack moves his girlfriend into a rental…Heather is seen with bruises often…Heather disappears…Jack moves his slut into his house….

All the way around, it looks bad to me. I can't help being suspicious once again that Jack may have killed Heather.

My thoughts are interrupted by Tish. "What did Chuck just say about Jack? I could only hear a few details."

"It seems Jack moved his girlfriend into his house a few months after Heather disappeared. Chuck says Jack had been having an affair with her for quite some time," I said in a low voice.

Apparently, it was not low enough. "That is right," Marcia said from across the table. "I have met Jack's girlfriend, and she told me she and Jack were in the military police on the same base. I guess she had seniority since she was getting out before Jack. When Jack's father asked Jack to take an early out due to his mother's illness, Jack jumped at it."

Tish asked Marcia a few questions. "Did Jack's girlfriend say she followed Jack to town or what?"

"Oh yes, she said they had it all planned out. She said Jack found the apartment for her. It was only two blocks away from where Heather and Jack lived. She also said Jack was over to her apartment every opportunity. I guess it was quite a love affair," Marcia said, beaming that she knew much, and enjoying the fact that everyone was listening to her with intensity.

Jillian added her comments, "That is just sick! Heather didn't deserve that kind of treatment. Heather was too good for Jack!"

I wanted to jump in and agree with my whole heart. A small voice in my head told me to be quiet. It was hard not to say Jack was a total jerk, and someone should make him pay for what he did to Heather and her baby.

Tish was watching me closely. I was glad I kept my mouth closed. Biting my tongue produced blood. My dessert did not taste as good as it should have with the taste of blood mingled in with the cherries.

Plates were quickly cleared, and Tran's brother once again stood up and went to the podium. He introduced himself to those of us he never met. Riley Tam reminded us of our investment contract with his company. Bragging about how well his company was doing, Riley produced a chart to demonstrate his point visually. He droned on, with most people glued to what he was saying...starting when he announced how much the investments had increased in value.

Riley asked for questions from the group. As individuals asked questions, Riley moved from the podium to be closer to the questioner.

Suddenly, I was jabbed in the ribs. I turned to Tish to see why she elbowed me. Leaning over to whisper in my ear, making sure no one else would hear, she says, "Look at Riley's shoes!"

I could not see well from where I was sitting as Riley had just moved from one table to another further away. I whispered back, "What about his shoes. I can't see them."

Continued whispers came from Tish's lips. "Look closely when you can. I think they are Italian driving shoes just like the assassin wore. I need to find out for sure."

"Just how are you going to do that?" I asked, wondering what excuse Tish could come up with to ask about his shoes.

"Easy," Tish said. "Once the questions stop, I will get up and ask him. I will say something about noticing his shoes, and I want to get you a pair. If they are super expensive, Riley is going to want to brag about them. Those junior execs like to seem important."

I wasn't sure it was going to be that easy. I did not say as much to Tish. She had proven to be resourceful in the past. Why not trust her instincts now?

Sure enough, once questions stopped, Tish jumped up and went straight to Riley. They chatted, and I could see Riley looking down at his shoes. They were too far away for me to hear anything they said.

As Tish returned to my side, I was not thinking of shoes any longer. Instead, I noticed that Riley, Tran, and Jesse were huddled together in a corner close to the door where Riley entered earlier.

"I was right! They are the exact brand and style of driving shoes that were identified by the police lab. Riley is the murderer of Rose Lee and Ray!" Tish said excitedly.

"Look," I said, "all three of them are huddled at the door."

Tish turned her attention to where I was looking. "I need to follow Riley. He is our best lead right now. I suggest you follow Jesse or Tran."

"I've got Jesse. If your theory is correct, Jesse is the other killer. Great, they are splitting up. Go!" I said, and Tish immediately sprinted towards the door with me in pursuit.

Tran and Riley went down the hall towards the elevator, and Tish followed them at a discreet distance. Jesse went in the opposite direction, and I followed him, also at a discreet distance.

Jesse seemed in a big hurry. I followed as closely as I could without him seeing me. He turned a corner, and I quickly rushed to where I had last seen him. I peeked around the corner, and he was nowhere in sight.

I checked all the options. At the end of the hall was a door marked stairs. The elevators were further down the same corridor. I did not see any motion indicating an elevator door closed. I was not ruling out the possibility Jesse sprinted down the hall and jumped into an elevator before it descended.

While trying to decide whether I should take the stairs or the elevator, I found myself looking at a room with the door wide open. By chance, I might see something that would help me decide which direction to go, I headed into the vacant room to the sliding glass doors opening to the balcony.

I leaned over the balcony and was just about to give up and toss a coin to decide which way to go when I saw Jesse heading for the door to valet parking. I sprinted from the vacant room and ran to the elevator. I pushed the button to the ground floor and rushed to the door leading to the hotel entrance.

The bus hired to take my classmates back home was sitting at the entrance. The driver was nowhere to be seen. I could only assume he was in the lobby waiting for my classmates to descend from the meeting.

I was about to go back inside when I noticed someone wriggling out from under the bus. It was Jesse. He had a gym bag with him, and when I hollered at him to stop, he ran down the exit ramp into the underground parking lot. Next, I saw his car speeding out of the exit ramp onto the main street.

I ran back inside the hotel to try to find Tish. I was fortunate to see her in the lobby.

"Tish, I just saw Jesse doing something under the bus. He took off like a bat out of hell when he saw me," I said.

"It looked to me like Riley was settling the meeting room and dinner bill at the front desk, and now he is about to leave by a limo. I am certain he will head back to the airport where his private jet is waiting. I need to follow him.

"You must find a way to phone Captain Jones and tell him about our suspicions, then stop the bus from leaving. Who knows what Jesse was doing under the bus?" With those words, Tish headed out to get on her Harley and left me with the job of phoning the police.

I ran to the desk and asked if I could use the phone. "It is an emergency," I said when the clerk hesitated.

Luckily, I knew Captain Jones's number by heart. I dialed and was relieved when he answered on the second ring. I informed him about Riley's shoes and that Tish was following him to the Executive Terminal at Midway Airport. I described seeing Jesse under the tour bus and my suspicions that Jesse tampered with it. He told me he would send officers to the airport as well as to the hotel. I hung up, thanked the clerk, and rushed back to the hotel entrance only to find that the bus was gone.

Running down the parking exit ramp to where I parked my Ford, I fumbled for my keys as I ran. I unlocked the door, started the engine, and put the car into reverse. I knew Tish would be taking I 55 towards the airport. Now, I had to decide what would be the quickest route to cut off the bus.

I could imagine my old classmates laughing and joking as they returned home. I was sure everyone was drinking soft drinks and eating chips or whatever the tour bus company might supply for the return trip.

It was suspicious enough that he drove to the hotel separately instead of coming with the group. I know I saw him crawling out from under the bus. There were many ways to sabotage a vehicle, but what had Jesse done? I just knew, in my gut, he did something that would endanger the lives of our former schoolmates.

My first thought was of Chuck. He had been my best friend for years, and I could not imagine the world without him. It was bad enough that Wally, Tommy, Rose Lee, and Ray, and well…okay, Lucy was also dead. There was no way I was going to let my other friends die.

I kept my eyes peeled for the bus ahead of me. It wasn't dark yet, but soon, it would be dusk. It would make it more challenging to see the bus if I did not find it before it got dark.

I was out of the Chicago traffic and onto the road that led to my hometown. There would be a curvy stretch of the road soon. My hope was that Jesse did not tamper with the brakes. That stretch of road ahead would be impossible to navigate without brakes.

In the distance, I finally saw the bus. I stepped on the gas and let my Ford's turbo engine do its thing. I hit 70 miles an hour and then 110 in mere seconds, and the distance between myself and the bus decreased dramatically. I pulled into the oncoming lane with my lights flashing and my horn blasting. The bus driver looked at me like I was a lunatic. I kept motioning him to stop.

Slowly, the bus driver pulled the vehicle to the side of the road. I rudely pulled the double-nickel in front of the bus and turned the engine off. The bus driver opened the folding door and stepped out. He was being followed by half of the occupants.

"Scott, are you mad! What in the world kind of stunt are you pulling?" Chuck said as he jumped from the bottom step onto the ground.

Just then, a patrol car came into sight with lights flashing and siren blaring. The patrolman pulled in behind the bus and got out.

"Hey, big guy! Are you Scott McFarlan?" he said as he approached the group. I said I was.

He went on to say Captain Jones had sent him to the hotel to check out the bus, but the bus was already gone. "I radioed the station, and they told me to take the road to Stanton. So, what's the problem?" the officer asked.

I told him how I thought someone had tampered with the bus, and I needed to stop it before there was an accident. The officer said he would call the State Police and a tow truck with a mechanic on board, who could check it out.

Just as he said those words, a car went driving past. It was Tran's car. I told the officer I needed to catch that car. The bus driver interrupted the officer, saying there was a truck parked on the side of the road that pulled out and raced past his bus. I asked the bus driver to describe the vehicle, and he said it was a loud old black rundown pickup truck. I knew then, Tran was following Jesse, and Jesse was leapfrogging the bus waiting for something to happen.

I headed for my car when the officer stopped me to ask more questions. I was trying hard to explain why I needed to follow the vehicles that just went past. I was wasting time trying to explain to the officer who was not understanding me. I finally just said I would be back, ran to my car, and burned a long tire patch as I left the bus and police officer in my rear-view mirror. I had a feeling I was going to be sorry for that decision.

It was getting dark. I could see rear lights far ahead of me. Quickly, I was catching up to the taillights and realized the cars were stopped. As I slowed down, bullets whizzed past my car. One hit my headlight, and another hit my windshield. I veered off the road and slammed on my breaks.

My one headlight illuminated the scene in front of me. I could see Jesse lying on the ground and Tran running into the bushes. I opened my car door and ran into the bushes on the opposite side of the road. I knew I would be a sitting duck if I followed Tran with my headlight, acting as a spotlight. I thought about turning it off before I ran across the road. Thinking twice, I decided to leave the light on as a decoy. I figured Tran's attention would be on the car and my approach from that direction.

Quietly, I maneuvered through the bushes. I knew how to move efficiently through the brush from my many years of hunting with my father. The darkness was now in my favor.

I inched through the undergrowth. It took several minutes to get beyond where I imagined Tran would be waiting. I needed to make sure I came from behind him. There were enough bushes to cover me as I crept across the road. Now, I was on the same side of the road as Tran.

Slowly, I sneaked closer and closer to Tran. I could see the scene backlit; Tran's silhouette dark against the lighter background of my vehicle's one headlight.

Tran was hunkered down with his gaze focused on the light streaming in from my trusty Ford. He seemed frozen, stiff as a wooden board. I knew Tran was dangerous at this point. I suspected he shot Jesse and had nothing to lose by shooting me. If I got careless, I would be the next victim.

Time was not going to be on my side. Tran must realize if I took much longer, it would be less likely I would approach from head-on. It was best to rush him now.

In a flash, I bolted from my cover, and before Tran could stand and turn around, I flattened him to the ground with my bulk. The gun remained in his hand, with one quick movement, I grabbed his hand and slammed it repeatedly into the ground until he dropped it.

One final punch to his face assured me Tran was unconscious. I took my belt from my jeans, glad that I was not wearing my best belt, and secured Trans hands behind his back. I left him lying silently on the ground and proceeded to Jesse's body.

I knelt beside Jessie and let my fingers search for a pulse. I found none... Jessie was lying in an ever-expanding pool of his own blood. Sadly, there was no doubt in my mind...Jesse was dead.

I went back to Tran and heaved his body onto my shoulder. It took minimal effort to carry him back to the trunk of my car. He barely weighed more than Tish.

It was hard for me to figure Tran as a cold-blooded killer. It was harder for me not to believe my own eyes. Jesse was lying dead, and Tran had the gun. Not only did he have the gun, but he fired it at me...repeatedly. I guess I should acknowledge Tran can kill after all.

I made a U-turn and headed back to the bus. When I arrived, there were city police and several state vehicles, and a large tow truck. I got out of my car and went to the officer who initially responded.

"I told you I would be back," I said flippantly.

The officer took one look at my '55 Ford and said, "You know I am going to cite you for driving with only one headlight, don't you?"

"Fine, cite away...but before you do, I need you to arrest the guy in my trunk and send another officer down the road where you will find a dead body and the revolver further back in the bushes, that the guy in my trunk used to kill Jesse and put two holes in my car. Also, I need someone to check out Jesse's truck to get the gym bag he had with him while under the bus," I said, annoyed by the little game the rookie officer was playing.

Another State Police officer, hearing our conversation, came over. Having listened to what I said, he offered to go down the road and check out the crime scene himself. About a half-hour later, he returned, saying he collected all the evidence.

"Question? Why do you suppose a county sheriff's deputy would arrive this far east of his county? Do you know a guy named Jack Johnson?" the state police officer asked.

I was immediately apprehensive. "You did not leave Mr. Johnson there by himself, did you?"

"No, the coroner and the state crime scene investigator were there before I left. Jack Johnson did not stick around. I was just puzzled how he knew about the accident this far away from his jurisdiction."

The State Police officer left and joined the other officers working on the case. That left me alone, wondering why Jack arrived just when he did. Was he supposed to have arrived at the scene of the bus accident to sterilize the scene before real police arrived? I also wondered if Tran was supposed to have killed Jack as well as Jesse?

My thoughts were interrupted by a city police officer who introduced himself and told me Captain Jones was on his way. He went on to say Captain Jones wanted me to stay put. He had news about Tish.

Hearing Tish's name startled me. I was so involved with the bus, Jesse, and Tran that I had not given a thought to Tish. I felt infuriated at myself for not thinking of her safety. What was wrong with me? Here the woman I love was chasing after a probable killer, and I was self-absorbed. I did not even think about her situation until I was hit in the face with it.

My former classmates were huddled together, talking. I avoided them altogether. I went back to my Ford and sat in the front seat, waiting anxiously for Captain Jones to arrive.

I knew Tish was alright by the comment the officer made. What the officer said was Captain Jones wants to brag about Tish. He went on to say he wasn't supposed to give me any details.

"Details? How can I give you the details? All I know is the little bit of chatter I heard on the radio. It wasn't as if I was at the airport when the culprit was apprehended," the officer answered when I pushed for more facts.

The mechanic found a timer that went off while he was under the bus. I wished the rookie officer was the one under the bus when the brake fluid gushed out.

Another bus was on its way to pick up my friends and return them home. They would have a story to tell everyone. At this point, I couldn't be sure anyone knew Tran was in the backseat of a police car and that Jesse was lying dead a couple of miles down the road. The whole story would be known before long. They could wait to read about it like everyone else in town.

Captain Jones pulled in just as the replacement bus was being loaded. The officers had everyone's name and a statement from each. Any other questions will be asked later if need be.

I went straight to Captain Jones and asked how Tish was. I was surprised by his laughter.

"You have one tough lady on your hands, Scott," the captain said before he turned his back on me.

He barked a few orders to his officers and then returned his attention to me. "I guess I can give you the low-down now that the officers have everything under control here. Back to Tish, one of the rookies she trained, was in the squad car with his partner, heading to the airport. They said they were approaching the Executive Terminal at Midway Airport. They stated they were told to go to the hangars where the private jets would be loading passengers.

"As they approached one hanger, the rookie said he could see a private jet getting ready to receive a passenger. Two people were fighting on the asphalt near the plane. As the rookie and his partner approached, the rookie said he could see one of the fighters was Tish. The other opponent was an unknown man."

Captain Jones continued the rookie's account by saying, 'The rookie said it was obvious the man was trained in some form of martial arts specialized in kicking. The man moved like a cat, but Tish was faster. The rookie said Tish was all over him. She blocked every move he made. The man was maneuvering and throwing kicks at her head, body, and legs. Tish blocked every kick and threw rapid-fire punches and kicks of her own. Her speed and accuracy were far too much for the assailant to handle. The man Tish was fighting, dropped to one knee, and Tish fired one last flying leg kick to the side of his head that nearly decapitated him." Captain Jones said the rookie finished his accounting of the fight he witnessed and waited for further orders.

"Captain Jones was laughing once again. "I told the rookie and his partner to make the arrest, of course. So, what do you think of the account of Tish's fight?"

I was in awe. I witnessed Tish as an instructor and saw her in action when Jesse confronted her at our Senior Ball, but I have never seen her in full-on battle mode. "I wished I was there to see her moves first-hand. Well, maybe not. I would have been a mess the whole time. It doesn't surprise me, as you said, she is one tough lady. So, Riley is in custody?" I asked, wanting more information.

"He has two officers with him. Right now, he is in the emergency room being checked out. Tish is at the police station, making a statement. I doubt she will still be there when we get there. Who knows, she may stick around," the captain responded.

"I got a chance to talk to Tran just now before the officer took him to the police station," the captain continued. "I think Tran will be willing to give up his brother. Tran's brother, Riley, kept saying everything was Tran's fault, while in the emergency room, and he had nothing to do with anything. I am willing to bet Tran will say the same thing about Riley."

"Jesse is dead. Tran killed him. I am wondering how Jesse fits into these murders. Tish and I are quite sure Jesse killed our friends, Wally and Tommy, but the shoe prints and gun casings prove Riley was the murderer of Rose Lee and Ray. Tish and I suspect Jack was involved in

Lucy's death, but we have no proof. I sure hope they all get what they deserve," I said to Captain Jones as he walked me back to my car.

"Looks like your car came out the loser in your gunfight with Tran." He shook his head, and I could tell he really was saddened by the hits my car took.

"Badge of Courage?" I said, looking appraisingly at the damage done to my car. "My dad can have it fixed in a jiffy if I take it down to him. However, he might take it back if I do. He loves this car about as much as he loves me. I think maybe I should find a garage here in town. Any suggestions?"

"Sure, I can give you the name of a guy who will have it back in ship-shape in no time. Now, get down to the police department and give your statement. Then go home and see how Tish is faring," ordered the captain.

I drove straight to the station and gave my statement. The captain wanted a more detailed report than what an officer would take at the scene. It took much longer than I thought it would take. I crept into the house around midnight, expecting Tish to be sound asleep.

"You are finally home!" Tish greeted me at the door with a kiss. As I closed the door behind me and locked it, I turned around to see tea was being poured.

"I want to hear all the details about Jesse, Tran, and the bus," Tish said as she handed me a cup of hot tea.

I started, "Jesse is dead, and Tran is in jail." Tish sat being very quiet as I told her the whole story, including Jack's peculiar arrival at Jesse and Trans crime scene. It was 1:00 a.m. before I finished my story. "Now, tell me your story."

"First off," Tish said. "I am sorry, Jesse is dead."

I was shocked knowing that Tish could not stand Jesse. Then Tish voiced her real thought.

"Now, we are going to have a hard time incriminating Jack. If Jesse were still alive, we could get him to buckle and turn Jack in."

It seems clear to me there were initially two isolated groups with the same intent. Tran and his brother worked this from the very beginning, from getting us all involved in the stock purchase to the murders of Rose Lee and Ray.

Jack and Jesse began their escapade with the drowning of Wally and the chainsaw murder of Tommy. Lucy Loose was most likely one of Jack's murder victims. Killing most of the rest of the investors on one big bus accident would have been the culmination of the murders. At some point, the four began working together...sort of. We need to find evidence that ties them together... Then we'll get Jack. Jack had to be the one pulling Jesse's strings. Jesse was too stupid to do anything on his own."

My tea was gone. I noticed Tish still had some. "Do you want a fresh cup of tea while we talk about this more?" I asked. I really needed more tea if we were going to stay up. My head was hurting from the whirlwind day.

"Tish, can you go back to some details about Riley and your encounter with him at the airport. I know how the fight scene played out from the captain. I don't know how you intercepted him in the first place?" I asked as I poured more tea, whether she wanted it or not.

Tish began her story. "When he left in the limo, I knew what route he would probably take. I assumed he would take I55 to Highway 50 to South Cicero Avenue to West 63rd Street.

I rode my Harley on I55 to South Central to West 63rd to cut him off. I arrived at the Executive Terminal first. Riley's limo was only minutes behind me. It was enough time for me to find out which jet was his company jet. I put myself between the plane and the limo.

Riley started out all pleasant and smiles. I knew it was an act. I could see distrust in his eyes as he approached me to talk.

I asked him where he got his shoes. He said at Nordstrom's here in Chicago but wanted to know why I was obsessed with his shoes." Tish took a short break to sip her tea.

"He must have thought you were a nut case. You asked him at the meeting, and now you hunt him down to the terminal to ask him more about the shoes. Did he finally make the connection or what?" I asked, hoping to get Tish talking again.

"He did say something more about them being too expensive for me to buy for you. I went on to tell him if they were ridiculously expensive, why did you wear them to murder Rose Lee and Ray? That is when the shit hit the fan.

He said something like, "So you know, do you?" and took a step closer to kick me in the head. The rest you have already heard."

Now, I felt terrible that I did not let Tish finish the story in her own time. It was apparent to me she condensed the story to finish quicker. "Is there anything else you want to add?" I said, hoping to draw out the rest of the story.

"Not really," Tish said with a yawn. "The police arrived just as I took him out. They knew from Captain Jones that Riley was a murder suspect, and he was to be detained. When one of the officers asked me if I needed to use force to hold him, I answered yes. He would be long gone, and besides, he attacked me first.

The officers said they saw the fight from start to finish, and they would collaborate my story that Riley took the first punch, well, kick."

I could see Tish was tired. We both had long days. While I was stalking Tran, Tish was fighting Riley. I had a feeling her day was more exhausting than my day had been. I knew I needed to cut her a break and let her go to bed. If my head was hurting, I could only imagine what her whole body felt like after her fight.

"Want a back rub before you go to sleep?" I asked with genuine concern.

Tish smiled. "I might take you up on that. You do have magic fingers."

I pulled her to her feet and led her to the bedroom. She followed along like a puppy.

CHAPTER THIRTY-FIVE

My dad insisted I bring the Double-Nickel to their shop for the repairs. One of my classmates told him about the incident before I could get my Ford fixed on my own. I informed my dad we would be down. The Jamiesons said nothing was pressing for Tish and myself to work on today anyway.

Tish and I talked all the way down about the possibility Jack was in on the killings. The problem was, how were we going to prove it. He seemed to have an alibi for each murder. That did not mean he did not orchestrate them. With Jesse dead, it was going to be harder to prove unless Tran and Riley were aware of his involvement and would be willing to testify.

As we drew closer to town, my fears switched to what our parents were going to say. Nothing was reported on the phone as to the danger we put ourselves in. I knew we were not going to escape a lecture or two or four. I was dreading the encounter. The realization that we could have been killed was too fresh in our parents' heads, not to expect some reaction or another.

Tish was probably thinking the same thing since she was quiet as we entered the city limits. We were just a few blocks from the garage, and there was no way to stall the inevitable at this point.

We parked the car in the lot and took deep breaths as we walked into the showroom entrance. We were greeted with confetti, horns, and lots of shouts and cheers. The whole busload of former classmates was applauding us as we entered.

Both of us were overcome with emotions. I was embarrassed, and Tish was on the verge of tears. We were immediately surrounded by our friends. 'Thank you' came from different voices all around us. I could not distinguish one voice from another. Finally, my father separated the crowd and made his way towards Tish and myself.

"Let them take a deep breath, people," my dad said as he took Tish by the hand and led us both out of the crowd. I could see my mom and Dorothy entering with a cart full of food, drinks, and a congratulatory cake. That refocused the group, and they descended on the food like vultures.

I was feeling overwhelmed by all the hero talk. Tish was uncomfortable with it. I could tell she was bothered when she blushed and withdrew from the animated conversations around her.

When choruses of "speech, speech" were chanted, I knew Tish was not going to be able to talk. I rose to the occasion and stood beside an empty food cart.

"First off, thank you for the surprise party and all your congratulatory remarks. Neither Tish or myself," looking at Tish for her approval to talk on her behalf, "feel like heroes."

I paused at this point. I was trying to decide what I wanted to say next. "As you know, way too many of our friends were killed over this silly contract we made in our senior year. I, for one, never thought twice about the consequences of our actions. Who could have guessed the driving force of greed, would lead to some very decent people being killed. It is even more unsettling when one realizes any one of us were next on their hit list. It made us terrified and sick. Even so, we felt we needed to figure out who was the killer and stop him or them before another one of our friends met their fate.

"You need to thank Tish twice as many times as myself. She was the one who knew something was wrong, and she was determined to find out who the killer was. I, on the other hand, fell for the red herring and thought Wally and Tommy were just accidents, plain and simple. Not Tish. From day one, she knew something was amiss. She was like a dog gnawing on a bone." I looked at Tish and said, "Sorry about the dog comment. You know what I am trying to say, remember, I didn't get an A in Public Speaking class as you did. Do you want to get up here and finish the speech before I put my foot in my mouth?"

Tish shook her head, indicating a negative response. I guess it was my job to continue until she either was forced to take over due to my stupid remarks or until I got the facts wrong.

"Well, you can also thank Tish for getting Captain Jones from the Chicago police involved. It was his resources that helped us tie in Riley. And while I am pointing out people deserving thanks, you can also thank Tish's dad and my dad. They found and captured clues at two of the crime scenes. If it had not been for them, the tampered brakes that killed Lucy, the bullet casings, and shoe prints that were instrumental in the capture of Riley would not have happened.

"What I am trying to say is there are many heroes in this case—not just Tish and myself. As I said before, we don't think of ourselves as heroes. We think of ourselves as concerned citizens and your friends."

I stopped since I was starting to sound syrupy even to myself. Once the crowd knew I was not going to continue, applause erupted, and I knew I could step back into the group.

Tish was being hugged by individuals, and I was getting claps on the back or high-fives. I was starting to feel exhausted from the displays of gratitude and was wishing everyone would go home until I thought about the lectures that were yet to come. I decided I could put up with the hero-worship a bit longer to avoid what would be coming next.

Unfortunately, one can't stop the inevitable. The group of friends said their last thank you and goodbyes and left Tish and me alone with our parents.

"Erik and Chris will have the Double Nickel looking like brand new in no time," my dad said once everyone was out the door.

I was relieved. It looked as if there was not going to be a lecture after all.

"You will take better care of it in the future, won't you? I would hate to need to confiscate it for the showroom permanently. What were you thinking...driving it straight into bullets?" And the lecture began....

I could see Tish was enduring an equal amount of ear burning. It was her mom, though, who was wagging her finger and screeching in a high voice. I suppose we deserved some of the sermons. Neither of us had thought through our plans as well as we should. In our defense, things happen rather quickly. Plans sometimes need to be made by the seat of our pants.

Finally, I was starting to tire of the words and said so. My mom still had to have the last word. "You won't understand how we feel until you have children of your own. We worry about you two, day and night, and the fact we supported your decision to go into a job that has dangers does not mean we love you less...we love you more than you can imagine. It is because of the strength of our love we can stand by and watch you do dangerous things and yet be very proud."

All I could do is hug her as tight as possible. When she squealed, my dad came to her rescue. "Let her down, Scott. Your mom isn't as young as she used to be."

I set her feet back on the ground and released my bear-hug grip. "Mom, Dad, Dorothy, Cliff, both Tish and I want to thank you for your support and love. We wouldn't be where we are today if it was not for you." I was starting to sound saccharine again, but I meant every word. We did have the best parents ever.

Tish jumped in and saved me from total embarrassment. "We can promise to try to think things through better. We will try our best not to put ourselves in danger. Captain Jones and the Jamiesons have given us the same lecture. I hope it makes you feel better knowing three knowledgeable people hold us accountable for our decisions?" More hugs and tears followed as well as small talk about our mentors. Before long, Mom and Dorothy left pushing the cart away.

Gabriel hadn't spoken much during all the festivities. When he finally did speak, it was to say Jack made an appearance at the showroom earlier in the day.

"It was certainly odd he showed up here. He has never made a visit to our place since the day he took office as a deputy. We could not figure out what he wanted. We found him looking at our display case, studying your newspaper articles."

We walked over to see which article captured his interest. "It was the one about you, Tish. The one where you helped a Chicago lady who was being abused by her husband."

Tish froze. I observed her closely. I could tell she was visibly shaken. I reached for and held her hand. I decided not to ask her why until we were alone. The fact we were holding hands did not go unnoticed.

Our moms, exchanged knowing glances and smiles, brought in bags of groceries for us to take home, as usual. We knew it was another way for them to show us how much they loved us. We took the sacks gratefully. There was no invitation to stay for dinner. Everyone knew we needed to get back. We were not on vacation.

As Tish and I drove back to Chicago, I decided to ask why she reacted the way she had about Jack reading the article on her. I wasn't ready for her answer.

"Scotty, there is something I need to tell you," she said, and I got a hard rock in the pit of my stomach feeling. I waited for her to continue.

"I know where Heather is," Tish said meekly.

"What do you mean, you know where Heather is?" I asked, wanting her to tell me more and yet dreading it.

"I got her into a safe house," she said just as meekly.

"You have known Heather was alive and safe all this time. Why didn't you tell me? Why? Why would you let me worry like that? Why would you let me think Jack killed her? Why wouldn't you have told me?" Lightly pounding the steering wheel, I was almost shouting; I was that mad.

Quietly, Tish answered. "She asked me not to tell anyone, especially you. She was afraid if anyone else knew, Jack would find out."

"You don't trust me enough to know I wouldn't leak a word to anyone. You don't trust me!" I was yelling now.

"A partnership is supposed to be based on trust! What am I supposed to think? Are we partners or not?"

Tish did not say another word, and neither did I. When we finally got home, I went to our bedroom and removed all my stuff and put it in my old room. Tish quietly put away the groceries.

CHAPTER THIRTY-SIX

Tish was still asleep when I dressed and left the house. I needed time away from her and someone to use as a sounding board. Patrick would be the perfect person.

I arrived at the Jamiesons' office before they arrived. I decided to go and buy donuts and coffee. Sitting down with breakfast might make talking easier for both of us.

The coffee was getting cold. I knew we could heat it up if we needed it. As the Jamiesons pulled into the parking spot, I got out of my car loaded with trays of coffee and donuts.

"You are certainly early," Aileen greeted me as she walked over to give me a hand. Patrick was unlocking the office doors, and we all entered.

"What brings you here this early, Scott," Patrick said, not missing the hidden signal that I was upset.

"I have a little problem with Tish that I want to talk to you about," I said in response.

Aileen quickly said, "Oh, girl trouble. Let me have a donut and a cup of coffee, and I will be out of your hair."

"No, Aileen, I would like your take on this, too," I said and stopped her from rushing off.

We all sat down with a donut and coffee in front of us. I stalled a few minutes, pretending I was famished, and finally, when I felt four eyes on me, I began.

"It seems Heather is alive and well, and Tish knew it all along. Tish is the one who personally went down and picked up Heather and brought her to a safe house here in town. The problem is, Tish never told me a thing about it even though she could see I was worried sick. I am feeling betrayed. I also feel as if Tish does not trust me, and if there is no trust, how can we be partners?"

Aileen and Patrick both sat quietly, waiting to see if I was going to add something to what I had already said. When I did not say anything else, the questions began.

"How did you find out Heather is alive, and Tish is the one who got her to a safe house? Patrick asked.

"Tish told me herself that she put her in a safe house," I said grudgingly.

"Okay, why did Tish suddenly tell you after all this time?" Question number two was asked by Aileen.

"Our dads said, Jack stopped into the showroom for the first time ever, and he paid a remarkable amount of attention to one of the newspaper clippings in their display case. It happened to be the newspaper article about Tish helping the abused woman.

"I noticed Tish becoming very nervous when she found out Jack was scrutinizing the article. Later, I asked her why she became agitated. She told me everything." I stopped talking again.

"Are you concerned that Jack is suspicious Tish might have something to do with Heather's disappearance?" Patrick asked pointedly.

"I haven't really given it much thought," I said. "I am mainly upset that Tish didn't tell me about Heather, and she let me be in such pain."

"There is more to all this than just Tish protecting Heather, in my opinion. You said you were once in love with Heather. Could this be part of the reason Tish didn't want you to know about Heather?" Aileen asked.

Questions were starting to pile up on my head. I just wanted someone to tell me that I was right. Tish should have confided in me since I am her partner. Instead, I was getting more and more questions.

"I don't know what Tish was thinking. Why didn't she confide in me? I am over Heather. I love Tish. How can our relationship continue if she is not honest with me?" I said, almost in a pout.

Patrick, the voice of reason, was the next one to speak, "Scott, partners are supposed to be honest with each other. You are totally right about that. If Tish was keeping Heather's whereabouts from you, I am sure she thought she was doing it for the right reasons. We agree, she should have told you. However, you need to give Tish the benefit of the doubt and talk things out with her."

On cue, Tish rode up on her Harley. It was late…almost ten-thirty. I knew Tish did not oversleep. I wondered where she had been to get to the office late. I excused myself to go to the smaller office and work on entering some data on their computer.

I overheard Aileen and Patrick greeting Tish when she entered. I also heard her tell the Jamiesons she was with Captain Jones for the past two hours. "Where is Scott? I need to talk to him."

Aileen said I was in the smaller office and to go on in. She and Patrick had some shopping to do. They would be gone for a while. I heard Patrick saying something about what shopping? Then I heard Patrick being rushed out the door.

I faked being busy on the computer and did not look up when Tish stopped in the doorway.

"Scott, I spoke with Captain Jones." I slowly turned my chair and looked at her. I was alarmed to see Tish's eyes were swollen. I almost blurted out, 'what happened to you?' when I realized Tish was crying.

"Don't talk, okay? Let me apologize before you say anything. First off, I am sorry I didn't tell you about Heather. It was wrong of me to keep it from you. I promised Heather I wouldn't tell anyone, and that included you."

I started to stiffen up and interject; Tish cut me off. "That is only part of the reason I did not tell you. The main reason I did not tell you was that I was afraid I would lose you if you knew Heather was in trouble and was also going to be free from Jack."

Tish started to cry. In fact, she was sobbing…she no longer could talk. I could not stand it. I hated to see Tish upset. I rushed to her and held her in my arms. I did not say a word; I just held her.

When her sobs slowed to whimpers, I led her to the small sofa in the office, and we sat down. I continued to hold her.

"Tish, I love you. I don't love Heather. I have never really loved Heather. I know now I have always loved you and only you. I need you to trust me on this and on everything else. If we are going to be partners, there can't be secrets. We need to trust each other in all things." I stopped talking and let my words sink in. I waited for Tish to think about what I had said and digest it.

I lifted her chin up to allow her eyes to meet mine. Even swollen, Tish's eyes were the most beautiful in the world. I could see relief and something more in her eyes. I kissed her lips and let the kiss linger.

"Tish, I want Evers and McFarlan to be a reality. We are progressing quicker towards that goal than I ever imagined. Do you still want our partnership to continue?" I asked her.

Her answer was quick, "With all my heart and soul. I want us to be partners for the rest of our lives. Do you think you can ever trust me again?"

"The question is not whether I can trust you. The question is whether you can trust me. I know you have issues with men…because of your uncle. Do you think with time, you can put your issues aside and really trust me?" I asked her without releasing her from my embrace.

"You deserve my trust. You are a good man, Scotty McFarlan. I want to be your partner for life, and I want you to come back to my bedroom," Tish said and broke into tears again.

"No. We moved in too soon. Let's give it a bit more time. It is too hard for me to sleep next to you without wanting more. I will move back in when you are ready. In the meantime, I love you too much to put any pressure on you. When you are ready, know I will be too. No pressure, okay?"

Tish, my tough lady, was nothing but a soft little kitten. I wanted to protect her forever. I knew in my soul; I would be able to trust her. I hoped she would be able to trust me in time. I could wait. She was worth the wait.

The Jamiesons returned without a single shopping bag. "I'm sorry. I couldn't keep Patrick away any longer. Are you two... alright?" Aileen asked.

"We are great!" I responded.

"Good! We have some news for you. Remember the insurance case you helped us with earlier this year. The fire fraud...well, we got several big checks from solving that case from several different insurance companies. The really good news is half of it is yours! Not only that, but there are also two more insurance cases that we will receive checks from soon," Patrick said with glee.

When he handed us a big check, my eyes popped out. "Whoa! That is one big check." I made sure Tish could see all the zeros. She did not comment. I could tell she was more than amazed; she was in shock.

"Our proposition is this," said Patrick. "Soon, Aileen and I will want to retire. We discussed this, and we want to know whether the two of you would like to buy us out. We wouldn't put the company in your names yet since you aren't twenty-one, but we certainly could start the paperwork, and you would be junior partners in our company until you are ready to take over completely. What do you say?"

I looked at Tish, and together we both said in unison, "Yes!" I asked a quick question, "Hopefully, you will be available to consult for a few years, right?" We were feeling hopeful. Our dreams were going to materialize much sooner than we had ever imagined. Evers and McFarlan were going to be a reality soon.

"Of course, partners, let's celebrate!" Aileen said with enthusiasm. "We are going to take you to the nicest lunchroom you have ever been to, and we are going to order anything or everything on the menu. What do you say to that?"

Tish was the first to say something, "But I am a mess. Look at my swollen eyes, and I am dressed to ride my Harley."

"A cold washcloth will work wonders for your eyes," Aileen said as she led Tish to the washroom. "As for your attire, this place will let you wear anything you want if you can pay their prices." I heard Tish giggle and was heartened to hear the sound.

Patrick leaned over to me and asked, "Everything seems to be fine with the two of you. Have you proposed to her?"

I was taken aback. "We aren't there yet," I said. "But we are moving in that direction." And I winked.

"Don't wait too long. Girls like Tish are hard to find. You sure wouldn't want to lose her to some sweet-talking guy, would you?" Patrick also said with a wink.

"We are working on trust. If that means I must trust Tish not to be taken in by a sweet-talking guy, then that means I can wait a bit longer to propose." I heard the ladies coming out of the washroom and dropped the subject.

"Are you ready?" Aileen asked. "Scott, you are going to love this place. They have the best steaks in the world. Don't worry, Tish. They also have seafood to die for."

"Where exactly are we going to eat?" I asked.

"We are going to go to *Gene and Georgetti Steakhouse*. Gene and Georgetti have passed away. We are still friends of the family. Gene's daughter and husband run the place now. I know they will make sure we have a great meal. You can have steaks, veal, pork, chicken, seafood, pasta, or all the above. Let's go. My mouth is watering just thinking about it," Patrick said, licking his lips.

We talked through lunch about the junior partnership and the details involved. Aileen told us we would not be getting an hourly wage any longer. "From here on out, you would be getting half of the proceeds brought into the business. Maybe we forgot to tell you…the checks you now hold only represent one-quarter of the total. We have another one-quarter check ready for you if you do not wish to acquire our business. If you agree to become our partners and the purchase of our business, then the remaining one-quarter will make a substantial down payment on the business."

I would agree with any business deal at this point. The prime rib was fabulous, and I was stuffed to the gills. We sat back and talked before coffee and dessert. There were many questions we needed answers to from the Latimer case.

"Please, if this is an appropriate time, fill us in on what happened in the safehouse with Maurice," Tish said. "We were so involved with our hometown murders last night that we did not have a chance to find out if Maurice is in jail and whether he turned in the other ladies."

Patrick answered, "Maurice didn't suspect he was set up at all. He went to the safehouse and broke into the back door. Even though he memorized the combination to the safe, you never gave him the second critical code that he needed, so he was unable to open the safe. However, the police caught him in the act of trying to open it. They held him for breaking and entering and attempted theft. Mrs. Latimer's statement regarding Maurice's masterminding the fraud is what really is going to put him away."

"What about Mrs. Latimer?" Tish asked with concern.

"Wendi will go before the courts. We promised that we would be a character reference for her, and the insurance companies are willing to withdraw their prosecution if she is willing to be a witness in the other fraud investigations. Unfortunately, Wendi will probably spend a couple of years in jail for fraud and enlisting others to fraud. There is a chance the judge will be lenient if she cooperates. The judge may allow her to spend her jail time at home under house arrest," Aileen said.

"Wendi is going to be miserable over her inability to fulfill the $500,000 pledge to save the elephants," Tish said sadly. "My hope is, eventually, she will understand how close she came to being put away in prison for many years."

"In that regard," Patrick explained, "the insurance companies involved in Mrs. Latimer's fraud case will continue to investigate the other jewelry fraud cases. Hopefully, with Wendi's or Maurice's cooperation, they will close more of these fraud cases. In the future, we could see more checks from this case, thanks to your solid investigative work."

I joined Patrick in trying to cheer up Tish by reminding her of our own good fortune. Now that Tish and I were patching things up, we are going to be junior partners, and my '55 Ford is fixed, I, once again am feeling life is good, and all is well with the universe, and I was hoping Tish was feeling the same way.

Tish and I spent the next several days doing our regular routine. I missed going to bed with Tish and waking up next to her. We needed to start over again. Trust needed to be re-established between both Tish and me. I knew it would take some time. I only hoped that it would not take too long.

The human mind is fragile in many ways. Something that happens in childhood can cause many problems well into adulthood. I sure hoped Tish's sexual abuse would not be a problem for us forever. Thinking of her uncle made me wish I had been the one to kill him.

I wondered, too, would we ever find out who really killed him…would it matter if we did? Knowing that someone killed him, removing another monster off this earth, is what really matters.

I know these thoughts would have my mother on her knees, praying for my salvation if she knew what I was thinking.

Days turned into weeks, and one day, Tish came in with two letters. One for each of us. They were from the Texas-based investment company that represented Riley's computer company.

"What do you suppose this is about?" I looked at Tish as she handed me one of the envelopes addressed to me.

"Only one way to find out. Open it." Tish said with annoyance. Tish was back to her sarcastic self. I was glad to welcome the old Tish back. Her repentant-self was a bit aggravating. She was just too sweet to me these past few weeks.

We both quickly read the letter. It seemed the investment company reviewed the 'Stanton's '92' Alumni Agreement' once the reasons for Riley's arrest became known. Both the Texas-based computer company and the investment company felt the agreement should be dissolved, and everyone should receive a new stock purchase agreement with a stock certificate for the amount we each invested initially. There was a place for us to have notarized with our signature.

"This is great news!" Tish said as she folded up the pages and placed them back inside the envelope. "Now, each of us will have our own stock certificate, and we don't need to worry about being killed to be the final alumni standing. I love it! This is how it should have been from the very beginning. I can't believe we all agreed to this stupid, asinine contract to begin with. It just goes to show how immature we were and what peer pressure can do."

"What a relief. I bet even Chuck and Douglas will sign the new agreement. Are you going to let your stocks ride, or are you going to cash them in?" I asked Tish.

"Definitely, let them ride. We don't need any extra money now. We may need more to buy out the Jamiesons when the time comes for them to retire. Remember, that insurance check is just a down payment," Tish answered.

"Speaking of the Jamiesons, we need to get over there," I said, rushing to the door. When Tish did not rush, I stopped and asked her if she was coming.

She hung her head a bit and said, "Scotty, sore subject. I should go and see Heather first. I am trying to convince her to go to the police and tell them what she knows about Jack."

Now my curiosity was peaked. "What does Heather know about Jack? She can't prove he deliberately tripped her, causing her to fall down the stairs and miscarry the baby. What else does she have on him?" I asked, really wanting to know."

"You are right," Tish said. "Anything Heather would say would be conjecture or her word against Jack's. She did overhear Jack and Jesse talking, and something they said scared Heather to death, but she wouldn't tell me what it was when she phoned me to help her. Yesterday Heather told me the reason she left was when she heard Jesse ask if he should cut Heather's brakes like Jack did Lucy's. I have been pressing her to contact the police even though I promised not to tell anyone anything that she told me. Again, I am truly sorry that I didn't tell you."

"No, Tish. You did what you thought was right to make sure Heather was safe. I have no problem with your helping her. I hold you in very high regard because you do want to help...even a classmate you never really liked. Back to the subject, what does Heather have on Jack that could be used in a court of law?" I asked.

"It is all Jack's word against Heather's word. She overheard that conversation, and Jack's response to Jesse was not to cut the brakes. He did not want two accidents to look the same. Jack told Jesse they needed to find another way to get rid of Heather. I think at that point,

Jack became suspicious Heather was listening because she said they stopped talking abruptly.

Another time, Heather overheard Jack laughing with Jesse about how sad it was that Wally could not swim. She said they continued laughing about Tommy being clumsy with his tools. When they finally stopped joking about the two boy's deaths, she heard Jack saying something about how to get rid of a large number at one time to speed things up." Tish stopped reiterating Heather's conversation.

"It is all still hearsay," I said. "It could sway the jury. The lawyer would probably dismiss Heather's testimony and tell the jury to strike what she said. I don't know what good it would do to have Heather go to the police. I think she is better off hiding out for a while longer until we can get some concrete proof Jack was in on the plot."

"Captain Jones said Tran only implicated Jesse. I don't think Riley and Tran even know Jack was the one manipulating Jesse. It could take years to catch Jack or maybe never. Heather can't put her life on hold that long. She needs to get her life back.

You should see her, Scotty. She is afraid to leave her safe house. I must bring her groceries every couple of days. That is what I am doing today. I need her to get some help, and she won't do that until she feels Jack isn't around any longer. She is totally paranoid right now." Tish seemed upset as she spoke these words.

"Hold on a minute. This whole thing was a conspiracy from the beginning. Maybe Heather's hearsay evidence is admissible in court," I said, having an epiphany.

"Way to go, Scotty!" Tish said with a sudden smile appearing on her face. "Now, I need to convince Heather to come forward. It isn't going to be easy, judging by how afraid she is now. I think I can talk her into meeting with Captain Jones."

Tish had a spring to her step as she went out the front door. My eyes lingered on her hips swaying as she trotted out to get her Harley. I was still in the doorway as she left. I suddenly felt my heart drop to my stomach. As Tish pulled away, a car pulled away from the curb down the street to follow her. I know that car! It is Jack's.

Carole Walker Carter

Starting life in a small town in Nebraska, Carole and her family moved from the Mid-West to the West Coast. Carole continued traveling from California to Texas, Ohio, back to Nebraska and finally settling in the Pacific Northwest with her husband, Don, her childhood sweetheart and partner, their dogs, and a few fish.

Carole's career involved working with children from pre-school through high school, dealing with special needs, and "at-risk'" children as an Occupational Therapy Assistant and Educational Assistant.

Meeting unique people throughout her life, fascinating characters formed in Carole's mind. These individuals shaped the basis for real and imagined characters found in her various forms of storytelling from Science Fiction, Detective, to her Children's Books.

Find her books on Amazon, Kindle, Nook, Apple Books, and Barnes & Noble Now by searching for *Carole Walker Carter*!

Aztara, The Mastel Kingdom
By
Carole Walker Carter

Aztara, The Mastel Kingdom, tells the background story of the majestic mastel creatures that roamed the rugged mountains and the fertile valleys of Aztara. The setting for this book is two generations before the plague that killed all the Aztarian women during Volume I, *Surtees, Science Rules.*

Idyllic as the lush lavender summer pastures might seem, the mastels are forced to be nomadic, dependent upon the weather and growing cycles for their diet. Equipped with spiraling horns and clawed feet, the stallions are always at the ready to protect the herd against terrifying river monsters and voracious tree-dwelling beasts.

The newly established bond between the cave-dwelling griswells and the mastels seems destined to fail, until Morsian, an inventor from the eastern factory villages, creates a symbiotic relationship that will change everything on Aztara…forever.

Explore the early world of Aztara and enjoy the Mastel's unique story.

Find this book on Amazon, Kindle, Nook, and Barnes & Noble Now!

Surtees, Science Rules
By
Carole Walker Carter

Surtees, Science Rules, is Volume I in the *Aztarian Series.*

In *Surtees, Science Rules*, we discover how ruthless a dystopian society can be when the ruler is a despotic scientist determined to achieve longevity to remain in power forever.

Ananaya brutally seizes power from his father, Ryndor, who set up several senior scientists as the leaders of scientific research centers. Under fear from retaliation, the scientists carry out the plans of Ananaya, which in turn, causes destruction to the air, water, and food supplies for the citizens of Surtees. As the Surtarians' lives crumble under the oppressive rule of Ananaya, two unlikely young females, Tawtanya and Myana, rise from champions of the Surtees Zrymir Games to become heroes of the planet.

Find this book on Amazon, Kindle, Nook, and Barnes & Noble Now!

AZTARA, A Galactic Love Story
By
Carole Walker Carter

AZTARA, A Galactic Love Story, Volume II in the *Aztarian Series*, centers on two main characters from two different planets whose lives are turned upside down by the ruthless scientist, Ananaya.

Shayla, an Earth woman, grieving for the loss of her only child and deceived and abandoned by his father, is close to suicide. A unique bond with fantastical creatures on her new home of Aztara helps Shayla to return to a balanced life in a strange new world.

Ty, having lived through a plague killing all the females on Aztara, finds refuge in his work, mining the mineral, phyrium, instrumental to all aspects of life on Aztara, including telepathy, longevity, and levitation.

Ananaya, the Chief Scientist from Surtees, leaves a dying planet to relocate on Aztara to seize control of the mineral phyrium for his own benefit. In his attempt to rebuild his army of Enforcers, he abducts Earth women who carry a specific gene, the warrior gene, to mate with the Aztarian men. This momentous event brings our two main characters together to face the seemingly insurmountable challenges of an intergalactic romance.

The story is about finding internal strength, trust, and love. Intrigue and thrilling moments prevail while the two main characters come to grips with a situation, not of their own choosing.

Find this book on Amazon, Kindle, Nook, and Barnes & Noble Now!

AZTARA, Secrets Revealed
By
Carole Walker Carter

AZTARA, Secrets Revealed, Volume III in the *Aztarian Series*, is the culmination of Ananaya's ultimate plan. The offspring of the intergalactic mating produce some surprises for the peaceful Aztarian men. Shayla's and Ty's love produced twins.

Nayela is the only interspecies girl on Aztara that bonds telepathically with a mastel. Kestle, jealous of his sister's abilities, has his hands full with being a gang member.

A tragic event occurs, changing everything for Kestle. Self-banished to the Wildlands leaves Kestle alone to deal with situations for which he was unprepared. Going deeper into the Wildlands brings Kestle to the dreaded Orange River, where dangerous monsters lurk. Saving a young runaway girl, Sinaka, from certain death. He discovers, however, there is more to this young girl than he first thought.

Sinaka finds it is her turn to save Kestle when a monster wounds him. With unexpected help from a beautiful creature and Sinaka's psychic and empathic powers, Kestle finds healing.

The Surtarian Chief Scientist, Ananaya, accelerates his plan to genetically modify the Aztarian/Earthling boys' Warrior Genes. Ananaya's plot is to create a daunting army of new Enforcers. All hell breaks loose when the usually passive Aztarians decide to fight to get their boys back.

Find this book on Amazon, Kindle, Nook, and Barnes & Noble Now!

Final Alumni
By
Carole Walker Carter

The Final Alumni is Volume I in the *Evers and McFarlan Detective Series.* This series follows two high school best friends who join forces to start careers as private investigators. Tish, haunted by a childhood experience, enables herself mastering many disciplines of martial arts, while Scotty falls back on his expert firearms training and physical prowess as a football quarterback.

Out of high school, the two go to Chicago, Illinois, to pursue their career through education and on-the-job training. Mentored by a well-respected couple who owns The Jamieson Detective Agency, Tish and Scotty are enlisted to assist Aileen and Patrick Jamieson in solving cases in Chicago while pursuing a series of unsolved murders in their own hometown as well.

Find this book on Amazon, Kindle, Nook, and Barnes & Noble Now!

Shadowy Faces
By
Carole Walker Carter

Shadowy Faces is Volume II in *the Evers and McFarlan Detective Series*. In *Shadowy Faces*, Tish and Scotty are confronted with the lives of three young women who have been ruined. Each young woman deals with lost weekends where all they can recall are vague faces tormenting them. The shadowy faces become the focus of the investigative team of Evers and McFarlan along with the Jamiesons and the Chicago Police department. The team works methodically to discover what happened to each of the women to bring the criminals to justice.

Tish needed to lean on a secret discipline her Grand-Master taught her even with the warning of what could happen to her if anyone should learn of her new martial arts fighting technique. Scotty also faces the threat of losing the love of his life

Find this book on Amazon, Kindle, Nook, and Barnes & Noble Now!

Carole Walker Carter

Nine Points of a Circle

Evers and McFarlan Detective Series

Nine Points of a Circle
By
Carole Walker Carter

Nine Points of a Circle is Volume III in the *Evers & McFarlan Detective Series.* In *Nine Points of a Circle*, Tish and Scotty are fully licensed detectives in The Jamieson Detective Agency. Even though the Jamiesons are preparing to retire, they continue to mentor, advise, and direct Scotty and Tish on new cases.

Captain Jones tries to block Tish and Scotty from getting involved in what appears to be an intelligent yet spine-chilling serial killer. Three homeless girls were murdered over the past five days, and their bodies were dumped on different streets in greater Chicago. At the same time, Tish and Scotty are assigned to a serial robbery case and are approached by a well-known Chicago business executive regarding his missing daughter.

All three of the cases challenge Scotty's mathematical and technical expertise and Tish's detective and martial arts skills to solve. Follow Tish, Scotty, and Duma, their tracking canine, as they plunge themselves into the plight of the homeless on the dark and perilous Chicago night streets.

Find this book on Amazon, Kindle, Nook, and Barnes & Noble Now!

The Child Rowanda, Little Dragon
By
Carole Walker Carter

The Child Rowanda, Little Dragon Volume I, Twelve-year-old Rowanda lives with her mother and grandmother, an elder sorceress, in the lush garden planet of Neslora. Seemingly an idyllic world with endlessly blooming flowers, buzzing bees, and birds chirping...until.

A tyrannical king's guards abducted and transport several women of Neslora to the desert world of Arolsen, where they are being kept as slaves.

Rowanda and her friends discover, with horror, the abduction of their mothers. Armed only with four talismans, chosen by mystical means, Rowanda goes through a portal to Arolsen where her fate is intermingled with two desert dwellers. Together they join forces to brave the scorching desert days and frigid desert nights to rescue Rowanda's and her friend's mothers. Rowanda learns to use her magic to defend against nomads, desert serpents, sand dragons, and vicious felines.

The Palace City of Arolsen reveals the true identities of Rowanda's traveling companions and the reasons they accompanied her on her quest.

Find this book on Amazon, Kindle, Nook, and Barnes & Noble Now!

The Child Rowanda, Return to Arolsen
By
Carole Walker Carter

The Child Rowanda, Return to Arolsen, Volume II, Alarm spreads through Neslora as unexplained destruction occurs to the bountiful planet. The Elder Sorceress discovers the evil king, Nashua from Arolsen is using charms Rowanda left for her friend Boultori to use to turn their barren desert into an oasis.

Now, Rowanda, with the help from her father, her grandmother, and best friend, must right the wrong by retrieving Rowanda's talisman and exchange them for charms that Boultori might use to overthrow his evil brother's rule of Arolsen.

Two new talismans, chosen by magic, assist Rowanda as she learns to control the most feared, yet fascinating creatures on Arolsen. These creatures aide Rowanda on her quest for justice.

Magic abounds in this second book of the Child Rowanda series as good battles evil to rescue a world from slavery and hardship and to keep Neslora from the same predicament.

Find this book on Amazon, Kindle, Nook, and Barnes & Noble Now!

The Child Rowanda, Underworld
By
Carole Walker Carter

The Child Rowanda, Underworld, Volume III, Rowanda, attempts to rid the world of Neslora of the evil wizard, Nashua, Rowanda finds herself dragged into the Underworld with the evil sorcerer.

Navigating the terrifying darkness of this new world, Rowanda finds a mysterious and mystical guide who reveals that Rowanda can only exit the Underworld the same way she came in, with the evil sorcerer at her side. However, Nashua must be truly repentant of his depravities before he is allowed to leave, which means Rowanda cannot depart the Underworld if Nashua does not repent.

Trying to find Nashua in the darkness and convince him to repent, becomes a complicated and dangerous process. Making matters worse are the demons, intent on making both Nashua and Rowanda one of them, meaning living an eternity in the Underworld in agony.

Find this book on Amazon, Kindle, Nook, and Barnes & Noble Now!

The Child Rowanda, Dragon Princess
By
Carole Walker Carter

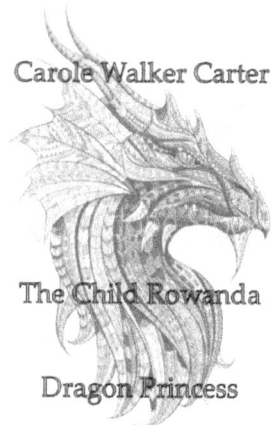

The Child Rowanda, Dragon Princess, Volume IV. Leaving the Underworld through another portal, Rowanda finds she has not returned to her home-world of Neslora but finds herself on another parallel world with the devious Nashua. Here Rowanda is elevated to a princess.

Friends and members of her family are in this world, but they are not as they should be. They are doubles with a different personality and…no recollection of Rowanda.

Rowanda finds herself at odds with her look-alike parents, the king, and queen of Soleran.

Rowanda's magical talent of charming animals allows Rowanda to help the enslaved citizens of this world by joining the rebel army in opposition to the king and queen.

Wanting nothing more than to return to her own world, Rowanda seeks the aid of an ancient fire-breathing dragon.

Find this book on Amazon, Kindle, Nook, and Barnes & Noble Now!

Childhood Stories My Dad Told Me
By
Carole Walker Carter

Childhood Stories My Dad Told Me, is about growing up on a farm in Nebraska during the Great Depression. It was difficult, but for two young boys, life on the farm was also filled with fun and adventures.

This book is based on stories my dad told me about the amusing antics that he, his siblings, and friends found themselves in during these hard times.

The stories, filled with insights about rural schools, country social events, and harvest time, as well as the day-to-day chores of a working farm, are informative as well as enchanting.

Find this book on Amazon, Kindle, Nook, and Barnes & Noble Now!